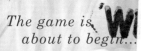
The game is 'W...
about to begin...

A Beginner's Guide to Rakes

SUZANNE ENOCH

St. Martin's Paperbacks

For my editor, Monique Patterson—I think this is the beginning of a beautiful friendship.

And for my agent, Nancy Yost—you're simply the best.

This is a work of fiction. All of the characters, organizations, and events portrayed in this novel are either products of the author's imagination or are used fictitiously.

A BEGINNER'S GUIDE TO RAKES

Copyright © 2011 by by Suzanne Enoch.
Excerpt from *Taming an Impossible Rogue* copyright © 2011 by Suzanne Enoch.

All rights reserved.

For information address St. Martin's Press, 175 Fifth Avenue, New York, NY 10010.

ISBN: 978-0-312-53451-6

Printed in the United States of America

St. Martin's Paperbacks edition / October 2011

St. Martin's Paperbacks are published by St. Martin's Press, 175 Fifth Avenue, New York, NY 10010.

10 9 8 7 6 5 4 3 2 1

Chapter One

Very few things in the world could make Oliver Warren, the Marquis of Haybury, flinch. He could count
these things on one hand, in fact. The yowling of small
children. The squeak of rusted metal. And the mention of
that name.

Stilling, he looked up, the stack of coins between his
fingers forgotten. "What did you say?"

To his left James Appleton nodded. "I thought the
Benchleys would have found a way to keep the manor, it
being in the family for so long. But it's the widow opening up old Adam House. Just arrived last night, from what
I heard. At any rate, it's the first time in better than three
years that anyone's lived there."

Oliver placed his wager on the three of spades, keeping his eyes on the game as the dealer turned over a four,
a nine, and the queen of hearts. "Hm," he said, deciding
vague interest would be the expected response to this particular gossip. "Lady Cameron. She's been on the Continent, hasn't she? What's her name? Marianne?"

"Diane," Appleton corrected, finally noticing that he'd
lost the wager he'd just placed on the four of spades. "Blast
it all. I heard Vienna or Amsterdam or some such. I suppose

with Frederick dead for more than two years now, she decided she missed London."

"That seems likely." A flash of long, raven black hair and startling green eyes crossed Oliver's mind before he shoved the image away again. *Damn, damn, damn.* He sent a glance at the man seated to his left. "London must be dull as dirt indeed, Appleton," he drawled, "if the most intriguing bit of gossip you can find is that a widow is settling back into her late husband's town house."

Across the table Lord Beaumont laughed. "You've hit on the Season's failing, Haybury. No good gossip. I don't think we've had a scandal since January, and that one doesn't even count because no one was in Town to enjoy it." The earl lifted his glass. "Here's hoping for some bloody entertainment soon."

Oliver drank to that. Anything that kept him from having to hear damned Diane Benchley's name on everyone's lips for the next six weeks had his vote. "Are you finished with wagering for the evening, Appleton?" he pursued. "We could fetch you an embroidery hoop, if you prefer to continue your tongue wagging."

Appleton's cheeks and throat flushed a ruddy red. "I merely thought it interesting," he protested. "The former Earl of Cameron and his wife flee London just ahead of the dunners, and now she comes back alone in a half dozen of the grandest black coaches anyone could let—and in the middle of the night."

"Perhaps she found herself a Prussian duke," the fourth of their party, Jonathan Sutcliffe, Lord Manderlin, finally put in. "She always was a pretty thing, as I recall." He patted Oliver's shoulder. "You weren't in London back then, were you? In fact, didn't you spend some time in Vienna?"

"Among other places." A sideways glance accompanied by a lifted brow convinced Manderlin to release his shoulder. "I returned in a grand black coach as well, Appleton. My own. Did you gossip about me?"

Finally, Appleton grinned again. "Did and still do. Almost constantly."

"Good. I work very diligently to keep all the wags occupied."

"That's true!" Lord Beaumont motioned, and one of the club's liveried footmen approached to refill his glass. "You're the one to blame for the quietude, then. Give us a damned scandal, Haybury."

Oliver inclined his head. "I shall do my best. Or worst, rather."

Diane Benchley, Lady Cameron, in London. And he supposed they'd run across each other at some soiree or other now. After all, Mayfair was a small place. Smaller even than Vienna. He downed the remainder of his glass of whiskey and poured himself another.

Mention of her name might have caught him unawares tonight, but if—when—he saw her face-to-face, he wouldn't be the one flinching. Not a muscle. Not any muscle. And she'd best keep her pretty mouth shut as well, or he would be forced to do something unpleasant.

"Are you wagering, Haybury?" Manderlin asked. "Or are *you* taking up embroidery?"

Gathering his less than pleasant thoughts back in for later, private contemplation, Oliver glanced at the rack of spent cards and put two pounds on the knave. In his experience, the knave always won.

"Diane, you have a caller."

Diane Benchley, Lady Cameron, looked up from the spread of papers on what had been her late husband's desk. "I'm not seeing anyone," she muttered, and returned to sifting through the figures and decimals and subtractions every sheet seemed to feature. "No exceptions."

"I know that, my dear," her companion returned, not moving from her position in the office doorway. "It's Lord Cameron."

For a heartbeat, ice ran up Diane's spine. In that swift moment, every hand she'd shaken, every breath of wind on the passage from the Continent, every thunderclap to her chest since she'd left Vienna, caught in her throat. It had all been for nothing, if . . .

Swearing beneath her breath, she shook herself. Frederick Benchley had died. Two years ago. She'd been by his bedside when he'd drawn his last breath. She'd stood at his graveside when the pair of workmen had shoveled dirt into the hole where they'd placed his cheap pine coffin. "For God's sake, Jenny, don't do that," she stated aloud, setting her pencil aside and rubbing at her temple with still-shaking fingers.

Alarm crossed her companion's face, and Genevieve Martine hurried deeper into the room. "Oh, good heavens. You know I meant the new earl, of course. I never thought—"

"Don't trouble yourself, Jenny. You did startle me nearly out of my skin, however. Where is Anthony Benchley?"

"In the morning room. He asked for you, and then for tea."

Diane pushed away from the desk and stood. "Well. At least we may assume that word of my arrival in London has traveled swiftly. That's something, I suppose."

"Yes, we may count one fortunate thing since our return here, then." Jenny blew out her breath. "And two dozen unfortunate things. To which column do I add Lord Cameron?"

"The unfortunate one. Come with me, if you would. I want to be rid of him as swiftly as possible."

"What do you think he wants?" Genevieve asked in the light French accent that seemed to fade or intensify according to her mood.

"Money, of course. That's what all the men of the Benchley family want. And as far as I've been able to determine, none of them are capable of keeping their hands on any of it they touch." She frowned. "And Adam House, most likely. He can't have that, either."

"Perhaps he only wishes to reminisce," Jenny suggested dubiously. "You were married to his brother, after all."

"There is very little about my life as part of that family that I care to remember," Diane retorted, lowering her voice as they reached the foot of the stairs. She'd known that eventually she would have to speak with a Benchley, but for heaven's sake, she'd been in London for less than two days.

In that time Jenny might have compiled a list of two dozen unfortunate things, but it had merely taken one disaster to set Diane's entire plan on its ear. In fact, the only happenstance she could imagine that would make things worse would be if it were Oliver Warren, the Marquis of Haybury, waiting for her in her morning room. Anthony Benchley was an annoyance. Nothing more.

That thought actually steadied her as she stepped into the room. Her former brother-in-law stood looking out the front window. His dark hair and ruddy complexion and even the way he tapped his fingers against his thigh reminded her forcibly of his older brother, and she didn't like that. Not at all. "Lord Cameron," she said aloud.

He started, then turned to look at her. "Diane," he returned, and walked forward to take both her hands in his. "Please, do call me Anthony. We were once siblings, after all."

She nodded, withdrawing her hands as swiftly as she could. "Anthony, then. Is there something you wanted?"

His brow furrowed and then smoothed again. "Ah. Don't mistake me for my brother, Diane. He did me no favors, either, by gambling away the family fortune."

That was true, she reluctantly admitted to herself. "You t—"

"But you're wearing black," he interrupted. "I apologize if I've off—"

"You haven't. It's only that I've just arrived, and the fellow with whom I'd intended to . . . do a bit of business met with an accident. I'm rather frazzled, I'm afraid." It wasn't entirely the truth, but it was as much as she was willing to divulge to anyone. The fact that Anthony was a Benchley only made her more cautious. She'd learned her lesson.

"Business?" he repeated. "You know, I'd heard that you arrived the other night with a dozen carriages full of your possessions. And— Well, I'm not certain how to be delicate about this, but my solicitors keep telling me that Frederick signed Adam House over to you. I thought perhaps you might consider . . . especially given that you have other business and matters of finance to attend to . . . returning the house to the Benchley family. God knows I could use it to settle some of Frederick's remaining debts."

"Yes, you wrote me about that last year, as I recall. But I believe I've settled most of Frederick's debts," she returned, keeping the abrupt surge of anger from her voice. "You still have Benchley House and Cameron Hall, Anthony. Adam House is all I possess."

She glanced at Jenny, who sat in the corner playing her role of companion. Adam House *was* all Diane possessed. And considering the news about her investor that had greeted her upon her arrival in London, she needed to make use of it. Fortuitously enough, she knew just how to do so.

"Well, then. I'd hoped you might be more amenable, especially considering that most everyone knows why you and Frederick were forced to flee the country, but if you wish to face the censure of your fellows, there's nothing I can do to protect you."

As if she needed his protection. "Thank you for thinking of me, Anthony, but I'll manage somehow." She drew a breath. "And now if you don't mind, I have some correspondence."

"Yes, of course." He headed into the foyer, with her and Jenny on his heels and keeping him, whether he realized it or not, from venturing any farther into the house. "I look forward to seeing more of you, Diane. Feel free to call on me as you would a brother."

"I will."

The moment he left the front step, she closed the door. "I have an idea, Jenny."

"I do hope it's a good one, considering that your business partner, as you call him, is being put beneath the ground this very afternoon."

"We need a venue. I think Adam House would suffice, don't you?"

"Good heavens." For a long moment Genevieve gazed at her. Then the overly thin blonde smiled. "I think it would, at that."

For three days following her late-night arrival, Lady Cameron didn't stir from Adam House. Oliver knew that because whatever he privately wished, no one seemed the least bit interested in discussing anything else. At Gentleman Jackson's he heard that she'd been glimpsed through an upstairs window of her home, her gown the black of full mourning despite the fact that it had been two years since the earl's death. Oliver refrained from scoffing in response, but only just.

During luncheon at the Society Club, Patrick Banfer informed the table that Lady Cameron had received a visit from her former brother-in-law, but that the earl had only stayed for ten minutes and then left again to go to Boodle's Club and drink an entire bottle of whiskey. And as Oliver refastened his trousers in Lady Katherine Falston's lavish green bedchamber, she relayed the news that Diane, the Countess of Cameron, had sent for a certain well-known jeweler who worked almost exclusively with the most precious of stones.

"Are you hinting at something?" Oliver asked, sitting back on the edge of the bed to pull on his Hoby boots.

A bare arm slid over his shoulder, warm breasts pressing against his back through the thin material of his shirt. "Neither of us is the marrying sort," Kat murmured, nibbling his earlobe, "but a pretty bauble or two—well, most ladies would welcome an expensive gift from an intimate friend."

Oliver shrugged out of her loose embrace and stood again. "I prefer to leave nothing behind to cost me more later." Retrieving his tan jacket from the back of a chair, he pulled it on. "Though perhaps I *should* send you a bauble. At the least it would give the wags something to chew on other than who might be calling on bloody boring Adam House and its so-called mysterious resident."

Kat sank back into the voluminous bedsheets. "Don't you dare. You know I was teasing you. I may enjoy an intimate evening in your company, but you keep your scandals away from me. If you wish to give me a gift, do it privately, and make it very, very expensive."

"I'll keep that in mind." Of course she'd made light of it; she knew as well as anyone that he didn't care for entanglements—in or out of bed. "Good evening, Kat."

"Mm-hm."

Most of Lady Katherine's household knew he was there, but he nevertheless kept his boot steps quiet as he descended the main staircase and let himself out the front door. Habit, he supposed, as not all of his lovers were unmarried. Though whether their husbands were concerned or even surprised over his presence was another question entirely. And a husband's possible reaction was one that Oliver always kept in mind. Not, however, tonight. With her status and connections, Lady Katherine likely thought as little of husbands as he did.

As he reached Regent Street, he slowed Brash, his gray thoroughbred. Adam House lay just out of sight past the tall hedgerows. Oliver clenched his jaw. *Damned woman. Damned, damned woman.* Yes, he'd thought the Season dull, but that hardly merited the dusting off of old morality lessons—the saying "be careful what you wish for" being foremost among them.

He supposed he could stop by some morning and pay his respects—well, not his respects, precisely, but make his presence known, at least—but Diane Benchley seemed to be in no hurry to reveal herself to her curious peers. Despite his desire to be strictly annoyed by her in general, that made him a touch curious as well. And all things considered, encountering her first in public would likely be wiser for both of them. The burning question seemed to be why she was waiting.

Rolling his shoulders, Oliver clucked at Brash and sent them trotting west to his rented town house on Oxford Street. He knew he was far past sentiment, and he'd never believed in allowing the passing of time to soften the hard edges of memories. And he never—*never*—let anyone else see an ounce of weakness. Not his own, anyway. Exposing that of others was so lamentably easy that on occasion he couldn't restrain himself. If Lady Cameron knew what was best for her, she would take care to keep him well away from whatever she might be plotting.

Though if she truly had her own best interests at heart, she would never have returned to England in the first place.

Chapter Two

D iane Benchley, the Countess of Cameron, took the
liveried footman's proffered hand and stepped down
from her rented black carriage. "All ready, Jenny?" she
murmured.

The tall, willow-thin woman descending to the cob-
blestones after her, nodded. "Just as we rehearsed, yes?"
Genevieve Martine returned in the same tone, her slight
accent that intriguing mix of French and German and English finishing school.

Tonight the severe pull of Jenny's blond bun made her
look like a governess or some companion to an elderly no-
blewoman, but that was deliberate. Tonight all eyes would
be fixed on Diane, and tongues would be muttering all nature of interesting things out of her hearing. But not out of
Jenny's; the woman was a marvel at going unnoticed.

"Yes. And I apologize for even asking; tonight has become more significant than I'd anticipated. You know I
generally prefer more than four days to plot out the entirety
of my—our—future." Diane pretended to adjust one of
her silky black elbow-length gloves, taking the moment to
gaze up at the large town house before them. Candlelight
glowed from every window, voices and the strains of a

country dance spilling out to the street. "You're certain Lord Cameron won't be here?"

"His invitation never arrived at his residence," Jenny affirmed, a brief smile softening her features. "Such a shame, I know."

"Splendid. He's an annoyance, but one I could do without this evening. I believe this party is going to be more than interesting enough without him." Diane made her way around the crowd of arriving and departing vehicles.

As she walked, she glanced at the various coats of arms emblazoned on the passing doors. A duke here, an earl there, along with brothers, cousins, nephews, and sons—all of the wealthy and powerful together with those who envied and emulated them. And all at the Duke and Duchess of Hennessy's grand ball. If not for the herd of other females fluttering about as well, she would very nearly have called the evening perfect.

No one would realize it, of course, but she'd planned her arrival in London to coincide with this soiree. Back then, however, she'd had only one goal for the night. Now she had two. At that thought, a red painted dragon twined about a bloody sword caught her gaze just in time to add the exclamation to her point. The quick breath she drew was entirely against her will. *Oliver Warren.*

"Haybury?" Jenny asked, following her gaze. "You're not having second thoughts, are you?"

Diane leveled her shoulders. "No. I'm not. Ideally this wouldn't be necessary, but as the ideal plan was just buried in York, necessity is what remains. Now that I've considered it, he's the better choice, anyway."

"Which is fortunate, since he is now the only choice." Under her breath Jenny uttered something in German about Henry, Lord Blalock, and a deep pit of hell.

Silently Diane seconded the curse. Whatever Shakespeare wrote about best-laid plans, however, hers was not going to go astray. Some of the players might change, but she'd literally and figuratively journeyed too far to turn back now. "In all fairness, I don't think Lord Blalock intended to expire," she returned in the same low tone. "And certainly not from a broken neck."

Jenny made a derisive sound. "What else does a sixty-year-old man expect when he rides after foxes? In the rain, yet?"

And that was the problem with several late aristocrats formerly of her acquaintance, Diane reflected. Despite all evidence to the contrary, they thought themselves invincible, untouchable, and immortal—until they fell. And they did fall, with rather alarming regularity. Diane shrugged out of her wrap as they reached the foyer. She could blame herself for being some sort of widow maker, she supposed, but then the one man of her acquaintances who most deserved to drop stone-dead had recently inherited a marquisdom and a great deal of money.

"How will you approach Haybury?" Jenny asked on the tail of that thought.

That very question had kept her awake most of last night. "I've an idea or two. Leave it to me."

With a brief nod, Jenny slipped past the butler amid a group of giggling girls undoubtedly enjoying their very first Season in London. For a moment Diane watched them, uncertain whether she envied their naïveté or pitied them for it. But then she'd begun the same way and she'd learned her lessons. The price might have been a bit steep, but perhaps because of that fact she'd learned them very well indeed.

The party was lavish enough that the butler was announcing the newly arrived guests to the rest of the crowd. She'd anticipated that, as well, and she'd dressed accordingly. Black silk draped from her waist to the floor. Her bodice was of the same color, intricately embroidered and glittering with black glass beads. Black lace sleeves ended halfway to her elbows, and a swoop of more lace circled her low, curved neckline. Together with her black elbow-length gloves, the ensemble had cost several pretty pennies. And she knew it would be worth every shilling.

She handed the butler her invitation, listened to the murmurings already whispering behind her. "Ladies and gentlemen," the fellow intoned from the top of the two shallow steps, "Diane Benchley, Lady Cameron."

Diane lifted her chin just a fraction, the better to show off her glinting black teardrop necklace of onyx with its matching ear bobs. The bustle of conversation in the large ballroom faltered and then resumed, changing from the level hum of bees to the buzz of hornets. And there she was, deliberately stirring them up. Giving a slight, deliberately secretive smile, she descended to the marble floor. *Look,* she urged them all silently, inclining her head at the Duke and Duchess of Hennessy as they came forward to greet her. *Be intrigued.*

By noon tomorrow anyone who hadn't already heard about her and her return to London would know. And that was precisely what she planned. Because after that she would own them all. Or at least the bits and pieces of them she wanted.

"It's so good to see you, Diane," the duchess cooed. "You've been away for so long!"

"Thank you for inviting me this evening, Your Grace," Diane returned, reflecting that she'd only met the Duchess of Hennessy once and that the woman had spent the entire time complaining about her husband's gout.

"My condolences on Lord Cameron's passing," the previously gouty duke rumbled, with a marked glance at Diane's all-black ensemble. "Two years now, isn't it?"

"Just over that, yes." She gestured at herself, the tips of

her fingers lingering for just a moment at her neckline. "I do so adore wearing black. Once I donned it for Frederick, I simply never gave it up." She smiled. "It's a very underused color for females, don't you think?"

"Yes," Hennessy returned, his gaze following her trailing fingers. "Very underused."

The duchess cleared her throat. "Do enjoy yourself this evening, Lady Cameron."

"Oh, I shall. Thank you."

She did intend to enjoy herself, or she had when she'd originally planned her reentry into Society. The architecture of her plans up to the tiniest of details was to have been laid out by now, with only the pied piping to remain. Things had changed, things not even she could have foreseen, but she would make do. It would take more maneuvering than she'd anticipated, and it would mean involving that . . . man, but perhaps even that could be turned to her advantage.

At the least she chose to think that with a bit of strategically applied effort and perhaps a pinch of blackmail the end result would be what she wanted. What she required. And that hardly seemed too much to ask.

A tall fellow with a glittering emerald pin through his cravat approached her and bowed. "Are you dancing this evening, my lady?" he asked, his affected lisp reminding her why for a time she'd actually preferred Vienna.

"Introduce yourself, and I shall decide," she returned, favoring him with the cool smile she'd perfected over the past year. The one that said she knew more than she was revealing. It had certainly served her well; in fact, she would place it just below money in the ranks of useful things to have.

"Ah, of course. I am Stewart Cavendish. Lord Stewart Cavendish. My father is the Marquis of Thanes. And you are ravishing."

A second son or below, then. But still a lordling. "For that kind compliment, I shall grant you a quadrille."

His own smile deepened. "And what would it take for me to earn a waltz?"

An inheritance and a title, she thought to herself. "Better than one moment of acquaintance," she said aloud. "We shall see how you manage the quadrille."

He bowed again, reaching for her dance card until she took a step backward and inscribed his name on the thing herself. When they danced was her choice, not his. She ticked off the spaces with her forefinger.

"I shall see you for the fourth dance then, Lord Stewart, son of Lord Thanes." She deepened her smile just a touch.

"And I shall be practicing the steps in anticipation."

As he strolled away to regale his friends with their conversation, Diane turned, taking a heartbeat to sweep her gaze across the many pairs of eyes watching her. No sign yet of Oliver Warren, but he was likely in one of the gaming rooms. Which meant she needed to find her way there as well—no easy feat considering that ladies were discouraged from visiting the sites of such vices.

By the time she'd made her way across the room to the doorway of one of the three temporary gaming rooms set off the main ballroom, she had seven dances spoken for. Only the evening's first dance and the two waltzes remained, just as she intended. Diane crossed the doorway, managing a surreptitious glance at the billiards table inside. A dozen gentlemen stood about, but not the one she sought.

A cool breeze brushed across her back. "You are making quite the impression," Jenny's soft voice came. " 'Where has she been?' 'Where did she find her wealth?' 'Why is no one escorting her?' 'Does she mean to remarry?' "

Diane gave a slight nod. "It doesn't take long, does it?"

she murmured from behind her dance card. "If I can find Lord Haybury, this next bit will be even more interesting."

"I heard two women complaining that he was spending all evening in the card room and wouldn't come out to dance," her companion returned. "They are very disappointed."

"Sometimes I think Bonaparte would have won the war if you'd been on his side, my dear."

"Of course he would have."

Diane caught the smile before it could touch her mouth. Instead she continued with her search, declining two more invitations as the music for the night's first dance, a quadrille, began on the overlooking balcony. The dance floor filled, and the space around her opened. And then her pathway was blocked again.

"Diane."

She looked up into pale gray eyes cooler than the fabled ice of the Arctic. "Oliver. There you are." Before she could take the moment to consider just what she was about to do, she stepped forward, taking both his hands in hers. "So good to see you again." She set her mouth into a deep smile, far more than she'd favored anyone else with that evening.

His hands felt warm even through her gloves—and thank God she was wearing them, or she would have been tempted to scratch out those lovely eyes with her nails. His fingers, though, remained in hers. And they were very still. A heartbeat later he withdrew them. "Yes, it's been a while, hasn't it?" he said, though the expression deep in his eyes was far more murderous.

"It has! Do call on me tomorrow. At ten o'clock. We'll have tea. I do so want to announce the news of my new gaming club, you know."

There. Before she could even turn away she heard the echoes of her conversation spreading through the guests like a ripple of water in a pond. Or fire in a wheat field, more like. Yes, she'd just said she was opening a gaming club. Yes, Lord Haybury knew all about it—indeed, they were old friends.

A hand grabbed her elbow. "What the dev—"

Diane blinked, pulling in her thoughts even as she faced Oliver again. His expression hadn't altered, but his eyes weren't cool any longer. "Not here, Oliver," she cooed, holding still despite the fact that she had the sudden urge to yank herself free and run. Swiftly. "We must discuss the details first." With her free hand she reached up and touched his cheek, brushed her fingers against hair the brown of richest chocolate.

The murmuring became peppered with gasps of surprise. "Whatever you're attempting to tangle me in, I will destroy you for this," he breathed.

She smiled again. "You may try," she returned. "Now unhand me or I shall kiss you."

The trap of his fingers snapped open, and feeling rushed back into her arm.

"A pity you aren't dancing this evening," she continued in a more audible tone. "Ten o'clock. Don't forget."

His hard gaze held her in place for a moment. "I don't forget anything."

"Hm. Neither do I."

As she glided over to meet her partner for the next dance of the evening, she used every ounce of willpower to keep her hands and voice steady. Yes, she knew precisely what she was doing and no, he didn't frighten her in the least, but being face-to-face with him again . . . It reminded her of more than how much she disliked the man. Touching him sparked the memory of things that she'd already resolved were not to be dredged up again. Not for anything.

By the second waltz of the evening Lord Haybury was

nowhere to be found and the gossip about her plans had spread so far it was coming back to her. She stood to one side, intentionally in sight of all the men who'd asked her to waltz and been refused. Yes, they were on the dance floor while she wasn't, but each one knew—as did she—that he was partnered with his second choice.

Yes, the night was proceeding perfectly. The only thing that could have made it better was if Oliver had demanded a waltz as well, so she could have turned him down just as she had all the others. More than likely he'd known that, though. Oliver Warren was no fool.

"You should sample the parfaits," Jenny said from beside her. "They are exquisite."

"The Hennessys' chef is a fellow from Sicily," she returned. "I won't have him."

"I didn't mean you should hire him. I meant the sweets are tasty."

Diane rolled her shoulders. "Yes, yes. I'm sorry, my dear; I'm obsessing again. But I won't be eating this evening."

"I shall eat two, then." Genevieve seated herself, using a stand of ferns to shield her from the majority of the room. "Everyone wants to know if you've gone mad. 'A club? What sort of club? If Haybury is involved it must be for wagering.'"

"I told you he was the better choice, however willing Lord Blalock was to open his purse. Blalock wasn't known for anything but having deep pockets and a penchant for the ladies. Oliver Warren is synonymous with wagering. It saves so many steps."

Even without looking, she knew Jenny's expression would be skeptical. It didn't matter, however. She'd taken the first step and had already laid out the pathway all the way to the front door. And Oliver had best walk it with her, or he would regret it. Because arrogant as he was, she knew just where to find the chinks in his armor. Nor was she afraid to exploit them. With Lord Blalock dead, everything depended on it.

"As you said, we have no choice," her companion agreed softly.

"As I said. More gossip, if you please."

"I'll be close by the refreshment table. And not because of the parfaits. The sweets seem to loosen tongues."

"I'll not begrudge you a parfait, my dear. Merely keep your ears busy, as well."

"Mais oui."

Partway across the room Diane noticed a young lady looking at her. That wasn't so unusual, though the woman's expression wasn't the vaguely resentful one she'd already become accustomed to seeing on female faces this evening. Finally the lady clasped her hands together and approached. "Has it truly been so long that you don't remember me?" she said, stopping a few feet away.

Diane looked at her more closely. "Jane Lumley."

Jane smiled. "You see? Four years hasn't altered me so much. You, on the other hand . . ." She gestured at the sleek black gown Diane wore. "You've become some sort of goddess of temptation, I think."

"Oh, please. It's only clothes." Abruptly less certain than she had been since her return to London, Diane gestured her old friend toward the open balcony doors. She hadn't had many close friends before Frederick, and fewer after, and this was not a conversation she looked forward to having. But if she'd learned anything over the past four years, it was that no one else would look after her with the same care and cunning she used. And looking after herself took precedence over everything. Even old friends.

"For someone who so quietly absented herself from Society you certainly know how to make a grand entrance," Jane observed as they stepped out on the balcony. Two couples had preceded them, but it was still a hundred times quieter than the ballroom.

Of course quiet also meant they could more easily be overheard. "Frederick's decision to leave England was rather . . . impulsive. Leaving Vienna took a bit more forethought. It's such a lovely city, you know."

"So I hear." Her expression cooling a fraction, Jane sent her gaze over the rooftops behind them. "You're not still in mourning, are you?" she asked in a quieter voice. "Because as I recall, you and Frederick—"

"Vienna is quite romantic as well," Diane broke in. "You really should make an effort to visit." *There.* Whatever her motives, it would never do for her to be seen as mercenary. Everyone had to see something in her plans for themselves, or her ship would be sunk before it ever left port.

"I shall, then." Jane favored her with a sideways glance. "I would be delighted if you would call on me, you know. For tea, or luncheon, or shopping—whatever pleases you."

"Well, I'm frightfully busy with my new hobby, but we shall see. Thank you for the invitation."

"Your new hobby being opening a gaming house?"

"A club. A magnificent, very exclusive club."

"A club, then." Jane drew a breath. "We were dear friends once, Diane. If you ever wish to chat, I shall lend you an ear. Two, if necessary."

"Thank you, but I'm not harboring any dark secrets. Not very exciting, I know, but there you have it."

When Jane excused herself a few moments later in favor of a clearly nonexistent appointment, Diane let out her breath in a small sigh. Yes, they'd been friends, but the last thing she needed these days was a combination of confidante and reminder of her unfortunate, naïve past. Diane chose her companions and associates with great care now, mostly because she could. In fact, she refused to be a victim of circumstance or tradition or—or anything, any longer.

This was her venture, and no one else would be allowed to guide, assume, or abscond with it. Ever. And the sooner one particularly arrogant man learned his place in the scheme of things, the better for everyone concerned. She would tell him that tomorrow. At ten o'clock.

Chapter Three

It was the first time, Oliver reflected, that he'd ever been threatened with a public kiss and backed down.

Any chit who delivered such a challenge to *him,* of all people, deserved every ounce of ruination he could send in her direction—which was quite a bit, given his reputation. In his own defense Diane had made her threat quietly enough that no one had overheard, so if he'd answered her challenge he would have looked the bully. Aside from that, Diane Benchley was up to something.

He had no intention of stumbling into some plot of hers mouth first. Or anything else first. No, today he would be treading very carefully. And she'd best be as well, for her own sake.

He swung down from Brash and handed the thoroughbred's reins to a waiting stable boy. "Keep him walking; I won't be long."

"Yes, my lord." The gray-haired fellow bobbed his head and led the gelding around the side of the large town house.

It was common knowledge that the fortunes of the Benchleys had been falling for years, which if nothing else left them with a string of impressive properties they had

married into in an ongoing search for wealthy in-laws. Such
was the case with Adam House; the earl two or three generations ago had snared the eldest daughter of Maximillian
Adam, the Marquis of Wright. The house had been a wedding gift from the marquis.

Oliver had done some checking in the last few days,
and since Adam House wasn't entailed, he was rather
surprised the late Earl of Cameron hadn't sold the place
to keep the dunners off his trail. But perhaps he'd intended to regain his fortune in Europe and then return to
London and Adam House in the rather spectacular manner his wife had managed. That might even be what Diane wanted everyone to think. It was only because of a
quirk of fate that he knew otherwise about her fortunes.

A young woman opened the front door as he reached
it, and Oliver paused for a moment. He'd seen attractive
women before, of course, but this one wore breeches. And
a butler's jacket and waistcoat. Whatever Diane was up to,
apparently she'd lost her sensibilities in the process.

"My lord," the woman intoned, inclining her head.
"Lady Cameron is expecting you. If you'll follow me."

Once he'd entered the foyer, the lady butler shut the
door and led the way upstairs. Oliver occupied himself
with watching her hindquarters—a surprisingly sensual
sight in those breeches and long jacket tails—and nearly
ran into her when she abruptly stopped outside a closed
door. She knocked twice, cracked open the door, and then
returned down the stairs.

So he was expected to make his own entrance. That
was nothing new, except that he knew Diane Benchley.
This would be a chess game, and in her home, at her request, he'd already lost several pawns.

And she was undoubtedly counting the seconds between the knock and his entrance, estimating whether he

was hesitating or plotting, or both. Oliver pushed open the door with one fingertip and stepped inside.

Diane sat behind a desk. "Are you trying to look busy, or to keep me at a distance?" he asked, closing the door behind him and leaning back against it.

Lifting one forefinger at him, she continued to scribble in a ledger. She wore black again, this time a simple, straightforward muslin that still managed to make her look sleek and stunning. Black hair swept back into a simple knot might have been meant to look severe, but the strands that escaped to frame her face were far too artfully placed to be accidental.

"You were wearing black when I last saw you in Vienna," he commented, studying her lowered face. "You didn't mean it then, either."

"When last you saw me I'd been widowed for less than a month. Of course I meant it."

Oliver lifted an eyebrow. "How closely do you wish me to recall the events of Vienna? Because I wouldn't have called it mourning."

With a sigh she set down her quill pen and steepled her fingers in front of her. "You didn't care what I called it. How could the color of my gown signify when you only wanted me out of it?"

"Is this the game we're playing, then?" He folded his arms over his chest. "I wanted you in it, but I could only have you out of it."

"Until you ran home to London like a scalded dog. That is what *I* recall about Vienna."

He pushed upright again. "I returned home to claim my inheritance."

"Ah, yes, I nearly forgot. You're a marquis now. What a fortunate bit of timing that you can blame your cowardice on your uncle's demise."

Oliver took a step closer. "I suggest you stop referring to my uncle's death as fortunate," he said, his jaw clenched. "That sort of talk causes rumors to start."

"I will, as soon as you cease referring to my period of mourning as gown deep."

Well, she had him there. As for the scalded-dog reference, she had him there as well. That part, however, he had no wish to admit to. Not to her, or to anyone else. "Agreed," he said aloud. "We shall cease insulting one another about our feelings or lack thereof upon the death of near relations."

"Good."

Reaching behind him, Oliver pulled open the door again. "Then good day, Diane."

"I'm not finished with you yet."

"Unless you have something to say that involves money or sex, I'm not interested."

"Money."

Finding that he would much rather have left Adam House regardless of her answer, Oliver forced himself to close the door again. "Speak."

"Sit down, why don't you?"

"Not until I know whether your conversation will make me money or cost me money."

A muscle in her cheek jumped. "First one, and then the other."

As little information as she was feeding him, she was replying. And he remained curious despite himself. Oliver released the door handle and strolled forward to sit in one of the large chairs placed opposite the desk. "I'm listening."

"I had a plan for my club," she said without preamble. "Lord Blalock signed papers agreeing to lend me five thousand pounds and to lease the old Monarch Club property in his name and for my use."

"Blalock broke his damned neck out riding after foxes with his latest mistress."

"Yes, I know. I discovered that the morning after I arrived in London."

Oliver gazed at her. Emerald green eyes held his steadily; she knew what he was deciphering, and she wasn't attempting to keep any information from him. Not about her finances, at any rate. "That must have been quite a shock."

"You have no idea."

"I'm to be Blalock's replacement, then. You want me to lend you the money."

"A bank won't."

"What about the money your late husband owed nearly everyone?"

"I've either repaid it or made arrangements to do so."

"With what? You were, as I recall, left penniless in Vienna."

"Frederick signed over all his unentailed property to me."

Sinking back in his very comfortable leather chair, Oliver crossed his legs at the ankles. "No, he didn't. Not before he died. You complained about having nothing the night we met. Or the morning after that, rather."

"I have a talent for forgery. And I had been signing most of his papers for him since our marriage, anyway."

"You're not even going to attempt to fabricate a lie? I'm disappointed."

"Lying takes effort, and I don't see the point." She gestured toward the trio of bottles set on a small table beneath the room's large window. "Do you wish something to drink?"

"No. Go on."

"Very well. I sold off everything Frederick willed to me with the exception of this house, and I was able to settle most of his debts. I'm only telling you this so you'll realize that the money you lend me will be used solely to establish my gaming club."

Ignoring for the moment that she'd assumed he would be amenable to giving her anything, he nodded. "Tell me about this club, then."

"No."

"No?"

"No." Diane shifted a little to partially pull open the desk's top right-hand drawer.

The thought that she likely had a pistol in there didn't do much to cool his temper, but it did tell him quite a great deal about how importantly she viewed this conversation. "Then I'll bid you good day, Diane." Mentally he began counting.

Before he'd reached five, Diane stood. "Oh, very well. You may listen. I do *not* want your opinion."

"Get on with it, then. You're the one who called this little meeting."

Slowly she took her seat again. "I have learned a great deal about the power of wagering. I have also determined that the only party who is guaranteed to have money at the end of the evening is the gambling establishment."

"There are a dozen high-class gentlemen's clubs here already, my dear. You're not the first to come to this conclusion."

"Frederick's idiotic wagering took everything from me, Oliver. Now it is my turn. My club will be extremely exclusive. And given that the Monarch Club property was just sold to some merchant wanting to open a shop in Mayfair, my club will be here, at Adam House. The architecture and floor plan are nearly ideal, and very little need be done to render it perfect. Every one of my employees will be female, well educated, and attractive. The—"

"So you're going to manage a brothel."

Her cheeks darkened. "Absolutely not. Sex is not the vice I aim to exploit. I am invariably disappointed by its brevity and arbitrariness."

Whether she meant to aim that particular barb at him or not, Oliver wasn't about to lose the path of the conversation because of an insult. "That explains the lady butler at your door. You do have an elderly fellow in your stable, however."

"I never said men aren't capable of shifting manure. You seem supremely well suited for it, in fact."

"And this is how you ask for money? I'd hate to hear you flat-out insult someone."

She hesitated. It was only a heartbeat, a brief lowering of her eyes, but he saw it. Not very long ago he'd earned his way by finding weak points in others and making them bleed any blunt he could get his hands on. This time he waited. Whatever it was about her that irked him also made him curious. Lamentable but true.

"Whatever my employees choose to do privately will not be my concern, as long as it doesn't reflect badly on the club. So no, I am not opening a brothel. If anyone should choose to think so and decide to pay my membership fee because of that . . . misapprehension, I have no objection."

"You have some interesting ideas, I admit, but I've never heard of a woman opening a club that didn't feature sex. And if you're assuming you'll remain Society's new darling once words become deeds, you're sadly mistaken." He pulled out his pocket watch and clicked it open. "It's an unsound enterprise, and I won't throw money at it."

"What would convince you to do so?"

"In general? Partial ownership, a guaranteed percentage of the profits, a say in which games were offered and who was granted membership. Specifically? I've been in bed with you, Diane. I don't care to repeat my mistakes."

She sighed. "I'd hoped you would see that I don't much

care what Society makes of me, as long as they continue speculating. And I thought you might realize that I intend to do this, whatever your unasked-for thoughts on the matter."

"Determination does not make a business successful, my dear."

"Men who flee my bed so swiftly they leave their waistcoats behind aren't permitted to call me 'my dear.'" She pulled a folded piece of paper from that half-open drawer. Considering he'd expected to see a pistol or a dagger, he was slightly relieved. "And before you pretend to be insulted and slink off again," she continued, "you should read this."

Frowning, he sat forward and pulled the paper toward him. "If you mean to publish a memoir about my 'slinking,' as you call it, pray keep in mind that I know a few unpleasant things about you, as well. Aside from that, I don't embarrass easily."

She flicked her fingers toward the note. "Read."

Oliver unfolded the paper. In neat cursive two lines curled across the otherwise bare page: "I have a sworn statement from Tomas DuChamps affirming that you cheated him and four other gentlemen at cards in the amount of 812 pounds on the twenty-seventh of April 1816."

Murder. That was what the chit deserved. Murder. Black fury flashing through him, Oliver snapped to his feet. "You little b—"

The pistol in her hand stopped the insult he'd been about to utter, but not the biting anger behind it.

"I know you don't embarrass easily," she said coolly, the pistol unwavering and aimed directly at his chest. "Losing your reputation as a cardplayer, however, is, I believe, another matter entirely. Sit down."

He nearly refused, until it occurred to him that not only would she more than likely pull the trigger, but she also might even enjoy it. Slowly, every muscle taut, he sank into the chair again. "I hope you've considered how you mean for this conversation to end," he murmured.

"I have," she returned. "I've done nothing else for five days, in fact, since I learned of Lord Blalock's death and that little nuisance Anthony Benchley made me realize that I have quite the prize in Adam House."

"Get to it, then."

"It's actually quite simple. Wagering took very nearly everything from me. I mean to turn the vice to my own use now. As for you, Oliver, though you weren't my first choice, when I consider matters I believe your participation is quite fitting. After all, thanks to Frederick and you I've learned a great deal about how men attempt to take advantage, and about how . . . ill-advised it is to rely on anyone else."

"This is all a rather overelaborate means to tell me to go to the devil, then? You might merely have sent a letter. There's a chance I would even have read it."

"Don't be an idiot," she retorted, true emotion pitching her voice a breath higher. "This has nothing to do with you, other than the fact that you're knowledgeable about wagering and that I can compel you to assist me."

"By threatening to ruin me and have me banned from every club in London? That's not a wise approach, Diane."

She gazed at him for a long moment. "I'd rather not ruin you, or even shoot you. But I suppose that's up to you now. Shall we discuss my business requirements, or would you prefer to continue with the threats?"

Oliver eyed her. "Two years ago you were much more weepy and . . . soft."

"Two years ago I'd just buried an idiot husband who'd left me destitute in a foreign country. And I was not weepy. I was angry."

A flash of her moaning beneath him, her nails digging

into his back, crossed his mind. "You were, at that. It was quite invigorating."

"I have a pistol pointed at you. Do you truly wish to discuss that particular fortnight? You didn't precisely look anything but cowardly by the end of it."

"No, I don't suppose I do. What am I being compelled to do, then? Loan you five thousand pounds and then what, gamble at your club? Very well. I will lend you the blunt for one year, at the end of which you will return to me *six* thousand pounds. As you said, no bank would do business with you, so accept the offer or walk away."

"I have a counteroffer."

"Do tell." Her statement didn't surprise him in the least. What she said, however, just might. And that at least made it interesting.

"You will lend me the money, and you will keep a private lodging at the club. Th—"

"What? You must be joking."

"Your presence here will both provide me with a shield against unwanted attention from others of your gender and make me sought after. You see, via you I will have made myself unobtainable, and you're quite aware, I believe, that men most want what they cannot have."

"So you want me to live here, under your roof. You do wish to be murdered, don't you?"

She actually smiled. "I should have mentioned— I'm not in direct possession of that statement from Monsieur DuChamps. I've put it somewhere safe, to be opened in the event of my death or disappearance."

"Good thinking."

"I agree. You are also a master at card playing, so in addition to lodging here you will provide me with every bit of information you have on odds and wagering and the rules of particular games, and you will train my employees."

"I'm not going to assist you with cheating anyone. Best shoot me now if that is your—"

"There will be no cheating of anyone. You will teach them how to take advantage. How to know when to encourage a wager from a gentleman, or when to send him away from the table so that he will return with more money later. Everything you know."

Oliver considered her demands. In truth she could have required the five thousand as payment for her silence rather than as a loan; he wagered heavily and with influential men, and any document proving that he'd cheated would see him ruined and reviled. No matter that he'd done it once and out of desperation. A scandal was a scandal, and this would be a delicious one. The *ton* would feast on it for months. Years.

"What is the name of this club of yours?" he finally asked.

"I've decided to call it The Tantalus Club."

He snorted. "Really? You've had two years to contemplate every aspect of this little plot of yours and the best you can come up with is The Tantalus Club?" Oliver reached into his coat pocket for a cheroot, which he lit on the lamp set at one corner of the desk. "An unrealized temptation? Rather . . . literal of you, isn't it? Why not The Tangled Web, then? Or the Toss Your Blunt down the Well Club?"

Diane gazed at him levelly. "Firstly, 'The Tangled Web' implies deception or dishonesty. My club will be neither of those, and I certainly will not put that thought into any potential member's head."

Hm. She *had* been considering things. But then, he'd never thought she was dull-witted. "And secondly?" he prompted, taking a long, herb-scented draw on the cheroot and breathing it out again.

" 'Tantalus' is a very honest name. They come through my doors tempted by fortune or fame or beauty. And realistically, they won't acquire any of the three. Not here. Not at any wagering club, really. Therefore, they've been warned." She leaned forward on her elbows, her right-hand fingers still curled around the butt of the pistol. "And thirdly, y—"

"A thirdly, even. No wonder you point pistols at everyone you invite in for a chat, with the amount of criticizing and insulting and exposition you do."

"And thirdly," she repeated, more forcefully, "you are providing funds and training and your presence. Not your ideas, opinions, or your thoughts. We are *not* partners."

"If I'm to invest my money and my presence and my expertise, I believe we *are* partners."

Her lips tightened. "You are a lender. A bank with, unfortunately, a mouth. I've had the papers drawn up. Sign them, and then have your man transfer the funds to my use."

If this had been a game of cards, Oliver reflected, he likely would have raised the stakes and dared the opposing player to show his—her—hand. In this instance, however, the surest way to learn what his opponent was thinking—and what she might ultimately be pursuing—would seem to be to surrender. For a long moment he studied her expression, but she'd learned a thing or two over the past two years about hiding her thoughts and emotions. Cool emerald eyes gazed back at him, revealing . . . nothing, which in itself meant something.

Two years ago he *had* fled Vienna, very like the scalded dog she accused him of being. And so, he supposed, there existed no better way for him to prove to himself that he was beyond such nonsense, beyond being seduced by wit and a pair of pretty eyes, than by agreeing to work with her.

"This project of yours is nonsense," he said, sitting forward and motioning for the contract papers, "but very well."

"Excellent." Swift relief crossed her face, then was gone again.

"I will sign over the blunt, but I'm not putting my signature on any further agreement."

"That is not accept—"

"I'll take a room at your club, and I'll instruct your so-called employees and lend you my expertise. The specific terms of that, however, will remain solely between you and me. Subject to further negotiation, of course."

Diane didn't like that. He didn't need to be schooled in reading anyone's expressions to know she was tempted again to shoot him. Oliver held still, keeping his alert but relaxed pose. If he'd been a believer in fair play, then he might possibly have conceded that he deserved a ball in the chest. Fortunately or not, his own philosophy leaned more toward getting whatever he wanted at whatever cost—within reason. Being shot didn't quite fall into that "reasonable" category.

Finally she shoved the pen and inkwell in his direction. "Do keep in mind that I still have the letter from DuChamps. You'd be better served by signing precisely what we agreed to. But if you wish to continue with negotiating, well, I know how to do that as well."

Oliver signed over five thousand pounds for the period of two years, with repayment at the rate of three percent. *Hm.* That seemed very reasonable of him. There were, however, other ways to better his position. In for a penny, in for a pound—or five thousand pounds, rather—as the saying went.

Chapter Four

W hen Oliver set down the pen, Diane tightened her grip on the pistol. Simply because it seemed as though the danger had passed didn't mean it had. Especially where Oliver Warren was concerned.

Finally, though, he pushed his chair back and stood up. "When do I move my residence?" he asked.

"Just for your information," she returned, standing as well so he wouldn't loom over her, "if I had a choice, you and I would be on separate continents. Once I begin hiring employees, you may begin calling on me. I will, of course, be intrigued but cautious."

"And ruined, once I move into your home."

"You're moving into a room above my club—not my home."

"Semantics, Diane. No more invitations to Society events for you. No more teas with duchesses or luncheons for church charities."

The odd thing was, a few years ago that might have hurt. "I have no doubt I'll be invited to fewer events. As long as I remain a mystery and a curiosity, however, I shan't lack for invitations."

"Care to wager on that?"

Of course he'd chosen those words on purpose. "Still scratching about for weaknesses, are you, Oliver? Be cautious about with whom you choose to play. I have claws, too."

He walked to the office door and pulled it open. "Yes, I know. I've felt them digging into my back."

"These days I aim for the throat. And I'll expect to receive the funds by the end of the day."

"You'll have them by noon. And I'll be giving up my house at the end of the month. That gives you a fortnight, I believe."

So he wanted to push at her already. Diane nodded. "I'll be summoning you before then to instruct my employees."

With a slight grin that looked much more predatory than cowed, the Marquis of Haybury left the room. A moment later she heard Juliet open and close the front door.

Heaving a deep sigh that shook along the edges, Diane dropped into her chair again. "Damn that man," she muttered.

The side door leading from the adjoining sitting room opened, and Genevieve glided soundlessly into the room. "You weren't exaggerating," she said, taking the chair Oliver had just vacated. "That man is a terror."

"No, he's formidable. But so am I."

"All the same, you might have compelled him to sign *all* the papers."

Yes, she could have—but she doubted she or any portion of her reputation would have survived the resulting carnage. "Let him think he can still negotiate. I can do the same. By the end I'll have him wishing he'd agreed to all my terms right from the beginning."

"Blalock would have been easier to manage."

"Haybury knows more about wagering than anyone else in the country, and he has more money, these days. I suppose I'll trade compliance for knowledge." She sent a glance at her companion. "Not that we have a choice in the matter. I refuse to go live in some rented cottage in the middle of nowhere because my late husband couldn't stop with ruining his own life and had to drag me down with him."

"You know you will always have my support, Diane, whatever happens."

She drew a breath. "Yes, I know. Thank you, Jenny. That man does tend to make me wish to hit things." Standing again, she brushed her palms down the front of her gown. She hadn't so much as shaken his hand, but heat seemed to cling to her regardless. "You put the advertisement in the newspaper?"

"*Oui.* Beginning tomorrow. And I sent a note to Mr. Dunlevy. He will call at four o'clock today."

"Good. Considering that we've relocated the club to these premises, we'll have to alter the floor plans somewhat." Drawing her arm around Jenny's, she forced a smile. "And we will make certain to put a brick wall between the club residences and my part of Adam House."

"A very thick brick wall," her friend agreed.

That left Diane the remainder of the day to revisit her decorating plans and see to the removal of the last vestiges of the Benchley family remaining in the house. Thus far the sale of a pearl necklace, two old vases, and a portrait—of someone who looked enough like Frederick that it actually gave her a nightmare—had only earned her ten pounds. But considering that that was more than Frederick had left her when he'd died, she considered it a fair beginning.

"So all that nonsense about you not recalling who Lady Cameron was," Jonathan Sutcliffe, Lord Manderlin, commented, whipping his rapier up and toward the ground again in a swift salute, "that was what, you having a laugh at the rest of us?"

Oliver adjusted his mask, flicked his own rapier sideways, and then lunged, digging the tip into the padded material covering Manderlin's heart. "Perhaps."

"Touché!" the referee called, and the two men resumed their original places.

"Good God, Haybury, do you have to go directly for the kill?"

Beneath the mask, Oliver grinned. "Your heart is a very small target, Jonathan. I doubt that blow would have been fatal."

"Oh, very amusing. If my heart is small, yours must have turned to dust years ago."

"Fence!"

This time Oliver feinted for a shoulder, waited for Manderlin to push his blade aside, then whipped the weapon down across the fine mesh of the viscount's mask.

"Touché!"

"Are you attempting to dismember me, then? Generally you let me have a point or two to build my confidence before you destroy me."

"Apologies. I'm not feeling particularly charitable this afternoon, my friend." In fact, he was quite happily imagining Diane Benchley standing opposite him, in her hands a parasol or something equally useless as he poked and prodded her at will. Yes, it was likely sexual, but he could hardly blame himself for that. The woman had been a tigress in bed. A demon, ripping beneath his skin to places he'd thought completely invulnerable. Taking his—

"Touché!" jabbed into his ears a half second after Manderlin stabbed him in the gut. Oliver blinked.

"Ha! Not invincible, are you?" Jonathan danced back and forth, swatting the empty air with his weapon.

The half smile still on his face dropping into a scowl, Oliver backed to his beginning position. She was not allowed to make him weak. If it took living under her roof and playing her little game to prove that he'd moved well beyond whatever it was she'd nearly done to him, then so be it.

"What, no chitchat now?" Manderlin taunted. "No witty ripostes or insults to my manliness?"

Oliver jabbed a finger of his free hand at the referee, who swallowed. "Fence!"

A minute later, Viscount Manderlin was flat on his back, suffering from a triplet of blows to his face, chest, and gut. Before their referee could finish calling out points or the outcome of the set, Oliver pulled off his mask and tossed it at a servant.

"Oliver!" Jonathan called out as he struggled to his feet.

"I don't like to lose," Oliver replied, striding toward the private dressing room to change back into his clothes.

He knew Diane's plans now. She'd already managed to pull him into her plot, and as long as she had that letter he hadn't much hope of escaping unless she allowed him to do so. And if he knew anything, he knew how very unlikely that was. Therefore, he needed to discover every detail, rule, and flaw of her game. Because not only did he dislike losing, but he also had no intention of doing so.

Once he finished dressing he went to find Manderlin again. "Are you free for dinner?"

"That depends. Are you going to gloat?"

"No. *And* I'm buying."

"Then we're going to White's."

Forty minutes later a footman seated them on one side of White's large dining room. Oliver spent several minutes doing something unusual for him—observing not the diners but the actual lay of the room. The number of tables, servers, the distance from the kitchen, the easily available liquor, and the enticing view into the closest of the gaming rooms.

The decor itself was overtly . . . stuffy, pretentious in a way that blatantly appealed to the wealthy and exclusive membership. Christ, there was a five-year waiting list for new member applicants. A prospective member had to have a sponsor, and even that was no guarantee for entry.

"I'm relieved that you've kept your word about not gloating," Jonathan said around a mouthful of roast pheasant, "but some conversation would at least assure me you don't mean to tip the table over on me or some such."

"To how many clubs do you belong?" Oliver asked.

"That depends. You aren't going to blackball me, are you?"

Oliver scowled. "Why are you so convinced I mean to maim you? I've never done so before."

"Because something clearly has your spine in a twist, and I seem to be the handiest surrogate target. I'd ask you what might be troubling you, but I value your friendship. I am therefore sitting here quietly eating this very expensive dinner and waiting to be enlightened. Or for you to begin a fight with me. I'm generally more certain which I'm facing, but you've got me a bit on edge tonight."

"That was long-winded. Why not just say, 'Out with it'?"

Manderlin gazed at him for a heartbeat. "Out with it, Oliver."

Oliver took a swallow of wine. "No."

"Bastard."

"For the moment, suffice it to say that if I were to confide in anyone, it would be you. I have a few things to decipher in my own mind first."

With a nod, Jonathan returned to his meal. "Fair enough. And five."

"Beg pardon?"

"Five clubs. White's, the Society, The Army, the Tory, and Boodle's."

"The Tory? Really?"

"I inherited the membership from my father. I don't think I've been above twice, but the fee's reasonable." Jonathan took a breath. "Is this by any chance about Lady Cameron announcing she's going to open a gaming club?"

Of course word of that would have spread to every corner of Mayfair by now, damned chit. But that was undoubtedly precisely what she'd intended. "If it was about that, what's your opinion on it?"

"What's *your* opinion?"

"I asked first. Don't be such a coward."

"Fine. My second thought was that she hasn't been in Vienna for the past three years—she's been in Bedlam."

Oliver nodded. Jonathan was a more . . . decent man than he was, so the viscount's opinion was likely that of the majority of Mayfair's male residents. "But you said that was your second thought. What was your first?"

"That I want to see this club. I mean, she's a countess who's pretty enough to net another husband in five minutes. For her to be willing to risk her standing in Society it would have to be extraordinary. I know Cameron was a gambler—a poor one, from all accounts—but just what was the countess up to in Vienna?"

Now *that* was interesting, Oliver decided. Perhaps he'd weighed shock and dismay too heavily against curiosity and possible fodder for gossip. He did tend to misestimate propriety—one of the consequences of trampling it so often, he supposed.

"Now will you tell me your opinion?" Manderlin asked.

"I also admit to some curiosity."

"And do you know anything more about it than you did when you pretended not to remember her name? Everyone up to and including my groom knows you were to meet with Lady Cameron this morning."

Had she intended that, as well? That his involvement, unwilling or not, would help spread her chosen gossip? She had turned him into an investor, after all. "It's to be called The Tantalus Club, and she means to employ only females. Apparently lovely and untouchable ones."

"Saint George's buttonholes!" came from behind him. "Chits?"

Oliver turned his head. "Henning. Didn't see you lurking there."

Francis Henning gulped down a mouthful of ham. "Employ only females? To bank at the tables and serve the drinks?"

"And to take hats and shuffle cards, apparently."

"But chits can't manage money or cards," the rotund fellow continued. "She'll have to close the doors in a month."

"But what a month," Lord Bentson broke in from opposite Henning. "I'll be happy to take some of Lady Cameron's blunt while it lasts."

That seemed to be the consensus at the surrounding tables. Diane was a fool about to lose everything, and every man wanted to be a part of taking it from her. Which would have been his opinion as well, Oliver reflected, except for the fact that it was his blunt she would be using. And once he moved his residence to The Tantalus Club, it would be his reputation as well.

Very well. He could acknowledge that Diane Benchley had outmaneuvered him. This morning, however, had only been a skirmish. He had every intention of being declared the winner at the end of the war—once he figured out what a victory would entail.

* * *

"I can break out this wall," Mr. Dunlevy grunted, slapping his broad hand against the salmon-colored blockade currently separating the downstairs sitting room from the library. "That gives you the most floor space."

Diane looked up from the house's floor plans. "If we close off the foyer, add entry doors, and tear down the hallway walls as well, I can use the entire front of the house as the main gaming room."

The builder lifted one caterpillar of an eyebrow. "That much renovation ain't inexpensive, my lady."

"Can you do it?"

He looked more assessingly at their surroundings. "It'll take a few pillars to bear the weight of the upstairs, but aye."

"Then let's get to it. I intend to open my doors in a month."

"A mo— Yes, my lady."

The money she'd given him this morning undoubtedly had a great deal to do with his enthusiasm, but she was more concerned with his speed. Making grand statements and piquing everyone's interest had been the first step. Now she needed to follow through with the club's opening before a new bit of scandal or gossip made her potential clientele lose interest.

Once she and Mr. Dunlevy agreed on the revised layout of her club, Diane made her way past what seemed like dozens of workmen already pulling down the terribly dated wallpaper, replacing carpet, and repairing stairway bannisters. The entire front of the house would belong to The Tantalus, with the large gaming room downstairs, the sitting rooms and private apartments upstairs, and the employees' quarters in the large, renovated attic.

The rear wing of the house remained hers, and the dozen rooms would be her sanctuary from what would, she hoped, become a very busy life. The irony that this small portion of the house was larger than her lodgings in Vienna didn't escape her, either. Wagering was already beginning to pay her back. As long as she wasn't the one doing the wagering, it would continue to do so.

If Lord Blalock hadn't broken his neck and his solicitors hadn't taken the liberty of countering his instruction to lease the old Monarch Club for her use, she would have been much closer to opening her own establishment. Even with the added expense and the . . . annoyance of recruiting Oliver Warren into her plans, however, she couldn't deny a certain sense of satisfaction at turning Adam House into something that would no doubt have horrified the Benchley ancestors who'd gone to the bother of acquiring it.

"A gaming club?"

Diane looked down into the foyer from her vantage point up against the balcony railing to see her former brother-in-law gawping up at her. *Damnation.* "Anthony. I'm afraid I'm not seeing visitors today."

"You can't turn Adam House into this . . . thing," he pressed, heading for the stairs leading up to her. "It's been in the family for fifty years."

"And now it's mine. Your brother did one good thing before he expired, and that was to see that I had a place to live. What I choose to do with it is my own affair." She took a half step backward. "And be cautious of the stairs; they haven't been repaired yet."

He stopped his ascent and gingerly returned to the foyer floor. "My brother signed over every unentailed bit of property in the family to you. Why do you need this one?"

"I used the others to pay off his debts—which I believe saved you from having to do so. And while we might once have been siblings-in-law, we are no longer any relation whatsoever. I must ask you to leave. When the club's doors open, you may apply for membership."

"Diane, this is ridiculous. What would your parents think?"

The same parents who'd bartered her off in order to have a countess in the family? She drew a breath, shaking herself. Anger led to mistakes, and she could afford to make none. "Ask them. I certainly don't care to do so. Good day, Anthony."

She left the balcony, stopping just out of sight to be certain he wouldn't attempt the stairs again. Once she heard Juliet bid him good day, Diane resumed her way toward the back of the house.

"He doesn't worry you, then?" came from just below her.

Turning around, she stopped to wait for Jenny to top the stairs. "The man climbed those stairs a week ago, and now he thinks they're perilous simply because I said so. I'm not terribly concerned."

A workman tipped his hat at her with his free hand as he carried one end of a rolled carpet past her. When she'd told Oliver—damnation, she needed to become accustomed to thinking of him as the Marquis of Haybury now, rather than as the marquis' nephew—that men were fit at best to run her stables, she'd neglected to include their worth in toting and hammering things.

"Then I shan't be, either." Genevieve shifted her ever-present notebook from one arm to the other.

"What do you think, then? One large gaming room on the ground floor, taking up the entire front of the house, with a larger dining room behind it on the left, and a smaller gaming room and a breakfast room on the right, a library and billiards room behind that. Though I'm beginning to wonder whether a narrow corridor running up either side might be more beneficial for the hostesses' and the servants' use."

"Ah. To keep the ladies out of sight until the last moment? I do like that."

"I do, as well. Have Mr. Dunlevy see me again, will you?"

"Of course. Do you wish me to interview the applicants, then?"

The discreet advertisement had appeared in the London *Times* this morning, where it would remain for precisely one week. Any longer would make her seem desperate and already fighting to sustain a failing scheme. If she hadn't filled all the necessary positions by then, well, there were several governess schools about where she might find a capable, attractive young lady or two who didn't wish to follow children about.

"After I see Mr. Dunlevy I'll be free until luncheon. If anyone appears, have Juliet or Margaret inform me."

"Diane, there are two dozen young ladies presently waiting in the rear sitting room."

"Two dozen?" She stopped. "It's barely nine o'clock."

"Yes, I know."

At Jenny's tone, Diane lifted an eyebrow. "You find this amusing, do you?"

"Not amusing. Encouraging. After all, if two dozen well-bred young women apply for employment at a gentlemen's gaming club, that implies a certain . . . acceptance of the idea, does it not?"

"Women are generally more difficult to convince than men where sin is concerned," Diane agreed. "What remains to be known is their quality. Would you and Margaret chat with each of them? With two dozen this morning, we shall hopefully be able to be a bit more . . . particular than I'd anticipated."

Jenny nodded. "*Mais oui.* I'll bring you the results after your meeting."

Though Mr. Dunlevy clearly didn't understand the

importance of adding a factor of teasing and mystery to the club, he *did* understand the additional hundred pounds Diane had added to the agreement for two more walls and strategically placed doors.

Once he returned to his work, Diane sat back and sipped at her cooled tea. When he'd first arrived, her foreman of construction had been less than comfortable first with the idea of taking orders from a woman, and second with meetings where she disdained the use of a chaperone. It seemed to have finally occurred to him that her money spent as well as any man's and that she knew her business.

Of course not everyone would be so easily convinced of her sanity or her reasoning. All she had to do, however, was make them want to visit The Tantalus Club. And then, if she'd managed to lay the path correctly, everything else would take care of itself.

Genevieve knocked at the half-open office door and then slipped into the room. "Do we have corridors for mystery?" she asked, holding onto the *r*'s and giving a deeper French lilt to her accent.

"We do. Do we have any possible employees?"

"I'll leave that to you. Margaret and I gave brief interviews and made notes on all forty women, and I sent them home. The rooms were becoming very crowded."

"Forty now? Good heavens." Diane gestured at the stack of papers her companion held. "I hope you took addresses."

"*Oui,* for the ones willing to give out such information. I instructed the others to return tomorrow for possible interviews with you."

Diane frowned. "I don't want whores working here, Jenny. If they can't give an address, then I—"

"Read the notes. Your order of sconces and table lamps arrived, so if you need me I shall be downstairs polishing and adding lamp oil."

Well, that was less helpful than Genevieve generally was. Frowning, Diane read through the first neat paragraph of notes. Then she read the next one, and the next.

"I'd ask if I'm disturbing you, but as we both know the answer to that, I'll just come in anyway."

Jumping at the low drawl, Diane nearly ripped the corner off the paper she held. "You aren't required yet, Haybury. Go away until I summon you."

Light gray eyes beneath a mass of unruly mahogany hair met hers. It wasn't that he looked untidy; in fact, Oliver Warren was always impeccably dressed and groomed. Rather, the too-long windswept hair and the simple knot in his snow-white cravat gave the impression that he was more relaxed than he was, that his mind wasn't running swift circles around everyone else in the room. With a few exceptions, of course. She knew his game, how he played it, and the moves that he preferred.

"From the destruction going on below, I assume you received the money," he said, strolling to the window behind her.

Diane turned her chair, unwilling to have him at her back. "You're not fooling me."

"That's . . . good, since I'm not attempting to do so."

"Yes, you are. You mean to ask an innocuous question here and there about renovations, floor plans, et cetera, until you've maneuvered yourself into giving advice, making suggestions, and then attempting to alter my plans to suit yourself."

"Am I? God's blood, I'm devious."

"No, you *think* you're devious. And I'm not interested in anything you offer unsolicited. As I said, when I require your presence, I'll send for you. At the moment, you're interrupting."

"You know," he returned slowly, reaching around her for one of the interview sheets she hadn't yet read, "as much as you don't want my opinion, I'd like to point out that in your general disdain for men you might have neglected a thing or two. For instance, ordering me to leave would be more effective if you had a large footman or two, say, to encourage my exit."

Her heart drumming in an annoying combination of anger and alarm, she twisted to dig into the drawer where she kept her pistol. Even as she moved, she realized that he'd turned her away from it deliberately, damn it all.

One booted foot jammed the drawer closed before she could do more than touch it. "Be nice," he cautioned. "It was only a suggestion. Not a threat."

"Get your boot off my desk."

"Certainly." He straightened. Before she could dive for the weapon again, however, he nudged her chair aside with his hip, opened the drawer, removed the pistol, and tossed it out the window. "There."

She glared at him as he sank back against the sill again, cleverly placing himself so she couldn't push him out the window after the weapon. "If you've killed any of my flowers I'll expect you to replace them," she finally said, and deliberately lowered her head to resume reading.

Though she couldn't ignore him, she could at least pretend to do so. She would, however, consider hiring a large footman or two. But only because aristocrats who'd lost all their money and had too much to drink might become unruly, and she hadn't considered that.

" 'Blond hair, blue eyes, approximately twenty years of age,' " he read aloud. "What's this?"

"None of your business," she snapped, drawing a pencil line through a description of a young lady Jenny had noted as being illiterate.

" 'A pleasant voice, claims to have a passing talent for the pianoforte, and speaks French.' " Oliver rattled the paper. "You know what I think?"

"I have no interest at all in knowing what you think. Haven't I made that clear enough to you?"

"I think this is one of the chits answering your advertisement in the newspaper." Handing the page back to her, he reached into his pocket and removed a folded newspaper clipping. " 'Seeking for the purpose of legitimate employment: ladies aged between eighteen and twenty-six, educated and pleasant of manner and appearance. Room, board, and salary will be provided.' " He dropped it onto the desk in front of her. "This is your address."

"I told you I mean to hire young ladies. Don't act as though you've discovered something nefarious. I'm hardly impressed that you know how to read, either. I believe I already knew that."

"It occurs to me that I should be present for these interviews. After all, being pretty and literate does not make anyone a good faro dealer."

Diane stood. With him leaning into the sill they were very nearly the same height, and she glared straight at him. "I will hire whomever I choose, for whichever reasons I deem appropriate for my needs. After I've hired them, I shall summon you to give instruction. At that point—"

"And if they can't manage wagering?"

"At that point," she repeated, ignoring his interruption, "I shall . . . permit you to voice an opinion as to which of them might be more suited than others for the various positions available at The Tantalus Club."

Slowly he straightened, and she found herself craning her neck to keep her gaze on his face. "You may have a damning letter," he said, "but you'd be better served to keep in mind that I have a great deal of money and influence, Diane. If you turn this into a battle, I will crush you."

She sniffed. "Color me unimpressed. I've been penniless and friendless already, Haybury. You may grind me into the ground again, but I'll see that you find yourself in that same patch of mud. Now go away until I send for you."

For a long moment he held her gaze, and she scarcely breathed. She was serious, and once he accepted that, perhaps dealing with him would be at least a little easier. Or so she hoped. Finally he nodded. "I've been invited to the Dashton soiree tonight. Dashton's an inveterate gambler, and so are most of his friends. What time shall I send my carriage for you?"

"I'm not accompanying you anywhere."

"If we're going to make our so-called mysterious connection believable, Lady Cameron, you will need to be seen with me. Eight o'clock." He headed for her office door. "And consider widening your front drive. Hopefully you'll need to accommodate traffic in the evenings."

And he still couldn't resist giving her advice. Which she would have tolerated better, except for the fact that thus far it had been good advice. "Eight o'clock," she said aloud, sitting behind her desk again. "Don't be late."

"Don't change your mind."

Chapter Five

O liver had his driver take the coach to Adam House by the most indirect route possible, ensuring he would arrive on Lady Cameron's doorstep precisely twenty minutes after he'd said he would be there. This was a game of wits and nerves he'd entered into, and every move counted.

Piles of wood and plaster lay to both sides of the drive as one of Diane's liveried footwomen emerged from the house to pull open Oliver's carriage door. If not for the fact that he'd shared a bed with Diane on several occasions, he would almost have been willing to think her one of those ladies who preferred the intimate company of other women.

Was he the reason she'd developed such a dislike and mistrust of men? *Hm.* More likely it was the three years of marriage to a man who'd left her penniless and abandoned in the middle of Europe. And apparently she meant for the rest of mankind to pay forever after.

On the other hand, perhaps the ambiguity of her preferences was intentional; after all, she had even him speculating about her, and he knew better. He glanced at the butleress as she stood back from the front door. Hiring all females. It seemed very much like something he should have considered himself.

"My lord, if you'd care to wait here, Lady Cameron will be down momentarily. I apologize for not being able to offer you a seat; we haven't any in this portion of the house at the moment."

"As you told me this morning, I believe."

"Yes, my lord. I've also been ordered to inform you that if you attempt to enter the depths of the house again without permission, I am to shoot you."

"I see." While he was tempted to inform her that she could certainly *try* to do so, he had other things on his agenda this evening. And apparently several minutes to kick his heels while he waited until Diane deigned to appear. "What is your name?" he asked the butler.

"Juliet, my lord. Juliet Langtree."

"Well, Langtree, what was your employment before Lady Cameron hired you to buttle?"

"I was a shopkeeper's assistant, my lord," she answered without hesitation. "In an establishment that sold weapons."

For a heartbeat he wondered whether she was having him on. Before he could decide, the air at the top of the stairs stirred. "Diane," he said, turning to face her as she descended. "Black again?"

He'd nearly said something more complimentary, because whatever the sleek ebony material was, it clung like water to her slender frame and every soft curve. But she knew that. That was why she'd chosen to wear it.

"It suits my mood," she returned. At her gesture Langtree pulled open the front door once more. "And cease pestering my employees. They've all been warned that . . . fraternizing with you is grounds for immediate dismissal."

"Jealous?"

"Wise to your very transparent lack of character." A second female, blond and whip-thin, appeared behind her to drape a black wrap across Diane's shoulders. "Shall we?"

The blond chit followed them outside. "You're to guard Lady Cameron's reputation, then?" he asked, offering a hand to help her into the coach. "Considering her plan of action, you're somewhat behindhand."

"I'm to protect *you*, my lord," she returned, her soft voice touched by a half-dozen accents but settling on none of them. "If Diane were to murder you, it would upset our schedule."

Once the ladies were settled inside, he stepped up after them. "Interesting that you've so completely misread the situation," he commented as the coach rolled back into the street. "If something were to happen to either of you, it wouldn't upset *my* schedule at all. And you said *our* schedule. Are you partners?"

"Oliver, this is Genevieve," Diane said into the following silence. "Jenny, Lord Haybury."

"You're new," Oliver continued, dividing his attention between the two women. They were of an age, he estimated, both in their early twenties, but whether they addressed each other familiarly or spoke about *their* schedule or not, he knew precisely which one of them commanded this little performance. "You weren't in Vienna when last I was there."

"Suffice it to say that Jenny and I have known each other for a very long time. I sent for her shortly after you fled Vienna."

Well, he'd brought it up; it served him right, he supposed, if she flung Vienna back in his face. "You know, I suppose I should thank you for driving me to flee," he responded, keeping his jaw clenched tightly so he wouldn't sneer. "After all, I arrived back in London just in time to reconcile with my uncle and inherit his wealth and title. All in all a very good summer, I think."

"For me as well, considering that Frederick expired and then you left just as you were becoming annoying." Diane straightened a finger of her black silk glove. "Now. We will remain at this soiree for two hours. Dance with whomever you please; the more the merrier, actually. Every waltz in that time, however, will be mine."

He could have disagreed with all of that, of course, but his curiosity to discover her plan outweighed his annoyance at being dictated to. "And what will you be doing when you're not in my arms?"

"I will *not* be dancing with anyone else. I did that at the Hennessy soiree. Tonight, let them wonder."

"And when anyone asks me about our connection?"

She glanced at him, then turned her gaze out the coach's window. "We are old . . . friends."

"Ah. 'Friends' with a hesitation. Secrets and such."

"I prefer to think of it as mystery." She looked back at him again, her startlingly green eyes softened to nearly black in the lamplight. "And you know nothing about the club other than its name and that it will open in one month."

"Shall I add my advertisement fee to the amount of the loan? I'm not your gossip column, Diane."

"Then say nothing. That's even better."

They rounded the corner, and the lights of Dashton House came into view up the street. When she glanced toward them he caught it—the very slight tightening of her mouth. However confidently she'd learned to speak and behave, she was nervous. Of course, if he'd wagered the amount she had and placed it all on one house of cards, as it were, he might be nervous as well.

"If Blalock hadn't expired," he asked slowly, half-wishing he'd decided against voicing the question because first, he didn't care, and second, it was a complication, "how would you be proceeding? Would you have demanded that fat old lecher take a room above your club? Would you have intimated that you and he were old . . . friends?"

"Now who sounds jealous?"

"I'm merely curious. I was a last-minute replacement, after all."

She sighed. "If you must know, in return for leasing the old Monarch Club for my use, Blalock would have been able to entertain there when he wished, with the intimation that yes, we were lovers."

"Well, you'll just pretend to be lovers with anyone, won't you?"

"Why not, if it serves my purpose?"

Oliver lifted an eyebrow. "Why do I have the distinct feeling that Blalock didn't know you only wanted to appear to be his lover, rather than actually stooping to sharing his bed?"

"He would have discovered that, eventually."

"You've lost every ounce of your heart, haven't you?"

"Your kettle is blacker than mine. And I didn't lose it. I disposed of it. It was only getting in my way, the useless thing."

The coach stopped, and a footman flipped down the steps, then pulled open the door. Oliver stepped down first and caught Diane's elbow as she descended. "You're a liar," he whispered.

"And you're a coward." She straightened her gown. "Offer me your arm properly."

"Yes, my lady." That last bit stung some, but he supposed he deserved that, too.

"And if you ruin this for me, I will destroy you."

As much time as he spent deciphering his fellows across a gaming table, Oliver had no trouble at all reading

Diane at the moment. She meant it. What she didn't realize, however, was the deeper the play, the more he liked it.

The difficulty with threatening a man who spent as much
time beyond the fringes of propriety as Oliver Warren did
was that he simply didn't frighten easily. Diane could see
it in his eyes as he accompanied her into the crowded
Dashton House ballroom. She'd very clearly threatened
him with ruination, and all she received in response was
mild, brief appreciation.

It didn't give her much reason to believe that fear would
compel him to behave as she required. Without that letter
she'd carefully locked away, she would have gotten nothing
at all from him. And even though she should—and did—
know better, it greatly irritated her that the skills she'd
worked so hard to master didn't seem to affect him at all.

"Two waltzes," Jenny murmured, appearing at her free
elbow. "The first one as soon as this quadrille is finished,
and the second one directly after refreshments."

Damnation. She would have preferred a bit of time
to observe the guests and to decide whether to attack or
defend before she stepped onto the dance floor with the
devil. Diane took a slow breath. Then again, she reminded
herself, she was no angel. Without much effort at all she'd
managed to send him fleeing the Continent two years ago.
Surely she could spar with him for four minutes and not
resort to physical violence.

"Is that what she does?" Oliver asked as Genevieve
slipped into the crowd again. "Flit hither and thither spying on people?"

"When I ask her to. And she's quite good at it. So
watch yourself."

"I'll be too occupied with watching you, and wondering when you'll realize that threatening me with every other sentence is nothing but a waste of syllables."

"It's habit, I suppose. In our brief previous acquaintance you ended by disappointing me." Whether that word was sufficient to describe her feelings after she realized he'd left Vienna she would contemplate another time. It was more important that he realize she was no longer the weak, panicked ninny she'd been two years ago when they'd met. She was as immune to him as he was to her.

"Haybury. Been wondering if you'd appear this evening."

Oliver's arm muscles tightened beneath her fingers, then relaxed again. "Manderlin," he said. "Have you met Lady Cameron?"

A tall mop of light-colored hair half-obscuring one brown eye bowed at her. The figure beneath wasn't bad at all and his features were quite pleasant, but that hair—*my goodness*. Someone badly needed to take a barber to that man.

"No, I haven't had the pleasure," the fellow drawled. "Introduce me, will you?"

"Jonathan Sutcliffe, Lord Manderlin," Oliver said without preamble. "Diane Benchley, Lady Cameron."

"I could have done that much," Lord Manderlin returned, shaking his head. "I know her damned name. A good introduction includes details. How each of us met you. Whether we're married or available. A favorite wine or sweet, perhaps."

"Do your own research." The music for the waltz began, and Oliver closed his fingers over her wrist. "After this dance."

She wanted to pull away from his grip, but resisted doing so. The decision to actually take to the dance floor was supposed to have been hers, but then she hadn't told him that. Thus far he'd tolerated her orders and demands, which gave her the superior position. If she pushed too hard and he balked, she would lose that measure of control—or the illusion of it, which was nearly the same thing.

Still holding her beside him, Oliver made his way to the middle of the dance floor. She approved the location—those not dancing would have only glimpses of her and Haybury, while the couples immediately around them would be able to see but not to hear any conversation. And it would look like they were conversing, whether they actually said anything to each other or not.

Then Oliver slid an arm around her waist, and she jumped before she could stop herself. The marquis cocked his head at her, his own steps unhesitating as he turned her into the dance. "If I were you," he murmured, "I wouldn't allow me to see that a simple touch unsettles you so."

"I wasn't unsettled," she returned, favoring him with a cool smile for the benefit of any onlookers. "I was repulsed. I am tolerating you for the sake of The Tantalus, and nothing more."

"Hm. You've generally been less direct with your jabs. You know, statements like that might injure my feelings."

"It would take more than words to score that rhinoceros hide of yours." Steeling herself, she looked directly at him—no small feat given the fact that he was at least eight inches taller than she was. "We can attempt to be civil, however, if you prefer."

"You're serious? I don't know which part of me to guard now."

It would help her cause if they looked friendly, so she smiled. "What is your opinion of current fashion?"

"I prefer black."

"Very amusing."

"What do you think of the London aristocracy, now that you've returned?"

"I don't actually wish to tell you anything you might later use against me," she said.

"You're too suspicious, Diane."

"Ah. Well, you taught me a great deal over a very short acquaintance, Oliver. Lessons I shan't ever forget."

"You're welcome, then." He drew her a breath closer to him as they turned. "Oh, that wasn't meant to be a declaration of gratitude, was it? You were attempting to shame me or something." Oliver grimaced briefly. "Hm. Care to give it another go? I can't guarantee I will appear contrite, but I'm willing to make the effort."

Resorting to physical violence had never crossed her mind—until that moment. If she attempted to slap him, however, two things were likely to happen: first, he would block the blow; and second, he would push her to the floor in front of everyone and ruin any mystery and dignity she'd managed to build since her arrival in London. "I don't require contrition. I stated a fact. And here's another fact: I don't trust you. And because I don't trust you, I can never like you. Ever again."

He lifted an eyebrow. "You've decided to abandon civility already, then?"

"Yes. It clearly serves no purpose with you."

Oliver stopped. In the middle of the Dashton ballroom, in the middle of a waltz. Lady Hubert and her escort nearly crashed into them, and Diane shifted a step to avoid the couple. For a heartbeat she noted that a few years ago such a move would have embarrassed—mortified—her, while now she was only concerned with how to turn the incident to her further advantage.

Offering him a soft smile, she kissed her palm and then placed her hand over his mouth. "You do say the most interesting things, Lord Haybury," she commented, then whirled away through the tumble of disorientated dancers. Somehow Jenny met her at the edge of the floor and fell in silently beside her. "We're leaving," Diane murmured at her companion, keeping the faintly amused expression on her face. "Get us a hack."

With a slight nod, Jenny vanished again. As soon as Diane passed out of the ballroom and through one of the hallway doors, she slowed, then ducked into the first empty room she glimpsed. *That . . . man. That arrogant, awful man.*

He'd tried to embarrass her. Tried to gain ground in what was already turning out to be quite the chess game. And the most annoying part of it all was that until she'd threatened him with blackmail she hadn't done anything wrong. Not where Oliver Warren was concerned, anyway. He'd found her in Vienna. He'd seduced her—though she'd certainly been a willing enough participant. He'd fled without a word. And now he, what, threw a tantrum because she wanted things her way?

She needed to make it perfectly clear that this was business and nothing more. Private personal feelings of wounded pride, animosity, revenge—well, they would both simply have to put such things aside.

And just to be safe she would ask Juliet's former employer if he could equip her with a less visible pistol or two. She didn't want to have to come up with a third plan to see The Tantalus opened, but she would do so if necessary. Lord Haybury needed to realize that what he wanted and what he thought didn't matter. And the sooner he did realize that, the better for both of them.

"I thought I saw you come in here."

The hard responding thump in her chest eased immediately. Oliver did not have a high-pitched voice or a Cornwall accent that even the very finest finishing school hadn't quite been able to erase. "Lady Dashton," she said, turning around. "I hope you don't mind. I saw the Gainsborough painting as I passed down the hallway, and I had to stop and admire it."

The viscountess's gaze shifted to the large family portrait hanging above the mantel. "It is fine, isn't it? Of course my sons are much older now, as are Stuart and I, I'm afraid."

"It's lovely," Diane commented, without looking at it again. Lady Dashton's fists were clenched; hardly what Diane would generally expect to see from a hostess chatting with an admiring guest. "And you all look very happy. I've never understood why so many painters settle such dour glares on their subjects."

"My husband is quite interested to learn more about your . . . club," the viscountess said abruptly, ignoring Diane's conversation.

"He won't have long to wait, then. I mean to open the doors of The Tantalus within a month."

"You know, Harriette Wilson became famous because of her impropriety with some quite distinguished gentlemen. But she's still never been invited to a proper Society event, and we still call her a whore."

Now Diane knew what the conversation was about. She clucked her tongue. "Such language, Lady Dashton. And yes, you're utterly correct about Harriette Wilson. But in her favor, she's never claimed to be anything but what she is." Curving her lips, Diane took a half step forward. "Allow me the same credit. Some of the gentlemen's clubs in Vienna and elsewhere on the Continent were magnificent. I am bringing that refinement to London."

"The idea th—"

"And who knows?" she pressed, shrugging. "If other ladies are as interested in The Tantalus Club as you are, I may institute a ladies' evening. A bit of genteel wagering and some Madeira and biscuits, perhaps. Served by handsome young men."

"Is that meant to sway me toward approval? Because I do not approve."

Deepening her smile, Diane inclined her head. "Then you needn't attend. Now if you'll excuse me, I have a coach waiting."

"I wonder how much longer *you'll* be invited to proper Society events," Lady Dashton returned, stepping out of the doorway to let her past.

"We shall see. It will be interesting, won't it?"

As she turned down the hallway she caught sight of Oliver leaving the ballroom at the far end. If she had to fence with him again this evening her head—and her temper—would explode. Hurrying without appearing to do so was something of an art, but one she'd mastered shortly after her marriage. In a moment she was outside and climbing into the waiting hack.

"I know you did your research, but are you certain there isn't anyone else from whom we could secure financing?" Jenny asked from beside her.

"I imagine we might," Diane said slowly. "But I don't want word of my cash difficulties getting out. More than anything else, that could ruin me. Gentlemen attend clubs for prestige and amusement and to risk. If I appear to be desperate for money, they will all assume I mean to cheat them."

"But Haybury isn't proving to be at all amenable."

She sighed. "He's a stubborn blackguard. I'll give him that. At the same time, he's more likely to keep certain of my secrets safe than anyone else I can imagine. After all, I hold one of his secrets. It's a balance, and one I simply don't have with anyone else."

"Until he throws you out a window."

"It would still be a balance. I would be dead, but his reputation as a man would be destroyed."

Jenny sank back into the corner of the small coach. "I

did not anticipate that this task would be a simple one. But neither did I expect that we would be having this much difficulty less than a week after we received our funds."

Disquiet stirred in Diane's chest. "I know how much I'm asking of you, Jenny. If you don't wish to continue, well, I'll figure out something el—"

"Nonsense, Diane. You found me again at a very . . . difficult time. If for no other reason than that, I would remain. But to have rediscovered a friend, as well—I will travel down any road you choose."

Diane grabbed her friend's hand and squeezed it in hers. "Thank you. But because we *are* friends, you must tell me if I'm driving us off that road and into the hedgerow."

With an uncharacteristic chuckle Genevieve squeezed back and then retrieved her fingers. "In some ways I hope this ride will continue to be as exciting as it's begun, as long as we reach our destination."

"And *I* hope I don't have to shoot the horse." The very troublesome stallion was going to have to be convinced to follow her rules before he ruined everything. And no man was going to ruin things for her ever again. Not even the Marquis of Haybury. No, *especially* not him.

Chapter Six

"M y lord, a message just arrived for you."

Oliver wiped butter from his fingers and gestured at the silver tray his footman held. "Let's see it, Myles."

The moment Oliver saw the elegant swirl of his name on the outside of the note, he knew who'd sent it. Three days, just as she'd informed him. Despite the constant and almost palpable urge to stride through the front door of Adam House and inform her that he'd been the one delivering the lesson and that no one left him standing on the dance floor, he'd resisted. He'd gone about his usual activities—or most of them, anyway—and waited for her to make the next move.

"That'll be all," he informed the footman, and rose to head for his office. As he walked the short distance down the hallway he passed the familiar painting of Aphrodite rising from the sea. When he closed the house, that would be joining him at The Tantalus Club, mostly because the depiction of a naked and openly seductive female would likely annoy Diane no end.

He walked to the window that overlooked the carriage path and Lord Penbridge's underused billiards room next door and took a seat. Manderlin and others had asked why he didn't purchase a house in Town now that he'd inherited the wealth of the Marquisdom of Haybury, but he didn't see the point. The only entertaining he did was of the very intimate variety, and he spent very little time at home, anyway. Outside the walls was much more interesting.

"Speaking of which," he muttered, and unfolded Diane's note.

" 'Haybury,' " he read aloud, " 'you are to sit down at noon today with a group of potential employees. I expect you to arrive at half eleven so I may go over your instructions with you. C. of Cameron.' "

The damned chit excelled at giving orders. And of course he would have to arrive on time, or he would look like a petulant schoolboy. Pushing at her control would take more sophistication than being tardy—and he hated repeating himself, anyway.

Swiftly he scribbled out a note to Amelia Lawson canceling their luncheon engagement, setting aside the realization that he'd meant to do that regardless of his orders. Playing about with pretty chits was a pleasant enough diversion, but he was waging a battle. And he would unfortunately have to discuss with Diane what he was supposed to tell the various females of his intimate acquaintance. He refused to let them believe he'd suddenly become either smitten or impotent.

He rang for Myles, one of only four servants he employed at his small residence. Haybury Park in Surrey was where the bulk of his employees worked and resided, but in the two years since he'd inherited his uncle's title, Oliver hadn't spent that much time there, either. For most of his life he'd been transient—boarding schools, university, London, Madrid, Rome, Vienna—and settling into one home, or even one country, still felt uncomfortable.

"Yes, my lord?"

"Send someone for my horse, will you?"

"Right away, my lord. Mrs. Hobbes inquired whether you would be in for dinner tonight, as she's just purchased a suckling pig."

"I don't know what my plans are. Have her roast the pig; the lot of you might as well enjoy it."

Myles gave a rare smile. "That is very generous of you, my lord. Thank you."

"If anyone should call, inform them that I'm out paying a visit to an old . . . friend."

"An old friend, my lord. Very good."

"No. An old . . . friend. With the implication that 'friend' isn't the correct word, but merely the most proper one."

"An old . . . friend. I understand, my lord." Myles turned for the hallway door, then hesitated. "I hope you know, my lord, that I would never promote gossip in such a manner without your express instruction to do so."

"If I thought otherwise, Myles, you wouldn't still be in my employ."

Oliver headed out the front door as a groom from the stable where he lodged the five horses he kept in London arrived with Brash in tow. He flipped the lad a shilling and set off at a trot toward Regent Street.

Had Diane given him such short notice of their meeting to keep him off balance? Or to prevent him from planning a rebellion? If either was the case, however, she'd badly underestimated him. He'd been conjuring scenarios and possible responses to her theoretical demands for three days. That still left her ahead at plotting, but he reckoned he was catching up.

The butler chit opened the Adam House front door as he topped the worn granite steps. Diane would need to have them and the door replaced before her club opened. He could point that out, he supposed, but it would likely cost him more money.

"Lord Haybury, Lady Cameron is expecting you. You'll find her upstairs in her office. I believe you've been there before."

"Aren't you supposed to deliver me there, Langtree?"

"Not today, my lord."

If he asked why she was unable to leave her post at the door she would only tell him it was none of his business. He was not going to lose ground to a damned female butler.

For the same reason he refrained from asking about the curtain of sheets that ringed most of the foyer. While the material hid the sight of the ongoing construction from any callers, it did nothing to muffle the sounds of hammering and sawing and the low buzz of men's voices.

The office door stood open, and Oliver stepped into the room without bothering to knock. "It's half eleven, though you likely know that because you've been looking at the clock for the past twenty minutes, haven't you?"

For God's sake, she was wearing black again—this time a straightforward muslin that would have looked fetching and fresh in any number of colors but that she managed to make . . . alluring. Quite a feat, really.

She indicated the chair opposite her desk. "Gentlemen's games. Faro, vingt-et-un, whist, hazard, and what?"

Oliver took a seat. "No. I demand a bit of social chatting before we get to business."

Diane cocked her head at him. "Very well. Have you bedded anyone interesting lately?"

Despite the sharpness of the conversation, he had to admire her skill at stabbing at him. But he had those same skills himself. "Interesting. Hm. Compliant, accommodating, yes. Now that I consider it, however, I have to concede that you were a more interesting lover than the chits I've run across lately." He deliberately lowered his gaze to her pretty bosom. "In fact, parts of me missed parts of you quite a bit, I think."

"How sad, considering that I forgot you the moment you walked out of the room."

Leaning forward, he set his elbows on the desk and his chin in his hands. "Did you now? Is that truly the tack you wish to take? Because I could always remind you."

"Yes, I imagine one of us would enjoy that quite a bit. Not me, however." She tapped her fingers against the paper in front of her. "Now. Tell me about games of chance."

Evidently he'd pushed her far enough this morning. "Very well. Men will wager over anything. How many times a friend says 'ain't' in the course of an hour. Whether a chit will step out of a carriage right foot or left foot first."

"Yes, that's all very well, but not terribly organized. Do I need to be more specific? I require a list of games and amusements they may play *here,* and preferably ones where the bank has the best chance of profit."

"Why don't you just rob them when they come through the front door?"

Diane didn't even blink. "Because then I would only gain what they had in their pockets on that particular evening. I imagine only a very few of them would return to be robbed again."

"True enough. It's all about subtlety, I suppose."

"Precisely."

He eyed her for a moment. "Two years ago you detested both wagering and the weak-minded men who failed to recognize their own lack of skill. And while I have to applaud the way you've moved beyond your contempt to see where wagering can be used to your advantage, I have to wonder at something."

She gestured at him. "Pray continue. I know I won't be able to get any use out of you until your girlish curiosity is satisfied."

The insult was rather blatant. To him that signaled that she wasn't comfortable with the path of the conversation. *Good.* "My girlish curiosity wants to know whether you've considered that you're planning on doing to other women what was done to you."

"Oh, good heavens!" she exclaimed, putting both hands to her mouth. "You're absolutely correct! How could I have been so blind?" Her horrified expression lifted into a faint smile. "I will no longer be trod upon, Oliver. I chose a wagering club because I appreciate irony and because it's a splendid way to make money. What is that old saying? 'The house always wins,' I believe."

"And the other women?"

"I'm not a tutor or a morality lesson. They are on their own, just as I was." One long finger tapped the sheet of paper in front of her. "Games. What have I missed?"

She *had* changed in two years. But he'd been attempting not to. In fact, that was why he'd left Vienna. To keep his life from upending. As she continued to gaze at him with thinly veiled suspicion, he shook himself. Contemplation was to be done in private, preferably with a large bottle of spirits at hand.

"In addition to cards and dice, there are wheel games and even some exotic Oriental fare."

"Tell me everything."

As he went about explaining the more basic rules of piquet and faro, he kept his attention on her. Most women took care not to be in a room alone with him unless it was intimacy they were after. But Diane simply wrote out her notes and glanced up at him from time to time when he intentionally shifted the path of the conversation. Did she truly see him as only a means to an end? Had she truly forgotten—no, not forgotten, but discounted—what he considered to be an extremely memorable fortnight?

And why the devil did he care if she had? *That* was the

aggravating part—that he couldn't seem to stop dwelling on it. "Have you found anyone to share your bed since I left?" he asked abruptly.

Diane didn't look up. "You rather put me off all that." Then she glanced at the mantel clock and stood. "Time to meet the first group," she said, and left the room without a backward glance.

"Like hell I did," he muttered, and followed her. After all, out of all the men in England, she'd gone looking for him. As a second choice, perhaps, but it still counted.

Twelve young ladies waited for them in a spare upstairs room. Diane had instructed that all furniture be removed and a card table and chairs be brought in. These women had passed her first three criteria of being young and literate and attractive, but she was aware that the ability to read was quite different from being able to converse—especially while managing gentlemen, money, and a game of chance.

"Ladies," she said as they all curtsied in ragged unison, "this is Lord Haybury. He will be discussing the game of faro. If you have any questions, feel free to ask him. I will be observing your aptitude, not just for the game, but as hostesses. You should think of your gaming table as your home, and you must entertain your guests well enough that they want to stay all night." There was of course much more to it than that, but with sixty-two women to choose from now, she needed to prune out the weeds, as it were.

While she remained at the back of the room, the thirteen seated themselves around the table. Oliver explained the basics of the game in a surprisingly understandable manner, and Diane allowed herself a brief moment of self-congratulation. Perhaps Blalock had been her first choice, but despite the irritation of having Oliver entangled in all this, he seemed to be the better choice.

Two seats around from Oliver on his right, a striking

brunette lifted a hand to ask her third or fourth question. Oliver sent the chit a glance, his mouth dipping a fraction, then looked away again as he answered her and went on with the lesson.

"You," Diane said, flipping through her notes. "Miss Carlysle, is it?"

The brunette nodded, her eyes darting in Oliver's direction and back to Diane again. "Yes, my lady. Mary Carlysle."

"You may go, Miss Carlysle."

"But—"

"If you can't control your tongue or your eyes when you know you're being observed, I can only imagine what might occur later. I don't blame you; Lord Haybury is evil." She turned to the group in general. "Anyone else who has been or who intends to become intimate with Haybury might as well leave now, too."

Miss Carlysle sent her an angry look, grabbed up her reticule, and stomped out the door. Oliver stood. The girls nearest to him actually shifted away, Diane noted. *Good for them.*

"A word, Lady Cameron?" he grunted, and walked out to the hallway.

"You may practice a round, ladies. I'll return in a moment."

As soon as she left the doorway Oliver stalked up to her. He lifted a hand as though to grab her arm, then clenched his fingers and backed away a step. "What the devil was that?" he demanded in a low voice.

"Why is it that as rakes get older, their mistresses get younger? She's barely nineteen, Haybury."

"Firstly, I am only nine-and-twenty, which is hardly anything close to being old. Secondly, Mary Carlysle is quite experienced for her age. Thirdly, you—"

"I already told you that I won't employ anyone with whom you've shared a bed."

"Which leaves you as the exception."

"I'm not an employee."

"Yes, well, you're beginning to sound jealous." He took a half step closer again. "Are you? Jealous, that is?"

Her cheeks heated. "Don't be ridiculous. I am not jealous. I am realistic. And realistically I know you are likely to do something to disappoint me. I'm attempting to prevent that. Or at least make it more difficult for you."

Oliver closed the scant remaining distance between them. Damnation, she wished he weren't as tall and physically imposing as he was. All she could do was lift her head and squarely meet his glare. Then he took her chin in his fingers, far more gently than she expected.

He meant to make her flee, no doubt. To run away trembling and lose ground to him while he returned to the room and more than likely ravaged all the remaining eleven women while each one stood in a queue waiting her turn.

"Well?" Diane demanded, inwardly delighted that her voice remained steady.

He leaned down, his breath close and warm against her lips. "Liar," he breathed. "You know I won't touch any of them."

"I know no such thing. Now unhand me."

His gaze lowered to her mouth. "I do wonder if you still taste as sweet, with all the sour things you say these days."

"Keep wondering."

"Do you dream about me?" he murmured, then abruptly released her and straightened again. "I imagine you do." He took the sheaf of papers she'd somehow raised to hold over her chest like a very ineffective shield. "I'll let you know whether any of these chits can manage a table. *You* decide whether they can sit back and watch men be ruined."

Diane took a deep breath. "Finish with them by two o'clock. You have another group at half past."

He nodded just before he stepped back into the room. Diane stood in the hallway, glaring after him. *Very well.* She still had several initial interviews to conduct, and given his conversation with her earlier, she also needed to look into ordering a pair of roulette wheels and something to contain rolling dice.

And she supposed with eleven ladies present in the practice room they didn't require a chaperone. Given the employment they'd chosen to pursue, perhaps this would be a valuable first lesson in other than faro, as well. After all, if they could resist the Marquis of Haybury, then they would have little difficulty turning away Lucifer himself. Her, jealous. *Over him. Ha. Ha twice.*

Diane headed down the hallway to the sitting room she'd given over for Jenny to interview the applicants who continued to appear on the doorstep at the rate of one or two per hour. If gentlemen showed themselves as eager to enter the doors of The Tantalus as the ladies clearly were, she would have no worries at all.

Inside the room Jenny sat across the small desk from a large bonnet. Someone, presumably a female, sat beneath, but the chapeau very nearly shielded every inch of her but her feet. And those were hidden beneath a rather drab gray and blue muslin. For a moment Diane nearly turned around and left the interview to Jenny—so far she'd managed to avoid speaking with the most insipid applicants. If she did leave, however, she would be sorely tempted to hover outside the practice room and fume over the nonsense Oliver was more than likely spewing.

"Jenny," she said before she could change her mind, "would you mind taking a look at the paint color I've chosen for the ceiling? I'm having second thoughts. I'll see to this."

Her friend nodded. "Certainly," she replied, rising. As

she passed through the doorway she brushed her fingers against Diane's elbow. "Be nice," she whispered, and was gone.

Stifling a frown, Diane sank into the vacated chair. When, precisely, had it become necessary for anyone to remind her to be nice? Pushing that thought aside, she pulled Jenny's notes closer and read through them. *Hm.* Evidently the interview hadn't progressed very far. "You are Emily Portsman," Diane stated, and finally looked up.

"I am."

The face, shadowed though it was by that voluminous hat, looked pretty enough. Hair color was even more difficult to determine—somewhere between blond and brown. "I am Lady Cameron."

"I have to ask, my lady. Your advertisement said you were looking to hire ladies to work at your club, but it didn't specify . . . Anyway, I . . . There are things I won't do, no matter the salary. So I wanted to know if you might be more specific before we began this, so as not to waste your time or mine."

Diane nodded. "I am not opening a brothel. What my employees choose to do on their own time is not my concern, as long as they are discreet about it. Or to be more direct, I will never ask you to sleep with anyone. I require employees to work at wagering tables, serve food, keep count of money, et cetera."

Miss Portsman reached up to untie her bonnet strings. Pulling the monstrous thing off, she set it on her lap. "Then I wish to proceed with the interview."

Chestnut. That was the color of Miss Portsman's hair, a still somewhat indecipherable combination of brown and blond and red. Diane jotted the notation down on the interview page, along with noting that the applicant had brown eyes. "Your age?"

"One and twenty."

Diane made another note. "You can read and write?"

"Yes."

"Languages spoken? Other than English."

"French, Spanish, and a smattering of Italian."

Well, that was commendable. She jotted that down as well. "Mathematics?"

"Passable. Sufficient for card playing and wagering and percentages."

"Did you attend a finishing school?"

"Yes."

"Splendid. Which one?"

"I prefer not to say."

Diane stopped in midscribble. "Beg pardon?"

"I attended finishing school and was considered an exceptional student, particularly of the fine arts. I prefer not to tell you which school I attended."

Well. She should have been offended, she supposed, that a prospective employee was unwilling to supply the most basic of references. She should likely end the interview and send the girl packing. Diane slowly sketched a light half-moon on the interview page. "References?"

"I have served as a governess in two distinguished households, neither of which I will name."

"I see." Diane set down her pencil, lifting her gaze to meet the direct brown eyes opposite. "Is Emily Portsman your real name?"

Silence. "No, my lady."

"You are aware that working here is likely to be seen as scandalous, whether you actually engage in any scandalous behavior or not. You may not be able to find employment as a governess again. Not for some time, anyway."

"Yes, I'm aware. I do not mind the appearance of scandal, as long as the decision of whether to actually sin or not remains mine."

"That's very . . . unusual of you."

"Is it? Are most of your applicants living comfortable, tidy lives, then?"

Diane had assumed that to be the case, she realized. Perhaps not entirely comfortable lives but . . . yes, tidy ones. The idea that she might be misreading her own potential employees troubled her. She didn't know everything, of course, but she had learned how to read people. Men, mostly, but certainly the ladies she'd allowed into her house. The ladies she'd left in the Marquis of Haybury's company.

The girl shifted forward in her seat a shade. "The position does offer room and board, does it not?"

"Is having you here going to cause me trouble?" Diane asked slowly.

Finally the supposed Miss Portsman looked down, pulling on her bonnet and settling it over her hair again. "It might. Thank you for seeing me. Next time I shall invent something more creative." Inclining her head, she stood and picked up her reticule.

"This trouble," Diane said to Miss Portsman's retreating back, not certain why she felt compelled to continue. "Would a man be to blame, by chance?"

Miss Portsman turned around. "I give equal credit to a man and to my own naïveté."

That certainly sounded familiar. "If your skills are as you claim, Miss Portsman, you're hired."

For the first time uncertainty crossed the other woman's shadowed features. "I . . . thank you."

"With a caveat: Keep the secrets you have now if you wish. But from this point onward, you will be honest with me. And if something from your past looks to impact my club, you will inform me of it."

Emily Portsman, or whatever her name might be, inclined her head. "You have my word, my lady."

"Good. I have a mathematics examination for you to

complete. I imagine you won't have any difficulties with it. When you've finished, we'll find you something to do, shall we?"

It belatedly occurred to her that her new employee hadn't asked about wages or days off or specific duties, something Jenny said most of the other girls had immediately wanted to know. After Diane looked at the completed examination and put Emily to work organizing the arrangement of the beds in the attic rooms, she went to find Genevieve.

"What did you think of the small thing with the large hat?" Diane's friend asked, not moving from her place in the doorway of the main gaming room. Beyond her several workmen perched on scaffolds and applied pale gold paint to the ceiling.

"I hired her."

"I thought you might."

Diane sent her a glance. "How could you possibly think so? You barely spoke with her."

"The look in her eyes reminded me of you."

"Oh, really? How so?"

"A determination not to be vulnerable." Jenny shifted. "I do like this color. It doesn't look so much like a home any longer. And it will complement the gold thread in the curtains and wallpaper."

"Jenny, were there any other applicants who didn't inquire about salary?"

Genevieve faced her. "Others who had that same look about them, you mean? Yes."

"I'd like to see those applications." At Jenny's stifled smile, though, she frowned. "This is not a charity or a home for wayward girls. I want charm, not desperation."

"There were a few. I'll gather the papers together for you."

"Thank you." Diane smoothed her skirt. "I think it's past time I looked in on our gaming instructor."

"I'm a bit surprised you left him alone with those young ladies in the first place."

Yes, so was she. But she wasn't about to admit that she'd been outmaneuvered. Not even to Jenny. "If they can resist his so-called charms, avoiding succumbing to any other temptation—or man—will be simple."

"But do the right-side-up cards always have to be spades?" the generous bosom asked.

Blinking, Oliver lifted his gaze from the table. Him, in a room with eleven very attractive young ladies and no one but the naive little ninnies to naysay him. He'd thought himself in heaven, but after an hour he was nearly ready to call this the other place.

"No, the face-up cards do not have to be spades. It's merely tradition."

"In my establishment the faro face-up cards will always be diamonds. That will be *my* tradition."

His spine straightened before he could tell his body to keep its relaxed pose against the card table. "Lady Cameron. You might have told me about your new tradition earlier."

The bosom bounced. "I asked that question because I thought diamonds would be more clever. Because we're ladies, and ladies love diamonds."

Oh, good God. In a more social setting he could have had the bosom ungarbed and spread upon the table by now, if he'd so desired. After the time spent listening to her and the other chatty, eager chits, however, what he most wanted was a drink and then another drink.

"Ladies, that will be all for today. Please be here at eight o'clock tomorrow for my final decision regarding your employment." As the chits left the room, Diane caught the arm of the bosom. "What is your name, my dear?"

"Charity. Charity Evans."

"Thank you. I'll see you in the morning."

"Oh yes, my lady." With a last bounce the bosom hurried from the room after the others.

When Diane remained in the doorway, Oliver took his seat once more and stacked the two decks of cards he'd been using for demonstration. She'd stayed away for the entire hour, which surprised him. And he didn't like being surprised. "A game, Diane?" he asked, setting one of the decks aside and shuffling the other. "Or are you afraid to play?"

"Disliking something and fearing it are two completely different things." She came forward. "Vingt-et-un."

"But then I don't get to play against you."

She lifted an eyebrow. "You think not? Never mind, then."

That was what he got for speaking plainly—a figurative slap to the jaw. "Sit down," he grumbled.

Apparently she considered that to be a signal of his surrender rather than an order, because she pulled out the chair opposite him and took a seat. "So you disliked Miss Evans, did you?"

"Did I?" He shuffled once more, then dealt each of them one card, hers face-down and his face-up, then dealt them each a second card, face-up. "If I say I found her attractive you'll send the poor half-witted chit away, and if I say she made me wish to put a ball through my head then undoubtedly you'll have the luscious young thing trailing me everywhere."

Diane lifted the corner of her hold card and glanced at it. "Another card," she said. "And you might consider that I won't suffer fools even if they do annoy you. Fools will cost me money and reputation." She looked down as he placed the four of clubs in front of her. "Now if she were secretly brilliant and only *playing* a fool, that would be something else entirely. I will stay."

"The dealer takes a card." He flipped over a five of hearts, which together with his king of hearts and the two of spades gave him a count of seventeen. "The dealer stays. And she was not playing at being a fool. She may not even be able to find her way back to her residence this afternoon."

"Then I won't hire her. How were the rest of them?" She turned over her hold card. "Twenty."

He nodded. "Seventeen. Player wins. Half the chits were rubbish, but four of them seemed fairly trainable. One of them already knows the game, and seems to have a talent for it." Taking the spent cards, he stacked them to one side and dealt again. "But you do realize that teaching them to play doesn't mean they can hold their own even as dealers or bankers."

"I'm aware. That's why I'm giving you the entire six weeks to train them. I'll keep on the five you mentioned for at least another few days. When I open I think thirty girls for the tables and serving drinks and general pleasant conversation will be sufficient."

"So you're listening to my opinion? Color me surprised." *And intrigued. More intrigued.*

"You know about wagering and presumably who has a talent for the cards. I may detest you on moral grounds, but I'm not a fool."

"I would be cautious where you fling your accusations of immorality, lady proprietor of a wagering club. You're taking sin in an entirely new direction for London."

"I suppose I am. Doing the sinning is much more pleasant than being sinned against, I'm discovering."

She meant that as yet another insult to him, of course. She thought she'd learned all the lessons of the world. But clearly she hadn't. Not yet. "Being sinned against may hurt, of course," he said, "but sinning has its own set of consequences."

She glanced up at him. "Do you have regrets, then?" she asked, her tone genuinely surprised.

"Of course I do. Beneath my monstrous exterior I am, after all, human."

"So you say. I shall withhold judgment until I see actual proof."

"Well then." Standing, Oliver shoved back his chair and reached across the table. Before she could shift backward he grabbed the front of her black muslin gown and yanked her forward. Lifting her chin with his free hand, he lowered his mouth over hers.

Heat slammed down his spine at the contact. He wasn't gentle about it, either, pulling her halfway across the table as he plundered her mouth. Her tongue flicked along his, drawing him harder against her. When he felt ready to combust, he straightened his fingers and let her go.

Diane plopped backward into her chair with none of her usual grace. Breathing hard and wishing he weren't, Oliver stayed on his feet and walked around her to the door. *Bloody hell.* He'd meant to remind her that she'd enjoyed him in Vienna just as much as he'd enjoyed her. Instead all he could conjure was the image of her beneath him, her midnight hair wild around her face and her green eyes sharp with excitement and passion.

"How is that for proof?" he said over his shoulder, his voice low and rough. "I'm going to get something to eat before my next so-called class begins."

He was halfway through the door when she shot him.

Chapter Seven

Diane dropped the spent pistol onto the table. She couldn't very well return it to the small band tied around her thigh, because the barrel was quite hot. And the room still seemed to echo with the loud roar.

In the doorway, Oliver staggered around to face her. "You shot me!"

"It's not as though I didn't warn you," she returned, lowering her skirt from where she'd lifted it to get to the pistol.

"You kissed me back! Shoot yourself if you're angry at someone for that!"

"Oh. I'm not certain I agree with you, but I'll remember for next time."

He clapped his right hand over his left shoulder. "See that you do," he snarled, and stumbled to his knees.

Jenny charged into view and then skidded to a halt, Margaret on her heels. "What— Margaret, fetch water and bandages. And keep the men downstairs. Tell them we shot a mouse."

"You're very quick with the excuses," Oliver noted, sinking onto his backside and no longer looking particularly alarmed.

"Yes, well, I've had practice." Jenny turned her head to look up at Diane. *You shot him?* she mouthed.

"He kissed me," she whispered back. And now she supposed she needed to assist Jenny, to keep the rat from expiring on her floor. Because that would certainly frighten away potential club members.

"Diane, do you need smelling salts?"

"No! I'm fine." *What a silly question.* Though she did seem to be swaying a bit. Diane gripped the edge of the table. For God's sake, she'd *shot* Oliver Warren. Yes, she disliked him—well, not precisely disliked, but loathed maybe. Or wanted to punch him in the nose—but not enough to shoot him. It was just that he'd—he'd kissed her. And that he'd been correct just then. She'd kissed him back, even knowing that he'd fled her bed like a fox with its tail on fire.

"Come and help me with his jacket," Jenny instructed, her voice sharp.

"Yes. Yes, of course." Blinking, Diane moved forward and knelt beside him to yank Haybury's jacket down his arms.

Oliver cursed blackly, using a selection of profanity so varied that some of it she'd never heard before. "I'll do it," he barked, pushing her back with his elbow.

One of the maids arrived with water and cloths, then hurried away again. This wouldn't be the first test of her household's discretion, but a shooting would be of far more temptation and interest to everyone than a countess's monochromatic wardrobe. Better to know now if they could be trusted, she supposed, rather than later.

"It looks to be a deep graze, my lord," Jenny said, ripping the sleeve of Oliver's lawn shirt off at the shoulder. "No ball to dig out."

"And yet I don't feel so very grateful," Oliver retorted.

"Be thankful that I can aim, then," Diane commented,

sticking her finger through the hole in his jacket sleeve and attempting to rid her head of the last of its cobwebs. "And that I decided your heart was too shriveled to make a decent target."

His right hand jabbed out and caught her around the wrist. "We're even now, Diane," he breathed, pulling her closer and off balance. "I damaged your pride in Vienna and now you've shot me. Attempt something like that again and I won't be so charitable."

She kept her arm relaxed, refusing to pull against a grip she couldn't break without putting both feet against his chest. So he thought he'd done nothing more than damage her pride. God knew he wasn't a stupid man, though. Had he not even realized how much he'd hurt her? It was so odd to think she might have misread things. And even odder was the way she abruptly seemed willing to look at them—at him—again. After all, she had shot him. Perhaps he'd earned a moment of consideration before she began loathing him again.

"If you attempt to kiss me again without my consent I will aim my pistol much lower," she returned, because she had no intention of letting him know what she was thinking.

He released her arm, his gaze sharpening. "Not without your consent, then."

"You both baffle me," Jenny muttered as she wrapped the deep gash high on Haybury's well-muscled left arm. "That's the most civil conversation I've heard you have. Now, have a seat back in the sitting room, my lord, and I will fetch you a whiskey while Diane finds you one of Lord Cameron's old jackets."

Oliver sent her friend a dubious look. "I am not going to wear a hand-me-down, and certainly not one worn by that fool."

Diane stood once more. "You have another group of

ladies to assess in ten minutes. And keep your opinion of my late husband to yourself." Whether she agreed with it or not.

To her surprise, Oliver pulled himself to his feet and followed her down the hallway, denying her the moments she needed to think. Of course he was *much* more to blame than she was, because he'd stepped into the illusion that she had control of the entire situation and he'd stepped into her memories. And he'd found the chink in her armor.

She'd wounded him, but now he knew that physical contact with him rattled her. Diane scowled at the air before her. *Damn it all.* When she'd realized she needed to include Oliver Warren in her plans she'd known he wouldn't be happy about it. She knew how he conducted both his business and personal affairs, and she'd thought herself prepared for it. Clearly she'd been wrong. Because whether she wished to deny it or not, she had kissed him back. And for the maddest, briefest of moments, she'd enjoyed doing so.

"I have a question," Oliver said from just behind her.

She resisted squaring her shoulders. "If the question is about why I shot you, I believe you can figure it out on your own."

"Yes, I know precisely why you shot me. You hoped it would keep me from noticing your tongue dancing with mine." He paused, undoubtedly to increase the dramatic effect of the statement. "My question is, why do you still have pieces of Lord Cameron's wardrobe?"

"There were a few things left behind when we departed London." She shrugged. "I've been back for only a fortnight, after all."

"It's just that the last time I saw you with one of Cameron's shirts, you were ripping it to shreds. With a knife, as I recall."

"I was a bit angry then. I've had two years to consider things since that day."

"Ah. And now that you've witnessed the results, was shooting me as pleasant as you imagined it would be?"

Oh, that was enough of that. Diane stopped, turning on her heel to face the absurdly tall marquis. "What *you* should have considered is that I have no tolerance for men who attempt to ruin my life." She lowered her gaze to the bandage around his upper arm. Red slowly stained the middle of it. She'd done that. And it troubled her that injuring him bothered her. "I will, however, apologize for shooting you," she forced out. "I confess that you . . . disturb me more than I'd anticipated."

Astute gray eyes met and held hers. "Likewise," he finally said, and motioned for her to continue forward.

Little as she liked having him behind her, the sooner they could find him appropriate clothing, the sooner she could have a moment or two on her own to think. The way he lived his life, this most likely wasn't even the first time he'd been shot. It was, however, her first time shooting someone.

"Are you going to open The Tantalus with a grand party, or simply invite prospective members to stop by?"

"None of your business."

Silence. "I'm not suggesting anything," he finally commented. "I'm only asking a question."

"Very well. A party. And don't give me your opinion of that."

"Wouldn't think of it."

"Good." She turned into the small bedchamber where most of Frederick's remaining things seemed to have accumulated since her return to London. "The jackets are in there," she said, gesturing at a half-open wardrobe. "A shirt or two as well, I think, though the quality isn't as fine as yours."

Favoring his left arm, Oliver began shuffling through drawers. After a moment he lifted out a lime-and-olive-colored jacket and held it by the collar with his fingertips. "Truly?" he asked.

Memory flashed through her, images of her thin, stern-faced husband remarking that when Prinny wore something it immediately became fashion and that fashion bespoke confidence and competence. And then him returning after a night in his fashionable attire a hundred pounds lighter in the pockets and forbidding her to speak of either.

"Diane?"

She shook herself, turning away from the brown-haired devil and his lifted eyebrow. "Just choose something and get back to your classroom."

With a noncommittal grunt he returned to digging. "If anyone sees me in this I'll be ruined," he finally said, and she faced him again.

The brown of the jacket was a fairly close, if less rich-looking, match to the one he'd worn to visit The Tantalus. The problem was the way his own shirtsleeves—sleeve—ended at his wrist while the jacket's extended somewhat short of that. And he couldn't have buttoned the thing if his life depended on it. "You two were of a height. I thought it would fit."

With a grimace he shrugged out of it again. "He didn't have much meat on his bones, did he?"

Diane frowned. "No."

"Well, I suppose I'll have to be attired more casually. I can only hope your prospective employees don't all throw themselves at me and leave you without assistance." Looking down, he began unbuttoning his waistcoat.

"What are you doing?"

"Putting on a fresh shirt," he said, hanging his tan-colored waistcoat over one of the wardrobe's doors and then pulling his one-sleeved shirt off over his head. "With the sleeves rolled up, I would presume."

Memory touched her again, this one much more pleasant. Those same arms and shoulders, that fit, muscled abdomen, golden with firelight and settling over her in what had only a fortnight previously been her husband's bed. Belatedly she turned half around to find a small pile of clean cravats.

"You aren't being bashful, are you?" he drawled. "It's nothing you haven't seen before."

"Precisely." Pulling a cravat free, she intentionally walked over and draped it with the waistcoat. "And I'm afraid the detriments of your character far outweigh the benefits of your body."

"You didn't think that then."

"I was stupid and lonely. Now I am neither. Get dressed. I want you out of my private rooms."

"I'll leave your rooms," he agreed. "For now. But I'll wager everything I own that I won't be leaving your thoughts."

Arrogant man. "No, both you and the rats in the cellar have my attention. Jenny will bring the ladies up in a moment. Be there waiting."

With that she slipped out of the room and down the hallway to her own bedchamber. It was the largest one in Adam House and had been Frederick's. Now it and its sturdy lock were hers.

For a minute she fought the urge to collapse on the bed. Instead she concentrated on easing the shake of her fingers as she paced to the window and back. Generally these days she was far beyond panic and hysterics. They had no place in her life any longer.

What Oliver had said made a surprising amount of sense. Not that silliness about them being even, but the bit about which of them presently deserved the blame for to-day's fiasco. She'd demanded that he be involved in all this, had thoroughly sought about for weaknesses, and then had shot him when she'd found one that had also turned out to be hers. Her mind might still mistrust him keenly, but her body was rather more forgiving.

"You're leaving?" Manderlin opened the lid of the nearest trunk and peered inside. Then he moved a step over to the next one and repeated the action. "And you're taking that Prussian beer stein with you? I rather like that one myself."

Oliver walked back into the morning room where most of the full crates and trunks had ended up to wait for transport. "I've decided not to renew my lease here," he commented, closing the lids Jonathan had opened. "When I expire you may have the stein. For now, it's going with me." And so was the nude woman painted on the outside of the mug, along with her head—which lifted off when the thing was opened.

"Are you finally purchasing a place, then? I heard that Simwell House was going on the market."

"I'm moving into one of the rooms above The Tantalus Club."

"You're bamming me."

Oliver glanced at his friend as Jonathan seated himself on a crate of books destined for storage. "I nearly moved into the Society last year. And who can resist a club stocked with pretty chits?"

"I can't decide if I should point out that the book at White's has The Tantalus at eight-to-one odds to close within ten weeks of opening, or if I should fall on my knees and worship you."

"I prefer the worship."

"That's an awfully close association with a near-certain failure, Oliver. Not the way you generally do business."

"It's not going to fail."

"Hm." The viscount slapped his hands on his thighs and stood again. "Purchase me luncheon at White's and we'll chat about your connection with Lady Cameron then, why don't we? And don't tell me you don't gossip when you've been supplying the wags with half their fodder for years."

"I'll keep my own counsel, thank you very much."

"That's damned selfish of you, Oliver." Jonathan strolled to the door, then stopped. After a brief hesitation, he closed it and turned around again. "I've known you for a long time, if you'll recall. I know, for instance, that your uncle cut you off five years ago because you called him a horse's ass. I know that—"

"No, I called him a poor excuse for a horse's ass." Oliver looked at his friend. Jonathan was sober, interested, and genuinely concerned. Over him. And however reticent he generally was to speak of his own situation, the viscount could be trusted—if the secrets had been Oliver's to share. "What do you want to know, Jonathan?"

"You met Lady Cameron in Vienna, didn't you?"

"Well, clearly I met her somewhere. Vienna does seem like the most likely place."

"And now you're moving into her house. Not a very subtle way to begin a scandal."

Oliver forced a grin. "I'm not moving into her house. *That* place practically has steel walls separating it from the club. On the other hand, The Tantalus Club boasts two private apartments above its main dining and gaming rooms. I'm taking one of them. Perhaps both of them. I haven't decided yet." In fact, he just that moment had, but he wasn't idiotic enough to announce it publicly before he did so to Diane. He had no wish to be shot again this month.

"When do I get a look at your new residence, then?"

Manderlin still had his doubts about what Oliver was up to with Diane Benchley. Considering how long they'd been friends and the sort of behavior Jonathan was used to from him, that wasn't much of a surprise. "How about today?" he decided. Diane's obsession with mystery was one thing, but mistrust from a good friend was quite another. And Oliver had few enough friends that he wasn't willing to set this one aside because of that damned woman. "After I purchase you luncheon at White's."

"Well, that's a generous offer. Thank you, Haybury."

"Half-wit."

Over the next two hours he learned that most of London seemed to know he'd been calling on Adam House almost daily and staying for hours at a time. Apparently everyone believed that he and Diane had a . . . connection, as Manderlin put it, and that Oliver was one of the reasons she'd chosen to open her club in London.

The speculation over the precise nature of The Tantalus Club was even more varied, but he refused to either add to or quell the flames. That was Diane's grand experiment. Not his. He was there only to share his expertise and to add to the spectacle.

As he listened and continued to turn away or misdirect questions from Jonathan and everyone else in earshot of his table, it occurred to him that so far Diane was accomplishing exactly what she intended. The Tantalus Club would open in one week, and no one—none of the men, at least—wanted to speak of anything else.

"Good afternoon, my lord," the senior Adam House groom greeted Oliver as he and Manderlin reached the front drive.

"Clark. How many men in residence today?"

The grizzled groom snorted. "More'n her ladyship likes, and that's for damn certain. I've two new lads myself." As he took Brash's reins and stepped over to collect Manderlin's Phoenix, he lowered his voice. "Just so you know, she hired on two large fellows this morning. From the docks, I think."

Oliver nodded. Though he ordinarily didn't make a habit of conversing with the help, Clark seemed to consider him an ally in a household where he was very much outnumbered. The information with which the groom supplied him had on occasion been quite useful.

The front door opened as he and Manderlin topped the steps. "Langtree," Oliver said, moving forward.

The chit stepped up at the same time, blocking the doorway. "Lady Cameron isn't entertaining callers today," she stated, with a pointed glance at the viscount.

"We're not calling on her," Oliver returned, reflecting that where he might have been willing to set an uncooperative butler on his arse, he wasn't so certain he wished to do that to a butleress. "We're viewing my new apartment."

With a nod she shifted sideways. "The secondary staircase was finished just this morning. Be careful of the bannister; I'm not certain the varnish has set."

He meant to ask Diane whether the new staircase at the very front of the house was for anyone wishing to reach the club's upper rooms or if it had been installed solely to keep him out of the main part of the house. The question would have to wait until he didn't have Manderlin tagging along, however; Oliver preferred to hear his landlord reply candidly—even when firearms were involved.

"I was in Adam House once eight or nine years ago," Jonathan commented as they ascended the new staircase, set at ninety degrees from the main one. "I don't recognize anything but the outside walls."

Oliver nodded. "She's been busy." A walkway along the right ran to the upstairs gaming and sitting rooms, while two doors stood on the left-hand side of the landing. He pulled out the key Diane had very reluctantly given him yesterday and unlocked the right-hand door.

Everything still smelled of fresh construction, but he'd become more than accustomed to that particular scent over the past five weeks. The door opened into a large, comfortable sitting room, with two bedchambers, a library, and an office all branching off from a short hallway just beyond it.

"This is rather ingenious," Jonathan commented as they walked the rooms. "Larger than the apartments at the Society by a good deal. What about servants?"

"The Adam House maids will clean, I've use of the club kitchen staff, and Langtree answers the door. I'm only bringing along Myles and Hubert, and they'll reside in the attic."

"If you weren't Beelzebub himself, I would say you'd found a room in heaven, Haybury."

Oliver grinned. "I doubt heaven has gaming tables and a billiards room or is populated solely by pretty chits."

"What are you doing up here?"

At Diane's sharp tone he turned around. She stood just inside his door, at her shoulder a pretty girl with ash-blond hair. "I'm showing Lord Manderlin my new residence," he stated, squelching the abrupt feeling that he was back in university and the headmaster had just caught him with a chit in his rooms. "What are you doing here?"

A muscle in her jaw jumped. "You know how I dislike having surprises spoiled, Oliver," she continued in a much more sensual voice, gliding forward.

Good God, he remembered that tone. His cock jumped, and he shifted. "Then you have nothing to fear. Manderlin is very nearly the soul of discretion."

"Thank you for very nearly complimenting me," Jonathan put in, his gaze shifting from the advancing Lady Cameron to the tall chit behind her. "I beg your pardon, but you're Lady Camille Pryce, aren't you? Does Fenton— Are you . . . working here?"

The chit paled. Before Oliver could get a closer look at her, Diane stepped between them. "You'll have to join The Tantalus Club if you wish to find that out, Lord Manderlin."

The viscount sketched a bow. "Yes, my lady. If I may say, what little I've seen of The Tantalus Club is very impressive."

"Thank you, Lord Manderlin. When you have a moment, Oliver, the main room is finished. As long as you're here, you and Lord Manderlin may have a closer look, if you wish."

As soon as she and her companion left the room, closing the apartment door behind them, Oliver turned on Manderlin. "What were you stammering about? Who's Camille Pryce?"

"You haven't heard?" Jonathan returned, raising both eyebrows. "I know something you don't? Hold a moment. I need to jot this down for my memoirs."

Clearly he'd been spending too much time at Adam House, if he'd missed out on gossip about the aristocracy. "It'll be your obituary if you don't tell me."

Manderlin eyed him. "You may be terrifying, but I'm going to take a stand here. You tell me what the devil is between you and Lady Cameron, and I'll tell you who Camille Pryce is."

Oliver snapped a curse. "I don't like bargaining."

"Yes, but you like not knowing things even less."

For a long moment Oliver glared at the viscount. "Remind me why we're friends?" he suggested finally.

"Because no one else tells you the truth about yourself," Jonathan said easily. "And because I don't pay attention to what other people say about you."

Oliver took a breath. "Yes, well, likewise. We were acquainted in Vienna. It didn't end well."

Manderlin nodded. "So I surmised. Camille, Lady Camille Pryce, that is, was engaged to marry the Marquis of Fenton. She fled the church on their wedding day. No one's seen her for weeks."

"Apparently this is becoming a home for wayward chits." It was all interesting, but something that he needed more time to contemplate. "Now let's go see Lady Cameron's gaming room, shall we?"

"I may trample you on the stairs to get there first."

Oliver refrained from confessing that he'd already seen The Tantalus's rooms, and on numerous occasions. Diane had managed to purchase his silence by threatening blackmail, but even more troubling was the way she'd managed to get him both to comply and even to willingly cooperate with her subterfuge.

It was past time he begin taking steps to see that if this little battle of wits ever became a full-out war, he would win. What he needed to do now was see how far he could raise the stakes before she felt compelled to risk her one hold card. Anything short of that, well—that left a very large field in which he could play. And he knew just the game.

What better way to prove to himself that Vienna had been nonsense, a moment of weakness, than to repeat the experiment? And to be sure that this time *she* would be the one fleeing like a so-called scalded dog. Because he didn't leave a table until the game was finished. Not any longer. And not until he'd won.

Chapter Eight

He recognized me," Camille Pryce said, her hands gripped together over her chest. "I told you that would happen, my lady."

Diane stopped halfway through the main gaming room. "It takes too long to say 'main gaming room,' doesn't it? I should name it. Something that flows off the tongue. Every room, in fact. What do you think?"

The Earl of Montshire's daughter wiped at her face. "I . . . Are you certain you know what ruin could fall upon you by employing me, Lady Cameron?"

"What I know, Camille, is that men will wish to see you here. They'll likely make comments, and one or two of them may sneer or scowl. If they wish to pay twenty pounds a year to scowl, however, they are welcome to do so."

"It's not you they'll be scowling at."

"Oh? You think not?"

Camille's too-pale cheeks darkened. "Well, perhaps they'll frown at you as well, but only behind your back."

"Where I shan't see it, and where I shall care even less. The worst they can do is not come here. Once they've paid to walk through my doors, well, let them do what they will, as long as they spend their money. Which I shall use to pay you and the other ladies in my employ. What do you think of 'the Persephone Room'? We'll have to paint the names in all the doorways, but . . . oh, yes. I think that would be splendid."

When Camille began to calm a little and join in with suggestions to call the other rooms after goddesses and mythological females as well, Diane shifted position. She wanted to know when Haybury and Manderlin entered the room.

She'd never expected to be reassuring young ladies or providing shelter for others of dubious background, but now that she'd begun it with Emily Portsman and Camille Pryce, it seemed . . . fitting. And even a little satisfying.

At three-and-twenty Diane was hardly of an age to feel motherly toward them, but a sister—yes, she could do that. They weren't her confidantes, because that was Jenny's role. But some of them had been placed in the position of *needing* to work for her, and they'd been put there not through any true stupidity of their own devising. No, men were much better at being stupid and arrogant. In that she had no difficulty agreeing that they were superior.

"Good glory!"

Diane stifled a smile at Lord Manderlin's exclamation. "Welcome to the Persephone Room," she said, trying out the name and liking it. She would have to meet with Mr. Dunlevy again, to have him do a bit of scrollwork for the lettering, but he'd managed an additional staircase with fewer than a dozen curses. Painting a few words above doors should be simple in comparison.

"It doesn't have enough tables," Oliver stated.

He'd said that before, and she'd ignored him. This time, however, he'd brought along a witness. Oh, and then she'd invited the two of them into her parlor, damn it all. She cleared her throat. "We have additional tables. They can easily be brought in and set within minutes, if necessary."

"I like it," Manderlin commented before Oliver could say something disparaging. "I always hate squeezing past empty tables at the Navy. Far too cluttered."

"Thank you for saying so, my lord." This time she did smile. "I think I've found the balance between intimacy and practicality."

"I'd love to see the rest of the rooms, if you'd indulge me, Lady Cameron."

She dipped her head a little, to look at Manderlin from beneath her eyelashes. "Your friend is quite charming, Oliver." Ah, men were so . . . transparent.

"Leave my f—"

"A lady must keep some mystery, however," she interrupted. "I will send you an invitation for opening night. Will that suffice, Lord Manderlin?"

"I suppose it will have to. You've definitely whetted my curiosity."

"Mm. Good." She drew a quick breath as if shaking herself free of the viscount's spell. He was a handsome man, after all, if not as devastating as the devil beside him. "If you gentlemen will excuse me, I have some things to see to." She walked to a bell rope hanging against one of the mystery doors, as she and Jenny had taken to calling them, and pulled it. Less than a dozen seconds later the door opened. "Mr. Jacobs will see you out," she said, keeping her gaze on Oliver.

One of the very large men she'd hired earlier sauntered into the room. She would have to thank Gentleman Jackson for his recommendations. She'd had no idea that there were so many former boxers willing to work for a lady in search of strong, intimidating help. If Mr. Jacobs and Mr. Smith were as effective as they looked to be at keeping order, she might even hire a few more of the fellows.

Once Lord Manderlin and Satan left the room, she sent Camille to find Emily. The supposed Miss Portsman had shown herself to be quite proficient at organizing both the ladies' private quarters and their work and training schedules. And whatever her past, Diane liked the way Emily had stepped in to see to the employees who'd survived Oliver's lessons.

Diane looked around the large room with its generously spaced tables, low-hanging chandeliers, and burgundy carpet with pale gold walls. The Benchley family wouldn't recognize Adam House any longer. Of course they likely wouldn't recognize her, either—and both realizations suited her just fine.

"The Persephone Room?" Oliver's low drawl came from the doorway.

She continued jotting down the names of Greek goddesses and muses. "I believe Juliet informed you that I'm not entertaining today. And your . . . services aren't required, either, as the ladies are learning the menu schedule and how to go about asking noblemen for money. To pay for their food and drink, to answer your next question."

"Are you going to offer lines of credit, then?" He strolled closer, his expression cool and otherwise indecipherable. "With my money?"

"It's *my* money until your repayment comes due. And no, I won't offer credit."

"Then you'll be seeing less wagering and fewer dinners and drinks purchased."

"Do you always pay off your bills at your various clubs?" He pulled out the chair opposite her and sat. "Yes."

"Frederick didn't. At the time we left London, he owed something near four hundred pounds just at the Society. I can't tie up that amount of funds for the pleasure of men who gamble more than they can afford to lose." She set down her pencil and sat forward. "Convince me that

Frederick was an exception, that everyone else pays their debts in a timely manner, and I'll reconsider. Otherwise I prefer to learn from my mistakes and to avoid repeating them. Or having them repeated against me."

"Hm." Oliver pulled the paper on which she'd been scribbling around to face him. "In that case and at the risk of being shot again, I suggest that you place a notice in plain view in the foyer, then. Something akin to: 'Play only with the cash you have to hand; you'll receive no credit here.' Otherwise you'll run into gentlemen who just assume they can make good later."

It was actually a very good suggestion, little as she wanted to admit it. "That's somewhat long-winded, but I'll consider it."

He fiddled with the paper for a moment, then picked it up. "'Persephone,' 'Psyche,' 'Aphrodite,' 'Demeter,' 'Hera,' 'Ariadne,' and 'Athena.' Ariadne's not a goddess, you know."

"I'm not creating a thesaurus listing. And it fits for my purposes."

"Why not Artemis? Or Diana?"

"Diana is Roman, and either one sounds too self-congratulatory."

"And they are the goddesses of the hunt. Perhaps too aggressive for a wagering club owned by a female?"

She glanced up at him. "We defend ourselves when attacked, if that's what you mean."

"I think you know it isn't, but I clearly won't win this argument." He looked at the paper again. "Room names is a fairly clever notion, I have to say."

"They go with the name of the club. And saying 'the Demeter Room' is easier than saying 'the billiards room in the northeast corner on the first floor,' don't you think?"

"I can't argue with that."

"For once," she muttered.

"Beg pardon?"

"I said, 'for once,'" she repeated in a louder voice.

"Ah. That's what I thought you said. So are you going to paint the names above the doors?"

Diane scowled. "That is my intention, yes. The easier the club is to navigate, the more inebriated the guests can be. And simply because I said I would consider your placard doesn't mean I want to hear any more of your suggestions."

He slammed the paper back down with the flat of his hand. "We are in a unique position, you and I," he said in a low, intimate voice. "I am at your disposal until I either decide that no man's reputation is worth this insanity, or I steal that letter from you. However, I think it's only fair that I share one or two facts with you in the meantime."

Her small pistol lay beneath her pillow upstairs. Haybury hadn't been expected today, and she'd yet to encounter anyone or anything else she couldn't conquer with her wits. She tightened her fingers around the pencil. It wasn't much of a weapon, but stabbed into a sensitive area it would at least give her time to summon assistance. "Enlighten me," she said in her most disinterested tone.

"Two years ago I may have had no money and no home to return to," he commented even more quietly. "But those two things were not all I left behind in London. Most women, for instance, learned quite some time ago to not attempt to order me about or dictate to me the terms of my life. The one *man* who attempted it—well, I now hold his title, his property, and his rather substantial fortune."

"If you're attempting to convince me that you murdered your uncle, I'm afraid you're wasting your time. Unless you employed a witch who cast a spell to have him drop dead in the middle of the House of Lords. Because darling, poison just doesn't suit you."

Gray eyes held hers in a steady, even gaze. "I wasn't

implying anything. I'm telling you—people don't cross me. They don't toy with me. They don't blackmail me. I believe some of them are actually frightened of me."

"You're not a nice man." She forced a sigh, relieved that it sounded just a touch bored, rather than edged with wariness. This was a game of chance, just as every encounter with him had ever been. She'd merely been a fortnight too late in realizing that fact. "I do know that, Oliver." She took the paper back from beneath his hand. "I only hope you've realized by now that I am simply not afraid of you."

To her surprise, he smiled. "'Afraid' is not a word I have ever used to describe you, Diane."

That almost felt like a compliment. "Then may I assume you're finished with wasting my time today?" she said aloud.

"Not quite. How many invitations are you sending out?" He lifted a finger. "And before you tell me to mind my own affairs, I'd like to mention that you wanted me about because of my expertise. Most clubs have a membership committee to decide who may or may not be admitted. Once you send out an invitation, everyone who receives it will assume they've been admitted."

"The invitations state very clearly that they are welcome to come and view The Tantalus Club for one evening. Membership applications will be handed out then."

"How many?" he repeated.

"Fifty, you annoying man."

"Fifty invitations, or fifty applications?"

"Applications. Three hundred invitations."

For a moment he sat silently. "You need more than fifty members. White's has hundreds, as well as a four- or five-year waiting list."

Clearly he wasn't going to go away until she'd discussed club membership with him. "I've a budget to follow, as you know. Five thousand pounds with which to open a club, hire employees, fund the club's bank, purchase food and liquor, renovations, furnishings, invitations, enlarge the stable and the front drive, feed the ho—"

"Then ask for more money," he interrupted. "Fifty members who are also members of other clubs won't appear here every night. Nor will they fill seven grand rooms. The place will look deserted, not exclusive."

"You would loan me more?" she asked, reluctance making the words catch in her throat. All her plans had been made with Lord Blalock's budget in mind; when Oliver had been dragged in she hadn't actually taken the time to consider that he might be able to afford to lend her more. A stupid, behindhand mistake that could now put her in a defensive position. "You made it very clear you were only willing to risk five thousand."

"I find that I'm willing to negotiate."

And there it was. The sound of the second shoe dropping. She'd been waiting for it, but it still managed to make her heart stutter. Diane sat back. "I won't pay you a larger percent in interest. That wouldn't gain me anything."

"That's not what I want. I don't need more money."

"Then what, pray tell, *do* you want?"

"You."

Her jaw dropped before she could stop it. A thousand thoughts spun through her mind. At least half of them involved her with a weapon and him lying dead. The other half, though . . . "But I hate you!" she exclaimed.

"What does that have to do with anything?"

Diane pushed away from the table and stood, her mind working furiously. She could not afford to spend her time retreating from him. "You are a despicable man. Go away before I have you removed."

He rose as well, moving around the table toward her.

"You could do that. Or attempt it, anyway. But consider my offer. Another five thousand pounds, with the same terms as previously. And one night—no, twenty-four hours— with no one but you and me. At a time and place of my choosing."

"I don't need to consider anything." Turning, she stalked toward the wall where the rope pull hung even as another avenue of attack occurred to her. "In fact," she continued, "I've been thinking. Your friend, Lord Manderlin, is quite charming and handsome. And *you* certainly lead him about by the nose. It shouldn't be difficult for me to do so. I imagine convincing him to lend me—"

"No."

The single word was abrupt, guttural, and spoken directly behind her. Before Diane could process just how close he was, Oliver had her by the shoulder. He yanked her around to face him, and her spine thudded against the wall.

She lifted her chin, balling both her hands into fists. "You do not get to tell me what to do, Oliver," she snapped, putting the tremble in her own voice to anger. "And be careful; you almost sounded jealous."

"You may play your games with me, Diane," he retorted, planting his hands against the wall on either side of her shoulders and trapping her there. "But you will leave my friends alone."

"'Friends'?" she retorted. "You have more than just the one? And here I was surprised to see *anyone* with you willingly."

Oliver leaned in until only an inch or so separated his mouth from hers. "We both know you could have found some rich, naïve pup to fund your venture, darling. Over the past two years you've perfected the art of manipulation, after all. Or so you want everyone to think."

If there was one thing she detested, it was being dissected and cataloged. Wife. Property. Powerless. Penniless. Well, now she was charting her own course, and no one else was allowed at the wheel. "You're mistaken," she forced out through her clenched jaw. "I don't care what anyone thinks. I only care what they do."

"Do you truly think you're that invulnerable, Diane? Because you haven't convinced me."

"And I care what you think least of all."

His gaze lowered to her mouth, and her breath wobbled. Did he mean to kiss her again? She tried to convince herself that it was revulsion roiling low in her gut, but it didn't feel like revulsion. It felt like excitement. Anticipation.

But she would not give up her control. And certainly not to him. Diane took a breath and met his gaze. "Attempting to prove me wrong?" she prodded. "Do you expect me to melt into your arms and beg you to take over this little venture?"

His eyes narrowed almost imperceptibly. "Any begging from you to me won't be about business." Moving slowly, he leaned in closer and touched his lips to her forehead.

The gesture didn't feel at all fatherly, which she would have disliked as much as anything else. And damn it all, he might as well have kissed her properly—improperly— and let her yell at him for it. Before she could punch him in the gut, he backed away and turned on his heel. "An additional five thousand would give you the opportunity to admit enough members to keep your club solvent, and allow you to purchase those additional tables I know you don't have. Consider my offer, darling."

Diane grabbed a candelabra off the side table and hurled it at him. If her aim had been as sharp as her anger, the brass tower would have slammed into the back of his head and sent him to the floor bloody and unconscious. Instead it brushed his jacket sleeve as he sidestepped but kept walking.

"You're better with a pistol," he commented without turning around and left the room.

Diane glared after him for a long moment, then strode over to retrieve the candelabra. How the devil he'd realized just how closely she'd had to trim her budget she had no idea, but his estimations were so near the target that arguing them even in her mind made no sense.

Blast it all. Yes, she'd had to do some quick reestimations of expense when Lord Blalock and her plans to lease an already existing facility had both dropped dead. And yes, she knew she needed a larger club membership—but that meant more upfront purchases of liquor, tables, hay, employees, everything. And a larger amount of cash on hand for those evenings when the players had better luck than the house.

An additional five thousand pounds would see her precisely where she needed to be. The terms, however . . .

"Diane," Genevieve's voice came from the doorway behind her, "Juliet informed me that Haybury brought a visitor to see his apartments."

"Yes, he did."

"Why are you carrying a candelabra?"

"Because it landed on the floor after I threw it at his head."

"I see." Jenny continued to approach until she could carefully remove the brass fixture from Diane's fingers and set it back in its place. "And was there a particular reason you wanted to kill the Marquis of Haybury again?"

"I didn't want to kill him. Maim him, yes, but not kill him. *That* would have caused too many difficulties."

"Well, I'm pleased to hear you haven't lost your mind,

then. Since I don't see him on the floor may I assume you missed?"

"Yes, dash it all."

"And why did all this happen?"

Diane clenched her jaw. Perhaps Jenny's reputation wasn't tied into this venture the way her own was, but Genevieve Martine was the one person in the entire world she trusted. She took a breath. "He offered to lend me an additional five thousand pounds."

"That's excellent news. Isn't it?"

"One would think so."

From Jenny's expression, she clearly knew she was missing part of the equation. Rather than explain, though, Diane excused herself and retreated to the private part of the house—her sanctuary.

Once there, she closed the door to the solarium so she could pace undisturbed. Oliver Warren wanted her, and he was willing to pay five thousand pounds for the privilege. Interesting, considering he'd had her for free two years ago and then fled.

If she refused, of course she could still keep the club, because that was, after all, the reason she'd returned to England in the first place. There was more to the additional funds than easing the strain of beginning a new venture, however—or at least he would see it that way. It would mean he'd made a challenge and either gotten his way or made her back down. And damn it all, the man knew precisely how attractive he was and how . . . proficient he was in bed. But then, she knew that as well. Surely for five thousand pounds she could tolerate his touch for one night.

And if she accepted, what would that mean? For her, a night of very troubling reminders of how alone and angry and desperate she'd been and how very nice it had felt to be preferred over a deck of cards or a pair of dice. How hungry she'd been for affection and for someone who didn't see returning to her side each night as merely holding on to the last remaining vestiges of a marriage that had long since failed in every other way possible.

That was her, however. What did *he* want? Oliver Warren could easily have a multitude of other women without offering up money. Diane made her way slowly to the nearest window and ran her finger along the bottom casement. In offering her precisely what she needed, he expected her to accept.

Did he wish another chance to earn her affections, then? Or was he attempting to prove something to himself?

She scowled. Or it could simply be that he was a man and that she'd made herself unobtainable and that running her thoughts around in circles was only going to give her a megrim. Pressing her fingers to her temple, she resisted the urge to go and see to some task or other and instead stayed where she was.

Because all speculation aside, he'd made her an offer for a substantial amount of money. And she needed to decide whether to accept it—not because of any plots on his part but because she'd literally staked her entire future on this venture. And those additional funds could make all the difference in the world.

What was that compared with a night of painful memories and the unabated company of a man with whom she'd once, and fleetingly, felt a connection? In fact, it should have been an easy decision. Why, then, was she being so . . . impractical?

Just at that moment the reason rode by on a fine gray thoroughbred, clearly heading from her stables to somewhere in the direction of Grosvenor Square. Perhaps he had other debts to collect on, or, more likely, other women to attempt to seduce.

If she agreed, would he claim victory? He could certainly attempt to do so, but if she viewed it merely as a business transaction, then what had she to lose? She'd survived him before, after all. And this time, at least, she knew the rules. Quite possibly better than he did.

With a slow smile she rapped her knuckles against the glass and then went to find Jenny. With additional funds coming in, she needed to make a plan. Or two.

Chapter Nine

Oliver stood back and watched as two large fellows carried his mahogany desk into Adam House. The matching bookcase had gone into storage, but in truth he spent so little time at home that he didn't much care what ended up above The Tantalus Club—except for his bed, of course.

"Haybury!"

He managed to arrest all expression except for the twitch of one eye and turned to face the barouche parading down the street in his direction. "Lady Katherine," he returned, inclining his head.

"It's true, then!" she exclaimed, calling for her driver to stop beside him. "You're actually going to reside above a gambling club."

"A fitting address for me, don't you think?"

Light blue eyes glanced toward the large building behind him. "A club employing only females and owned by a woman. Yes, I should think so. If I were the kind of female who became jealous, however, this would be a stab to my heart."

"Lucky for you, then, that you aren't that kind of female."

She tapped her delicate blue ivory fan against her palm. "I think I would very much like a tour of the premises, when you're available to guide me, of course."

The idea that he'd been forbidden to dally hadn't much amused him from the beginning, whether he'd particularly felt the desire to do so or not. A kept mistress was supposed to be faithful to her benefactor, of course, but here *he* was the benefactor and he was being blackmailed into keeping his breeches buttoned. It might have been amusing, if he'd discovered someone else being managed in such a way. "Perhaps when I've settled in," he hedged.

Katherine Falston leaned over the side of the carriage. "You moved very quickly to take these rooms, Haybury. Especially for someone in no particular need of them."

"Ah. Well, simply because I never discussed my plans for shifting my residence with you, Kat, doesn't mean I never had any."

"Be a beast then if you wish to," she returned mildly. "It's what I enjoy most about you." At her order the barouche clattered off again, trailed by the half-dozen carriages forced to stop behind it.

With a silent curse, Oliver turned his back on them. In addition to his movers, Diane had most of her hired chits running about putting the final bits and bobs together for the evening's soiree. He'd never received an invitation himself, but a brigade of the Coldstream Guards wouldn't have been able to keep him out of The Tantalus Club tonight. He wondered, though, if Diane had realized that once he'd made it past Langtree and into his own quarters he was essentially inside the club and halfway into her private house, anyway.

He glanced through the open door, past the additional door at the rear of the foyer, and into the depths of the club. She hadn't given him an answer yet about his offer of additional funds, which did not help his growing level of frustration any. Instead she'd spent the last few days not being in the same room as he, while her damned silent-moving shadow delivered her instructions.

When another laden wagon stopped behind him he ignored it. At least he did so until all four of the club's hired bruisers clomped outside and began unloading gaming tables and chairs. Oliver turned around. Two more wagons carrying identical furniture turned onto the street behind the first.

"Hubert!" he yelled.

His valet scampered out of Adam House. "My lord, I don't know why you leased rooms with an east-facing bed-chamber window. Those draperies are *not* heavy enough to k—"

"Hubert," Oliver cut in, "calm yourself. And keep an eye out here. I have business with Lady Cameron."

Before the valet could reply, Oliver strode into the foyer. "Langtree, where is Diane?"

The butleress looked up from a list she had clutched in both hands. "She isn't seeing visitors, my lord. The grand open—"

"This is business," he interrupted, and pushed past one of the arriving tables to stride through the Persephone Room.

He had to concede that naming the rooms was a rather good idea, and the way Diane had managed to work the goddess's myth into each room's decor would make it possible for all but the most inebriated gentleman to at least know where in the club they were.

In the doorway to the Demeter Room he caught sight of Pansy Bridger, one of his more promising—and hostile—faro students. "Have you seen Lady Cameron?" he asked.

"In the Athena Room," she returned, then went back to arranging lamps.

With a nod he walked through the doorway into the

generous space Diane had designated as a library and smoking room. She stood on a stool, placing a last few books on the deep-set shelves. As she lifted her arms, her sleek black skirt rose to expose her black slippers and bare ankles.

He stood back, watching. Whatever might or might not have been between them, she was a lovely woman. In truth, when they'd first met, her appearance was the only thing he had admired about her. Now, however, she'd displayed spleen he never would have expected from that weeping, vulnerable widow. However, her positive qualities were far outweighed by one horrific fact—Diane Benchley was the only person in the world of whom he'd been afraid. And allowing her to remain in that position simply wasn't acceptable.

"You know I can see your reflection in the window," she commented into the silence.

So much for the element of surprise. "You've purchased more tables and chairs."

She continued shelving. "I won't use them tonight; we'll need the floor space."

"That wasn't my question."

"You didn't ask a question."

He stayed where he was, safely across a good portion of the room from her. "I thought it was implied. As you wish, then. Where did you get the money?"

Setting a last book into its place, she stepped to the floor and went to put the stepstool back into the corner. "I decided to accept your offer," she said, so coolly that for a heartbeat he thought he must have heard her wrong.

Abrupt, raw . . . hunger stabbed through him, so strong it was almost painful. By sheer willpower alone Oliver kept his feet from moving. Of all the things he'd expected to feel when she agreed to his proposal, it hadn't been need. "And when were you going to tell me?" he asked, making certain he sounded even more disinterested than she had.

"I thought you would figure it out when you saw the furniture, which you evidently did."

"Perhaps, but that's not how gentlemen make agreements."

She wiped her hands on a rag. "I'm not a gentleman. Nor are you, I daresay."

"Nevertheless, I expect you to walk up to me, offer me your hand, and say, 'I agree to your terms, Oliver.' And then I will summon my solicitor and have the funds transferred to your account posthaste."

He added that last part to remind her that at the moment he hadn't given her anything, so she'd best cooperate.

She eyed him, then set down the rag and approached. "Very well. Make whatever silly rules about this you want; after all, it's clearly about pleasing you." She stuck out her hand. "As for me, this is business. Twenty-four hours of my time in exchange for five thousand pounds."

So she thought she had him figured out, then. How could she, though, when he didn't know what he was doing himself? He took her hand in his. "You still have to say it."

Diane blew out her breath in an exaggerated sigh. " 'I agree to your terms, Oliver,' " she recited.

He kept hold of her hand for a heartbeat longer than he needed to. "I'll consult my calendar, then. You're mine for twenty-four hours—whenever I choose."

"I'm not yours, Oliver. Nor will I ever be again. As I said, this is business."

"Call it whatever you like, darling. We'll see how clinical you can be when I'm moving inside you."

Just before she pulled her hand away, he felt the shiver in her fingers. He hoped to hell it was anticipation making her shake, because as coolly as he generally liked to play his games, he was fairly shuddering with lust himself. At least he presumed it to be lust. He couldn't imagine what else it might be.

"You'll be happy to know that I'm nearly moved in," he continued when she seemed to have collected herself enough to turn away. "By the time your soiree begins tonight you'll be able to claim me as your . . . whatever. What am I, again?"

"You should know better than to leave your skin so exposed, darling," she retorted, dragging a chair back to its place closer to the bookshelves. "I don't know what you are. You are *posing* as my protector. A man interested in me but vague about how intimate we have been and continue to be. Enough to make other men both see me as desirable and realize they can't have me."

"You *are* desirable, Diane. You hardly need me to convince anyone of that."

She tapped her chin with one finger. "I'm more interested in being able to turn them away without insulting them. Attempt to be formidable."

"Shall I frown relentlessly, then?"

Diane shot him a look that contained more humor than he expected. "We've discussed this already. Stop pestering me and go prepare to play your part."

"And what will you be doing?" he asked skeptically. "Aside from being mysterious, desirable, and unobtainable."

"I will be preparing to make as much money as possible."

She started for the door back into the Demeter Room, but he moved forward and blocked her path. "Someone will ask about my involvement with the club."

"The club is mine, Lord Haybury. You are an employee."

"I'm not telling them that."

Diane blew out her breath. "Fine. Tell them you are a consultant. You do know a great deal about wagering and clubs after all, since you've wasted most of your adult life doing one while inside the other."

That blow was a bit direct, especially for her. Sensing that he had her on the run about something, Oliver stepped closer. "I'll tell them that, then."

"Good."

"If you kiss me."

"I—I am not going to kiss you."

"Yes, you are."

"You will do as I say, Haybury, or I'll ruin you."

"You'd use that letter now? To make me say I'm your consultant? That seems a waste, Diane. Your club isn't even open yet."

Her emerald eyes snapping with anger, she strode up to him, grabbed him by the lapels, and smashed her mouth against his. Before he could even respond she'd pushed backward, moved around him, and left the room. "There," she said over her shoulder. "You're my consultant."

"That wasn't much of a kiss," he called after her, and saw her shoulders stiffen.

"You aren't much of an inspiration."

The hell she said. At the moment he felt quite inspired. And according to the amount of spirit she showed arguing with him, she was inspired as well. She was saying drivel, nonsense to make him angry and cause him to forget that, first, she *had* just kissed him, sloppily or not. And second, she'd agreed to come to his bed on a date and at a time of his choosing. A damned fine morning's work, if he said so himself. Which he did.

Jenny stood supervising as the last of the new tables was carried into a back storage room and covered with a sheet.

Tonight the club would be crowded enough that adding the extra seating would only get in the way, but Haybury had been correct in noting that they needed the additional gaming tables if they wanted to keep the rooms from looking too empty.

Halfway across the room from her friend, Diane stepped aside as a pair of her large bruisers, as Haybury called them, nodded politely at her and returned to polishing the few existing tables that had yet to receive the treatment. At least thus far no one had complained about her policy of having everyone lend a hand when required. Tonight they could look large and stand ready to step in if needed, but for the moment moving and polishing furniture was far more necessary than appearing formidable.

"Everything here?" she asked as Jenny faced her.

"*Oui.* And the cook has just received the last bucket of strawberries, so the tarts should be well on their way to the oven."

"Excellent." Diane took Jenny's arm as they returned to the main part of the club. "And I have to say, the ladies have come along quite well."

"Are we giving credit to the marquis for that?" Jenny asked.

"No, we are keeping it for ourselves, since we hired him."

"You hired him, you mean."

"Well, yes."

"And you agreed to whatever his terms were for the additional funds."

"Yes."

Jenny paused for a heartbeat. "But you aren't going to tell me what those terms are."

"Not at the moment, no. Suffice it to say that on paper this five thousand pounds is to be repaid in the same manner and under the same terms as the original loan."

Her friend nodded, then tightened her arm, keeping Diane close against her. "Lord Haybury has had little incentive to change his ways, my dear," she said in a low voice.

Diane pulled free, scowling. "Whatever you're implying, Genevieve, I am *not* in pursuit of that man. Because even if I found him attractive, which I no longer do, I haven't forgotten that he . . . very nearly broke me," she finished in a whisper, wishing she could stop the tremor in her voice.

"But he didn't." Jenny gripped her shoulder. "You are my dearest friend, Diane. If you wish Haybury to disappear, I believe I can see to it."

"Oh, for heaven's sake," Diane returned, snorting. "However determined I am to have this go my way, I am not prepared to resort to murder. Thank you for the offer, though."

"Just keep it in mind."

"Certainly. I do believe in reviewing every option."

That kept her smiling until her mind strayed back to the self-satisfied expression on that gray-eyed demon's face when she'd agreed to his terms. Something swirled down her spine, hot and shivering all at the same time.

That would be another battle, and she had quite enough madness through which to wade over the next few hours. In fact, that seemed to be the only way she could manage to keep her sanity for the time being. Because business proposition or not, she'd just agreed to share Oliver Warren's bed. *Good heavens.*

Attempting to shake off that rather persistent and unexpectedly heated thought, she did a last circle through the club's large rooms. The tips of her fingers felt electric as she adjusted a chair here or a festive ribbon there. The previous seven weeks—every conversation, every appearance she'd made, nearly every thought she'd had, had been about this night. Every man she hadn't invited needed to hear about it and wish they had been. And then she would choose who was allowed to come to The Tantalus and lose their money.

Deciding how lavishly to decorate for tonight had been a challenge, but as she continued her tour through the kitchen to speak with the cooks and then walked outside for a last word with Clark, her head groom, she thought she'd found the correct balance. Spectacle was good—it was only that extravagance didn't match with mystery. Elegance, however, did, and as she viewed the string quartets setting up in each room and her ladies making last-minute adjustments to hair and dress before they vanished behind the mystery doors, she didn't even bother to stifle her smile.

She sat down with her staff for one final meeting, ate a quick dinner with Jenny, and went upstairs to her private rooms to change into her evening attire. It hadn't taken much for her to be known as the lady who always wore black, and she'd actually debated whether abruptly appearing in crimson might be effective in keeping everyone's attention.

After all, every one of her guests tonight would be male, and every one of them would be gazing at the ladies swirling around them, wondering which of them could be seduced. Finally she settled on a sleek black gown sparkling with swirls of black glass beads—she wasn't the mistress of some bawdy house, after all. And while she didn't care whether or which of her ladies might accept the favors of a gentleman, that was not her purpose.

Once she'd made a final turn in front of the mirror, checked the fit of her elbow-length black gloves, and settled the onyx pendant on her throat, she stepped back. Sound didn't carry from the front into the back of the house; she'd made certain of that. But Adam House *felt* different. Occupied. A glance around the edge of the closed bedchamber curtains confirmed that bobbing carriage lanterns lined the street and filled the stable yard. The invitation had specified nine o'clock in the evening, and she'd been raised knowing the social importance of a fashionably late arrival. No one wanted to be seen as overly anxious to know what someone else might be doing.

"What time is it, Mary?" she asked aloud.

Her maid looked up from putting away the extra hairpins and combs they hadn't needed. "Ten minutes of nine, my lady."

Diane smiled. Early arrivals. This was going to be a very good evening.

A knock sounded at the door, and Mary hurried over to answer it. A moment later she returned with a folded note. Diane took the missive and opened it. Oliver's heavy but elegant scrawl crossed the paper, and the steady beat of her heart sped a little—in concern, of course, that he would be attempting something nefarious at the last moment.

Swiftly she read through it. *Are we lovers presently? Am I dancing attendance on you?*

She thought she'd made it clear to him; obviously he was only attempting to remind her that he was a necessary part of her plans. Crossing to her writing desk, she scribbled out a "Yes" beneath the first question, and a "Close enough to do so" under the second and then had the waiting footwoman return it to him. Then she sat down beside her window and picked up a book. Her part didn't begin for nearly an hour, after all.

Oliver chuckled as he read the note one of the liveried footwomen returned to him. Diane certainly had no trouble with pretending intimacy with him. When the terms of his loan came due, however, he doubted she would be as cavalier. Whatever she said or thought about him, he could feel the passion that still simmered between them.

He leaned against the wall to one side of the Persephone Room and watched the parade of curious males. Most entered The Tantalus Club in pairs or trios—much safer on the reputation than risking entering alone and finding no one else there. A few of Diane's black-and-yellow-liveried footwomen stood by the front entryway to collect coats and hats and gloves. Except for them and Langtree at the front door, the place was empty of chits.

"Haybury!"

Crossing his arms over his chest, he nodded. "Stanpool."

"This is early yet for you to be prowling about, isn't it? I thought you were more nocturnal."

"I'm not prowling. I live upstairs."

The baron lifted an eyebrow as he shifted to face Oliver straight on. "I'd heard that rumor. You mean to say it's true?"

"I believe that's what I just told you."

Stanpool took a half step backward. "No need to be testy."

"Then don't test me."

"You're acquainted with Lady Cameron, then, I presume?"

Oliver wondered if Diane had yet realized just how cooperative he truly was being. If he'd wanted her ruined he could have accomplished it two years ago, or any time since then. It would only take a word. That, however, wasn't the game he was interested in playing.

Since he wasn't finished with her yet, he needed her to be protected from everyone but himself. Yes, she was playing her own game, but cooperating with her was the surest way for him to win his own. "Lady Cameron and I are old . . . friends," he said evenly.

"Old *friends,* is it?" Stanpool's gaze shifted to look at something beyond Oliver's shoulder. "If I cared to plow the widow's field, then, you wouldn't object?"

Haybury clenched his right fist, real anger coiling through him. The strength of the emotion surprised him. "You might wish to rephra—"

"Ah, there you are, my dear," Diane murmured, and slipped her arm around his. "Do introduce me to your handsome friend, won't you?"

Good God. No wonder Stanpool wanted her. She sparkled like a midnight sun, lithe and mesmerizing and shimmering. Briefly Oliver wondered whether his fingers would burn if he touched her skin. "This is Lord Stanpool," he returned, indicating the baron with his chin. "He finds you attractive."

She inclined her head, a curling strand of her midnight hair falling forward along her cheek. "Very pleased, my lord. I hope you enjoy yourself this evening."

"I'm planning on it."

Oliver stroked his fingers along hers. "Come along and tell me who else you'd like to know."

"Oh, everyone. I only invited men I thought I could tolerate, you know. Lord Stanpool. I shall see you later."

"Yes, you shall."

As soon as they were out of Stanpool's hearing, Oliver pulled his arm in, drawing her closer. "Do you intend to make me look the cuckold after every introduction this evening?"

Sparkling emerald eyes looked up to meet his gaze. She was excited about this evening, though he would have been more surprised if she weren't, considering the effort she'd gone through to get here. "We are not a couple," she said softly. "Therefore I cannot cuckold you."

"Shall I pull out the note and point at the bit where it says we're lovers?"

Her lashes lowered a touch. "Are you jealous, darling?"

"Sleep with whomever you please, Diane. But if you attempt to make me look the fool, I won't be so cooperative." Even as he spoke the words he realized he was lying—which wasn't that unusual, except for the fact that he'd evidently been attempting to lie to himself. That was a damned useless waste of effort.

"I don't need your permission to keep company with anyone. For your information, however, I do intend to flirt quite a bit. I may even veer into being seductive." She patted him on the arm with her free hand. "You do know the game, I assume. I've seen you play it before."

"Generally when I play, the seduction doesn't end with words. Be cautious about with whom you toy; as a man I feel the need to inform you that a false seduction can have unpleasant consequences."

"As can an actual seduction." She took a half step away from him. "You know, I think you're put out because I'm playing what is usually a gentleman's game. I'm a widow and have no virginity to protect. I'm opening a business, and so have little hope of maintaining my grand social connections. I've already paid the price, and now I intend to reap the rewards."

"This is a larger game," he pointed out quietly, even as another guest caught her eye and she started to move away. "And you do *not* know all the consequences you could face."

For a moment she turned around to face him again. "And I give you the same advice. Or was it a warning?"

"Interpret it as you will."

She knew a handful of the men present, and he quickly noted that those were the fellows with whom she spoke most briefly, and the ones where she made certain he was present. *Hm.* It wasn't fear of being chatted at by an old lover, certainly; other than the Earl of Cameron's reputation for being a poor gambler, Oliver had never heard as much as a duck's quack about the man or his wife or any of their comings and goings. After an hour or so he'd formulated the opinion that she wanted him there because men were afraid of *him*. Or at the least they were hesitant to cross him. She used him to control the length, breadth, and depth of the conversation.

"I say, Lady Cameron," Francis Henning commented, approaching with a glass of wine in one hand and a biscuit in the other, "I heard that you hired half a hundred pretty chits. I only see half a dozen servants. Say that ain't the total of them, or I'll be damned disappointed."

She smiled. "So you'd like to meet my croupiers and dealers and bankers?" she asked in a carrying voice.

A round of male "Ayes" rumbled around her, and the low-pitched chatter that always reminded Oliver of a flock of grouse increased tenfold.

"I thought so." She nodded. And in impressive near unison all four of the half-concealed doors on either side of the room opened. Young ladies appeared in soft browns and beiges and golds, each of them as pretty as the last. He knew them all by sight if not by name. He knew which of them he would prefer to have at his table for faro or vingt-et-un or commerce or whist or hazard. But that was just him.

His fellows were buzzing like bees around flowers. Within the walls of The Tantalus Club, the conversations and flirtations abounded. For a few minutes the Persephone Room more resembled Almack's Assembly than a gentlemen's club.

He sent a sideways glance at Diane, who watched the unfolding scene with an expression of mild amusement. "But will they gamble here," he murmured, "or be content to turn your club into a bawdy house?"

Diane's brow lowered. "That I will not permit. These

ladies are under my roof and under my protection." She stepped forward. "Ladies, to your tables, if you please. Gentlemen, tonight The Tantalus Club's doors are open to all of you. Enjoy yourselves. As for the future, you'll find applications for membership in the Ariadne Room and in the foyer." She sent the room at large a slow, sensual smile. "And gentlemen, be persuasive. We intend to be *very* exclusive."

Amid the general appreciative laughter she took a step back, out of the way. Oliver followed her. "Outside this club most of these men wouldn't deign to talk with these ladies."

"We're not outside the club. And both I and these ladies know the possible consequences of our actions. I daresay I would prefer employment in a club like this to the only other alternative open to many of them."

"So you're their benefactor now?"

"I am not having this argument with you. You've had weeks to protest or be offended, and apparently it didn't occur to you."

"I don't get offended, Diane. I'm looking out for my investment."

"Ah." She put her gloved palm flat against his chest. It was more than likely his imagination, but he could have sworn her touch felt warm. "I daresay I've put more time and thought into this venture than you have, Haybury, so do as I've asked and keep your opinion to yourself."

She was so damned sure of herself. He opened his mouth to remind her once again that he wasn't her employee, but that argument was beginning to lose what little effectiveness it had had. He supposed he could point out instead that he would have her soon—at any time he chose, in fact. That might set her back on her heels.

Oliver looked down at the black-gloved hand pressed against his chest, her fingers curling into the edges of his waistcoat. He wondered whether she could feel his heart beating. Considering he'd been told more than once that he didn't have a heart, it was a rather interesting question.

"Tonight," he said aloud.

"Yes, tonight, and until I ask for your opinion."

Before she could walk away he covered her hand with his. "You misunderstand. Your soiree will end at what, three o'clock in the morning?"

"That is our aim, yes."

"Then at four o'clock in the morning I expect to see you in my front room. Per our agreement."

This time her eyes widened. "You can't be serious. I'm busy at the moment, if you haven't no—"

"I've noticed. Four o'clock." He lowered his gaze, taking in the beads sparkling across her bosom, her fingers twitching and clenching now over his heart. "Wear that."

Chapter Ten

William D'Arville, the Duke of Whiting, leaned one shoulder against the wall and eyed her. "And how do you reconcile your position in Society with the ownership of a gaming house?"

Diane watched a tray full of wineglasses go by and sighed in regret. As tempting as it was to imbibe, especially after her conversation with Oliver, she needed her wits about her to both entice and fend off the hundreds of men she'd invited to The Tantalus Club this evening. But it wasn't them she was thinking about.

It was him, the devil seated at one of the faro tables amid a crowd of onlookers. He certainly knew how to play the game. And how to distract her from the game she was in the midst of playing.

"Lady Cameron?"

She shook herself. Damnation, she was supposed to be convincing wealthy aristocrats that her club was well worth the twenty-pounds-a-year membership fee. "You own horses and hunting dogs, do you not, Your Grace?"

Whiting nodded. "I do."

"They are your hobby. This is mine." She smiled. "The

skills of the players, the give-and-take—I find it all very . . . exciting."

"You're willing to risk your reputation for the sake of some vicarious excitement?"

With effort Diane wrenched her gaze from her brown-haired nemesis to look at the lean-faced duke. "I consider excitement to be vital." Almost as vital as the money she meant to make from these men. "If it costs me a dinner or a quadrille or two, well, so be it."

"Would you be offended if I said I find you quite exciting, Lady Cameron?"

He and a dozen other men this evening. Men didn't even possess the self-awareness to be embarrassed at how easy they were to lead about. Men—most men, anyway—were so easily deciphered it was almost pitiable. Of course Oliver wanted her as well, but he'd managed to find a way to maneuver her into his bed. Or he would at four o'clock, anyway.

"I rarely find compliments offensive, Your Grace." When he would have responded, she deepened her smile. "At the same time," she continued, "I am not a flower swayed by every stray breeze."

The duke chuckled. "That is refreshingly straightforward of you, my lady. Most women claim to prefer pretty words and secretly wish for pretty things. I prefer your honesty."

And she preferred money with no strings attached. "It reduces the chance for any misunderstanding."

"I shall endeavor to acquire something appropriate, then."

Profitable as this conversation might turn out to be, she wasn't paying as much attention as she should have been. Instead, she kept glancing toward what had become the main faro table and the broad-shouldered male there who commanded everyone's attention.

She had intentionally left clocks out of the rooms of The Tantalus Club, because she didn't want her wagering guests to know how much time they spent beneath her roof. But tonight she could not help wondering every other moment what time it might be. Four o'clock seemed to be approaching at a full gallop.

"Do you have the time, Your Grace?" she asked, hating that she'd been unable to resist checking.

He pulled out an engraved pocket watch. "It's nearly half one."

She put a hand on his sleeve. "Then *you* should try one of the tables. Or the desserts being served in the Hera Room."

Whiting put a hand over his heart. "Am I being dismissed? I'm heartbroken."

Diane laughed. "Merely delayed, Your Grace. Do enjoy yourself."

As soon as she'd shed herself of the rather charming duke, Mr. Evans took his place. And then Lord Ackland. Evidently owning a club made her eminently desirable. At the same time, she doubted any of them had marriage on his mind, however wealthy she was rumored to be.

"It's fortunate you had those additional applications printed," Jenny said, approaching from the foyer. "Several guests in the Demeter Room have called for pen and ink to complete them tonight."

"Good." Diane sent another glance at Oliver's back. "Can you supervise the cleaning and restocking after we close? I want to be ready for tomorrow evening."

"Of course I can. But where will you be?"

Oh, she didn't even want to say it aloud. "I have an . . . obligation to see to. I'll be available again after closing tomorrow."

Genevieve stepped closer. "Is something wrong? You know I am quite . . . resourceful if you should require assistance." She followed Diane's involuntary glance toward the faro table. "Is it Haybury? What did he do?"

"He loaned me money, Jenny, and I agreed to his terms. By four o'clock tomorrow morning, I'll be finished with him."

Jenny took her elbow. "I saw you after he left Vienna," she whispered fiercely. "I knew it was a mistake to get tangled up with him again. Do not—"

"I know how to conduct my business, Jenny," Diane interrupted. "And I'm not the same woman I was two years ago. I think I can manage a few hours in his company. Stay out of this."

With a stiff nod, Jenny released her again. "If I don't see you at one minute after four tomorrow morning, I will make this *my* business."

"Agreed."

While in the future wagering would continue until the players retired from the table, tonight Diane wanted all of the gentlemen to leave with their thirsts unquenched. At ten minutes before three she had the various room supervisors go about to begin closing the tables. One by one the ladies vanished back through the mystery doors. As the last one exited, Diane stepped up to the raised dais placed by the main door.

"Gentlemen, thank you for sampling The Tantalus Club's hospitality. Our doors will be open to all again tomorrow for the same limited hours. Our full hours will begin on Thursday. On Thursday next, you will need to be a member to join us. Good evening."

With the temptation of the ladies removed, wagering ceased and in small, noisy groups the men of Mayfair left the premises. For over a year Diane had anticipated this moment, when she could call opening night a success and breathe a sigh of relief that she'd actually managed to make it all happen.

Instead her hands trembled and her insides quaked, simply because she would be spending the next handful of hours in the company of a man with whom she'd once shared a fortnight. And for some unfathomable reason, that shook her more than had the idea of beginning this entire venture.

As soon as the last of her guests left, she had Juliet close and lock the front door. Diane hurried upstairs to the large sitting room above the kitchen, the one she'd put in at the last minute to give her employees a place to relax away from the club. Nearly all of her female employees seemed to be inside, the sounds of chattering and laughter almost deafening.

"Ladies," she called, stepping onto a chair, "well done!" At her gesture, the footwomen brought around glasses of champagne for everyone. "After tomorrow, we will begin our regular schedule, but tonight I wish to say that I am very pleased with all of you. Tomorrow we'll begin at noon, and Jenny and Margaret will discuss any changes we need to make. For now, enjoy yourselves!"

As soon as Diane could break away from the rounds of thanks and congratulations, she escaped to her private rooms and paced while she stared at the clock and watched the hands race each other around the circle.

At two minutes of four she blew out her bedside candle, pulled her gloves back up her forearms, and headed down through the dark, empty club. She could do this. She'd faced creditors and poverty and solitude and had bested them all. This was twenty-four hours. She could survive anything for one day. Even Oliver Warren.

She stopped on the landing just outside his door and took a deep breath. If he'd been any sort of gentleman he would have called on her, but she already knew precisely what kind of man he was. And "gentle" didn't enter into the equation. Blowing out her breath once more, Diane knocked on the door.

Nothing happened.

Well, that was unexpected. She supposed he might have forgotten he'd played this particular hand and he was presently out sharing some other chit's bed. In that case, though, one of his servants should have reached the door by now. Silently Diane began counting. Twenty-five seemed a good, round number. If no one appeared by then, she would consider her duty fulfilled.

At number seventeen the door opened.

Oliver stood there, gazing at her. He'd shed his dark jacket and turned up the sleeves of his white lawn shirt. In his waistcoat, his boots and trousers still in place, he looked relaxed and . . . formidable all at the same time. The effect was rather breathtaking and didn't at all help the jangling of her nerves. "Are you going to ask me in?" she queried, using every ounce of will to keep her voice steady.

He stepped back, opening the door wider. "Come in."

Squaring her shoulders, she strolled into his front room. "When did you begin answering your own door?"

"When I told my servants to make themselves scarce until or unless I should call for them." The door closed with a solid thud behind her, the sound resonating down her spine.

She half-expected to be pinned against the wall and mauled, but instead he moved past her toward the back rooms. "Do you want some wine?" he asked over his shoulder. "Or something stronger?"

If she could become inebriated enough, perhaps she wouldn't even remember the next twenty-four hours. But that would make her a coward—and he would know it. "No, thank you. I am rather tired, though, so I would prefer if you would just get this over with."

"Yes, I know you would," he agreed. "This way."

The one good thing about her apprehension was that it kept her exhaustion at bay. And without them both keeping her in a tense standoff between panic and sleep, she doubted she would be able to move. "You might have waited for a decent hour to begin this; I doubt I'll be able to remain awake, whatever your plans."

"Mm-hm." He pushed open the bedchamber door to reveal a large brass bathtub filled with water. A mist of steam hung just above the surface, which had been liberally sprinkled with deep red rose petals.

"You mean to drown me, then," she commented, ignoring the abrupt satisfaction curling through her at the thought of a long, hot bath.

"Not at the moment. Get in. I'll be back." With that he left the room, shutting the door behind him.

As Diane looked from the candles on the small table to the bath and the door, she narrowed her eyes. The Oliver Warren from Vienna had been . . . fiery, drawing her into bed on their very first meeting. For that fortnight they'd barely been clothed—and even more rarely apart. The Lord Haybury of London had likewise been aggressive and arrogant, pushing at her with every opportunity. This didn't fit with either version of that man.

She stepped out of her shoes. "Well, you can figure this out standing here," she muttered at herself, "or sitting in the bathtub."

The water looked so inviting. Experimentally she dipped her fingers in, swirling the petals about. Delicious and almost too warm. He'd kept the staff busy hauling buckets. A shame to let all that effort go to waste.

Slowly she reached around her back and unfastened the trio of black buttons there. Then she shrugged out of the gown, letting it pool around her bare feet. Her shift followed. Then, with another glance at the closed door, she stepped into the brass tub and sank into hot, fragrant bliss.

She couldn't help the pleased groan that escaped through her lips as she sank down to rest the back of her neck against the edge of the tub. This was so much nicer than tepid water in a washbasin. If not for the man undoubtedly lurking just on the far side of that door, she would have been tempted to drift off to sleep.

The door opened again. Oliver walked into the room, a platter of biscuits and strawberries and two glasses of white wine in his hands. "Comfortable?" he asked, shutting the door with his foot.

"Surprisingly so," she returned. "I said I didn't want a drink."

"I already had it poured. Leave it if you don't want it." Setting the tray down on the floor, he dragged over a chair and stepstool beside the tub, transferred the tray to the stool, and sat in the chair.

"So this is how you mean to spend your time with me? I'll admit to being pleasantly surprised, but the clock continues to tick."

Oliver bit into one of the biscuits, chewed, and swallowed. "You didn't used to be such a stone-hearted chit."

"Ah. Well, I find that being twice abandoned—thrice, if we count my parents—has left me unwilling to consider anyone's well-being but my own."

He reached over to run his forefinger slowly down her bare shoulder. "Did I break your heart?" he murmured.

That wine was beginning to look better and better. "Was that your aim?" she countered. Never would she answer that question. He wanted to know too badly.

"You have to answer my questions for the next twenty-four hours."

Diane sank lower into the water. She closed her eyes, because that would perturb him. "It's twenty-three hours and thirty minutes now," she corrected. "And you have my body to use as you will; not my mind."

A moment later she felt his hands on her hair. She nearly flailed upright, concerned that he might attempt to push her head beneath the water after all. Instead, though, he began gently to pull the pins and combs from her hair until it hung loose and disheveled down the back of the bathtub.

The warm water and the tickle along her scalp felt quite . . . delicious. Keeping her eyes closed, Diane forced her mind to work again. He'd wanted her two years ago. He'd had her, and then he'd fled. Now he wanted her again. Why? He didn't wish anyone else to know, so this was about him rather than being some statement to the males—or females—of Mayfair.

Abruptly it occurred to her, and she opened her eyes again. "You're afraid of me, aren't you?"

Oliver dipped his finger into the water beside her hip and stirred lazily. "If I were afraid of you," he said slowly, his gaze trailing down the length of her and back again, "why would I have you here?"

"To prove to yourself that you aren't afraid of me."

His mouth curved upward. "That's so delightfully naïve of you. Adorable."

She cupped one hand and hurled water at his face. "I am not naïve," she snapped, sitting upright. "Nor am I adorable."

Water dripped from his hair and chin, but he didn't move. "So you have no trouble with the idea of selling yourself to me for five thousand quid, but you won't tolerate being called naïve or adorable? That seems somewhat unbalanced."

"I loaned myself to you. For one day." She leaned her chin on her arm, trying to gather her temper back in. He'd angered her on purpose; it seemed only fair that she attempt to return the favor. "My theory is that you found yourself falling for me two years ago, and, being the self-interested bastard you are, the idea of love frightened you—to the point that you fled the Continent. And now that I'm here, you feel the need to prove to yourself that I no longer affect you."

His finger wandered up her arm in slow swirls. "That's a fascinating theory. Have you ever considered that I left Vienna because my uncle sent for me, and that you're here in my bedchamber because you came to me for help? I think perhaps it's you who need to prove that *I* no longer affect *you*." He dipped his hand to caress her left breast, leaning down to kiss her at the same time.

Lightning flared through her. As soon as his soft, warm mouth left hers, she pulled in a hard breath. "It seems to me that if we're each convinced the other only wants to prove disinterest, perhaps we should simply call the night over with. It would seem to be a very large mistake."

He pinched her nipple between his thumb and forefinger. "I am inclined to keep you here," he mused, tangling the fingers of his other hand into her hair and pulling her head back for another deep, openmouthed kiss.

"Well, just so you know, I have nothing to prove to myself about you," Diane panted as his mouth trailed along her jaw. She clenched her fingers into the rim of the bathtub. "You're pleasant enough in bed, but you can't be trusted or relied upon."

"Because I left?" he asked, his very capable mouth nibbling at her ear.

"Because you seduced me a week after I put Frederick into the ground."

"Mm. I thought you seduced me. Or at the least I would call it a mutual attraction."

She could concede that he had a point, or at least that

the humming blood racing just beneath her skin was making her feel considerably more agreeable. And thinking, keeping her wits about her . . . Even when she knew he would take every advantage possible she couldn't seem to gather her thoughts together.

Oliver straightened again, his damp hands running up his chest to unbutton his waistcoat. He pulled it off and just as swiftly yanked his shirt over his head and cast it aside. Against the tan of his skin, the small white bandage high on his left arm was even more obvious. She'd done that to him. And it wasn't satisfaction she felt as she realized that. "Does it hurt?" she asked, gesturing.

"I've had worse." He rolled his shoulder to demonstrate. "Do you wish to come out, or shall I join you?"

"You're giving me a choice? Or have you forgotten what to do next? I thought this was your venture." Beneath the water she shifted her legs; this was a very large bathtub, and both of them would fit quite easily. But somehow it seemed even more intimate than a tumble in his bed.

"So it is." One by one he removed his boots and dropped them beside the chair. He reached down and handed her a small vial. "Rose oil. Make yourself useful while I finish here, will you?"

"Make myself useful? Whatever happened to the idea of romance?" she returned, taking the vial and pouring several generous drops into the warm water. Immediately the faint rose scent around her deepened, sweet and spicy all at the same time. Unless she was mistaken, this was some very expensive oil.

"You keep insulting me. I've decided to attempt a more direct approach." With that he stood up, unbuttoned his trousers, and shoved them down his thighs.

"Well, I do remember that." Diane spoke as coolly as she could, despite her abruptly dry mouth. The sight of his impressive arousal reminded her of several things, including how very good he was in bed. However that fortnight had ended, the fourteen days it encapsulated had been . . . exceptional.

"And clearly it remembers you, darling." He stepped out of his trousers and with a graceful shift of his weight climbed into the bathtub to sit opposite her.

The water rose to her armpits as he sank down, their legs tangling into one another. Oliver reached over for one of the glasses of wine and offered it to her. Deciding she wasn't accomplishing anything by abstaining, she took it from him and drank a generous swallow. It didn't help.

"What now?" she asked, setting the glass aside again.

He ran his palms up from her ankles to her knees. "Surely you haven't forgotten. How long has it been since you've had a lover?"

"The last one I had rather ruined my taste for them, thank you very much."

She'd meant it as an insult, but he smiled—that aggravating, charming, sensual smile that still had the power to affect her. "No one since me, Diane? I'm flattered."

"I doubt you can make the same claim."

His smile slipped for just a moment. *Regret?* Just as swiftly as that thought crossed her mind, she rejected it again. More than likely it was the realization that he'd lost the advantage for a moment.

"Suffice it to say that I've never loaned any of them five thousand pounds in exchange for a bath."

"The bath was your idea. I'd much rather be asleep at the moment."

He tightened his grip on her knees, tugging her closer. "Allow me to attempt to change your mind," he murmured, leaning forward to kiss her once more. Oliver nibbled at her lower lip, then backed away an inch or so. "You may as well enjoy yourself, Diane," he continued in the same tone. "Because while you may claim to detest me, you also want me."

It took a moment for her breath to return. "Don't be so certain of that."

"I am."

This time he didn't give her a chance to respond, instead drawing her up over his thighs as he kissed and nipped at her mouth. Good heavens, the man knew how to kiss. Almost unaware of the motion, she slipped an arm around his shoulder, holding herself against him. Heat flooded through her, alive and shivery.

When he dipped his head to pull one of her breasts into his mouth, she threw her head back and groaned. Logic, plotting, strategy, all fell away. As he'd said, with twenty-four hours in his intimate company she might as well enjoy herself. He was, after all, very good at this.

Oliver trailed his palms up her thighs, then slowly slid one finger inside her. Diane bucked, arching her back as he continued his ministrations, moving his hand in time with the sucking motion of his mouth on her breasts. Her breath escaping her in gasps, she tangled her hands into his mahogany-colored hair.

When he straightened again to take her mouth, she pushed against his chest. "Enough of the bathtub," she managed.

"I agree."

He slipped his arms beneath her shoulders and knees, then stood. The fragrance of roses followed them as he stepped out of the water and carried her over to his bed. Her body abruptly felt chilled everywhere he wasn't pressed against her, but she noticed the cool air only peripherally; inside, she burned.

He'd covered the bed with additional blankets, evidently anticipating that they would both be wet when they arrived there. Oliver settled her into the nest, tied the ribbon of the neat French condom around the base of his penis, then climbed up her body, kissing her thighs, her belly, and her breasts, and then taking her mouth in another deep kiss.

"Say you want me," he breathed, reaching between them to rub his thumb against her left nipple.

With his weight settled on her hips, his arousal pressed against her thighs, remaining objective was becoming supremely difficult. He made her want to move, to take him inside her, to groan like a moonstruck girl. But he wasn't allowed to know that. "You want me," she responded, running her own palms down his muscular arse and up again along his spine. The play of muscles beneath his skin was intoxicating, heady, and arousing, and she blinked in an attempt to clear her mind.

"So that's how it's going to be, is it?"

"Yes," she rasped as he took a breast into his mouth again. "Don't tell me you're surprised."

"Everything about you surprises me."

That seemed like an uncharacteristically straightforward compliment. Perhaps his head was as preoccupied with sensation as hers was. Because whatever her head thought of him, her body was very, very pleased. As Oliver parted her legs and settled her ankles around his hips, she forgot everything but the exquisite sensation of his hard cock sliding inside her. *Oh, God.*

He entered her again and again, his weight pinning her to the damp blankets. Diane couldn't breathe, couldn't do anything but clench her fingertips into his back and groan in time with his penetrations. Every muscle tightened and then released as she contracted around him.

"I knew you wanted me," he murmured, his gaze intent on her face.

Anything she could conjure at the moment would have sounded idiotic, so she settled for biting her lip and trying not to make the mewling sounds attempting to burst from her throat. Abruptly he rolled them so that he lay on his back and she sat straddling his hips, her hands splayed on his hard chest.

If she'd had any self-control at all she would have remained still; after all, this agreement was all his idea. But the sensation of him filling her took precedence over everything else, and she began to move, stroking up and down the length of him. This time *he* moaned, reaching up to fondle and knead at her breasts, pulling her forward for another hard, breathless kiss.

He thrust up into her faster and faster and then moaned as he convulsed against her, holding her close onto him as he came. More than anything she wanted to collapse on his chest, relax her tired, aroused muscles. But that would mean surrender—and she was not about to surrender. So instead she looked down at him and tried to capture enough breath to speak. "What now?" she asked. "You still have twenty-two hours remaining."

"Damned chit," he muttered, lifting her off him. "Lie down."

She started to lie back, resisting the urge to cover herself or attempt something equally girlish. She wasn't a girl. "Very original."

"On your stomach."

Diane frowned. "You are not g—"

"And shut up." He pushed her with his fingers until she lay on her stomach, her arms crossed under her head.

A moment later she felt him wrapping a towel around her hair and then tugging it down. He repeated the action, rubbing the wet strands between the folds of the towel. "You're drying my hair?"

"You'll ruin my bed otherwise. Go to sleep."

"So you're finished with me?"

"I'm tired. We can begin battling again in the morning."

She considered that for a moment, letting the feeling of him toying with her hair seep into her. Nothing had changed. They were still adversaries. It was only that she felt very relaxed at the moment. And very sleepy. "Agreed."

Chapter Eleven

I t hadn't precisely gone according to plan.

Oliver sat back against the headboard of his large bed and gazed at the dishevelment of blankets and sheets beside him. Barely visible but for one arm and a tangle of long, curling black hair slept the greatest conundrum of his life.

He hadn't meant to touch her until morning. A comfortable, confidence-lulling bath, a warm night in his bed while he slept elsewhere, followed by a decadent breakfast and then hours of even more decadent sex. And then he'd seen her sitting naked in the warm water, and he'd forgotten everything he'd planned.

People in general, and his peers in particular, thought him a hedonistic libertine. They thought he set his eyes on something and reacted to it as his gut—or slightly lower—wished. They were wrong, of course; he rarely acted without first considering where all the threads would lead. Of course, his only caveat of the past two years had been that the feminine distractions led him away from memories of Vienna.

Last night, however, his mind had evidently fled the premises. And the damnedest part of the disaster was that sex with Diane Benchley had not accomplished what he'd intended. Because while she'd clearly enjoyed the tumble physically, her mind and her heart had remained her own. Not that he'd intended to lure her into heartbreak again, but he found it aggravating that he'd lost control when she hadn't.

This was supposed to be about proving to himself that Vienna had been . . . unique, a fortnight-long instance of mental confusion and weakness on his part. He was now supposed to be done with her—except that clearly he wasn't.

Shifting carefully, Oliver slipped out of the bed, pulled on a pair of trousers, and went to his front room to ring the servant's bell hanging against the wall there. A handful of seconds later, someone knocked and he pulled open the door. "Langtree. Good morning."

Her steady gaze didn't even acknowledge his bare chest. Damn it all, he was clearly not up to his usual standards. "I require breakfast for two, and suitable morning attire for Lady Cameron. Gown, shoes, a hairbrush, and whatever else she generally has need of when she rises."

This time the servant blinked. "For Lady Cameron?"

"Yes, and be quick about it." Before she could say anything else, he closed the door on her.

Interesting. The servants didn't know where their mistress had spent the night. He wondered if the tall French twist had any idea about the terms of the new loan. The rest of Mayfair thought he and Lady Cameron were lovers already, mostly because she'd encouraged that interpretation herself. Evidently her own household wasn't supposed to have come to the same conclusion.

While he waited, he sat down and wrote out a note to Manderlin excusing himself from the planned excursion to Tattersall's, then another to Lady Katherine to inform her that he wouldn't be available for an intimate afternoon tea after all. She wouldn't be surprised; he hadn't been available for anything intimate or otherwise for nearly five weeks.

The siren in his bedchamber kept drawing him toward the back of his apartments, and he sternly resisted the urge to go see whether she was still sleeping. He needed a new strategy, and he needed it quickly. Because if he still wanted her, then he had to do something to make certain she wanted him. Which meant something different, something unexpected, something to shake her free of her heretofore very accurate perception of him—the him whose character seemed to . . . improve when he was in her presence.

His front door rattled and someone shoved at the heavy wood. Hard. Out of habit he always latched it—one never knew who might be displeased with one.

"Open the door at once!"

Ah, the French twist. "I'm not seeing visitors, Miss Martine," he said, stifling a grin. Genevieve Martine hadn't been informed of Diane's obligations for the next . . . eighteen hours, either.

"Juliet, fetch me an axe and Mr. Jacobs!" she called from the other side of the door, naming the largest of Diane's male club protectors.

Oliver unlocked the door and pulled it open. "I suggest you not attempt to break down my door," he said in the same tone that had convinced several men not to fight him and subsequently lose their lives in idiotic duels.

"You will release Diane immediately," she snapped back at him, her blond hair only partly put up and her gown slightly askew. "Or I will do worse than break down your door, you blackguard."

"Mm-hm. Breakfast and clothes. If you want an explanation for Diane's presence, you may ask her after four o'clock tomorrow morning."

"I'll ask her now."

"No, you won't."

"You h—"

He shut and locked the door again. Immediately she began pounding on it. Generally women were either intimidated by him or set on attracting his attention. Other than Diane, none of them were openly hostile. Well, her and this chit.

"What the devil have you done now?"

Oliver leaned back against the shaking door and folded his arms across his bare chest. Diane stood a few feet from him, clothed in his discarded shirt and nothing else. With her long, loose hair, bare legs, and sleeves rolled up to her elbows, she looked . . . delicious. And she knew it. Otherwise she might have donned her shift. Did she want him to fall on her again? Even acknowledging that it would likely cost him some ground, he couldn't help simply . . . gazing at her.

"Well?" she prompted.

"Your Miss Martine thinks I've kidnapped you," he answered. "I'm assuming you didn't inform your household about our agreement."

She frowned. "I was waiting for an opportune moment. You're the one who pounced on me before I could say anything to them."

"I did not pounce, and you had several hours to tell whomever you chose."

Diane waved a hand at him. "Oh, get out of the way before they break down the door."

He didn't move. "You aren't leaving." Even if he had to fight off a house full to the brim with angry, yowling chits.

"Not for eighteen hours." This time when she motioned him aside, he shifted.

"She's not allowed in, either," he added, reaching over to unlock the door.

From his place behind the door, keeping it from opening fully, he couldn't see the angry Miss Martine just on the other side of the oak planks, but he didn't need to. Considering that he hadn't been particularly unpleasant to the woman, he had to assume that Diane had spoken to her about the events in Vienna. Interesting, then, that Diane hadn't said anything about this.

"No, I'm quite well," Diane was saying as she curled her fingers into the half-open door.

She had elegant fingers. Perfect for a cardplayer, though she more than likely wouldn't appreciate hearing that. Oliver reached out, intending to run his own fingers along hers, then stopped the motion. This wasn't a seduction or a romance. This was him, attempting to purge her from his mind. Touching her for no damned reason was not going to help that.

"But *him*, Diane? You said you would rath—"

"I know what I said," she interrupted, her grip on the door tightening momentarily. "But I also told you that I had an agreement to see to. I'll attempt to explain it later, Jenny. In eighteen hours. Until then, you'll have to make do without me."

"The fiend asked for breakfast and clothes for you."

Oliver frowned. While he didn't give a damn what the French twist thought of him, he didn't particularly believe he'd been a fiend. He looked at Diane's profile. Had that been her word, or her friend's? Was that truly what Diane thought of him? He leaned around the door. "And tea," he added. "Now."

With the flat of his hand he closed the door again, this time leaving it unlocked. The chit began a stream of muffled curses in several different languages, but he doubted she would attempt to break down the door again. Turning around once more, he gazed at his guest.

"I have a question," he said, gesturing her to precede him to his small morning room.

"Did we decide that me talking to you was part of your agreement?"

Perhaps he should have kept her awake all night after all. That would have dulled her sharp tongue a little. "You can either chat with me or I'll remember we have more physical things we could be doing together. I'll let you choose."

Color touched her cheeks. "I believe you had a question, didn't you?" she asked, walking to the overstuffed chair beneath the window and curling into it like a cat.

He stayed silent as he sank onto the couch opposite, considering whether to ask the question foremost on his mind. It was a very poor idea, because it left him open to a riposte, but he genuinely wanted to know. "In Vienna," he began, "when we met, what did you think the outcome would be?"

She drew a breath, turning her gaze toward the window and the treetops of her garden beyond. "Clearly my thinking was impaired in Vienna. I can't answer your question."

"Yes, you can."

"You answer it first, then."

"Very well."

Visibly surprised, she shifted to face him again. "Well, this should be enlightening."

"Just remember that you have to answer the question as well. No matter what I say on the subject." This would have been an opportune moment for the tea or breakfast to arrive, but the front door remained closed and silent. "When we first met, I thought you were stunning, and so angry at the world that you would grasp at any way to defy it. And I thought you would be a fine addition to my bed."

"What about the outcome?"

Of course she'd noticed that he hadn't quite answered the question. "I reckoned I would spend time with you until I became bored or you began to cling, at which time we would part company."

Her eyes narrowed. "I didn't cling, so you must have become bored."

"Th—"

"What's this, then?" she pursued. "If I bored you, why arrange to have me in your bed again?"

"You didn't bore me."

"Then why did you leave?"

The front door opened. "In here," he called, rising and going to intercept the platter of food and the pot of tea entering his apartments. Once the footwomen had set the trays down on the table in between Diane and him, he sent them away in search of his other request. The longer Diane remained in his shirt, the more likely he was to peel her out of it. And while he had no objection to having sex with her again—in fact, he planned to do so—he wanted it to be on his terms rather than because she was purposely tempting him.

She sat forward to pick up a piece of toast and began munching. "Shall I repeat the question?"

"You can if you wish, but this is *my* dance, if you'll recall. And it's your turn."

Rather than answer, she finished her toast, then poured herself a cup of tea and sipped at it. Oliver selected a soft gold-colored peach and bit into it. He might have teased or taunted her into answering, he supposed, but if she wanted a moment to think and decide on her answer, in this instance he was willing to give it to her.

"I was eighteen when I married Frederick," she finally

said, standing to lean against the windowsill. "It was arranged, you know, but I was quite excited to be marrying an earl."

"Your grandfather was a marquis, was he not?"

"Yes. But the title went to my uncle, which my father never liked. The idea of his daughter being a countess made him quite happy." She took another sip of her tea. "I won't say that Frederick was a monster or any such thing, because he wasn't. He simply wasn't very . . . intelligent, or interesting. Of course he thought he was, the same way he thought he knew how to play cards."

"I think that ailment is common to most men."

"I did everything I could to keep our bills paid, but he was the master of his house, and he brought it down around both of our ears. And when he died, yes, I was angry. He destroyed everything, and left me to face the consequences. Not to mention the year I was forced to spend in mourning."

"You never told me this before," he commented, sitting forward to pour himself some tea.

"You never asked. When you appeared at Lady Darham's luncheon, I just wanted to forget everything."

"I'm glad I could oblige, then."

"Oh, please. Clearly you would have pursued me, regardless of what I might have been thinking."

"Fair enough." He gazed at her profile for a moment, but she remained silent. "And a fortnight later?" he finally prompted.

Taking a breath, she faced him once more. "Evidently I hadn't learned as much about men and their motivations as I'd thought. Honestly, Oliver, I'd never met anyone like you. You fascinated me. For a time I thought perhaps you were meant as compensation—a counterbalance for Frederick and his idiocy. And then you left, and I realized you were merely the final part of my lesson."

He didn't like the way she said that. "Which lesson was that?"

"The lesson about the peril of relying on men—on any man—for my security or happiness. I don't feel inclined to thank you, but I don't believe I would be here opening The Tantalus Club if I'd never met you."

She said it smoothly enough, but he knew damned well it wasn't a compliment. "If you detest me so much, you might have found someone else to fund your venture."

"Perhaps, but I have the means to compel you to help me. And I like seeing you inconvenienced. And in all honesty, there were pleasant moments in Vienna. I merely need to remember not to take them to heart." As someone knocked at his door again, she set down her tea. "That will be my clothes, I assume," she said, and left the room.

Oliver listened for a moment to be certain she wouldn't attempt an escape after all, but when he heard the door close and her bare feet padding in the direction of his bedchamber he rolled his shoulders. Then he dragged the end table closer and dug into the poached eggs and ham.

She *had* fallen for him in Vienna, however she chose to word it. And damn it all, he'd fallen for her. The only difference was that he hadn't liked the sensation and he'd done everything possible to expel it—and her—from his thoughts and memory. And he thought he'd managed it—until she'd appeared in London.

And now he'd made it worse. Had he been attempting to purge himself of his desire for her, or had another part of him wanted to remember how much he enjoyed touching her and feeling her skin against his? He liked their verbal fencing matches, even when she drew blood. Her damned rapier was much sharper these days. And evidently he liked being knotted up in her schemes, because Lucifer knew he could have convinced her to hand over that bloody letter if he'd truly wished her to. Doing that, however, would have left her destroyed; he couldn't imagine she would surrender her advantage willingly.

The question, then, became what to do next. He'd taken more money from men than they could afford to lose. He'd damaged the reputations of women when they'd attempted to make more of a connection with him than he'd wanted. And now this woman who hated him had tangled herself into his life and he'd allowed it. Even encouraged it.

And then there was the way she'd chosen to wear his shirt this morning, the way she'd agreed to his twenty-four-hour meeting. As he considered it, the most likely conclusion was either that she disliked him less than she pretended or that she was attempting to seduce him and then break his heart, as he'd broken hers.

Oliver paused in midbite. The Diane of two years ago hadn't been nearly as devious, but this one . . . He gave a slow smile. He couldn't even remember the last person who'd attempted to stand toe-to-toe with him. And if this was the path she wanted to take and if it meant letting her get closer to him—and him to her—then by God, he would make it a merry chase. He had no idea how it might end, but that thought didn't trouble him nearly as much as he'd expected.

Hm. Finishing off his bite, he rose once more and went to the bell pull. He had a few more plans to make this morning.

Diane left the top two buttons at the back of her simple black muslin walking dress open and finished pinning up her hair. Thank goodness Oliver had asked about Vienna. After last night she wanted to make certain he knew that she hadn't lost all her sensibilities and forgotten what a cad he was. And she wanted to make certain *she* remembered, as well.

Oh, he perturbed her no end. And what the devil was wrong with him, that she could appear wearing nothing but his shirt and he did nothing more than send for breakfast? Last night had given her an epiphany, among other things. The man needed a healthy dose of heartache. And as long as she kept their past firmly in mind, she would be just the one to give it to him.

She stepped into her shoes, then frowned as her left toes poked something stiff. Sitting again, she reached into the shoe and pulled out a folded piece of paper. *If you need assistance,* she read in Jenny's flowing cursive, *say "marmalade" when you leave the apartment.*

They'd used the same strategy before, when she'd first begun meeting with Frederick's rather angry creditors. Considering that she disliked marmalade, it seemed a safe word to use. Shifting the note to her pocket, she finished donning her shoes and left the room. Oliver still sat in the morning room drinking tea. From the look of the breakfast platter, he'd had a generous meal as well.

"Button me, will you?" she asked, turning her back on him.

A moment later she felt him approach behind her, and then his warm fingers trailed up her shoulder blades. "Do you own anything not in black?"

"Yes."

"When will you wear it?"

"When I wish to." She pulled the note from her pocket and held it up as she turned to face him.

Oliver took it from her and opened it. He read it swiftly, then looked up at her. "Your friend is very resourceful."

Diane grinned. "You have no idea."

"Why did you show it to me?"

"To prove that I'm honoring our deal. And so you don't say 'marmalade' by accident. She's likely to shoot you."

"I try to limit having holes put in me to once a month. Thank you for the warning." His jaw twitching, he handed the note back. "Who is she?"

Damnation. She should have known he would be putting all the puzzle pieces together. It was what he did. "She's an old friend. I told you that."

"Fine. I can do a bit of digging on my own. It's rather gratifying to realize how many people owe me favors."

Taking a moment to gather her thoughts, Diane picked through the remains of the breakfast platter. Being on the defensive wouldn't get her anywhere. "I presume you have something other than fornication in mind, since you sent for my clothes," she commented. "Or is it just that you wanted to tear them off me?"

"I have the ability to think of fornication *and* something else, all at the same time," he returned with a swift, attractive smile. "But you're correct; we're going out."

Considering that she'd thought he would keep her naked in his bedchamber all day, this was supremely unexpected. "Going out where?"

"You'll see." He took her hand and kissed her fingers. "I need to dress. I'll be back in a moment."

She shook out her fingers as he left the room. If he wished them to be seen together in public, she supposed that would only help the impression that she was both desirable and unavailable. In fact, she couldn't see how he would benefit at all from taking her about London.

With the grand opening and then the rest of the night spent in Oliver's bed, she'd barely eaten in hours, and the toasted bread hadn't done much to curb her appetite. Glancing toward the open door of his bedchamber, she sat in his vacated chair and quickly ate a slice of ham and the remainder of the eggs.

"Do you want more?" he asked, stepping back into the room.

She jumped. "No. Not unless you'll have us gone until four o'clock in the morning."

"I imagine we'll return to my bed before then," he drawled. "Button me, will you?"

Turning around, she saw that he'd donned a pair of black trousers, a black jacket, and a black waistcoat, which currently hung open over his white shirt and black cravat. "Are you making fun of me?"

"I thought we should match. I can hardly dress more colorfully without looking like a dandy now, can I? Button me."

"You don't need my help."

"Neither did you."

Diane blew out her breath in feigned annoyance. Or actual annoyance. He drove her so close to madness that she wasn't certain any longer. How could anyone be so aggravating and so compelling all at the same time? Standing, she stalked up to him and yanked the two sides of his waistcoat forward. It didn't budge him an inch. Refusing to look up at his face, she swiftly buttoned the half-dozen fastenings running up the black waistcoat and then stepped back again.

"Do you need me to comb your hair? Shave you?"

"No. Do you require a reticule?"

"That depends on whether you intend to abandon me somewhere to make my own way home."

He narrowed one eye. "I won't abandon you anywhere."

Ah, an opening. "Hm. Well, that will be a nice change."

Muttering something under his breath that sounded very unflattering, he led the way to his front door. When he pulled it open, Jenny stood just two feet away on the landing, already glaring at him. "Good day," he said, nodding at her. "I'll have her back before daybreak."

"I should hope so," Genevieve returned stiffly. "Diane, do you wish anything else for breakfast?"

She could escape if she wanted to, she imagined, but if she did so then Oliver would more than likely withdraw his support and his additional five thousand pounds, and The Tantalus Club would be forced to close before it had truly opened. And if she did escape, she wouldn't discover what he had planned for the day. "No, I'm fine. But thank you for asking. I'll be back later."

"Very well."

Halfway down the stairs it occurred to her that she'd forgotten something rather significant. She stopped. "Jenny, have we received any applications?"

"Forty as of this morning. Footmen have been bringing them by since just after daybreak."

Oh, thank goodness. "Excellent," she said aloud. "Are you certain you can open the doors without me?"

"They'll make do," Oliver cut in. "And you're impinging on my time. That's enough conversation."

Diane sent him an annoyed look for Jenny's benefit, then followed him down to the foyer and out the front door. His high-perch phaeton and pair of jet-black horses stood there, waiting for them. Wherever they were going, then, he meant for them to be seen. Juliet handed over her black bonnet, and Diane tied it over her hair.

It had been ages since she'd ridden in a phaeton, and despite herself a thrill of excitement ran down her spine. She took his hand as he helped her up to the high seat, then waited as he walked around the back of the carriage and clambered up the other side. Without another word he took the reins, nodded at the groom holding the horses, and flicked the ribbons. In a heartbeat they were off, trotting down the street in the direction of Hyde Park.

"Will you tell me now where we're heading?" she asked,

holding on to her bonnet with one hand and trying not to smile.

"No."

"Why not?"

"Because once I tell you, you'll begin plotting and planning your response to the setting. You'll have to tolerate simply . . . being surprised."

She sent him a sideways glance. "Do *you* know where we're going?"

Oliver laughed. The unexpected sound put a responding grin on her face before she could stop it. He didn't laugh often, she knew; she'd only seen him that amused once or twice in Vienna. And to hear the low, merry chuckle now . . . she liked it. Except that she didn't like that she liked it.

"Yes," he said. "I know where we're going."

Since her return to London she'd attempted to familiarize herself with the area; Frederick's family had been anxious for the two of them to marry, so she'd only spent a total of four weeks enjoying her debut season in Town. All she knew for certain at the moment was that they were heading south toward the Thames and that they were west of the shopping on Bond Street.

They passed a barouche going the opposite way, and the three ladies inside sent her clearly curious stares before they began whispering and giggling together. "If you're showing me off, shouldn't we be in Hyde Park?" she ventured.

"I don't need to show you off; everyone knows who you are."

They turned onto one of the bridges spanning the Thames and crossed to the south bank. Rows of trees and a distant Oriental pagoda came into view as he pulled the phaeton into a large public stable yard, and she abruptly realized where they were.

"Vauxhall Gardens?"

The moment a groom appeared to take charge of the horses, Oliver jumped to the ground and came around to her side of the carriage. "Yes," he said, lifting his arms to her. "It's a bit shabby and past its prime, but it does have its amusements."

She started to take his hands to step down, but he moved closer to grip her about the waist. Before she could complain that she was not some helpless young miss, he lifted her into the air and then set her down in front of him.

"And what amusements in particular interest you today?" Diane asked, stepping back from the circle of his arms as casually as she could manage. After all, while there weren't many people about, it only took one gossip to say that Diane had been seen recoiling from her rumored beau. "A deep pond for drownings?"

"I don't know why you've decided I mean to do you in," he returned mildly, offering her an arm.

"Ah. Perhaps I'm confusing my own whimsy with yours."

Oliver nodded. "That must be it. This way."

They crossed a footbridge and made their way through a pretty if overgrown trellised garden, then around a large grouping of mostly empty private boxes to the central pavilion and fountain. The farther into the pleasure gardens they walked, the more crowded it became, not only with aristocrats but with what looked to be everyone from merchants to brightly dressed lightskirts.

Everyone stood grouped around a roped-off circle in the adjoining clearing where a large dome towered above them. No, not a dome, she realized as they made their way closer. An orb. A very large one decorated with a horizontal patterning of yellow and red stripes.

"A balloon?" she commented, falling in behind Oliver

as he rather effectively made his way through the crowd to the rope boundary. "You've brought me to see a balloon?"

"No, I haven't." He lifted his hand, gesturing at one of the dozen men scurrying about the large woven basket resting on the ground beneath the anchored balloon. A large fire crackled to one side, while a much smaller burning caldron was secured between the basket and the balloon.

"Yes, monsieur?" the man said, approaching.

"We two wish to go up," Oliver returned in flawless French.

Diane's heart stammered. "No, we don't," she hissed.

Before she could back away, Oliver took her hand in his and drew her up against his side. "Yes, we do," he muttered.

"The rides begin tomorrow," the fellow said. "Today is only for show and to make certain we have patched all the . . . *les trous.*"

"The *holes*?" Diane squeaked, translating.

"Yes. Holes."

"I am the Marquis of Haybury," Oliver stated, this time in English, digging into his coat pocket with his free hand. "And I have twenty pounds to give someone in exchange for the privilege of ascending in your aero balloon in the next five minutes."

The balloonist repeated Oliver's request in French to his companions, then lifted the rope barricade as high as he could. Still pulling her along behind him, Oliver ducked beneath the barricade.

Oh, goodness. If they'd been alone she would have kicked him and fled, but with the vocal and highly interested audience of onlookers surrounding them, she settled for clenching her jaw and following him. She was supposed to be mysterious and fearless—the first for everyone else, and the second for herself. And still she couldn't help pulling just a little against Oliver's iron grip. "This is mad," she whispered. "What are you attempting to prove?"

Oliver put his hands around her again, this time lifting her into the waist-high basket. "I'm not attempting to prove anything. I want to ride in a balloon and see London from above. And I want you to go with me." He clambered rather easily into the basket beside her while a single balloonist followed less gracefully a moment later.

"Why do you want me to ride in a balloon with you?"

"Because you didn't expect it."

"I wouldn't have expected a nice diamond necklace, either."

"Next time, perhaps."

With a command of "Loose!" the other men released all the ropes tied to stakes around the basket. Held by a single long tether wound around a solid wooden crank, they began to rise slowly into the air.

Chapter Twelve

London from five hundred feet in the air. Below them the Thames wound through the middle of the city, while to the northwest Oliver could make out the dense green of Hyde Park, and St. James's Park farther to the east. St. Paul's Cathedral and its round-topped spire dominated the skyline to the northeast, and directly below them the circle of curious onlookers seemed as small as ants. Well, mice perhaps.

Spectacular as the aerial view of his city was, however, he was more interested in the reaction of the young woman standing beside him. He doubted she even realized that she had a bruisingly tight grip on his hand, because her gaze remained fixed on the landscape below them. The excited half smile on her face fascinated him even more than the view—though he would never admit that aloud.

She was so guarded in his presence. He was the same in hers, of course; neither of them wished the other to find a weakness, an unarmored chink to be exploited. But he'd never realized just *how* careful she was about what she showed him until he glimpsed this wide-eyed, laughing chit leaning out into open space. If he opened himself more to her, risked a wound or two, then perhaps she would do the same for him. He'd begun to think it was worth the risk.

"I feel like I'm flying!" she exclaimed, then pointed. "Oh, look! I can see my house from here!"

He had his doubts about that, but given the odd light-heartedness touching him this morning, he didn't see the need to argue her claim. Instead he twined his fingers with hers and took in the sights above London. And wondered abruptly whether he'd made a very large mistake two years ago. He hadn't wanted his life upended. Over the past few weeks she'd upended it anyway—and by God, it had been interesting so far.

A gust of wind canted them a little sideways, and her grip tightened. "We won't fall out, will we?"

"That almost never happens, miss," the balloonist returned.

" 'Almost' never?" she repeated.

"You will address her as Lady Cameron, monsieur," Oliver corrected.

The fellow tugged on his forelock. "Beg pardon, my lady."

"No harm done," she replied. "I'm certain Lord Haybury ascends with females of no breeding at least three days every week."

Oliver lowered his gaze to hers. "The wonder of floating above London is beginning to fade, then, I assume?" he commented, shaking the soft, pillowy edges of nonsense from his mind. "And I've never ridden the air in a balloon before, Diane."

A half smile touched her mouth again. "Then I suppose I still feel some wonder. This is rather remarkable." Her green eyes danced as she gazed across the city once more.

"Yes, rather remarkable," he echoed. As was the realization that this woman who had caused him to flee or risk losing . . . himself after only a fortnight had as many facets as a diamond. And the sparkle of her fascinated him. He'd never expected intrigue to outweigh the drag of entanglement, but as long as it did, he intended to continue both his exploration and his pursuit.

They spent nearly forty minutes in the air while he pointed out the sights around them and she laughed every time the breeze made them sway. When the crank finally returned them to the ground again, he vaulted over the lip of the basket and lifted her out after him.

As he set her on her feet, she looked up at the balloon again. "That was quite enjoyable," she admitted, straightening her black bonnet.

"Yes, it was. I may hire one this autumn for Haybury Park. It would be interesting to see my lands from above." He offered his arm, and she slipped her hand around his sleeve.

"You've truly never done this before?" she asked, sending him a dubious look.

"I never have."

"What made you think of it, then?"

Oliver shrugged. "I remembered reading that the balloon would be here this week, and I thought you would like it."

"Well. Thank you. I did."

"You're wel—"

"I could think of several less pleasant activities you might have decided on while I'm compelled to remain in your company, so this is especially nice."

Oliver stilled his expression. For a heartbeat he'd forgotten that while he might be contemplating pursuit, Diane was still attacking and retreating at a full gallop. "Back to being sharp-tongued again, are you? Or was that little statement supposed to convince me to send you on your way?"

She tilted her head at him. "Did it work?"

"No. I will give you a choice, though. Shopping, or a drive through Hyde Park."

"Oh, now I'm disappointed. You've already run out of unexpected jaunts?"

Good God, she was relentless. "How about luncheon at White's, then?"

This time she blinked. "You can't be serious."

"Why not? You're a club owner. It behooves you to make a study of your competition."

"I would agree, but there are several lamentable rules about no females being allowed at White's—or any of the other prominent gentlemen's clubs. And I do not wish to be seen as a crusader for women's rights. That will drive men away more quickly than anything else. This is about me earning my way, not about me being thrown out of somewhere on my arse."

"Leave it to me."

"I don't trust you enough to do that."

He helped her up to the phaeton's seat and strode to the far side of the carriage to join her. "Considering that you're mine for the next . . . fourteen hours, you don't have much of a choice." As he flicked the reins, he moved a breath closer to her. "You should have chosen shopping."

"Then I choose shopping."

"Too late." He glanced sideways at her. "I won't make things worse for you."

"If you do, the ten thousand pounds you've lent me becomes mine, along with an additional ten thousand pounds to see me on my way."

This was beginning to become expensive. Still, he did love to wager—and a wager where he would feel the loss came about too rarely these days to be allowed to pass by. "Then what do I get if we're allowed to eat at White's and the sun doesn't fall from the sky as a result?"

"I don't make meaningless wagers. I've lost more than enough to that nonsense."

"Then we'll also make it something unrelated to money." He considered for a moment. "If we're permitted to stay for luncheon, you will allow me to escort you to the Drury Lane theater on Tuesday next."

"*You* go to the theater?" she returned skeptically.

"I've found there is no better place to find young ladies who are bored witless and looking for a distraction." And he happened to enjoy the theater, but she would never believe that. "Do we have an agreement? With the caveat that if you sabotage us at White's, I win by default."

She pursed her lips. "Very well. I don't have to spit on my hand and shake yours, do I?"

"I believe we can forego the spitting." Shifting his grip on the reins, he held his right hand out to her.

Diane shook it, making the contact as brief as she could manage. The fact that she'd been touching him quite a bit today, and voluntarily, hadn't escaped her. And therefore it likely hadn't escaped his notice, either. Hiding her scowl, she turned her gaze forward again.

St. James's Street with its parade of gentlemen's clubs came into view ahead of them. She was far from fearless, but since Frederick's death she'd made a vow never to let fear stop her from doing what she needed to ensure her own survival. Luncheon at White's—while seeing the premises with her own eyes could be very helpful—was not necessary.

Rather, it was Oliver taking what she wanted and pushing it far past where she felt comfortable treading. But considering that she'd already spent part of the additional five thousand pounds and had plans for the remainder of it, she didn't seem to have much choice. Mainly, though, she couldn't help noticing that she'd very much enjoyed the first ten hours of this agreement.

"You're being rather quiet," he observed.

"I'm contemplating what I'll do with my additional ten thousand pounds and no debt," she returned, mentally shaking herself. Heaven knew she needed to keep her wits about her in his presence. "Travel, perhaps. I hear that Greece is lovely."

"Don't pack your bags yet, my dear."

They stopped outside White's Club and handed the phaeton over to a groom. She took Oliver's proffered arm again, willing herself to at least look calm. As she'd told him, she was no pot-wabbler; her concern was for her own well-being and that of her club. This wasn't about making a statement about female rights as much as it was about learning what she could about the competition. And about demonstrating to Oliver Warren that he couldn't intimidate her.

The unassuming door opened. A footman dressed in black livery sent her a dismissive glance and then turned his attention to Oliver. "My lord. Welcome."

"Hello, Winston. Are you crowded today?"

"Passable, my lord." When Oliver stepped forward, the footman took a half step back, then stopped his retreat. Clearly the poor fellow had no idea what to do. "You're welcome to enter, Lord Haybury," he said, his voice shaking a bit at the edges, "but of course your . . . friend isn't permitted."

"Fetch Mr. Raggett and allow us into the foyer, will you?" Oliver returned in the same easy tone he'd used previously.

"I— Yes, of course." Finally he stepped aside and let them through the door. "Please proceed no further."

Once the servant hurried out of the small entryway, Diane faced Oliver. "This is a very poor idea," she said in a low voice. "They'll never allow me inside, and you'll lose twenty thousand pounds for being so bloody arrogant."

"I thought you would wish me to lose," he returned.

"You've already lost. I'm only pointing out that you would be less embarrassed if you conceded now and took me to luncheon somewhere females are allowed."

"Spoken like someone about to lose a wager, my dear."

A short, whip-thin man with silver fringing his dark, short hair stepped into the entryway. "My lord. What is this? You know you cannot—"

"Yes, I know," Oliver interrupted, a slight scowl drawing his brows down. "This is Lady Cameron."

"Ah. The Tantalus Club. Everyone's been speaking about it today." Raggett favored her with an assessing look. "You're looking to take business from me, my lady."

She smiled. "Yes, I am."

"I've been attempting to discourage her from all this," Oliver put in, shaking his head. "You are my last hope. I thought, George, if she could see the interior of White's and have a taste of your famous roast chicken luncheon, she would realize that a gentlemen's club owned by a chit hasn't a chance against White's, or even any of the lesser clubs."

Oh, that was very clever of him. Appeal to the man's pride and vanity, belittle her, and get precisely what he wanted. And she couldn't protest his tactics or she would lose regardless of whether he succeeded or not. Neither, though, did she intend to aid him. Fixing him with an annoyed look, she stood silently and waited.

"I'd lose half my membership if she sat down to eat here today, my lord."

Oliver lifted an eyebrow. "And?" he drawled in a low voice.

Now that was something she wished she had the talent for: making a single innocuous word sound like a threat. It took her at least half a dozen syllables to accomplish that feat.

Raggett cleared his throat. "Perhaps a tour—a swift one, as a courtesy from one club owner to another. But no dining."

"Very well. Lead on, Mr. Raggett."

Taking her hand in his, Oliver placed it over his arm and followed the proprietor into the front room. On her left, at the infamous bow window once occupied solely by Beau Brummell and his cronies, sat a group of well-dressed gentlemen. As they caught sight of her, one of them choked on his drink, a second one shot to his feet and then sat again just as quickly, and the third one spat out his mouthful of whatever it was he was eating.

"What is the meaning of this?" an elderly man with a shock of white hair and a cane clenched in one fist growled. "Mr. Raggett, I demand an explanation!"

Oliver took a half step sideways in what looked, oddly enough, like he was moving to protect her. "Lord Frist," he said with a smile. "This is Lady Cameron. I insisted she tour the best of our clubs in the vain hope that she might improve hers."

"You will not belittle me," she murmured in his ear, "or I will remove that which qualifies you to attend any gentlemen's club."

He actually sent her a brief grin. "Though I do have to say," he continued, moving forward again, "The Tantalus Club serves an excellent dessert."

That elicited some chuckles. She didn't like it, but she supposed amusement was better than staves and pitchforks forcibly removing her from the premises. "This way, my lady," Mr. Raggett said, gesturing her toward the next room.

As they toured the famous club, Diane realized that the layout of The Tantalus was actually quite similar. Separate, more intimate rooms for quiet conversation, billiards, or tea and smoking, and larger rooms for dinner and general card playing. Silent footmen roamed about, seeing to every need of the patrons and toting drinks and platters of food.

White's, of course, didn't have the narrow corridors on either side of the main room for unseen transport of food and servants, and she much preferred her design. And The Tantalus boasted its private apartments—which were solely to accommodate herself and Oliver, but that was beside the point.

Oliver pointed out a few things as they walked, and one or two of them actually made a bit of sense. Considering that she'd never darkened the doorway of an English gentlemen's club before today, she thought she'd done an outstanding job with her own version.

And considering that this tour would not end with her eating on this club's premises and she was therefore earning twenty thousand pounds, it was turning out to be quite an exceptional day. And that after quite an exceptional night. She wondered if she would ever be able to smell roses without thinking of Oliver, though she would never admit that to the man walking beside her.

The kitchen was large and bustling with even more staff; clearly she would need to hire more servants as well, if attendance reached anywhere near White's levels. As Mr. Raggett explained that the kitchen never closed and that he had three master chefs, Oliver left her side and took the proprietor's arm.

She had no idea what Oliver said, but she was certain that money exchanged hands—especially when Mr. Raggett bowed and went over to drag a table to one side of the kitchen. As she watched, he and a footman brought in two chairs and then set the table for luncheon.

"This way, Diane," Oliver said, walking over and pulling one of the chairs out for her.

"This isn't White's dining room," she protested, following him.

"But it is White's."

Somewhat amused and impressed despite her best efforts to the contrary, Diane sat. "How much did it cost you?"

With a grin he took the seat opposite her. "Suffice it to say that this is the most expensive luncheon I have yet enjoyed."

While the kitchen continued to rattle and clank around them, she ate a rather plain chicken brisket and some bland meat pie. She glanced up at Oliver to find him watching her. "What?" she asked.

He leaned over the table. "Your food is better," he whispered.

"And less expensive, evidently," she returned in the same tone.

"True, but I've won the wager. I hope you enjoy Shakespeare."

Well, she had to concede that Oliver had just performed the impossible. Nodding, Diane returned to her luncheon. The Tantalus Club would be opening its doors in another five hours. While she had no doubt that Jenny would be a perfectly serviceable hostess, it continued to irk Diane that she couldn't be there to oversee the evening. She took a breath. "Oliver, you know this is my club's second d—"

"In exchange for my releasing you to your duties this evening," he cut in, "you'll owe me another night of my choosing."

So now he could read minds. Or more likely, he'd read her expression. She'd become better at hiding her feelings in the time since her marriage to Frederick, but Oliver had literally made a living by studying the men seated opposite him at the gaming tables of Europe. "Agreed."

"Good. Now finish your luncheon. I still have a few hours, and I haven't yet decided how to spend them." He tilted his head, gray eyes lowering to her neckline. "Though I do have an idea or two."

"Yes, I would imagine you do."

At some things, Oliver considered himself a master of self-discipline. Refraining from drink when playing a high-stakes game, declining a wager or an entanglement when the odds were too far against him. Women, however, had always appealed more to his body than to his intellect, and he rarely denied himself.

Except for this afternoon, apparently. Halting the horses, he signaled for the shaved-ice vendor to approach. "Two lemon ices," he said, flipping the fellow a coin.

"This is very . . . gentlemanly of you," Diane said dubiously, taking the ices as he flicked the reins again.

"And what were you actually going to say?" he prompted, guiding the phaeton off the Hyde Park trail and beneath a stand of oak and ash trees. "I know 'gentlemanly' can't have been your first choice of word."

" 'Pedestrian,' " she answered, setting the ices on the seat beside her and taking the reins when he handed them over and hopped to the ground.

Oliver tied off the horses and walked around to help her down to the grass. "Pedestrian" was likely the most accurate word for taking a lady for a drive when he could be wallowing in bed with her, but the word that had first come to his own mind had been "domestic." And that was at least as frightening as the other one and even more troublesome.

He wanted her again. Badly. In fact, he'd been conjuring images of pustules and drunk members of Parliament all day to keep from publicly . . . illustrating his desire. But at the same time he remembered last night. Physically she'd been his, and he would even venture a solid guess that she'd enjoyed the encounter. But at the same time she'd been very careful not to do or say anything that he might take as a sign that she'd forgiven him.

And he found the idea of experiencing that aspect of their encounter again distasteful. He wanted her to want him. Which was odd, considering that if she'd been anyone else he would have thought the night's encounter absolutely ideal. Physical pleasure with no emotional entanglement. Apparently, at some moment in the past handful of hours, he'd gone mad.

Or perhaps it was only his male pride that wanted him to be wanted. He hoped to God that was the case. Anyway, he clearly had her confused, which at least made him feel a bit better.

"You haven't changed your mind about letting me see to my club, I hope," Diane said, sitting on a stone bench beneath one of the trees.

"I gave my word. And you gave yours."

"Yes, I know. The Drury Lane theater, and a night to be claimed at a later date." She eyed him over her ice. "And you'll make another appearance tonight at The Tantalus. Perhaps play some whist."

So she wanted to take the reins again. Oliver nodded. "You know, I rather enjoy the idea that even if I lose to the house, the money will go to repay your loan. I actually can't lose, can I?"

"That's what Frederick used to say, several hours before he would return home with his pockets to let."

"I'm not Frederick."

"You're not invincible, either."

"I never said I was. Eat your ice. I imagine you want to get back in time to select the appropriate black dress."

"My wardrobe makes a statement."

He nodded. "Yes, I know. You're mysterious. Unless

you're belaboring the point, in which case you're being obvious."

Diane snorted, covering her nose with the back of her hand. "It's a fine balance, I'll admit. And nothing sounds mysterious when you say it so matter-of-factly."

The sound of her amusement made him pause in mid-bite. It wasn't something he was accustomed to seeing or hearing from her; two years ago she'd been lonely and angry but definitely not amused. And since her arrival in London she'd been entirely focused on opening The Tantalus Club. "Ah. I'll attempt to do better next time."

"Thank you."

They sat in silence for a few moments, eating their ices before the treats could melt in the warm London afternoon. Truth be told, he did feel somewhat domestic in her company—at least in his interpretation of what domesticity did indeed feel like. It was an odd, content sensation, and not nearly as uncomfortable as he would have expected.

"You mentioned holding a ladies' night at the club," he ventured, sending her a sideways glance. "I'm aware that you don't want my opinion, but I do know some chits who happen to be inveterate gamblers. And they have few places to gather in numbers."

"I've been considering it," she returned. "I think once the excitement around the club begins to fade a bit, holding a ladies' night might be a splendid way to return everyone's attention where I want it."

"Will you make it a regular event?"

"Perhaps. Once or twice a month or so. For the most part, the money lies with the gentlemen."

"Very mercenary of you."

With a frown, she gestured with her free hand. "Observing facts is not mercenary. Do you dispute that as a rule men have a greater control and quantity of funds than do women in London?"

"No, I don't."

"Good. I would like to return to Adam House now, if you please."

"You didn't send me an invitation to your party."

Oliver just refrained from jumping at the low voice close behind them. Diane flinched more noticeably, and they both turned. "And who the devil are you?" he asked.

"I'm her husband's brother," the sharp-chinned fellow said, his gaze disapproving.

"My late husband's brother," Diane corrected, standing. "No relation to me at all."

"Except that we share a last name and a title, at the moment." With an audible sniff the fellow turned his gaze back to Oliver. "And who the devil are you?"

"Haybury," Oliver said. "You must be the new Earl of Cameron. I haven't seen you about London."

"I haven't been much about London. I require a brief word with my sister."

Even if Diane's knuckles where she gripped the ice hadn't been white, Oliver wasn't much inclined to relinquish her to someone else. "Then call on her at Adam House."

"Diane?"

She didn't move. "I'm occupied at the moment, Anthony. As for your invitation, I sensed you were less than pleased at the use to which I'm putting Adam House. I didn't think you wished to attend."

"I do wish to attend."

"Then come tonight, after nine o'clock. I'll make certain you're expected."

Cameron gave a stiff nod. "I will be there. Haybury. Diane."

"Anthony."

From the way he pushed through the shrubbery to

claim a horse standing on the far side of the path, he'd obviously been stalking them. Oliver watched him for a long moment. "Your husband's family didn't welcome you warmly, I presume?"

"They welcomed my dowry. I could have been a potato for all they cared otherwise."

"Well, my dear, suffice it to say that you are nothing like a potato. A thorn-covered rose, perhaps, but never a vegetable."

Her jaw twitched as she faced him. "I don't require a compliment from you. Nor do I need your protection or your interference."

Oliver spread his one empty hand. "I'm not proposing an alliance. I'm merely commenting that you seem to have been improperly categorized, and I'm stating that I don't like the Earl of Cameron overly much based on this singular encounter."

Green eyes held his for a moment. "Very well, then. Shall we go?"

He had other questions for her and several suggestions about the club, but oddly enough he wanted her to take them seriously. He actually wanted to help and not to be seen as sticking his nose in where it wasn't wanted. Well, if he'd learned anything through an early career in wagering, it was how to bide his time.

The moment Diane set foot in The Tantalus Club foyer, she vanished. He hadn't expected thanks for a voluntary kidnapping, but a balloon ride and luncheon with him at White's weren't exactly everyday occurrences. "Langtree," he said, nodding at the butleress before he climbed the stairs to his own apartments.

"My lord, you have a note," she returned, holding out a silver salver for him.

Oliver turned around and retrieved the missive, then continued climbing. He recognized the writing—Kat

Falston. With an annoyed sigh that she'd interrupted his thoughts, he opened the note. It was short and to the point. Evidently she'd grown tired of her cold bed and found another benefactor. *Good.* That meant Oliver didn't have to bother with messy farewells. He cast the note into the hearth and walked into his bedchamber.

Inside his quarters his bed had been made, his clothes from last night folded and put away, and every trace of his female visitor erased from view. The bathtub had been emptied and every stray rose petal picked up and disposed of.

Generally he didn't care one way or the other if some chit left behind a stocking or a hair clip. Of course generally he shared their beds rather than them sharing his; it made separating at the end of the evening—or, more rarely, in the morning—that much simpler.

Why, then, was he looking for traces of her? "Idiot," he muttered, and went to find a glass of whiskey. Whatever stupidity wanted to roil about in his mind, it was just that—stupidity. And he'd never gotten anything by being stupid.

The question became figuring out what he wanted. And to begin with, that was fairly clear. The next time they shared a bed—and there would be a next time—she would want to be there, she would yearn for his touch, and she would be just as eager to touch him.

All he had to do now was make it happen.

Chapter Thirteen

H ow many this morning?" Jenny asked, slipping into the Adam House breakfast room.

"Another fourteen." Diane handed over the latest stack of applications. "I've been thinking that after we have our base membership, perhaps we should have members in good standing nominate new members. That's the way most of the established clubs do it."

"And perhaps your founding membership should have a plaque or some such thing," Jenny added with a nod, sitting down beside her to flip through the pages. "I see that Lord Cameron's applied. Are you going to admit him?"

"A plaque. Something to keep them returning here. That's a splendid idea." Diane motioned for another cup of tea and spooned in some sugar. "And no. He doesn't qualify. The new Lord Cameron doesn't have a large enough income or fortune."

"But if he did, would you—"

"No. I said I would allow him to attend the opening. I have no intention of making it easy for him to come by whenever he chooses. Next he would be offering suggestions."

"This *was* to have been his London home."

Sending her friend a sideways look, Diane sipped her tea. "He can continue to reside at Benchley House. It may be smaller than Adam House, but it's entailed. No relations, dead or otherwise, can sign it over to their spouses."

Jenny glanced swiftly about the room. "Be cautious, Diane. While I agree that you deserve Adam House and whatever good you can make of it, the courts would not see it that way."

"Yes, well, Anthony's already had his solicitors review the deed, and they are all convinced that Frederick's signature is legitimate. And *I* won't be stopped by a Benchley." She cleared her throat. "Now. Back to The Tantalus. Emily just reported that we have thirteen guests for breakfast."

After taking a deep breath, Genevieve nodded. "For our second day of serving, that's a fair beginning." She sipped at her own tea. "I'm glad to see Miss Portsman is working out so well."

"Or whoever she actually is. Thank goodness we've found ladies who can help us captain the various parts of the club. I don't think the two of us could oversee everything for twenty-four hours every day. I've also been thinking of moving Sophia White from the faro tables to seating the dining room. Gentlemen seem to like her . . . eyes."

"Mm. And her hair, and the rest of her." Jenny chuckled. "She's quite charming."

"Which is what I require."

Her companion carefully spooned marmalade onto her toasted bread. "You aren't concerned that her parentage might make some tongues wag?"

"I'm hoping it does."

"And how does Miss White feel about you using her as a curiosity?"

Diane frowned. "Clearly you don't approve. You might have simply said so."

"It's not that, *mein Freund*. It's that you didn't ask *her*. She may have been born on the wrong side of the blanket, but we all have our degrees of pride."

"Fine. I'll ask her."

"*Merci.*"

"Are there any other employees whose permission I need to ask for anything?"

"Diane, don't be angry. Sophia is a special situation. Her father's friends—even her father—may visit the club. And he has not acknowledged her. Can you imagine being the daughter of the Duke of Hennessy and his wife's personal maid? That is not a position I would envy."

That was true, Diane supposed. A dozen or more of her employees were of noble birth or background, and at least two of them weren't using their family names. Sophia, whether her father had acknowledged her or not, was certainly one of the best educated of the Tantalus girls. And she would never be invited to a proper soiree or be courted by any self-respecting aristocrat. *Men*. Sighing, Diane reached over to squeeze Jenny's fingers. "I concede your point. I will ask her. Nicely."

They chatted for another twenty minutes while Jenny finished eating and Diane finished up another cup of tea. It felt like the longest she'd sat still in the past three days. Even as well as the club was being received, there remained so much to do that she was considering acquiring a notebook like the one Genevieve carried about.

"Haybury."

Starting, Diane lifted her head to look about the breakfast room much as Jenny had a moment ago. Other than herself and Jenny, only two footwomen were in sight over by the sideboard. Diane looked back at Genevieve. "What about Haybury?"

Jenny waved at the two servants. "We need a moment, if you please."

"Of course, Miss Jenny."

As soon as they were alone, Genevieve laid both of her hands flat against the tabletop. "He's interfering."

"How? What's he done now?"

"Today? Nothing. Not yet, anyway, though apparently you are going to the theater with him this evening."

Accustomed as she was to thinking several steps ahead of everyone else, with Jenny, Diane had always been able to simply speak her mind. And generally Jenny agreed with her. "Drury Lane was because I lost a wager."

"Your luncheon at White's. So you told me." Jenny looked down at her splayed hands. "I understand why you agreed to his terms for the additional five thousand pounds. It's made things much easier. My . . . concern is that you didn't *need* to visit White's."

"It did turn out to be helpful. Make your point."

"Very well. I am concerned that you are looking for excuses to deal with Oliver Warren. To be in his company."

Diane snorted. "Oh, please. I detest the man."

"You detested him two years ago," Jenny countered. "Has his character altered since then?"

"I . . ." *Hm.* That was a very good question. He certainly hadn't apologized for abandoning her, and he hadn't mourned her loss or his actions by abstaining from female companionship since he'd fled Vienna. Of course, she would have flung any apology he attempted back in his face—and he knew it.

The two of them had a connection; if nothing else, the swiftness of his retreat and the speed with which she'd ended up in his bed again confirmed that—as had the bleeding hole in her chest when he'd left. But lately . . . *Bah.* It wasn't worth considering. "I don't know whether or not his character has changed, but my perspective has. I'll use him as I see fit to get what I want."

"You wanted to accompany him to the theater tonight, then?"

"I do like Shakespeare. And seeing White's with my own eyes *was* helpful. I simply never thought I could manage it. And I wouldn't have been able to, on my own."

"Just guard your heart, Diane. You've made your connection to him common knowledge."

"Don't trouble yourself, Jenny." Rising, Diane gathered up the membership applications. "If anyone's heart breaks, it will be his. I've learned my lesson very well."

"I hope so. At the least, do keep in mind that since you have him living under our roof, making him disappear would be a very simple thing. Escaping the blame for it, not so simple."

Diane pulled open the breakfast room door. She doubted he would be as easy to dispose of as her companion seemed to think, though Jenny was extremely resourceful. "Promise you won't make him vanish without first consulting me."

With a slow smile, Jenny inclined her head. "I promise."

Two steps down the hallway Diane stopped as Oliver came into view. Her heart sped briefly—with annoyance, she was certain. "Get out of my part of the house," she ordered, moving around him.

He fell in behind her. "I've ordered my coach to be brought around at seven o'clock," he said.

"I'll be ready; I haven't forgotten. Now go away."

"I've a question for you."

"Then ask me tonight. I'm occupied at the moment."

He took her shoulder and backed her into the wall. Damnation, she hated when he did that; it simply demonstrated that while she could be his equal intellectually, physically he was seven stone of solid muscle heavier and six inches taller—and he used that muscle to his advantage.

"Do I need to remind you again that I'm not a servant or an employee?" he murmured, his arm across her chest.

"My wish for you to leave me be has nothing to do with your rank or position, darling," she returned, glaring up at his steady gray eyes. "You annoy me."

He stood there silently for a moment. "You trouble me, but you've never annoyed me," he finally said, and walked away.

Her first instinct was to be moved by what he'd said, to consider that he had and still did like her more than he felt comfortable admitting. Once reason stepped in, however, she could acknowledge that perhaps she was finally getting to him. For the moment, at least, she was winning. And that was a good thing.

Once she decided that what she felt was triumph, Diane went up to the third level of The Tantalus Club to find Sophia White. A quartet of Diane's dealers were up in the sitting room playing a game of whist, wagering with peanuts. "Sophia?" she asked, not seeing her in the large, comfortable room.

"She's down in the Aphrodite Room with Emily, my lady. We thought more of us should learn the tables and menus."

"That's much appreciated," Diane returned, smiling.

They did continue to surprise her, with both their willingness to essentially throw away any chance at being seen as paragons of Society and their happiness at having found employment where they could use their intelligence as other than governesses or the companions of old, bitter ladies.

She returned downstairs to find the two ladies, along with a number of servers, chatting with the nine or ten men who sat at the breakfast tables. The room looked too empty, but she would have to be patient. As blasted Oliver had said, removing tables would give the appearance of failure.

"Sophia, may I borrow you for a moment?"

The Duke of Hennessy's daughter curtsied and left the room with her. "I know I'm not to work until tonight, my lady," the red-haired girl said with a grimace, "but Emily said if you or she or Miss Jenny were to fall ill, there would be no one to—"

"I appreciate your enthusiasm, Sophia," Diane broke in. "In fact, I was wondering if you would care to become our evening greeter, showing members to tables in the main dining room and generally making certain that all our guests are being seen to and are happy."

Light green eyes lowered briefly. "There are some men who might not look too kindly on me showing them about, my lady."

"Then they are not welcome here."

"My mother always said I was too lowborn to be a lady and too highborn to be a governess," Sophia said slowly. "Until I read your advertisement, I couldn't find employment anywhere. I was beginning to think . . ." She drew a breath. "I would welcome the opportunity to see to the Demeter Room. As long as you're aware of what might happen."

In her plans, Diane reflected, all of the girls had been of impeccable birth and unblemished character. And then she'd met the women who were willing to apply for employment here. If they needed a champion she was likely a poor excuse for one, but she was willing to give it a go. The idea actually . . . pleased her. Made her feel proud, even. And she'd never expected that.

"I'm aware. I'm going to the theater tonight, but Jenny will assist you. Agreed?"

Sophia grinned, dipping in another neat curtsy. "Oh, yes. Agreed."

While she would rather have been walking the floor of The Tantalus Club and seeing with her own eyes how everything was progressing, Diane spent most of the day going through applications. She supposed it would be more dramatic to limit the number of founding members to twenty or thirty or so, but whoever bore the label of "founder" would have more loyalty to the club—which meant the more there were, the better it would be for her. Or so she hoped.

But she didn't care to rely on hope. Hope had never served her well. Which left her with questions: Was two hundred too many? Would having too many founders reduce the impact of being named one? Diane scowled as she looked at the list she'd created. Oliver would know the answer, and ostensibly she was keeping him about for his knowledge about wagering and clubs, but she didn't like approaching him for help. Or rather, she didn't dislike it as much as she'd expected to and *that* troubled her.

She tapped her pencil against the wood-grain surface of the desk. He made her furious on a regular basis and annoyed her at every other moment. It was those seconds in between the fury and annoyance, however, that concerned her.

What she'd begun to realize in between balloon rides and lemon ices was that she'd hadn't really known him in Vienna. And that the man with whom she was becoming acquainted now was witty and interesting and perceptive. Had he changed? Or had she not been well enough acquainted with him to know?

She had no intention of falling for him again. That didn't stop her from being curious over whether he'd changed— and whether she might be the cause. If he'd changed, then she could at least justify her looking at him a bit more kindly. If he hadn't changed, then she was on the verge of being an idiot all over again.

"Damnation," she muttered, and called for Sally, one of Adam House's upstairs maids. "See if Lord Haybury is available for a meeting, will you?"

"Yes, my lady."

A handful of minutes later Oliver knocked on her half-open office door. "You called for me, my lady?"

"Don't you have Parliament to attend or something?"

"You are not in charge of my duties to Britain, if that's what you're implying, but for your information there is no session today."

"I'm not interested in influencing your voting," she returned, unsurprised that he would be annoyed. She had dismissed him from her presence a scant three hours ago when he'd come looking for her. "I was only wondering why you're always here."

He leaned against the doorframe and folded his arms across his chest. "Well, I live above a gentlemen's club, which provides breakfast, luncheon, and dinner as well as supplying me with a place to wager and the competition I require. You've requested that I forego seeing any of my intimate female acquaintances, so I actually have little reason to go anywhere."

He was leaving some things out, but she understood his argument. Diane set down her pencil. "That was rather long-winded of you."

"You asked the question," he returned. "What do you want? Or did you just want me here so you could dismiss me again?"

Oh, bother. "I need your advice."

Oliver straightened. "Beg pardon?"

"You heard me. Come here and sit down so I can get this over with."

He must have been surprised, because he dropped into one of the seats facing her desk without a word. Gray eyes took in the various stacks of applications, the list of names in front of her, even the cooling half-empty cup of tea at her elbow. She'd known before that he seemed to be aware of everything, but seeing him in the act of assessing a situation was . . . interesting.

"All right," he said after a moment, "I'm seated. What do you want me to advise you about?"

"We've been considering naming a number of the first applicants as founding members of The Tantalus Club."

Nodding, Oliver sank back. "They didn't precisely found the club, but it's a fair idea. It'll give them a reason to attend more often, and to bring guests—especially if you reserve tables or a sitting room or some such thing for their exclusive use."

Reserving tables. That was actually a good idea. "I thought a plaque of names would be flattering to them, as well." She grimaced. "How many founding members do you think The Tantalus Club should have?"

"Is that your prospective list?" he asked, gesturing.

"Yes."

Oliver lifted an eyebrow. "Did you actually leave anyone *off* the list?"

"All of these men applied the first night."

"So you're being fair."

"Yes. I don't want to offend anyone who has the funds to wager here."

"Then charge for a founding membership. Make it some exorbitant amount—five hundred pounds, say."

"Men would pay that?"

"Not all of them. Accept everyone who's applied, and send them all a letter stating that you'd like to create a founding membership to admit future club members and see to enforcing the bylaws. Tell them they'll have reserved dining tables and that you'll . . . waive the entrance fees for the first year, or something."

Diane gazed at him for a moment. "As much as I hate

to say it, I actually like that idea. But I insist on having a say about who belongs to my club."

"Set down your membership guidelines as part of the club bylaws."

Bylaws. She had her own set of rules, of course. Setting them down on paper for current and future members and even owners, however, had never occurred to her. And she knew why. Everyone else was to do as she commanded. Especially men. Explaining herself . . . felt odd. But now at least she could see why it would be necessary.

"Once everyone else knows the rules," he continued, apparently reading her mind, "enforcing them becomes a much simpler matter. Founding members or voting members or whatever you wish to call them actually do much of the policing at most clubs. If someone breaks the rules you may not even have to step in, because they will."

"How many should I accept?"

"Twenty-five or thirty seems a good number. You need to be able to have a majority in Town at any given time during the Season for voting in new members, et cetera."

Well, she'd never considered that, either. It was more than a bit unsettling to realize that there were some things she hadn't known—not about the opening of a club, but in the longer-term running of the establishment. "I'll take your advice under consideration."

"I'm glad." He sat forward. "Was there anything else?"

She sighed. "Yes. I'd like to know your opinion of these men." Diane picked up the fourteen applications she'd separated from the others and handed them over.

"My opinion in regard to what?" he asked, their fingers brushing as he took the pages from her.

Warmth slid up her arm. "I keep waiting for you to say something cynical or biting, you know."

He flashed her a grin. "After we're finished here, perhaps. I'm becoming quite the conundrum, aren't I?"

"That's one way of putting it." She gestured at the applications. "I won't have anyone here who has no money to wager. Especially if they're married."

For several moments he sat silently as he looked through the papers. Whatever she thought of him and his character, with his lean face, long eyelashes, and high cheekbones he was an exceedingly handsome man. He knew it, though. And he knew how to use his attractiveness to his benefit.

Finally he looked up at her. "Not everyone has as little self-control or as poor judgment as Frederick Benchley."

"I refuse to be responsible for seeing another woman, another wife, left penniless because of her husband's idiocy."

"Men—even ones who can afford to wager—win and lose fortunes every day at gaming tables. Ruination will happen at The Tantalus Club, Diane, and short of placing absurd limits on the wagers, as long as you keep the doors open there is nothing you can do to prevent it."

"I can prevent men with no incomes from walking through my doors in the first place," she retorted. "Frederick was in debt everywhere, and not one club turned him away. They sent dunners after us, but they still allowed him to gamble. This club will not do so."

It made sense to her, and it was one thing about which she didn't care to be advised. Even so, the muscles across her shoulders eased when he nodded. Perhaps he'd simply realized that arguing with her wouldn't do any good, but it meant . . . something that he'd accepted her explanation.

"I wouldn't admit any of these men, then," he said, setting the applications back on the desk. "I would say you have a good eye for detecting men who have more balls than brains, but then you'd be even more impossible to live with than you are now."

She chuckled. "I'll take the compliment, since you don't live with me." Diane took a sip of her tea, then made a face at the cold liquid and set it down again. "Blech. Thank you."

"And now I'm dismissed?"

It would likely be a nice gesture for her to ask what he'd wanted to talk about when he'd invaded her home earlier. "Yes, I'm finished with you," she said aloud. She wasn't prepared to make nice gestures yet. Not for him.

Oliver stood. Then before she could react, he leaned across the desk and gave her a swift kiss. "No, you're not," he returned, and headed for the door. "Seven o'clock. And I insist that you wear black."

Aggravating man. "Is that supposed to drive me to do otherwise?"

"I suppose we'll find out this evening," he returned, amusement in his voice.

Oliver descended to the foyer his apartment shared with both Adam House and The Tantalus Club. At two minutes before seven the entryway was busy, with small groups of peers entering for dinner or leaving to attend the theater or one of the trio of soirees scheduled for the evening.

"Your coach is waiting," Langtree said as she spotted him.

"Thank you." He stopped to one side of her. "Your duties have expanded of late, haven't they?"

"I knew they would when I accepted employment with Lady Cameron," she returned, sending a footwoman to the coatroom for Lord Avery's greatcoat and hat, and without pause directing Mr. Walter Jorie to the Hera Room for the best selection of wines.

"So you have no regrets over leaving your father's shop?"

Langtree smiled. "I earn five times what my father could afford to pay me," she said in a low voice, nodding to greet another group of gentlemen. "I'm not expected to wed Bertram Marks and move from being a shopkeeper's daughter to a baker's wife. So, no. I have no regrets."

Another chit Diane had apparently saved. Oliver wondered if she was doing it consciously or if the women she hired simply filled empty positions and she didn't care beyond that. From the way she spoke to him about her determination to reclaim a life that wagering had taken from her, she wanted him to believe that everything was simply the means to an end. But he was beginning to think that she was lying.

"Generally a gentleman escorting a lady to the theater brings her flowers, does he not?" Diane's smooth voice came from behind him, followed by a loud chorus of "my lady" from the men around them.

"Who's to say I didn't?" he returned, facing her. The next suave thing he'd been about to say, however, lodged in his throat and stayed there.

Diane Benchley, the Countess of Cameron, wasn't wearing black. Deep emerald silk clung to the curves up top and draped down around her legs like liquid. A single emerald glinted on her neck, drawing his eyes to the low, sweeping bodice that barely seemed to contain her charms. More emeralds dripped from her ears, and an emerald bracelet hung about her left wrist, circling one elbow-length black glove.

She lifted an eyebrow. "Are you well, or should I slap you on the back?"

He felt like he was leaning toward her. It took a great deal of effort to draw himself back both mentally and physically. "Save the slapping for a better occasion." Gesturing her toward the door, he intentionally moved between her and the three gentlemen who stood gaping at her from the entrance to The Tantalus Club. "Your coach awaits, my lady."

Outside he handed her into his large, black coach and

then stepped up behind her. His control, his decision not to claim her later tonight, felt frayed already, and he nearly asked her if she wished a chaperone. Him. As soon as he pulled the door closed the coach lurched into motion, and he sat back in the forward-facing seat, opposite her.

"Did you select that material simply because it becomes you, or because it precisely matches the color of your eyes?" he asked after a moment.

"Both, of course." She glanced about the coach. "Where are my flowers?"

"The horses must have eaten them."

"Mm-hm." She tilted her head at him, eyeing him from beneath long lowered eyelashes. His cock twitched in response. "You might have just said you didn't think to purchase any," she continued.

"In my defense, I don't actually have to leave my house to come calling on you." He shifted, trying to find a comfortable position in his usually comfortable coach. "Since we both know you didn't decide to alter your wardrobe because of anything I said, what prompted the emerald?"

Diane smoothed her palms down her thighs. If he didn't know any better, he could almost think she was attempting to seduce him. "The emerald is unexpected. And it's dark, which I believe still qualifies as mysterious." She flicked a finger at her dangling ear bob, making it wink in the lantern light. "These are faux, by the way. I don't want you thinking I've misspent the money you loaned me."

"The thought never crossed my mind."

He shifted again—anything to keep him from falling into that bottomless green gaze. If he fell, he would drown. And she'd probably aid the process by holding his head under. Thank God he was a worldly, jaded cynic wise to the folly of following his heart, or he would have been in very real danger of losing it.

"You do realize that when we arrive at the theater unescorted," he offered, "the rumors that we're lovers will be confirmed."

"Nothing is confirmed unless one of the two of us confirms it. Which we won't."

"Suit yourself. You may have men wondering if you're available, but there are scores of women who wonder the same about me."

"Are you trying to make me jealous?" she asked, then favored him with an amused grin. "Because it's not working."

That bucket of icy water cooled his ardor and cleared his mind, at least. "Don't be ridiculous," he retorted. "I'm merely offering advance warning. Men seek you out, and women seek me out. And now that The Tantalus Club is open and attracting even more interest, you may also find yourself the object of . . . censure."

"I fully expect to be insulted, both behind my back and to my face. I have no problem with that, though if I find anyone too petty or small-minded I shan't invite him—or her—to darken my doorstep."

"Very pragmatic of you. You're going to hold a ladies' night, then?"

"Yes. I was thinking of something like the first and third Tuesday of every month."

Oliver nodded. "Parliament has an early session most Wednesday mornings, so you would likely have fewer men in attendance on Tuesday evenings, anyway."

"Yes, I know."

Of course she knew that; she'd clearly done a great deal of research to learn every aspect of owning a gentlemen's club and dragged him in to supply her with blunt and the one or two bits of information she hadn't been able to obtain elsewhere.

She did like her facts. It was the other areas, the ones

that called for her to use her feelings, where the ground beneath her feet wasn't nearly as firm. The question was how best to use that knowledge and how to discover precisely what it was he wanted from her. Because he didn't think sex would be enough to satisfy him any longer.

"Stop being so quiet," she said abruptly. "It makes me think you're plotting something which can't possibly benefit me."

"I was considering where you could find male croupiers for two days a month. Because the ladies won't want your scandalous chits walking among them."

She flipped a hand at him. "Don't blame their snobbery on my club. If all of my 'chits,' as you call them, were employed as governesses and companions, they would be just as frowned upon."

"I don't want to debate degrees of frowning, but there's a difference between being seen as socially inferior and being avoided. Governesses and companions may not all be asked to dance, but they are allowed to enter good households."

"And yet not all well-educated women find themselves in the position to net more . . . acceptable employment. What are they supposed to do, become whores?"

Oliver swallowed the cynical comment he'd been about to make. She'd actually asked him for advice earlier, and he didn't want to lose ground. "You're beginning to sound protective of your employees," he said instead. "That makes you a rare flower, Diane."

She actually blinked. "Don't compliment me in the middle of an argument. It won't make me stammer or blush, and it just makes you look desperate."

Folding his arms across his chest, he gazed at her for a long moment. "And what I think," he commented slowly, hoping she didn't have another pistol strapped to her thigh, "is that whenever I say something complimentary, you snap back with an insult because you feel uncomfortable. Because you *like* when I compliment you."

"Rubbish." She scooted to one side of the seat and peered out the window. "Good. We're here."

"Coward."

"Ha. Just remember that your character was questionable long before I succumbed to pragmatism." The coach stopped. "And another thing," she continued, standing as the driver flipped down the trio of steps and opened the carriage door. "I may enjoy a compliment, but you'll never see one turning my head."

Hm. That felt very much like progress. In a dirty, clawing battle like this one was turning out to be, it was nearly a victory.

Chapter Fourteen

A ttending the Drury Lane theater was exactly as Diane had expected. Murmured conversations and sideways glances surrounded them, and even an offended gasp or two sounded behind them as she and Oliver made their way through the large lobby.

She kept her fingers wrapped lightly around the gray sleeve of his superfine jacket and listened and watched. Another female, one concerned with propriety or her standing among the social elite, would have been mortified. Diane, however, was not that female. Not any longer.

In a sense it was freeing to have lost everything. At the least it had broadened and altered her perspective on what was truly important. Her necessities were enough wealth to be able to live comfortably and the ability to determine the course of her own future. Those things were important. Being looked at in askance or having some marchioness turn her back—that was not worth losing even a single night's sleep over.

"You're being quiet," the tall, lean devil at her side commented, turning his head to gaze at her with those mesmerizing gray eyes.

"I'm busy being noticed," she returned, finally admitting

to herself that he was one of the reasons she could hold her head high tonight. Before they'd met, she'd known nothing about how to survive or how to stand her ground against men like him. "Keep walking."

"Yes, my lady." They continued toward the stairs leading to his private box. "If any of this nonsense troubles you, I'm happy to go tackle Manderlin and make a scene."

"If they're talking about me, then it's not nonsense; it's good business."

"But not terribly amusing for you, I would imagine."

Oh, this was too much. First she couldn't seem to keep herself from thinking about him more kindly, and now he was being solicitous. She stopped, fixing a look of amazement on her face so plain that even he would be able to make it out. "Are you having a sympathetic thought for someone other than yourself? Do you wish to lie down?"

"Ordinarily I would take that as an invitation and ask you to join me," he returned smoothly, "but since you first appeared tonight I've begun to suspect that you want me to collect on the remaining eight hours of our agreement and . . . get it over with."

Drat. "What makes you assume that, other than your own inflated sense of self-importance?"

He leaned closer. "It's not my self-importance that's inflated, my dear," he murmured, "but I'll collect what's owed me when *I* choose to do so."

Clearly he either had no idea that thinking about another interlude with him was keeping her awake nights, or he did realize that he unsettled her and he simply didn't care. More than likely it was the latter.

"So you actually intend to sit for three hours and watch *King Lear.*"

With a slight grin he maneuvered her around a trio of gawking overdressed fops who were *never* going to be granted membership at The Tantalus Club. "I imagine I'll enjoy it well enough." He sent her a sideways glance. "I lied, by the way."

It took some effort to keep the frown from her face. As far as she knew, he'd only lied to her once, and that hadn't turned out well for her. "Could you be more specific?"

"Very amusing. We're not here to see *King Lear.*"

"Then what are we here for?"

"To see a different play." Oliver pulled back the curtain at the back of his large box and gestured for her to precede him. *"The Taming of the Shrew."*

If most of the audience seated below them hadn't already been looking in their direction, she would have hit him. "If you're implying that I'm a shrew, Haybury, then I have sorely overestimated your intelligence and insight. And furthermore, if I *were* a chit who needed to be tamed, *you* are not the man to do it." Sniffing, she plunked herself down in one of the chairs at the box's front. "Such a man doesn't exist."

He took the seat beside her. "I don't feel the slightest need or inclination to tame you, Diane," he said in a voice so low she could barely hear it over the noise of the audience filling the theater. "I happen to like you as you are."

"Stop attempting to flatter me," she snapped back, keeping an expression of vague amusement on her face for the benefit of their growing audience. "Why go to the bother of lying to me about the play if you don't see me as a shrew?"

"Because we would have had this argument in private and I would have lost—and I wanted to see the play."

"Does one of your mistresses happen to be an actress?"

As soon as Diane asked the question, she had the oddest desire to clap her hands over her ears to avoid hearing the answer. Which was absurd, because she didn't care what his answer might be.

"Oddly enough, no." He brushed the edge of her skirt

with one finger. "Did I tell you that you look stunning this evening? If I were less jaded and cynical, I would call you breathtaking."

Well, that was unexpected. And the part of her that was still eighteen years old and wished she'd been wooed rather than bargained for was pleased that he thought so. And that he'd noticed. That silly girl, though, had never had her heart broken—by this same man. No doubt he expected her to bite back at him again, as she'd done every other time he'd attempted to compliment her. Diane took a slow breath. "Thank you."

Oliver gazed at her. "That's it?"

Shrugging, Diane sent a glance at the box opposite theirs. "It was a nice compliment."

"As was my aim."

She looked at the opposite box once more. "Who is that staring at me through his opera glasses?"

"Everyone's been looking at you. Why point *him* out?"

A low, delicious shiver went through Diane. If they hadn't just finished a discussion about jealousy, she would have asked him why his tone seemed so sharp. "Not a friend of yours then, I assume?" she asked him instead.

"Adam Baswich, the Duke of Greaves. He was in York for your grand opening, I believe. Must've just returned."

"And you dislike him because . . ."

"I don't dislike him."

"Then which word would you use?" she pursued. Anyone who upended Oliver Warren was worth knowing about, at the least.

"You're more damned single-minded than a dog after a bone, aren't you? Leave it be. The curtain's opening."

Oh, this was far too interesting to let go. Diane sat silently as Christopher Sly and the Hostess took the stage and the audience's attention moved to the front of the theater. Once everyone had settled, Diane edged closer to the formidable man seated beside her. "Is your disagreement with Greaves over a woman?" she whispered.

The muscles around Oliver's eye twitched. "Not yet."

"A horse?"

"No."

"Land?"

"No. Shut up."

"A wager?"

Silence. *Ah.* At the least, she seemed to be closer to the target. His expression, of course, hadn't altered a whit—at least not in her view of his profile as he faced the stage.

"He's lost money to you," she pressed, then frowned. That would account for Greaves's dislike, but not for Oliver's . . . reserve. "You lost to *him*," she amended.

"Technically." Finally he glanced sideways at her. "I have my doubts."

"Oh." Diane sat up straighter. "You think he cheated. I see this as somewhat ironic, considering you—"

"Enough," he growled, standing and yanking her to her feet in the same motion. The ease with which he did so left her a little breathless.

"Unhand m—"

Changing his grip to her left wrist, he yanked her to the back of the box and through the curtain into the rear corridor. Before she could even look around he pushed her back against the wall and pinned her there with a forearm. Diane lifted her head, trying to conjure what insulting thing she would say in response to his kiss—but the gray eyes glaring at her snapped with fury, not passion.

"Perhaps you've forgotten," he said very quietly, "that I am at your service for one reason only. If you discuss that event or even mention it within the hearing of anyone else, I will have no further grounds to assist you and every reason to cause you pain. Is that clear?"

She met his gaze. "You have already caused me pain,

Lord Haybury. If you think you can deal me anything worse than what you've already put me through, you are sadly mistaken." Her voice broke, but that didn't signify. He was not going to best her in a battle of wills. Or anything else.

He didn't move a muscle. For a long moment, while her heart pounded inside her chest, they simply stared at each other. Then, his jaw muscles clenching, he reached out one hand and brushed a finger along her cheek. It came away wet.

"I am not crying," she stated. If he disagreed with that, she would kick him. And she knew precisely where.

"I know," he returned.

Leaning down, he very softly touched his lips to hers. Diane closed her eyes at the warm, electric contact. Heat spiraled through her from inside her chest to the tips of her fingers. He'd never kissed her like that before. Nothing about Oliver Warren had ever been gentle.

As he finally lifted his head an inch or two away from her, Diane realized that she had one hand around his shoulders and the other splayed over his heart. The rapid thud drummed against her fingertips. His gaze searched hers, though for once she had no idea what to think. And he looked at least as baffled.

Oliver cleared his throat. "I'm afraid I lied again."

At least he'd changed the subject. "What now?"

"That letter of yours isn't the only reason I'm here." He took her hand, rubbing his fingers against her wrist where he had grabbed her. "And yes, I believe Greaves cheated me. I can't prove it, but it cost me a friendship."

"You and Greaves were friends?" she asked, far more comfortable discussing Oliver's wagering than what his true reason for lending his money and expertise to her and The Tantalus Club might be and if that reason had something to do with regret for hurting her.

"I thought we were. Evidently I was mistaken. It was quite a blow to my pride." Brushing her cheek once more, he reached past her to hold open the curtain at the rear of the box. "I count my . . . blindness to his true nature to be one of the two greatest mistakes of my life. Now. Shall we return to the play?"

She didn't want to ask what the second mistake was. If it was either leaving her or, worse, meeting her in the first place, she would be angry. If it was something else, she would be . . . angrier. "Yes. We've given the audience something else to speculate about, anyway."

And he'd given her something to speculate about as well. She wasn't the only one who seemed to be confused by the pull that remained between them.

By the middle of the next month The Tantalus Club boasted 23 founding members and an overall and still swiftly growing membership of 412. The first ladies' night was so successful that male staff from other clubs arranged to have Tuesdays off and signed up weeks in advance to work at Diane Benchley's club on two Tuesday nights per month.

"You know, Haybury," Jonathan Sutcliffe, Lord Manderlin, commented over the remains of a pheasant at White's Club, "people are beginning to speculate over whether you mean to make an honest woman of Lady Cameron."

Oliver finished his bite, a mix of amusement and annoyance running through him. "Diane's honesty has nothing to do with me," he returned.

"Yes, but Lady Kate Falston says you've fallen."

"She has to invent something, I suppose, to explain why she's now spending her nights with Whiting, of all people."

Manderlin snorted. "Why *is* she spending her nights with the duke now, my friend? Are you finished with her?"

Shrugging, Oliver gestured for a footman to refill his glass of wine. "I like Kate. I wish her well. But I hate trotting in place. It's dull."

"Which returns me to my previous question. Are you after Diane Benchley? Of course most of Mayfair thinks you've already got her. And since you haven't moved on after better than six weeks, of course they're wondering what you mean to do with her."

He hadn't had Diane for nearly a month. His cock likely thought he was dead, except for the blood rushing through him every time he set eyes on the confounding chit. Considering that she still owed him a night, he could only conclude that he'd gone mad. But the right bit of circumstance, the perfect moment, hadn't yet presented itself. And apparently he was willing to wait until he found it.

Manderlin continued to gaze at him, clearly still waiting for an answer. "As far as Mayfair is concerned," he said slowly, "they can spin any tale they choose."

"And me? Am I to be left to tale-spin as well?"

A few months ago Oliver would have told Jonathan to mind his own damned business. His first instinct was still to keep his own counsel. But lately the idea of having someone else with whom to speak had become much more appealing. Particularly when he seemed to be walking a path he'd never traveled before. He took a drink of wine, using the moment to survey the diners around them.

White's dining room actually seemed a bit less crowded these days, and he had to wonder whether that was because The Tantalus Club served a fine luncheon along with some pretty chits for decoration. Diane was doing well; much better than even he had expected. "I don't know what to tell you, Jonathan," he finally said. "I've had a taste, and I continue to crave more."

"Then you *are* in pursuit," Manderlin whispered, lifting both eyebrows and leaning forward on his elbows.

Oliver looked down at his hands. "I caught her once, in Vienna. And I let her get away. I'm attempting to be more cautious this time. I . . . want to be certain what I want. Because I won't get a third chance."

It wasn't until he said the words aloud that he realized he'd already decided his course of action. The fact that he had someone else to convince—well, that would be the most difficult part of all this. But antagonistic as they were—or perhaps even partly *because* she kept him constantly on his toes—he liked having her in his life again. He preferred that she remain there.

She was not some malleable chit looking for her first love or for a wealthy protector, however. Not her. And like him, Diane Benchley wasn't much for standing still. At the moment he could only hope they were moving forward in the same direction. Even if that was so, the odds of him succeeding were so poor he wasn't certain he'd be willing to bet on himself.

"You're paying her rent and you're a founding member of her club. That has to count in your favor, does it not?"

He'd practically been kidnapped and he *was* being blackmailed, but he could hardly tell the viscount about that. Nor did Oliver wish to discuss the . . . oddness that had penetrated him when he'd finally realized just how much he'd hurt her in Vienna. Until that moment he'd only considered his own feelings and how tightly he'd felt the ropes wrapping around him and threatening to drag him down.

The panic still touched him when he gazed into her emerald eyes, but it wasn't the dominant feeling any longer. He wasn't certain what was going on, but pursuing Diane Benchley was definitely the only way to figure it out.

"Well, isn't that interesting," Manderlin murmured, nodding his chin toward the doorway.

Oliver lifted his silver case knife and angled it so he

could see the reflection of the trio of men entering the
dining room. The Duke of Greaves caught his eye first,
and he clenched his jaw. That was one complication he
could have done without this Season. At least the duke
had been wise enough to avoid visiting The Tantalus Club
thus far.

The second man, however, made seeing the first considerably more troubling. Oliver immediately recognized
the fellow's darting, snakelike gaze and the pompous way
he held himself. Spying the third man, the Earl of Larden,
didn't leave him feeling any better at all. "Lord Cameron?"
he muttered at Manderlin, and lowered his knife again.
" 'Interesting' isn't the word I would use." "Trouble," yes.
That word he would use.

"I was actually referring to the combination of him
and his companions," Jonathan returned. "I didn't think
they traveled in the same circles."

"Neither did I."

One obvious reason for the odd trio did spring to mind,
however. The Tantalus Club. The strength of the urge to
leave White's and hurry off to find Diane stunned him;
generally he had a much stronger sense of self-preservation
than he did of philanthropy. "Diane won't allow Cameron
a membership in The Tantalus. Perhaps he's looking for
financial backing to make another go at it."

"That sounds humiliating."

"It would be, if he had to go crawling to his former
sister-in-law, hat in hand, to beg to be let into the club."

"You truly think it's that? Neither Larden nor Greaves
has much tolerance for paupers."

"No, they don't." And while previously Cameron had
been a minor irritation, every instinct Oliver possessed was
now yelling at him that things had just become more serious. And the abrupt strength of the . . . need to see that no
harm came to Diane stunned him. But if there had ever

been a time to be cautious over his approach, it was now. Greaves, and to a lesser degree Larden, was not to be taken lightly.

"Oliver? You have a very calculating look about you. It's rather off-putting."

He shook himself. "Apologies. I was calculating. Now. Are you going to continue gossiping, or shall we leave for Gentleman Jackson's?"

"By all means. I still owe you a dismemberment."

Oliver forced a grin. "Today is not that day, my friend."

Despite Oliver's boasting, he nearly did get his head taken off by a rather lucky flail from the viscount. Distraction was a damned nuisance. The two men who accompanied Anthony Benchley were keen-witted and deadly. And Oliver had never known either of them to be anything other than self-serving. The three of them together couldn't signify anything good.

Clearly whatever they wanted had little or nothing to do with him, and so as a rule he would have noted their appearance and with whom they spoke, and soon enough he would have deciphered their plan and then gone on with his own fun.

This, however, was different. This was more than a passing interest about what business a former friend and his cronies might be engaged in. No, today he was worried. Over someone else.

When he returned to Adam House late in the afternoon, two bouquets of roses sat on the table in the spacious foyer. "For Lady Cameron, I presume?" he queried as he handed over his hat and riding gloves. "Let me guess: Oberley and Henning."

Langtree inclined her head. "If I may be so bold, how do you always know, my lord?"

Because he couldn't seem to keep his eyes off Diane from the time she entered the club until she left it again.

"Oberley followed her about like a fat puppy all last evening, and Henning insisted on reading her a poem he'd written in her honor." He paused. "Is she in?"

"Lady Cameron is meeting with her captains. Shall I inform my lady that you wish to speak with her?"

He debated informing her about her former brother-in-law's new allies in London versus staying out of her business as she kept ordering him to do. "No," he said aloud. "I'll make do."

After all, it could be a coincidence. Perhaps Anthony Benchley had attended university with Larden and they'd decided to have luncheon at White's to chat about old times. Diane legally owned Adam House, at least as far as the world at large knew, so Cameron couldn't still be disputing that. He could be whining about it, which would be annoying but harmless.

Yes, and pigs flew. If he had any remaining sense of self-preservation he would note that any coming trouble wasn't his and he would have gone up to dress for dinner. That was by far the most sensible and logical course of action. Diane constantly flung the philosophy of logic and self-interest at him. Scowling, he descended the stairs to the foyer again. "Which room is this meeting in?"

Langtree faced him. "If you're out to make trouble, my lord, I'm obligated to stop you."

So the mistress of the house hadn't rescinded the order to have him shot if he misbehaved. "No trouble. Not of my making, anyway."

The butleress eyed him, then nodded. "The Aphrodite Room."

"Thank you, Langtree."

He walked through the nearly empty main dining room and through one of the two doors at its rear, then stopped just inside. Diane, Miss Martine, and five of her young ladies sat at one of the breakfast tables reviewing schedules, menus, and the merits of taking dinner reservations versus utilizing first-come, first-served seating.

"If you begin taking reservations," he broke in and seven pairs of pretty eyes turned in his direction, "they'll all begin competing for tables. First you'll have servants running you notes an hour beforehand, then two, then all day, then the day before, then—"

"Yes, I believe we comprehend your meaning," Diane interrupted. "What is your point?"

At least she hadn't thrown a candlestick at him and ordered him out of the room. "They won't all appear. You'll end up with half your tables reserved and no one sitting at them."

"Perhaps we should charge a shilling per reservation," the red-haired chit, Sophia White, suggested. "Or even more."

Diane shook her head. "We already charge them a membership fee and an entrance fee." She sighed. "I hate to say it, but Lord Haybury makes a good point. We're already holding five tables for founding members. No reservations."

He waited another few minutes until she finished the meeting and sent the chits who worked in the evening out to their places. Once it was just her and Miss Martine in the room, he came forward. "Do you have a moment, Diane?"

"What do you want?"

The French twist looked rooted to the floor. He wasn't surprised; since their outing to the theater, since that kiss that had stopped his heart, Diane had made it all but impossible for him to speak to her in private.

"I had luncheon at White's today," he said, unable to stop himself from sending Miss Martine an annoyed glance. "As I was leaving, I happened to notice—" He stopped. "The prologue doesn't matter, does it? Anthony Benchley has two new companions—the Earl of Larden and the Duke of Greaves. I've been attempting to conjure a reason they would all be together, and I can't conclude that anything positive is afoot."

Diane knew she should have been surprised. After all, she'd already decided that Anthony was nothing more than an annoying reminder of a past that no longer held any power over her. But the club's membership continued to increase, and they'd begun to make a profit. And so the part of her that still doubted whether she could accomplish all this wasn't surprised at all.

"Thank you for telling me," she said aloud, knowing some response was expected. "Was there anything else?"

"Diane, we need t—"

"This is my venture, Oliver. Not yours. Now. Was there anything else you wanted to discuss?"

"No. Not at the moment."

From the look in his eyes he clearly wanted to give her some advice or his opinion or to make himself available to commiserate with her. She supposed if she still entirely disliked him, a conversation would have been perfectly acceptable. But now everything felt much more complicated. And if he kissed her again the way he had that night at the theater, she might begin remembering the heat and life and . . . hope that had surrounded her in Vienna for that fortnight.

"Then I'll see you this evening," she returned, hoping he would take the hint and leave her be.

He nodded. "Come sit at my table. I'll purchase you dinner."

"We'll see."

"If you mean 'no,' darling, then say no."

"I meant precisely what I said. Now. Why don't you go away and test out my new roulette wheel?"

"I won't tell you this could be serious, because you already know that. I'm not trying to take the reins from you. I wouldn't even attempt it."

"Leave."

"Coward." With that he left the room.

Diane counted to five and then took a seat. Jenny hurriedly took the chair beside her and grasped her left hand. "Anthony Benchley can't make any trouble, can he?"

"From what I recall of him, being the earl should make him perfectly happy. He always seemed dissatisfied with being the second son."

"So the question is whether he is perfectly happy and going about town with his friends or whether Haybury has the right of it."

"Yes, indeed. And I will mention to Juliet that the new Lord Cameron might be calling again, just to be safe."

"You might consider that Lord Haybury is attempting to panic you so that you'll confide in him more deeply."

Diane frowned. "I don't think he would do that." Before they could begin arguing again that she was doing something as absurd as falling for Oliver all over again, she stood. "Whatever happens, for Oliver's sake he'd best keep in mind that this is *my* home. Given the state in which Frederick left the title, I doubt Anthony can afford to go about wagering, either. At any rate, I won't help him gamble away what's left of the Benchley properties. He should be thankful I turned him away."

"But what of these other men?" Jenny gestured toward the Persephone Room. "You encourage them to wager."

"And in case you've forgotten, I kept fourteen other applicants from joining the club. I've instructed my girls to inform me immediately if anyone drinks too much or gambles too deeply. I don't want to ruin families. Not even the one that ruined me." Retrieving her hand, she stood again. "And that is that."

Jenny rose and followed her to the door. "I will be very

angry if he attempts to make trouble. Gentlemen's club or not, you are doing good here. And not just for the two of us."

Diane laughed. "Don't let Lady Dashton or her 'Ladies of Moderation' hear you say that. To them I'm Eve, Jezebel, and Delilah, all in one."

"Did you happen to notice Camille today?" Jenny pursued as they made their way to the kitchen. "She laughed. Twice."

"I doubt she'll be laughing if her father or the man she refused to marry ever come calling at the club."

"Perhaps she believes you will help to see that no harm comes to her. You already saved her life by hiring her to work here, after all."

"Oh, please. Stop being so dramatic."

"I'm not being dramatic. A well-bred daughter of an earl who couldn't run to any of her family or friends for sanctuary or employment. What do you think would have become of her if The Tantalus Club hadn't existed?"

"Then it's a happy coincidence," Diane stated. For heaven's sake, she hadn't planned on being a nanny to wayward aristocratic females, however much it seemed to be leading that way. Yes, there was an unexpected . . . satisfaction in helping the girls find employment. But it was not her goal. It couldn't be. This was about seeing to her own independence. She hadn't factored anyone else into the equation. Taking a slow breath, she nodded at Mary and Fiona as they passed down the hallway. Perhaps it was time she found a different equation.

"And Haybury?"

Diane faced her friend, reluctant to discuss the most troubling part of any—all—of her equations. "He's doing his job well. Eventually he'll cease challenging me. And once I'm able to repay the loan, we'll have no need of him at all."

Jenny continued to look skeptical, but Diane left her with a smile. She could only juggle so many things before they all came crashing down around her ears.

The most pressing problem continued to be Oliver Warren. She'd steeled herself against him, because she'd known he would be razor-sharp and witty and argumentative and oh, so attractive. But that kiss—just thinking about it still curled her toes and made her heart pound. That, she didn't know how to defend against.

And she didn't quite know why she felt so certain that more trouble was coming—or that whether she was willing to ask for his assistance or not, Oliver would be willing to offer it.

Chapter Fifteen

And good evening to you, Lord William," Diane said with a smile. "I'm pleased Lord Cleves here has brought you along. Enjoy your visit."

The Marquis of Plint's son grinned back at her. "I say, this is rather marvelous. More pretty chits here than at Almack's, that's for damned certain."

Cleves gripped his younger companion's shoulder. "Behave yourself here, Billy, or two large gents lurking behind those doors there'll set you outside on your arse."

Apparently Haybury had been correct when he'd said the club's members would begin to enforce the rules themselves. Sending Cleves a grateful smile, she left the gentlemen and went to find Pansy Bridger to see that the baron received a complementary berry tart, his favorite dessert.

"I'll see to it, my lady," the petite brunette said, making a note on her tablet. "And Lord Haybury sat down in the Demeter Room ten minutes ago. You said you wanted to know."

"Thank you, Pansy."

Well, she needed to eat, and if she continued avoiding Oliver the number of flirtations she had to contend with every evening would increase, as would the bouquets the next morning and the letters and poems expressing undying admiration and even marriage. Squaring her shoulders, she strolled into the main dining room.

Oliver sat toward one side of the room close to the quartet of windows overlooking the lantern-lit garden, at one of the tables reserved for the club's founding members. Though he sat alone, the table was set for two and a glass of white wine, her favorite, waited at the place opposite him.

He stood up as she approached. "Good evening, Lady Cameron," he greeted her, moving around to hold out her chair.

"You're being quite the gentleman tonight," she observed, sitting.

"It's something new I'm trying," he returned, resuming his own seat. "You haven't worn that gown before. I know you don't need my approval, but it's lovely on you."

"It's a black dress. How do you know it's new?"

"I noticed."

He paid even closer attention than she'd realized. "And how did you know I would join you for dinner?" she pressed, lifting her glass of wine for a sip. "You didn't seem so certain earlier."

"You didn't say no."

Patricia came by to take their dinner order, and Diane requested the roast pork while Oliver chose the venison. The room was filling up nicely; Sophia had swiftly developed a true talent for seating club members at the appropriate tables and for encouraging the most easily persuaded ones to move on to the gaming rooms when the dining room began to back up.

"Will you keep the club open all year?" Oliver asked, his gaze studying Diane's face. He did that a great deal, she'd noticed, as if he was still attempting to figure her out. She liked that he didn't think he'd done so already.

"Do your other clubs close at the end of the Season?"

"Some of them do. The others reduce their staff and their hours."

Reduce their staff. That had been her original intention when the club had still been in its planning stages. It made sense financially. Fewer guests meant less money coming in, and fewer employees meant less money going out. Now, however, it felt infinitely more complicated. "What do the employees who aren't kept on do?"

"I have no idea. I've never had that conversation with any of them."

"Oh, what a shame. You were helpful for a moment, and then . . . well, it ended."

He grinned. "Being helpful is another new direction I'm trying. Shall I inquire at the Society? I'm meeting Manderlin there for breakfast before Parliament."

"Yes. Thank you."

He took a swallow of whiskey. "And you'll owe me . . . a walk through the park of your choice on Tuesday afternoon."

"No!"

"Then I'm afraid I won't be chatting with any footmen or waiters about their autumn and winter activities."

Diane narrowed her eyes, annoyed and a bit . . . flattered all at the same time—despite the fact that she knew him to be heartless and self-serving. "St. James's Park."

"Very well."

"And your idea of helpfulness needs some improvement."

"As does your impression of a ruthless club owner governed solely by logic and the desire for independence." He grimaced, no doubt sensing that she was about to stomp on his foot. "Ah. A bit too close to the mark, was I? Should I have said that I admire the way you're managing an enterprise no chit has ever attempted? And that the affection and loyalty your employees clearly feel toward you, and you for them, is even more admirable?"

"You adm—" She stopped herself before she could say something completely foolish. "You're bamming me, aren't you? That's just mean."

Oliver sat forward. "I am not bamming you." Reaching across the small table, he tapped her forefinger with his. "I admit that sarcasm is perhaps my favorite form of expression," he murmured, quietly enough that not even the neighboring tables could possibly have overheard him, "but for once I am being utterly sincere. You are a remarkable woman, and I do admire you."

She drew a slow breath, attempting to ignore that warm, lifting feeling she'd first noticed when he'd kissed her at the Drury Lane theater. Or had it been even before that, when they'd flown above London in a balloon? She couldn't quite recall when she'd begun . . . liking him more than previously. "Then I sincerely thank you."

"You're sincerely welcome." He pressed down on her finger briefly, then released her again. "But you still have to go walking in the park with me."

And she still didn't mind the idea as much as she should have. "That's why I haven't complimented you about anything."

For a brief moment he actually looked perturbed, but the expression was gone from his lean face so swiftly that she couldn't be certain. "I'll have to put a bit more effort into it, then."

Had she been too harsh? Yes, he was far ahead of her in cruelty, but he'd just handed her two genuinely splendid compliments. She had no intention of apologizing, but perhaps she could soften the blow a little. "Oliver, I do appr—"

"Bloody hell," he muttered, scowling.

"Well. Never mind, then."

"Not you, chit." He glanced away from her, then back

again. "Anthony Benchley just walked in. With his new friends."

And *that* was likely the nicest thing Oliver had ever done for her, giving her a moment to gather herself together before the next storm broke. She'd put Frederick behind her the moment he'd died, and with the exception of one large rut in her road she'd been moving forward ever since. Every time Anthony appeared she felt the drag back toward the abyss her life had been—when she'd been nothing more than Lady Cameron, helpless, hopeless, and destitute. In all honesty, that wasn't precisely Anthony's fault, but he had to know by now that she didn't want him anywhere near her.

"Diane?"

She looked up. And then she remembered that they were in *her* club, in *her* home, and he was only someone's guest. "Anthony," she said, standing so she wouldn't have to look up at him. "I see you can't resist The Tantalus Club." She wanted to add that unfortunately he wasn't welcome there but refrained from doing so. If she couldn't withstand such a pitiable nuisance as Lord Cameron, she had no business being a club owner.

"No, it doesn't seem that I can, does it?" He smiled, showing too many teeth, and a sliver of uneasiness slid down her spine.

At the same time, she heard Oliver's chair push back. *Oh, no.* "I know Lord Trainor, of course," she resumed, speaking to the only club member in the group, "but will you introduce me to your friends?"

"With pleasure. His Grace, the Duke of Greaves, and the Earl of Larden. Gentlemen, my . . . former sister-in-law, Lady Cameron."

As cordial as all that sounded, she didn't have to be terribly perceptive to feel the male aggression in the air. And a great deal of that emanated from directly behind her. If Oliver meant to play the part of her ally, he needed to calm down. "Have you met Lord Haybury?" she asked, taking a half step sideways so she could make a grab for him if he lunged at anyone. For heaven's sake, he was generally much more cerebral than physical with his violence. "Oliver, the Duke of Gr—"

"Yes, we're acquainted," Oliver interrupted. He'd moved up around beside her, she realized, close enough to touch. "Go take a table and enjoy your dinner, gentlemen. The cooks here at The Tantalus Club are exceptional."

Anthony scowled, sending his gaze around the room. "You think to put me off again then, do you, Haybury? You and your cow? I did some checking, you know. You were in Vienna when my brother expired. And now you're living under his roof, with his wife. Do you expect me to believe it's all just a coincidence? Diane, you stole—"

"If the next two words dribbling out of your mouth aren't 'my heart,' " Oliver cut in, his voice flat, "you and I are going to have a disagreement."

Lord Cameron snapped his mouth shut. "I won't be bullied any longer. I've been polite until now. And now I have my own allies, Diane. I want what's mine. Y—"

The Duke of Greaves clapped Anthony on the shoulder, though his dark gray eyes remained fixed on Oliver. "We're here to try your tables, actually, my lady," he interrupted. "There's no need for insults or raised voices. Passions may be high, but we are all gentlemen—and ladies—here."

"Indeed," Lord Larden took up. "Everyone wants a look at your unusual club. You can hardly blame us for our curiosity . . . and interest."

"Yes, this place is quite a feat, considering that when I last saw her she could barely put together a dinner menu." Anthony chuckled.

Oh, there were so many things she wanted to say in

answer to that, beginning with the difficulty of putting together a menu when the household could barely afford fish and boiled potatoes. She curled her fingers into a hard fist.

Warm fingers brushed against hers. "He wants a fight," Oliver whispered. "Don't play his game."

"You, either," she returned in the same tone, but flexed her hand again. She faced Anthony squarely. "I hope you're not jealous that I've been able to improve my life," she said in a more normal tone, batting her eyelashes.

"I don't care that you have; I only insist on knowing how you did so," her former brother-in-law pressed. "And I want you to prove that you didn't accomplish this by making some sordid pact with Haybury that involved doing in Frederick—or the former Marquis of Haybury, for that matter."

She was not going to fall into that hole. "I don't discuss my finances, Anthony. But you might tell *me:* how did you convince Lord Trainor to bring you here? I wasn't aware the Benchleys had anyone left in London who would do them a favor."

Beside her Oliver snorted faintly. The red of Anthony's face deepened, though in his defense the new Lord Cameron had never heard her speak up for herself before. This Diane very little resembled the one he'd known four years ago before Frederick dragged her to Vienna.

Greaves pulled Anthony back a step. "The tables," he said. "I'd like to do some wagering. Not argue with a chit in her own domain."

Settling for a graceless nod, Anthony backed away and turned around. Once they'd disappeared into the Persephone Room, Diane faced Oliver again. "How much of a threat to my club are Greaves and Larden?"

Of course she didn't care that Greaves and Anthony

had called her names; her life was tied into the club so deeply that only the club mattered. Briefly Oliver wondered if there could ever be room for him in her heart. "Larden's likely to attempt to wager so deeply he'll break the bank and force you to give the club over to him. Greaves is more devious. He'll look for a crack and dig into it until it breaks wide open." He put a hand on the back of her chair, half-encircling her. "You made Cameron go scrambling for reinforcements. Have I mentioned that you're fairly formidable?"

Forcing her shoulders to relax, Diane managed a grin. "Nice of you to notice."

"That's not all I've noticed about you, but we'll save that conversation for another time. Shall we finish dinner?"

As they sat down once more to eat, she realized that something exceedingly odd had just happened. Sometime over the past few minutes she and Oliver Warren had become allies. Even odder, lightning hadn't struck either one of them dead.

A pack of wolves had entered The Tantalus Club. Well, two wolves and a hyena. Oliver kept watch on the door as he and Diane finished their dinner. He needed to give more credit to Cameron. Evidently the man had seen that he was being viewed as nothing more than a nuisance and as a result he'd brought in allies who absolutely needed to be taken seriously. The question became whether Larden and especially Greaves were playing the same game as their new friend. Regardless, this all meant trouble.

"Tell me," Diane said unexpectedly, "is Greaves here because of you?"

"It's possible. He likely knows I live upstairs and that I spend most evenings here."

"And if *he* cheated *you,* what is he after?"

"I don't know." Oliver frowned at his nearly empty glass. "If Cameron approached him for a particular purpose, Greaves agreed to it knowing of the earl's connection to you, and yours to me." He glanced up at her to find her intense green gaze on his face. "I have a suspicion he's been promised a part ownership of The Tantalus Club."

"Well, he can't have it," she retorted. "And neither can Anthony or that Larden person. It's mine."

"You don't need to convince me of that, my dear."

With a deep breath she jabbed her knife into her roast pork. "When did this trouble between you happen?"

"Three years ago."

"About the time you left London for the Continent. Not a coincidence, I presume."

Fascinating as he found her, from time to time he wished she were a little less acute. "Not a coincidence."

"And Larden?"

"I've never liked him. He simply enjoys winning the property and lives of others."

"I won't tolerate that here." Diane pushed back from the table and stood. "I believe I'll visit the Persephone Room."

Rising as well, Oliver reached across the table to grip her hand. He liked touching her, and she didn't seem to be objecting. "Let me see what they're up to."

"This is my club. Whatever they're doing here affects me. Not you." She made a face. "I thought the trouble you'd bring me would be from some woman attempting to gain employment here and then slipping into your rooms at night. I should have realized that you've made enemies of both sexes."

He refrained from pointing out that the trouble had begun when she'd forged her late husband's signature on the deed to Adam House. If there was one thing upon which they agreed, it was that she deserved the opportunity to be happy. "Diane, I'll see to it."

"No, you won't. Thank you for dinner. Now excuse me."

Damnation. Every time he took two steps closer to earning her trust, someone—generally Diane—came along to push him back one step. Oliver left the dining room to circle around through the smaller Ariadne gaming room and to the rear door of Persephone. When he, albeit rarely, reflected on his life, it seemed as though he'd spent most of his adult years in the mud for one reason or another. He was tired of it—but he also knew how to navigate through the muck. In fact, he was quite good at it.

Interestingly enough, while all three of the club's new visitors stood around the roulette wheel, only Greaves and Larden were placing wagers. Cameron stood beside them, his attention clearly on the room at large, its layout and décor, and its occupants. He was likely taking mental notes about its value. He'd worn that look before, but no doubt this time he thought he had a chance to actually take the club from her. And whether by the strictest interpretation of the law it should have gone to Cameron or not, Oliver wasn't about to let that happen. Diane had earned this, for God's sake.

Halfway across the room she was playing the charming hostess, admiring John Welling's new watch fob and smiling as another of the club's membership flirted with her.

Oliver didn't mind the flirting overly much, because he was quite aware that she was merely playing a role, providing a bit of charm to earn The Tantalus Club a few more shillings by distracting the wagerers. It was the way some of the other men looked at her, generally while she wasn't looking at them, that he didn't like.

Greaves had his gaze on her in just that way, a wolf sizing up its next meal. Oliver's lip curled in a snarl. This club might be her business, but looking after her had become his. That wouldn't make her very happy, but he would accept the consequences. It was about time he began doing that, anyway.

With a last look around the busy room he left the shelter of the doorway and made his way toward the roulette table. As Miss Sylvie Hartford acknowledged him, he placed his wager—twenty pounds on number eleven.

"Only twenty?" Larden commented. "That's rather light for you, isn't it, Mr. Warren? Or Lord Haybury, rather. My apologies."

"Was that an insult, or is your mind failing you, Larden?" he returned. "I warned you about your fondness for pox-ridden chits."

The earl paled, a vein pulsing in his forehead. Greaves, though, cleared his throat, elbowing his companion at the same time. "You should know better than to begin a verbal battle with Oliver," Greaves commented. "Make your argument on the table."

"True," Larden put in. "We all know he's far from invulnerable there."

Before that night at the tables in Vienna, Oliver would have been able to claim the moral high ground on the subject of game play. In a sense, he could blame Greaves for his behavior—but that would mean he owed the duke just as much for what was happening now. Oliver preferred to leave Greaves out of it altogether and accept responsibility for his relationship, such as it was, with Diane.

"Were you chattering, or wagering? Or should we all wait while you decide?" he asked, placing a second twenty pounds on black. He nearly always bet on black. It had served him well thus far.

"Gentlemen, hold your wagers," Sylvie instructed, and sent the ball around the wheel. "Seventeen black," she declared after a moment, then paid off the winners and cleared the table.

"I can see why The Tantalus Club is becoming so popular," Larden commented. "Even losing has its charms." He tossed a shilling onto the table. "Pick that up, will you, my dear?"

Without hesitation Sylvie leaned across the table and retrieved the coin. "This one's mine," she said, setting it at her elbow. "The next dropped coin will go to him." With a charming smile she gestured at the gargantuan Mr. Smith, who'd seemingly appeared from nowhere. "Mr. Smith, though, will thank you outside."

Oliver realized he was smiling, and he belatedly pulled the expression back in. Of all the things he thought would come of this experience, feeling paternal pride was not one of them. For God's sake, he was nine-and-twenty, ten years Sylvie's senior—but he'd taught her how to manage the table and the wagerers and how to respond to general male idiocy. And she'd done it well.

"Well, where's the fun in that?" Larden protested. "If you're not for touching, and not for looking at, what good are you?"

Before Oliver could do more than curl his fist, Diane glided up to the table. "If that is your opinion, my lord, perhaps you would prefer to wager at a different club."

"Do you lead all your members about by the nose then, my lady? Or is it a lower body part you prefer to grasp?"

"Some gentlemen prefer an ordered, elegant setting where they can eat and wager and chat with friends, and not be disturbed by gauche displays of vulgarity, Lord Larden."

A chorus of "hear, hear" rang out behind her. Larden had made enough enemies during his reign at the Mayfair gaming tables that while not many would be willing to stand up to him, they were certainly willing to whisper their dislike from the safety of the shadows. Oliver took a half step closer to Diane.

"I believe I more than qualify for membership in your little embroidery circle," the earl commented, his expression cooling to the point of blankness.

"No, I don't believe you do," Diane returned. "Your friends are welcome to stay, but as I recall, you have an engagement elsewhere, anyway."

And she even invented a way for the fiend to save his pride. Unless Larden was a fool, which he wasn't, he would take the opportunity to avoid being thrown out of The Tantalus Club on his arse. If he hadn't thought it would make matters worse, Oliver would have applauded.

Larden, though, turned his pale blue eyes in Oliver's direction. "Do you actually allow this cow to speak to her betters like that?"

As if he would say anything now to ruin this fragile new alliance he and Diane seemed to have forged. "I don't believe Lady Cameron requires anyone's permission to conduct business in her own establishment," he returned. "As for you being her better, well, we'll have to agree to disagree. And if you insult Lady Cameron to her face or to her back ever again, I'll be calling on you. With a pair of pistols, if you were wondering."

"You'll regret this," the earl snapped. "And so will you, harlot." He turned on his heel and strode out of the room, the hulking Mr. Smith close behind him.

Diane sent a pointed glance at Greaves and her former brother-in-law. "Enjoy yourselves, gentlemen," she said coolly, and with a nod strolled toward the nearest of the faro tables. Halfway there, she paused and turned around. "Lord Haybury, do you have a moment?"

Oliver collected his blunt and left the table. "For you, of course."

She led the way into the Demeter Room and then through the nearest of the mystery doors into the narrow hallway beyond. "Lord Larden has nothing in particular against you?" she asked, facing him.

"I've beaten him several times at the tables, but not for any significant amount. So, no. I think he was tempted to come here by Anthony Benchley."

Green eyes studied his, though he wasn't certain this time what she might be looking for. "Yes, I do, as well."

Then she stepped forward, slid her arms up around his shoulders, and kissed him. He put his own hands up to her face, drawing her in closer as she sank into him, moaning against his mouth.

"This doesn't mean anything," she murmured, nibbling at his lower lip.

His eyes wanted to roll back into his head. "Of course not," he agreed, tangling his tongue with hers.

"I still don't like you."

"I don't blame you." Arousal tugged through him, heady and exciting.

"And I don't need your help."

"Only a madman would think so." With her fingers kneading convulsively into his shoulders, her breasts pressed against his chest, and one ankle wrapped around the back of his boot, she seemed fairly amenable to having him. And he was beginning to lose the ability to think. "Unless you move away from me immediately," he muttered against her mouth, "then I am going to collect on my eight hours. I want you."

He felt her hesitate, felt the jump of her muscles. Clearly she'd been swept up in the moment, her blood rushing after standing her ground in a confrontation with a pair of dangerous men. And he'd overplayed his hand. She didn't want *him;* she simply . . . wanted. *Damnation.* If there was one thing he'd been attempting to avoid, it was making a mistake that would set them—him—back to the beginning again.

Then Diane tangled her fingers into his hair and pulled his head down. "I do hate leaving debts unpaid," she whispered into his ear. "I'll go tell Jenny I'm leaving, and then I'll meet you upstairs."

If he gave her any time to think, she would change her mind. "No. You come with me, and we'll tell Langtree on the way upstairs." He kissed her again, hot and open-mouthed, for emphasis. Now that he'd shown his hand, there was nothing to do but pretend he'd meant to do so.

"Oh, very well," she breathed, licking his earlobe.

Good God. If he could have locked the mystery doors, he and Diane wouldn't be leaving the hallway. As it was, another minute of this would render his . . . interest visible to everyone at the club. Taking a hard breath, he grabbed her hand and towed her up the hallway. At the last door he released her, ran a hand through his hair, and looked sideways at her.

What an idiot he'd been two years ago. He'd abandoned this woman because he'd fallen for her, and that made him a complete fool and a coward. *W*hether he could make amends for that or not, if she would allow it he would spend the remainder of his life trying to do so.

Instead of speaking, he reached over to brush a stray strand of her midnight hair back behind her ear. "Shall we?"

Nodding, Diane opened the door and stepped into the ordered chaos at the front of the Demeter Room. As soon as she appeared, men noticed. She drew them to her like a magnet. Oliver didn't like it, but he understood it. However brilliant her plan and even the design of The Tantalus Club, she was the reason anyone wanted to be there, to be seen there, to be a part of this very unusual venture.

The face she showed them was . . . magical, for want of a better word.

She drew him as well. At least he was aware of it. And he'd seen more of her than her knife-sharp, seductive side. Even so, he couldn't help moving closer to her as they made their way to the foyer.

"Juliet," she said, flexing her fingers as if to be certain she still retained possession of all of them. "Please inform Genevieve that I will be . . . unavailable until five o'clock or so in the morning."

How pitiful was he that he took the words "or so" to be a sign that she might be softening toward him? Shaking himself, Oliver nodded at the butler chit. "Likewise, Langtree. I don't want anyone pounding at my door this time for anything less than a fire. Is that clear?"

"I'll see to it, my lady," the servant said, not even glancing in his direction.

Oliver stifled a grin. Clearly the chit knew who buttered her bread. "I'll remember this, Langtree," he commented, and gestured Diane to lead the way up the front stairs.

Once they were inside his front room, he closed and latched his door. That damned foreign chit was too unpredictable to risk leaving it open. Then he faced Diane again, to find her gazing at him. To his eyes, at least, her face in the lamplight seemed almost ethereal in its beauty. Every part of him, skin to soul, wanted her, and it took all his willpower to remain where he was.

Slowly she looked him up and down. "Well, come along," she said, her voice breathy and rough. "A bargain is a bargain."

He shook his head. "This isn't about a bargain."

"Then why am I here?"

Oliver took a slow, controlled step closer, halving the distance between them. "Because you want to be here."

She tilted her head. "Are you certain about that?"

For a heartbeat he weighed how much he wanted her against how much he wanted her to choose him. He swallowed, knowing he was an idiot for relying on hope after what he'd done. He much preferred skill, but that wouldn't serve him until after he got her clothes off. "If you want to leave, then go."

"And the eight hours?"

"Wiped clean."

"Are you certain of that?"

No. "Yes. That debt is finished with. You still owe me the walk in the park, though."

A grin, sultry and aroused, touched her mouth. "Then I can leave if I wish to?"

"Yes."

"Hm." She continued to look at him. "Why so generous?"

"There's something about compelling you to join me in bed that I find . . . distasteful." He shrugged. "Odd, I know."

"Very odd." Diane folded her arms across her chest, then lowered them again. "Step aside, then."

Cursing himself in every language he knew, Oliver moved away from the door. He'd played games of faro and whist with thousands of pounds at risk. He'd lost huge amounts of money, albeit rarely. And he'd just lost this game.

She walked past him and put her hand on the latch. "You truly aren't going attempt to stop me?"

"Truly."

"You don't want me to stay?"

He blew out his breath. "Of course I want you to stay."

"Then ask me."

Was she simply playing? Asking him to look even more foolish than he already felt? He deserved it, he supposed. "Diane, would you spend the night with me?" he asked, unable to keep his voice steady.

For a long moment she looked straight into his eyes. "Perhaps," she finally murmured. "But not tonight." She unlocked the door. "If you want me again, Haybury, then you're going to have to prove that you truly have changed." With that she slipped back out to the landing and closed the door behind her.

Chapter Sixteen

Diane had to give Oliver a great deal of credit for not pursuing her down the stairs.

Considering the raw ache coursing through her, however, perhaps he wasn't able to run. She stifled a somewhat hysterical chuckle and continued down to the foyer. Oh, she wanted him. But now, at least, they were a bit closer to being even. And with Anthony making much more blatant accusations and threats, she needed to think. In Oliver's intimate company, thinking became supremely difficult.

"My lady?"

She blinked as Juliet materialized in front of her. "Ah, yes. Never mind what I said earlier." Shifting to ease the material that abruptly seemed far too tight across her breasts, she grimaced. "Though I will be retiring to Adam House for the evening. Have someone prepare a cool bath, will you?"

"A *cool* bath?"

"I don't have to look at you to know you're smirking, Juliet," she said over her shoulder, heading for the half-hidden door that led through a short corridor to her private home. "A *cold* bath."

"Yes, my lady."

Even as she stripped out of her black gown and stepped into the uncomfortably cold water thirty minutes later, her mind continued to argue with her body. Why should she deny herself a night of pleasure—and being with Oliver Warren was infinitely pleasurable—simply because he'd erred two years ago?

"Erred," she muttered, stifling a shriek as she sat down in the bathtub and cold water rose to her chest. If erring consisted of abandoning people without a word—people who'd begun to care for him a great deal and deserved some kind of explanation, which he *still* hadn't offered—then yes, he'd erred. Very badly.

And she was not some fainting daisy who melted into his arms simply because he knew how to kiss and he knew how and when to say the correct thing to her and about her. Or because he'd proved to be quite helpful, more so than blackmail strictly required. The bastard.

At least the icy water cooled her ardor. For heaven's sake, twenty minutes ago she'd barely been able to put two sentences together. Blowing out her breath, Diane squeezed her eyes shut and splashed her face. If he deserved credit for not chasing after her, then she deserved credit for escaping from him when what she wanted to do more than anything was feel his weight on her and his cock moving inside her.

Growling, she splashed more vigorously, gasping as the water's wake reached her armpits. An abrupt solid thud seemed to rattle the room around her, and she gasped again.

"Mary?" she called, flinching as the thud repeated, reverberating against the ceiling. Her maid, though, would be down in the kitchen helping sort out the food orders during the Demeter Room's busiest hour.

Another thud. This time, dust and plaster shook down from above. At the next blow, the end of what looked like an axe carved a hole into her ceiling and then vanished again. "Good heavens," she muttered, and scrambled out of the bath.

Pulling her thin dressing robe over her shoulders and knotting the belt around her waist, she dove for her bed stand and the pistol she kept there. Wood and plaster dropped to the floor as she grabbed the weapon and cocked it.

With a last shuddering thud, the ceiling exploded. A good portion of it hit the floor a few feet in front of her, followed by a figure that fell and rolled to its feet. His feet.

"Oliver?" she gasped, leveling the pistol at him.

"Langtree and your damned behemoths wouldn't let me back into the club," he muttered, brushing plaster dust from his shoulders as he straightened. "And don't shoot me again, damn it all."

"You made a hole in my ceiling!"

"No, I made a hole in your floor above. Hope no one falls through it. I put a vase on either side, but you never know." He shrugged.

"You've gone mad!"

Moving faster than she could follow, he stripped the pistol from her hand and tossed it into the bathtub. "More than likely." Keeping his unreadable gaze on her, he moved sideways until he could dip his fingers into the bathwater. "Cold," he said, as though that meant something. Which it did, but she wasn't about to tell him that.

This was beyond mad. "You released me from your stupid bargain. Go away!"

"You said you wanted to be convinced that I've changed."

"Yes, convinced! Not . . . frightened half to death by men falling through my ceiling."

"And how am I supposed to convince you of anything

when you keep avoiding me? I know you, and you know me better than any other woman in the entire damned world. So you want flowers, I suppose? Jewelry? Fine gowns?" He walked toward her. "Poems? You would laugh in my face."

"Flowers are very nice," she returned, stumbling a little on the wet, debris-covered floor as she backed toward the door leading to her private sitting room.

"Men give you flowers every day. I'll wager you don't even recall the names of the men who sent you flowers today."

"I've told you numerous times that I don't wager."

"Lord Quence, Michael Penn-Haller, and Lord Peter Selse." He took another step closer to her. "I'm not giving you any bloody flowers."

Her heart skittered. "You make note of whoever sends me flowers?"

Oliver's gray eyes narrowed. "Every damned day."

Diane took another step backward, and her spine bumped against her bedchamber door. "I think you should know, cutting holes in my ceiling and refusing to bring me flowers is not how I would convince me of anything but your lunacy."

"Isn't it?" Stopping a foot in front of her, he reached out and ran a finger from her throat to where the neck of her robe closed over her chest. "I can feel your heart beating."

"That's what hearts do."

"You've risked your reputation, your money, *my* money, everything you own, on The Tantalus Club. And flowers are supposed to sway you? Don't be ridiculous."

She hated to admit it, but he made a good point. After an arranged marriage ended in ever-increasing poverty, flowers had struck her as being overly sentimental and useless. "Then destroying my home is *your* chosen method of . . . swaying me?"

"Was it successful?"

At the moment, with heat twining down her spine and excitement making her hands shake, she couldn't think of anything more arousing than a man—this man—breaking down walls or ceilings or floors to get to her. "So far." If she'd trusted him just a bit more, she wouldn't have hesitated at all. And that thought shook her a little.

Oliver hooked his forefinger into the material of her robe and tugged her up against his lean, solid body. She couldn't say who kissed whom first, but within a few hard beats of her heart she was so tangled into him that she couldn't tell where she ended and he began, even through their clothes.

"Tell me that you want me," he murmured, pushing her robe down her shoulders and kissing her throat.

The way he said it, the slight break in his husky voice, aroused her all over again. He might have broken in to get to her, but he seemed to need to know that she was glad he was there. It was very unlike the arrogant, self-assured marquis she thought she knew so well.

Some kind of game or not, however, these days she took what she wanted. She even had a rule about it. "I want you, Oliver," she breathed, tangling her fingers into his rich brown hair. "But not here."

He pulled back, scowling. "What kind of damned thing is that to say?" he demanded.

"There's a hole in my ceiling," she explained carefully, gesturing. Clearly he was just about at the edge of reason. "I refuse to have my staff listening—or watching—us."

His expression eased again. "Ah. I apologize. All the blood has left my brain and traveled downward." He sent her a sly look full of sex and secrets. "As you can likely tell."

"Yes, I can." With a slow grin she reached behind her and unlatched the door leading to her sitting room.

Half-stumbling out of the room, they ended up pressed

against the back of a couch. His mouth lowered over hers again, and she closed her eyes, drinking in the sensation of him around her, his hands on her bare skin.

"The door," she managed shakily, using all her will-power to push him away.

"Do you think I'll be followed?"

"The door."

Oliver leaned his forehead against hers, then kissed her again. "As you wish."

He closed her bedchamber door harder than he meant to; his control had clearly deserted him the moment she'd left him staring, alone, at his closing front door. For a few minutes he'd attempted to be logical and magnanimous and understand that she likely needed to hurt him so they would be, in some sense, even.

But then he'd realized that if he allowed her to dictate the terms of this relationship, he would lose too much ground. He would be the servant, the subordinate. While he had never been in that position with anyone, with her it was even more vital that he neither follow nor lead. And most important, he would be going to bed alone, hard, aching, and furious.

Returning to her, he untied the sash around her waist and pulled her dressing gown open. God, she was lovely. "You're breathtaking," he said aloud.

Diane responded by pushing his jacket off his shoulders and stripping him out of his waistcoat so quickly that one of the buttons popped off. "Oh, apologies," she muttered, tossing the garment to the floor.

He grinned. "A button versus a ceiling, Diane. I've no complaints." Dipping his head, he took one of her soft breasts into his mouth, flicking his tongue across her nipple.

At her responding gasp he turned his attention to her other breast, attempting to ignore the constricted ache of his cock. This was the Diane Benchley he remembered, free with her expressions of pleasure. She still might not trust him completely, but she'd begun to.

Thankfully the couch was both long and deep, and once he'd yanked off his boots he stretched out alongside her. Carefully he removed the clips from her curling hair, drawing the black, lavender-scented mass forward across her shoulders. When he lowered himself over her for another kiss, her wandering hands reached for his trousers.

In a moment she shoved the material down past his thighs, and he kicked it off to the floor. "You're so warm," she breathed, arching her body against his.

"You were just in a tub of cold water. Let me warm you." With a grin he sank down, kissing her breasts and her belly and her thighs, then parting her legs to work his way up again. When he brushed his tongue and fingers along her folds, she gasped and moaned throatily. *Good God.* If she made that sound again, he would likely come right there, like some virginal schoolboy with his first chit.

"I'm quite warm now, thank you," she rasped shakily, digging her fingers into his scalp as he lowered his head to her again.

He chuckled, then had to close his eyes and conjure images of dustbins and gouty old men when she bucked against him. Teasing and licking at her dampness until he couldn't stand not being inside her for a second longer, he slid up her body again.

Settling over her, Oliver kissed her again, relishing the way she pushed up, pressing her body close against his. She flung her ankles around his thighs and he angled his hips forward, pushing hard and hot into her. Everything became sensation: his mouth on hers, the slide of flesh around his, hands everywhere—time seemed to stop for those minutes, with nothing but the sound of breathing and moans and the slight, rhythmic creak of the low couch beneath them.

She climaxed around him, but he held on to his slipping control as best he could. Slowing his thrusts to prolong her shuddering, shivering pleasure, he watched those sparkling emerald eyes as she panted beneath him. He'd run away from this two years ago. What in God's name had possessed him? When her breathing settled a little he sped his own rhythm, burying himself in her over and over, hard and fast and deep. With a grunt he came, emptying himself into her.

For several long minutes they lay where they were, still kissing as he rolled onto his side next to her. He didn't wish to stop touching her, caressing her—and then he remembered. *That* was what had sent him fleeing. Not the very exceptional sex, but that need to be close to her that consumed him at every waking moment. That desire to please her, to shoulder all of her troubles, to see the concern and worry gone from her eyes.

But the oddest part of all this was that while he remembered his horror in those tangible memories, the idea of attachment didn't . . . trouble him as it had before. He didn't know whether it was the two years that had passed and everything that had happened in that time or the fact that he'd spent the past two years attempting to feel the pleasure without the need and had failed miserably.

"I have a question for you," she murmured, still sounding out of breath.

"My mind's not quite up to form, but I shall do my best to answer it," Oliver returned, abruptly fascinated all over again by the soft curve of her throat. He placed a kiss over the soft, quick beat of her pulse there.

"You gave up your eight hours hoping that I would be grateful enough to end up in your bed anyway, did you not?"

"No."

Diane lifted an eyebrow, looking up at him. He briefly wondered what she saw. "No?" she repeated. "You took some rather extreme measures to find me when I declined."

"I wanted us to end up doing this," he conceded, running his fingers in circles around her breasts. "But I wanted the odds to be even, so to speak."

"You didn't wish to force me, you mean?"

"I wouldn't do that regardless, but yes, I wanted you to want to be here." He was being very honest this evening; apparently whatever insanity had struck him when he'd decided that hacking through her ceiling would be the perfect way to get her attention hadn't abated.

"Ah, Oliver," she sighed, stretching in a way that made him hard all over again, "you and bed and I have always been very compatible. It's everywhere else I have my doubts."

"You know, living here is the closest to . . . domesticity I've had since I turned twelve. It may take me some time to become accustomed to it."

She chuckled, running her hand along his hip. "If The Tantalus Club is your idea of domesticity, it *has* been quite some time for you." Her smile faded. "Are you ever going to tell me why you fled Vienna? And not that nonsense about needing to reconcile with your uncle."

Whatever this thing forming between them might be, a lie would ruin it. But it was very likely that the truth would as well—especially when he was still attempting to decipher his feelings, old and new, himself. "I'll tell you," he said slowly, "but not tonight."

"That's not very reassuring."

"Suffice it to say that I'm not running now." He took a breath. "Nor do I intend to."

Her emerald gaze held his for a long moment. "I will require some convincing, and a bit of proof."

Oliver turned her onto her side, facing away from him, then reached around her to caress her breasts. "I shall do my utmost," he murmured into her ear, and, propping up one of her knees, slowly pushed into her from behind. As long as the task involved sex with Diane Benchley, he was more than willing to make amends.

It had to be near dawn when he fell asleep on the couch, Diane lying across his chest and a thin blanket covering the two of them from the late-night chill. And it couldn't have been more than ten minutes after that when he jerked awake again at the sound of a female screech.

"Diane!"

Her sitting room door burst open, the swinging door closely followed by the French twist and two of the stouter-looking chits. This time Miss Martine was carrying a damned pistol—and it very much looked like she knew how to use it.

"I'm well, Jenny," Diane said groggily, sitting up in front of him and taking most of the blanket to wrap around her. "I told Juliet I would be indisposed."

"Yes, but that was when you were in his apartments. When you left, she assumed your plans had changed." The chit scowled at him beyond Diane's shoulder. "You know there's a hole in the floor of the servants' hallway upstairs. It looks directly down into your bedchamber."

Diane cleared her throat. "Yes, I know," she returned, humor touching her voice. "We'll have to summon Mr. Dunlevy and have that repaired."

"And that's all you have to say?"

"At the moment, yes. That's all I have to say. We can talk more later, my dear. But I would truly like to get some sleep first."

"With him here?"

"Him would like to stay, yes," Oliver put in, becoming a bit annoyed at being spoken about as if he weren't there. "We can chat tomorrow as well, if you'd like."

"*Cochon,*" she snapped.

"It's far too early to be calling me names," he commented, lying down again and favoring her with his most porcine-like snort just to show that he understood the insult.

Diane elbowed him in the rib cage. "I will sit down to breakfast with you, Jenny," she said. "At ten o'clock."

"Yes, yes. I can see there is nothing to be done here now."

It had already been done, but if he said that aloud, she would likely raise that pistol again. Once Genevieve and her female guards left the room and closed the door again, Diane sank back down onto the couch. "That might have gone better."

"Considering that no one shot me this time, I have to disagree."

He felt rather than heard her chuckle. "Perhaps things are looking up for you, after all."

Oh, he definitely had to agree with that. And now he could begin to worry in earnest about what Cameron and Greaves might be planning.

"He wanted to get my attention," Diane said, beginning to lose her patience. She rose from the breakfast table to fetch another slice of ham from the sideboard. "Which he did."

"He smashed a hole into your bedchamber ceiling," Jenny retorted. It was the fourth or fifth time she'd made that statement—apparently she didn't think Diane actually understood what she was saying. "If he wanted your attention, he might have sent you flowers."

"I made that same suggestion." Sitting at the small table once more, she returned to her breakfast. When Jenny continued to glare at her, however, she set down her fork. "I'm not falling for him again, if that's what's troubling you. I don't repeat my mistakes."

"Then why have you been smiling all morning? You detest Lord Haybury—or have you forgotten?"

And that was the rub. She couldn't count the number of times she'd ranted about Oliver to Jenny. The curses hadn't been said to gain sympathy or to turn him into a villain simply because Diane felt she'd been wronged. She'd meant them all. But now was not then. "I haven't forgotten," she said aloud.

"Then what—"

"I do hope you've noticed how much more cooperative he's been lately. And I've no complaints about his overnight performance." *None at all.*

Jenny scowled. "I only hope you aren't being fooled in all of this. You may have caught him by surprise initially, but he is not a stupid man. And he does not like to lose. I can almost guarantee that he is making his own plans."

"I don't doubt it." What those plans might be, though—given the way he'd been mentioning domesticity and not going anywhere—disconcerted her.

"And do you think the Duke of Greaves and Lord Larden were here because of you, or because of him? He's bringing trouble."

"He didn't bring Anthony."

"That, my dear, I will agree with. The new earl spent the evening touching the wallpaper and fingering the curtains and counting every penny the club took in last night."

With a sigh, Diane set aside her fork. "Perhaps I've been a bit too clever at looking well-off. The costume might have convinced gentlemen to trust that I wouldn't cheat them out of anything, but obviously Anthony thinks that either I or The Tantalus have a very fat purse."

"And how do you propose we discourage his interest?"

For a moment Diane wasn't certain whether Jenny was referring to Anthony or to the Marquis of Haybury. *One problem at a time,* she reminded herself. First she needed to protect the club, and then she could worry about her heart. "I'm not certain yet. I can keep Anthony from becoming a member of the club, but if a current member invites him as a guest . . ." She scowled. "This is so annoying! It's *my* club, and he can't have any part of it. I'll see to that."

"Good." Finally Jenny returned to her own breakfast. "By the way, as long as Mr. Dunlevy will be returning to repair your ceiling, have you considered giving some of your senior staff their own quarters?"

Diane nodded. "I don't see the harm in taking one or two of the dormitory rooms and dividing them into individual bedchambers. I want my captains to feel secure here. And to be able to make a home of this place."

For a long moment Jenny gazed at her. "I never expected to hear you say that."

"I've read those idiotic pamphlets Lady Dashton and her stiff-spined cronies are publishing. I doubt they'd be calling my employees whores if they happened to have too many daughters and not enough money to support them. Not everyone wants to become a governess or a lady's companion, for heaven's sake."

"Or to marry," Genevieve put in feelingly. "The Tantalus Club is far more exciting than an embroidery circle."

Laughing, Diane lifted her cup of tea in a toast. "Darling, you have no idea."

"Then back to our starting point. Promise me you'll continue to be careful about whom you . . . trust, no matter how pleasantly that devil is behaving."

"I will. I promise." A knock sounded at the half-open door, and she turned her head. "Come in, Sally."

The footwoman sketched a quick curtsy. "My lady, Grace says you have a caller."

Grace had proved to be a fair butler as well, if not quite as . . . formidable as Juliet. Poor Miss Langtree couldn't be at the door for twenty-four hours each day, however. "Did she say who it was?"

"Oh, yes, my lady. I beg your pardon. It's Lord Cameron."

That ill feeling in the pit of her stomach, the same one that arose every time she thought of Anthony Benchley taking The Tantalus Club away from her, asserted itself again. "Have him brought to my office, if you please."

"Right away, ma'am."

"Damnation." Diane pushed away from the table and stood. "Be close by; whatever he wants, I intend to see that he doesn't get it."

"Mais oui."

Rather than go directly to her office, Diane detoured to her bedchamber and dressing room. Mr. Smith and Mr. Jacobs had cobbled together a patch for the hole in her ceiling, and she sat at her dressing table to remove the pearl necklace she'd donned when Oliver had left her for his own quarters. There were times when the appearance of wealth could do more good for her cause than actual wealth, but a meeting with Lord Cameron would not be one of those times. The pearl ear bobs went into the same drawer, and she put on a pair of green glass ones in their place and fastened a bracelet of matching glass beads around her wrist. Wearing no jewelry at all would be far too obvious.

At the same time, she couldn't help thinking that she should have taken such care earlier, back when Anthony had first appeared on Adam House's doorstep. She'd

underestimated him, lumped him into the same category
of uselessness where she'd relegated his brother.

In the strictest legal sense she'd stolen Adam House,
and that tiny cottage in Vienna, from Anthony, because
she felt she deserved . . . something for years of disappointment and deepening despair. The new Earl of Cameron still had a house in London and two ancestral—and
entailed—estates. He had a roof over his head, and he
always would. When Frederick had died, she'd carefully
counted every penny remaining inside the house they'd
shared. She'd had seven pounds and twopence with which
to make do for the remainder of her life. And so she'd
taken what she needed to survive. Anthony couldn't have
it back.

With that thought firmly in mind, she gazed at herself
in her dressing mirror and took a deep breath. She wasn't
Miss Diane Hastings, granddaughter of the Marquis of
Clansey, any longer. She wasn't subservient to anyone, and
she didn't rely on anyone but herself for her survival.

When she'd kept the new Lord Cameron waiting for
approximately fifteen minutes, she made her way to her
neat, large-windowed office. Behind her desk Anthony
sat hunched over, digging at one of the desk drawers with
a knife blade.

The sight actually reassured her a little. If that was his
tactic, she *hadn't* underestimated him. "Good morning,
Lord Cameron," she said pointedly.

He straightened. "Diane. I thought we'd decided that
you're to call me Anthony."

"Are we keeping up the pretense of civility, then?" She
stayed where she was. "Is there a reason you were attempting to break into my desk, Anthony?"

"That's rather direct."

"I don't see the point of subtlety after you dragged

Larden and Greaves here last night to attempt to, what, intimidate me, I suppose? So what are you after?"

His gaze steady on her, Anthony sank back into her chair and plunked his boot heels onto the top of her desk. As he crossed his ankles, he pulled a cheroot from his brown jacket pocket.

The elaborate show of relaxation meant one of two things. Either he was supremely confident that he had the key to evicting her from Adam House and The Tantalus Club, or he simply wanted her to think that while he sought about for a chink in her armor.

Well, she wouldn't be handing him any ammunition to use against her. Diane remained in the doorway of her own office and allowed one of the people she most disliked in the world to sit at her desk. The unobtrusive door behind his right shoulder remained closed, but she knew Jenny was just behind it.

"If you must know," he finally said, "I wanted a look at your books. From the crowd here last night and what I've already seen of The Tantalus Club, you must be pulling in the blunt hand over fist."

"Money comes in, and money goes out. I don't receive all those liquor bottles for free, and my employees don't work for free. It's a business, and that is what my books show."

"I'd still like a look at them with my own two eyes."

"No," she said, incredulous. *Of all the nerve.* "I have no connection to you, and I owe you nothing. You are here only because I was once married to your brother. Now is there anything else, or are we finished?"

"I am here, Diane, because as far as I am aware, Frederick was penniless and in debt when he died. And yet you've opened a gentlemen's club. I've made a few inquiries to some of his creditors, and you've also paid off most of them. And I heard that you arrived in London in grand style." Lowering his feet, he sat forward again. "Adam House is a separate matter in this. But if you had any money from Frederick, it's mine."

"The only things I had from Frederick," she said stiffly, "were a ring and our three-room house in Vienna. That money is how I repaid his creditors."

"And this?" Anthony gestured at the house and club around them. "He signed Adam House over to you, as well." A scowl crossed his face. "Or so you say. I had my solicitor peruse that very interesting document Frederic had drawn up just before he expired. Quite uncharacteristically thoughtful and intelligent of him, really. And disappointing, considering that Adam House was supposed to be mine."

"I've given up relying on 'supposed to,' Anthony. Frederick did neither of us any favors. Perhaps he felt a bit of guilt at the end for dragging me to Vienna. I imagine we'll never know for certain what he was thinking. Therefore, the facts before us will have to suffice." And thank God she'd learned her late husband's signature so well.

"You still haven't explained The Tantalus Club. Opening this place took considerably more than you claim to have gotten from my brother." Anthony waggled a finger at her. "Someone is lying, Diane."

"I'm not lying, and I don't need to justify anything to you. I am weary of your refusal to simply accept that. Now please leave."

"I don't think you understand. Unless you snare some other lord, you will remain Lady Cameron. That makes us connected. And *I* am growing weary of being referred to as the poor relation hanging about you hoping for scraps."

And she'd spent the last two years experiencing just how difficult it was for a female with no income and alone in a foreign country to keep herself away from genuine disaster. Considering their relative positions in the world, she had very little sympathy for the new Earl of Cameron. Even so, she needed to choose her next words carefully. It was, as Oliver would say, all about strategy. "Then cease hanging about me, Anthony. I won't apologize for the fact that things are as they are, but for both our sakes you need to simply accept it. I am not sharing. Not with you, and not with anyone."

"Hm. I still don't believe you." He stood. "In fact, I think I'll go have a word with the Marquis of Haybury. If anyone knows anything about how you ... earned the money to open this club, he will. He'll also know whether you're sharing or not. Or whether you do have a partner."

Anger began to replace her annoyance as he continued to gaze at her, an expression on his face she could only call patronizing and arrogant. Meeting his gaze, she folded her arms across her chest. "I don't particularly give a damn who you talk to, Anthony, as long as you leave. If you can find any club member willing to escort you back here, then you're welcome to visit The Tantalus. Otherwise, stay away."

"You *have* changed, my dear," he commented. "Clearly Frederick was too softhearted with you, if you think you can stand there and speak to one of your betters in that manner."

"One of my betters?" she bit out. "I see no one here who matches that description. Now leave my home."

He moved toward her and the door. Diane stepped backward, unwilling to be cornered in her own office. Over his shoulder the morning room door opened silently and Jenny appeared, a raised pistol in one hand.

"I'll be back," he said, keeping his gaze on Diane as he left the office and turned up the hallway. "I remain unconvinced of Frederick's foresight. Or his charity to you, of all people."

"Damn that man," she grumbled at Genevieve as he stomped down the hallway.

"Do I allow him to call on Haybury?" her friend asked in the same low tone.

Short of shooting her former brother-in-law, Diane didn't see how they could stop him. "Yes, let him," she returned. "Just make certain he doesn't cause any trouble in the club on his way through."

Apparently she had some faith in her altering assessment of Oliver Warren. Because she trusted that he wouldn't say anything to damage her or the club he was being blackmailed into aiding. God help them both if he proved her wrong.

Chapter Seventeen

"W inters," Oliver said, nodding at the morning butleress as he reached the foyer.

"My lord. Clark has brought your coach around."

"Thank you." She pulled the front door open for him,
but halfway through he stopped his exit. "Do I smell Ma-
cassar oil?" In other clubs the smell was almost ubiqui-
tous, but Diane didn't like dandies, and only dandies put
the damned grease in their hair.

"Lord Cameron arrived some thirty minutes ago, my
lord."

Oliver turned around. "To visit the club?"

"To see Lady Cameron." The chit blushed. "I'm not
supposed to tell you about her business, though."

Damnation. "I won't say a word," he promised. "Though
I do feel the need to ask Lady Cameron a question. Where
might I find her?"

"Her office. But—"

Before he could pull open the side door leading to the
interior of Adam House, Cameron himself shoved it open
from the other side. "Haybury," the earl said, starting. "Just
the fellow I was looking for."

Under any other circumstances Oliver wouldn't even

have bothered to acknowledge the man; most of what he knew about the Benchleys he'd learned from Diane, and that was more than enough for him. Cold, superior, grasping fools underestimating their own inadequacies and unhesitating about dragging others down with them.

"And why is that?"

"I've some questions I thought you might be more amenable to answering than Diane has proved to be."

Immediately Oliver swallowed the insult he'd been about to deliver. The fellow wanted information, and *he* wanted to know how much Cameron thought he knew. "I suppose you have something to offer to make me feel more amenable?"

The earl's cheek jumped. "You know I can't offer you money."

"I don't need money." What he did need, though, was something Cameron could use to bribe him with. *Hm.* How often did a man have the opportunity to designate his own flaws and weaknesses? "Your former sister-in-law is quite attractive, however," he ventured, then caught the earl's glance through the open door leading to the interior of the club. "Nearly as attractive as The Tantalus Club itself." *There.*

"You— I've already promised a partnership to Greaves and Larden."

"Then if you'll excuse me, I'm on my way to Tattersall's to meet Lord Manderlin."

"But—"

"Lady Cameron and I are . . . friends at the moment," Oliver interrupted, realizing now that that word was completely inadequate to describe his relationship with her. "If you expect me to chat about things I may or may not know, I expect you to provide something that will persuade me to do so. Good day."

"Ten percent ownership of The Tantalus Club."

Oliver slowed his exit. "Forty percent."

"The three of us agreed to an equal partnership. No one has forty percent."

Apparently Greaves and Larden were fairly confident this venture would succeed if they'd shaken hands on anything. "Equal, eh?" Oliver returned. "Very well. Twenty-five percent. As long as no one else knows." He smiled. "We can't have it getting about that I can't be trusted, can we?" He'd best get the information he wanted swiftly, because he was fairly certain he was going to vomit if he had to keep discussing any kind of betrayal of Diane's very hard-won trust.

"I— Very well, then. If I can convince Larden and His Grace to agree."

If Oliver had truly meant to follow through with this venture, that assurance wouldn't have been enough to convince him of anything. But the more quickly he could separate himself from this fool, the better. It wasn't only the mud that he could already feel rising around his ankles; it was what Diane would think if she saw him chatting with the Earl of Cameron. Being a hero was bloody complicated. "Care to join me at Tattersall's, then?"

"Well, I've an appointment of my own, but a morning in the company of such a well-respected judge of horseflesh is a rare treat." Lord Cameron nodded. "I would be honored."

"Let's go then, shall we?"

Cameron followed him outside, then made a show of noticing the hired hack waiting at the edge of the drive. "Damnation," he said, patting his pockets, "I've forgotten my purse. Lend a fellow a shilling, will you, Haybury?"

His estimation of Cameron and his character falling even further, Oliver took a coin from his pocket and flipped it at one of the grooms busily moving carriages and horses into and out of the drive. "Pay the hack, will you, Robson?"

The groom tugged at his forelock. "Yes, my lord."

That done, Oliver motioned Diane's former brother-in-law into his coach. He could almost swear that Cameron was twitching his fingers in imitation of the coin toss, practicing the move for his own later use. For the moment Oliver kept his steadily lowering opinion of the earl to himself, wishing he'd had the opportunity to speak with Diane before this little jaunt.

Now he needed to decide what he wanted to do about this conspiracy and, just as important, what Diane would want him to do about it. And the fact that he was more concerned over her well-being than his own convenience told him just how much he—and his life—had already altered.

"Are you looking to purchase an animal today?" Cameron asked, taking the front-facing seat.

"If I find one that appeals to me, I may," Oliver answered. In truth he had a very specific type of mount in mind, but now, unless Manderlin was indeed at the horse market and willing to make the purchase, he would have to wait for another opportunity.

"I have to say, I thought Diane had you wrapped around her finger, especially after that disagreement with Larden last night. Greaves warned me to stay away from you, said you'd want nothing to do with me."

"But you thought otherwise."

"I see things. Something's keeping you here, and it's not Diane's money. I reckon it's either *your* money or a bit of lifted skirt from the owner and her chits."

"Not to disagree, but a bit of lifted skirt has never compelled me to do anything." No, his heart seemed to be dictating matters currently.

"Greaves said you were playing deep at something. He thinks—"

"I don't actually give a damn about Greaves's cranial

endeavors, Cameron. I'm talking with *you*. And at the moment you're boring me."

"You don't care to speak about Greaves, then," Cameron pursued. "Why not?"

"No particular reason, other than the conversation's utter frivolity. I don't wish to speak about mutton, the stench of the Thames at low tide, or shoes, either. Or Cornwall, now that I think about it."

The earl chuckled. "Very well." He ran a finger along the seam of the carriage seat, no doubt assessing the quality of the workmanship. "So what can you tell me about Diane? Where did all that blunt come from?"

As if he would say anything that could hurt her. "First tell me what you were planning, before you recruited me into your little embroidery circle."

"Why?"

"Because I'm curious, know a great many things, and have an obscene amount of money at my disposal. If the pretty chit has secrets from me . . . well, I'd like to know about them."

"Five years ago I wouldn't have thought she was intelligent enough to have any secrets, the mousy little thing." Cameron shook himself. "My brother promised me Adam House for my London residence. You can imagine my surprise when I read in the newspaper that Lady Cameron was in London, and then when I heard that she was opening a gentlemen's club at my home. I spoke with her, then had my solicitor contact her man. We looked through all the paperwork she brought back with her from Vienna. It seems that Frederick signed Adam House over for her exclusive use shortly before his death."

"I know all this. It actually seems like the one decent thing your brother ever did for his wife," Oliver commented.

"I said that it *appeared* Frederick had signed over the property. Given the money Diane has been spending since her return to London, and the way she suddenly acquired property that has been in the Benchley family for generations, I have my doubts about the legitimacy of this entire enterprise."

"Do you, now."

"I believe she forged Frederick's signature. And I think the Old Bailey will be very interested in hearing a disagreement between the Earl of Cameron and a widow who mysteriously acquired a fortune to use for entertaining men and ruining my—and my family's—good name."

Oliver took a slow breath, anger beginning to simmer to life beneath his considerable annoyance. "Did you mention these . . . suspicions of yours to Lady Cameron?"

"Of course I did."

"And what was her response?"

"She ordered me out of the house. And I think that French chit of hers had a pistol. That's when I came to find you. She's become far too high in the instep, and with your help I can demonstrate to her the peril of deceiving her betters. You know the way of the world. A silly chit with grandiose ideas and no ability to see them through will only bring ruin down on herself. We, however, will be Corinthians. And I'll have what should have been mine all along."

So Diane had thrown him out. That made Oliver's path somewhat clearer. As a gambler, however, he liked to know all the cards the other player was holding, or thought he was holding, before he proceeded. "You're determined to take the matter to court, then? To take over ownership of a club with two—or three, rather—partners in tow? That's doesn't sound terribly ideal to me."

Cameron frowned. "What do you mean?"

"I happen to know something of Greaves's character.

And Larden's, for that matter. And I would imagine that their idea of an equal partnership varies somewhat from yours." He took a breath, hoping Diane wouldn't shoot him again for what he was about to do. But in a public setting, a public trial, she had a fair chance of losing. And that would devastate her. "You are the least among us, after all. To be blunt, of course."

The earl's face lost most of its color. "Adam House and, by extension, The Tantalus Club are mine."

"Lovely words, Cameron, but perhaps you need to consider what it is you truly want. A quarter interest in a club where within a month of ownership you'd have no say and likely the majority of the work to do, or something more . . . tangible?"

"More tangible? You mean Diane? I don't bloody want her. Aside from the fact that she was married to my brother, I detest the chit."

Good God. For a man determined to engage in a conspiracy, Cameron hadn't any clue at all. If Oliver needed to lead him by the nose in order to be rid of him, however, then so be it. "I was actually thinking that Diane's doing most of the work. Why should you want that to change?"

"I can hardly be expected to make my way about Mayfair penniless while the woman who still carries my family's name and title flaunts both of them while acting like a bawdy-house madam. I want what's mine. No more, and no less."

"Interesting." Oliver leaned over to the door and banged on the outside of the frame. "Audley, drive us through Hyde Park," he ordered, and sat back again. "Now we come to the crux of the matter."

Cameron smiled cynically. "I still fail to see what you mean to gain from all this."

Mentally sending up a prayer both that Diane wouldn't object to this degree of interference and that his past misdeeds weren't waiting for just such a moment to step in and drag him back into the mud, Oliver inclined his head. "Let's suffice it to say that Diane is a bit high in the instep for my taste. So, considering that she will want to avoid a public dispute and you want to avoid being entangled with men who are more interested in their own pockets than yours, how do you propose . . . settling the problem of your empty purse?" For God's sake, the fool had best take the bait. Otherwise Oliver would have to consider murder.

For a long moment the earl gazed through the coach's window. "I think in exchange for my keeping my suspicions out of court and allowing her to continue as hostess of what should be my club, three thousand pounds a month would be acceptable. Do you like the residence above The Tantalus Club? I heard there were two apartments up there."

Tattersall's nearly abutted Hyde Park, and Oliver glanced out the window as the coach rolled onto the path that paralleled the Serpentine River. "I'm renting both residences," he said, looking back at Cameron and altering his plans once more. The fool was cooperating; as much as he deserved to be booted out of the coach and into the river, that would likely dampen Cameron's enthusiasm for the more subtle course of blackmail. And blackmail would give Diane time and privacy in the way a legal hearing never could. "And yes, they're quite spacious."

"That's unfortunate. Perhaps we could make an arrangement, just between us, so that I could have the use of one of the residences. Diane and I are related, after all, even if it is only by marr—"

"One issue at a time, Cameron." He rapped on the door again. "On to Tattersall's, Audley."

"Yes, my lord."

"Why did we detour through the park?" the earl asked.

Because I was about to dispose of you. "I was making a decision about something," Oliver said aloud. "I'll assist you, if it will teach Diane some humility where certain other things are concerned."

"Excellent." Cameron grinned; then his face folded into another frown. "You wouldn't happen to have any idea how I might end a certain other partnership, do you?"

Oliver lit a cheroot on a coach lamp. "I have an idea or two."

"You're certain?" Diane asked, attempting to keep her voice level.

Grace nodded emphatically. "They drove off together, my lady. In Lord Haybury's coach. He invited Lord Cameron to go to Tattersall's with him. It's been three hours ago now."

"I told you he couldn't be trusted," Jenny hissed from beside her, then swore in German. "The two of them together? Do you have any idea how much damage they could d—"

"I'm aware," she snapped.

Damnation. Oliver might dislike personal entanglements, but she couldn't believe he would actively betray her confidence. And not just because she still held a letter that could discredit him at every wagering club in England. He was not that kind of man. Irreverent, cynical, underhanded, jaded, yes—but not . . . dishonest or dishonorable. Not to her.

"What are we going to do, Diane?"

"I need to think. If Haybury should return, inform me at once. I'll be in my office." She turned on her heel and left the foyer.

How in the world could she have neglected to seriously consider the new Lord Cameron? She'd factored in everything else. And however much she wanted to forget four years of cold disappointment, Anthony was not Frederick. Anthony understood his own shortcomings, and he was intelligent enough to look for a way to compensate for them. Which he apparently meant to do by trying to take her club away from her.

Perhaps she should have let him finish telling her what he wanted, but just the idea of that . . . man waltzing in to upset her apple cart made her want to be ill. And now that man was in the company of the one man she no longer viewed with disdain. Or she had ceased doing so, until ten minutes ago.

Why would Oliver want Anthony anywhere near him unless he had something nefarious in mind? The two men couldn't have been more different in temperament and character—or so she'd thought. One was a snake and the other one a . . . a lion, magnificent and regal, lazing about in the sun until something caught his attention. And then he was swift and deadly.

Unless she'd completely misread him again. After all, two years ago the last thing she'd expected him to do was vanish just when . . . just when . . .

"My lord, you are not permitted into Adam House!" Grace's high-pitched voice came.

"I need to speak with Lady Cam—" Oliver stopped, Grace and Jenny both on his heels, as he entered the hallway and caught sight of her. "I need to speak with you, Diane," he resumed. "Now."

"So I heard." For once she could read the expression on his face. He was angry, and worried. Swallowing back the remainder of her curt reply, she nodded. "My office. In private, Jenny."

Scowling as well, Genevieve inclined her head and

turned back toward the foyer with the butleress. No doubt she would find herself in the morning room pressed against the door, but for all Diane knew, she would require Jenny's assistance.

Oliver glanced over his shoulder before he continued down the hallway. "Some day you'll have to tell me precisely where you found that chit," he commented.

"If you don't have a very good explanation as to what you've been doing in Anthony Benchley's company, this will be the last conversation we ever have."

Diane entered her office, striding to the window as Oliver slammed and locked the door behind them. When she turned around he was eyeing her closely. Then he walked over to the door adjoining the morning room and locked it as well.

"We have a problem," he said, sinking one hip down on the edge of her desk.

"Yes, *we* do," she returned. "You know he's been threatening my club, so what the devil were you—"

"He came looking for me," Oliver interrupted. "And stop lecturing. I'm not going to tell you again that I am not one of your employees. Nor am I about to do anything to betray your trust."

Diane took a breath. If she needed proof that Oliver had changed over the past two years, it was that statement— and the fact that he'd uttered it in such a straightforward way. "Anthony said he thought you might be more amenable to answering some of his questions about me and The Tantalus Club. Were you?"

"Hm. Firstly, what precisely did he want from you?"

"He was pushing to convince me to admit that I don't have the proper title to Adam House, and that you were more involved than either of us admits."

His shoulders rose and fell with the deep breath he took. "Thank you for answering me. I know you don't wish a partner, but I'm attempting to at the least be a friend."

She tilted her head at him. "Would you still be a friend if I didn't have a certain letter hidden away?"

From his expression, her question had surprised him. As though he hadn't been thinking about the letter. "Not when you first arrived in London," he said after a moment. "It's taken a bit for me to realize that you're not the only one who's changed."

He had changed. She could simply no longer ignore that fact. Finally, realizing she'd been gazing at him rather intently, she shook herself. "That's enough about trust. You've been gone for three hours. You must have had quite a conversation with Anthony."

"He came within a heartbeat of being booted into the Serpentine on his head. I even had my driver detour us through the park for that very purpose."

"What changed your mind?"

Oliver looked down at his hands. "I hope you aren't armed," he muttered. "I had to do some quick thinking."

"Go on."

"He strongly suggested that you forged your husband's signature, and that Adam House is still his. And he stated that he looked forward to having the courts decide between an earl and a woman . . ." He paused, frowning. "These are his words, not mine."

"Go on. I'm far past being insulted by anything these frivolous people have to say about me."

"Very well. He's willing to let the courts decide between an earl and a bawdy-house madam. When he ultimately takes ownership of the club, he and Greaves and Larden are to be partners. Me, as well. I negotiated up from ten percent to a full quarter share."

Diane stared at him, feeling like her reality had just

fled out the window. The inside of her chest abruptly felt cold and hollow. "How . . . how could y—"

"No, no, no. I didn't. Let me finish."

"Oh, this tale had best have a very good ending."

"I don't know how good it is, but I think it's more workable than a legal fight."

"Workable? Like a game of cards? I—"

"Let me finish, damn it all."

Dread deeper than the worry already filling her pulled at her heart, but she crossed her arms over her chest. "Fine. Just speak quickly."

"I'm attempting to. Believe me. After we'd settled on my share, I pointed out that he was the least among us, and that before long he'd end up doing all the work while the other three of us reaped all the rewards that owning a prestigious club would bring."

He paused, as though waiting for her to interrupt, but despite her personal and keen interest in the outcome, she found herself fascinated by the conversation. His mind was a rather terrifying place.

"No? Then I'll continue. We sought about for several minutes until he finally took the bait and hit on the solution. Blackmail. Of you. Your former brother-in-law means to ask you for three thousand pounds a month in exchange for his refraining from any legal action."

Diane stared at him. Very few things in the world truly surprised her any longer, but this certainly had. "So you decided that my paying him an exorbitant fee every month was the solution to this little tangle? And why three thousand? Why not one hundred thousand? I can afford neither."

He leaned down, grabbing her clenched fists in his hands. "You misunderstand. That man knew you married Frederick because of an arrangement. He knew, clearly, that his brother had no skill at wagering and that the fool was dragging you into poverty. And he still had the gall to insult you for surviving, and then to claim a right to grab onto your purse strings—while he insulted you the entire time. So I gave him rope. Now we need to hang him."

"If this is a battle of morality, you seduced a widow a week after her husband's death and abandoned her a fortnight later."

Oliver closed his eyes for just a moment. "I expected a pleasant romp between the sheets," he bit out, "not an encounter that would set me back on my heels and cause me to question the entire way I'd planned on living my life. Now may we return to today's dilemma?"

Diane realized her fingernails were digging into her palms, and she flexed the hands he still held in his. Had he been as shaken by their first meeting as she had been? It made sense, but she'd simply never quite looked at it that way before. She took a shallow breath against the spinning of her thoughts. "Very well. I . . . understand your leading him away from any legal proceedings, but I do not have three thousand pounds per month to spare even if I was inclined to pay him. Which I am not."

His face quirked in a dark half smile. "Well," he said slowly, "there is still my original plan. I doubt anyone would miss a minor earl if he should happen to vanish."

Good heavens. "You're suggesting that I kill him, then?"

"No, I'm suggesting that *I* kill him."

"Even if it were something I was willing to consider, you don't owe me that much, Oliver."

He loosened his grip, shifting to run a finger lightly across the back of her hand. "It's not about what I owe you, Diane. It's about what you're worth to me now."

Oh, my. "That's very nice, Oliver, but—"

"But it doesn't solve our problem. I know."

Just when Anthony had gone from being her problem to one she and Oliver shared, she had no idea. And pride, independence, and oaths to the contrary, she was actually pleased to have an ally in this. To have *him* in this with her. She'd felt alone for so long, even with Jenny in whom to confide. "What is your idea, then?" Diane asked. "Other than killing him. Not that I object on principle, but I am attempting to live the life I want. And that doesn't include murder. So far."

Oliver gazed out her window for a long minute before his gray eyes met hers again. "Neither of us has the best of reputations; taking the high road, as it were, doesn't seem a likely option." Oliver moved to sit in the chair beside hers. "Regardless of anything else, I never meant that you would be expected to pay that rat anything. You needn't worry about that."

"I don't even like the idea of him thinking I've given in to his demands," she returned. "I mean, yes, legally Adam House should have been his. But I deserved something out of that wreck of a marriage. And I took it. I'm not giving it back."

"I don't expect you to. Just think a moment, and tell me what it is you want, Diane," he said quietly.

She had the distinct feeling that he was inquiring about more than the situation with Anthony. One peril at a time, however. "I want Anthony Benchley and his threats to go away and leave me be forevermore." She sighed. "You know, until he began threatening me and what I've done here, I didn't dislike him. Until Frederick died and left me with less than nothing, he never overly troubled me, either. They were both just . . . there."

"Like a dog is there?"

"No. Like a plant is there. You keep it pruned, you water it, and perhaps it provides you with a bit of shade now and then. But it doesn't provide any sustenance, and no affection."

Silence. Then Oliver half-stood and dragged her chair closer to kiss her. Sinking down to kneel in front of her, he pulled her face down, touching his mouth to hers in gentle kisses that made her ache inside. Diane ran her fingers into his hair, pressing him harder, closer against her. She didn't want delicate or gentle. Not now. She wanted real and solid and arousing.

Finally he sank back onto his haunches. "I can say with some authority," he murmured, running a finger down her cheek, "that *you,* my dear, are *not* a plant. Not by any stretch of my imagination."

Her mouth quirked in a smile. "Likewise. But I still won't agree to killing Anthony."

Giving a deep sigh, he returned to his chair. "Fine. If you insist. I do hope you won't object to something devious."

"Oh, I prefer devious." Diane cleared her throat. "And I assume you have something in mind."

"As a matter of fact, I do. But I won't—can't—proceed without your permission."

"Then perhaps you would join Jenny and myself for dinner at Adam House tonight and we could discuss strategy."

He inclined his head. "Certainly. But may I ask why you want Miss Martine present? I know you're not worried about being alone with me."

Actually, this new aspect of him, this man who encouraged and supported her, upended her more than the one who'd only wanted her body. "Jenny will have a unique perspective to offer," she said aloud. "And I trust her."

"Very well, then. At what time should I call?"

"Seven."

"I shall be there." Standing, he unlocked the morning

room door and pulled it open. "Miss Martine, I believe Lady Cameron wishes a word with you," he said, standing aside as Jenny slipped into the room. "And I shall see you at seven o'clock," he continued, glancing at Diane before he walked to the hallway door and let himself out of the office.

Despite the nonsense with Anthony Benchley, she found herself smiling. Whatever the outcome of this, it would affect not just The Tantalus Club but also her heart.

A few weeks ago Oliver would never have believed that Anthony Benchley would be the catalyst that gave him the opportunity finally to prove himself to Diane. Previously he'd thought Frederick expiring had been the best thing a Benchley would ever do for him. And yet it was because of the latest Lord Cameron that he stood in the drawing room of Adam House as an ally. Hell, he hadn't even had to break in to get there.

He'd been through the house's doors a handful of times previously, mostly when the premises had been under reconstruction. And of course he'd snuck in through the servants' entrance on several more occasions than even Diane likely knew about—and he'd searched thoroughly enough to know that the damned letter she held over him wasn't there.

Wandering over to the table beside the window, he poured himself a glass of whiskey from the well-stocked tantalus there. Lately he'd thought about that letter only rarely, and it concerned him even less. He wasn't inside Adam House because of blackmail—and he hadn't been for some time.

Through the window he could see the corner of the stable and a number of the carriages and horses awaiting the return of their masters. Perhaps it was too early to claim success, particularly with Cameron breathing down her neck, but Diane had managed something of a miracle. New gentlemen's clubs opened nearly every Season in London, and most of them didn't last the summer. But she'd created a haven where the wealthiest and most sophisticated gentlemen could go and gamble, and spend the evening eating fine food and being flattered by pretty, intelligent young women.

"What are you looking at?" Diane's voice came from the doorway.

Warmth spread through him, as though her presence brought him to life. "You've quite a crowd tonight, from the look of the stable yard."

"Our attendance keeps increasing. I hate to be overly optimistic, but it is encouraging."

He heard the hesitation at the end of her words. Interpreting what troubled her didn't take a soothsayer. The more successful The Tantalus Club was, the more determined Cameron would be to wrest it away from her, either wholesale through the courts or piece by piece through backmail. Oliver turned around—and stopped dead.

Instead of her usual sophisticated black, Diane wore a silk gown of deep, rich red. Red ribbons wound through her black hair, and red slippers peeked from beneath the lace hem of her skirt. He wanted to pull her into his arms and took a hard, deep breath to quell the impulse.

It didn't work, but it did give him a moment to recover himself. "I know that complimenting a woman on her attire is rather pedestrian," he commented, his gaze lingering for a long moment on her bosom before he lifted his gaze to her face again, "but you made my knees weak just then."

She smiled, the warmth in the expression touching her green eyes. "Tomorrow night is a ladies' night. I want the gentlemen in attendance tonight to remember to return on Wednesday."

Of course she hadn't worn it for him, but that certainly didn't stop him from appreciating it. "I don't think you'll have any trouble with that."

"Diane, dinner is served," the French twist said from the dining room doorway. With a glance at him, she retreated again. With the way Diane seemed to rely on her friend, clearly he had two women to win over now.

"After you, Diane," he said, leaning in to smell her lavender-scented hair as she passed him.

Platters of baked fish, potatoes, and a blood pudding lined the center of the table alongside a basket of bread and a large bowl of what smelled like pea soup. The footwomen who seated them immediately left the room and shut the doors behind them, so apparently the three of them were to serve themselves. *Good.* He didn't care to have anyone else overhear some of the things he wanted to discuss.

Deliberately he took the seat opposite Genevieve Martine, while Diane sat to his left at the head of the table. He approached nearly everything like a game to be won, assessing opponents and strategy with every breath. As he gazed at Diane spooning potatoes onto her plate, however, he knew this wasn't just another game—*she* wasn't just another game. He'd somehow found himself with a second chance to win her. This time he wasn't leaving the table until the game was over. Not until he'd won.

Realization hit him like a punch to the gut. Initially blackmailed into being there or not, he wanted Diane in his life. He wanted to be a part of her life. She was the one woman he'd ever met who didn't acquiesce to him, who wasn't afraid to stand toe-to-toe with him. And the changes he saw in her now made her even more attractive to him. These days he enjoyed her company as much out of bed as he had in bed two years ago. And it terrified and thrilled him all at the same time.

"Why are you staring at me?" the object of his affection and desire asked.

Thinking fast, he rolled his shoulders. "You said we couldn't kill Cameron," he returned. "How far are you willing to go?"

"The shorter answer would come from you asking me what I'm *not* willing to do."

He smiled. "That's what I hoped you'd say."

Chapter Eighteen

I think you need to be more specific," Oliver said, nudging the edge of her parasol so it would stop poking him in the head.

Diane stifled a grin. "About what?"

"What did you mean last night when you said, 'Jenny can convince him; she once fooled Bonaparte'?"

"I'm surprised you waited until this afternoon to ask me that." She was also surprised that she was enjoying the walk through St. James's Park in his company. It had seemed too mundane and domestic, and yet it was also something she'd never done with Frederick. He'd never asked her.

She had the sneaking suspicion that this was what was supposed to have happened five years ago—when she'd been eighteen and naïve and ready to fall in love. A simple walk in the park. Oliver had had to bargain her into it today because she'd ceased to believe in things such as romance, but in a sense the effort he'd gone through to get her here made the afternoon more . . . meaningful.

"I would have asked over the fish," he returned, "but I thought she might come across the table at me."

"She doesn't like you much. Of course, I don't, either."

He stopped, putting a hand on hers where it draped over

his arm. "At the risk of leaving my innards exposed to a jab in the heart, how *do* you feel about me? Not overall, of course; that's asking too much. But now, at this moment?" he asked quietly, his expression surprisingly serious.

Goodness. It *was* very unlike him to leave such a large part of himself so unguarded. She met his gaze, then looked away again, abruptly uncomfortable. "At this moment, I like you. Will that suffice?"

"Yes, quite well. And likewise, if I may say so. Now. Bonaparte. Miss Martine. Explain."

"I met Jenny when we were children. Her father was a diplomat serving in France, but her mother spent the summers here, at a cottage just across the valley from Fenhall, where I lived. She has an amazing grasp of languages, and even though she's always considered herself to be English, she's at least as fluent in French, German, Italian, Spanish, and I don't know what else."

"And Bonaparte?" he prompted.

"Five years ago, when she turned eighteen, she was approached by the foreign minister. And she spent the three years after that as . . . well, she spent them aiding England during the war."

He eyed Diane. "She was a spy, you mean."

"We don't generally tell anyone that. So don't tell anyone else."

A grin touched his mouth. "You do trust me a little, then."

"A little," she conceded, barely recognizing herself in the company of this man who had, after all, once broken her heart. Diane took a hard breath. "And she's very good with both pistols and knives. Don't forget that."

"I shan't."

They continued on their way. A barouche passed them, the trio of ladies inside staring openly at her, then looking away and whispering behind their hands. Considering that one of them had appeared at The Tantalus Club a fortnight ago and lost forty pounds at whist, aside from noting that they were hypocrites, Diane could not have cared less for their opinion.

"May I ask you a question?"

Even with her attention on the departing carriage, she could feel his gaze on her. It was the oddest thing; this was a simple walk, and on an afternoon when she should have been at The Tantalus Club making certain the temporary male staff were arriving and all positions were covered. And yet the sensation running through her was the same one she'd felt when he'd taken her up in the balloon—excited and electric and very aware of the handsome devil of a man standing beside her.

"What sort of question is this, if you need my permission to ask it?" she finally said.

"I'm attempting to be gentlemanly." Amusement touched his gray eyes.

"Just ask me, for heaven's sake."

"Very well. Have you seen your parents since you returned to England?"

Diane frowned. "What does that have to do with ridding myself of Anthony Benchley?"

"Nothing whatsoever. You left England nearly three years ago, when you were barely twenty. I'm curious." He paused. "My father died when I was twelve, and my mother seven years later. I say that to forestall any protests you may have about me sticking my nose into your personal affairs when I haven't told you anything of mine."

Simple, cordial conversation. With Oliver Warren. A few weeks ago, she never would have been able to even imagine it. Yet now it seemed . . . natural. Comfortable, even. "No, I haven't seen them. They have three other daughters and a son. I turned eighteen, married, and left home as I was supposed to. And that is that." Intentionally she bounced the parasol off the side of his head again. "It was a very efficient and proper household. They wouldn't approve of what I'm doing now, and I don't see the point of encouraging their interest or censure."

"Very logical of you."

"I'm not afraid of them, if that's what you're implying."

"I've never seen you afraid of anything, my fierce warrior queen."

"We are allies for the moment," she said, attempting to ignore the warm tingle of his words. "I am not yours. Or anyone's."

"Very well. *You* fierce warrior queen. Better?"

"Infinitely. Is your curiosity satisfied, then?"

"For the moment. I sup . . ." Oliver paused, then nodded and sent a grin at a passing acquaintance. "Appleton."

"Haybury." The fellow pulled up his bay gelding and tipped his hat at her. "You must be Lady Cameron. I keep waiting for Haybury to invite me to his new club, but I've barely seen him in the past month."

"I live above a gentlemen's club, James," Oliver returned. "Having found paradise, I'm reluctant to leave it."

Mr. Appleton grinned, nodding. "That I understand. I owe you a luncheon, however. The Society tomorrow?"

"The Tantalus Club, at two o'clock."

"That's good of you, Oliver. I'll see you there."

Diane watched the man ride off again. "I hope Mr. Appleton proves less troublesome than your other friends."

"Greaves and Larden are not my friends," he stated flatly. "Manderlin and Appleton are."

She reconsidered what she'd been about to say. "Greaves has applied for membership at the club."

"I'm not surprised. The Tantalus Club is becoming the place to be seen. I won't be voting in his favor, however."

He hadn't asked her to do the same. A small thing, perhaps, but she considered it significant. At the beginning he'd attempted to step into her business, but lately he'd seemed to realize how angry that made her. Either that or he approved of what she was doing. Not that she cared about that, but he had spent a great deal of his time in gentlemen's clubs. If an expert supported her efforts, well, naturally she would be pleased by that fact, she supposed.

Oliver glanced around them. "I was about to say that I can't imagine you simply returning to your parents' house and living off their good graces until you could marry again."

"Is that what I was supposed to do? It honestly never occurred to me to return home."

"Why would it? I've yet to see you retreat from anything." He cleared his throat. "I've another question for you."

"Aren't you the curious one today? Just remember that I may have some questions for *you,* and now I'll expect you to answer every one of them."

"Agreed."

"Then ask away."

"Before me, you had never been with any man but Frederick, had you?"

Her heart thudded a little harder. "No, I hadn't. You were the first time I realized that my 'wifely duty,' as my mother called it, could be so very pleasurable. Thank you for that, I suppose." Halfway across the park she caught sight of Lady Dashton in her barouche, two of the viscountess's Ladies of Moderation with her. Diane sighed.

She'd actually liked Lady Dashton on their first meeting, and she had the feeling that it was Lord Dashton's drinking rather than The Tantalus Club that had the viscountess squawking so loudly. The Ladies of Moderation were yet another problem she would have to save for another day, though it was beginning to seem that she would run out of days before she ran out of problems.

Oliver tugged at her arm. "What did y—"

"Oh, no, you don't," she cut in. It made her feel too vulnerable to have him asking so many questions of her. "It's my turn now. Why were you in Vienna two years ago? The truth, if you please."

"I never lied about it before; you just never asked me."

"I am now."

Oliver gazed across the park, though he didn't seem to be looking at anything in particular. "As you wish. Two years ago I annoyed my uncle one too many times and he cut me off. I had some blunt I could use to support myself through wagering, but after Greaves cheated me out of it I could no longer afford to live in London. Hence my holiday in Vienna. And hence my less than honest behavior at the table that night when I played against DuChamps." He glanced sideways at her. "Is that the one question you truly wanted to ask me?"

The other question took more courage. Still, she was apparently now a fierce warrior queen. What was a bit of painful reminiscing to a warrior? "You're certainly brave today," she said aloud. "You're actually encouraging me to bring that up?"

Stopping again, Oliver slipped his arm from beneath her hand and instead clasped her fingers in his. "Neither of us is ever likely to forget. I'm aiming a bit lower."

She snorted. "Forgiveness, I presume? This had best be a very good tale." The words didn't have quite the sting she intended. Apparently his recent good deeds and the very lovely afternoon were having a greater effect on her than she'd realized.

"Time to find out, I suppose." He took a breath. "When I arrived at Lady Darham's luncheon, I asked her who you were, sitting there in the corner by yourself and all dressed in black. She told me that you were English and your idiot of a husband had just died and left you penniless. You literally . . . stopped my heart, with that long black hair and your beautiful eyes. And I wanted you. I thought . . ." He stopped, keeping his gaze on her face. "I thought you would be easy to maneuver into bed."

"And I was. But that's the beginning of the tale. I asked you about the end."

"Diane, y—"

She pulled away from him. "I recognize that tone. Either tell me or tell me that you're not going to tell me. Don't attempt to change the subject."

Oliver caught her hand in his again. "Very well. But you're not fleeing after I speak."

From the hard grip of his fingers around hers, she doubted she would be able to manage it even if she wanted to. "I asked the question. I imagine I can manage hearing the answer."

"I left because I was seven-and-twenty, had no fortune, and was determined that I would not be some married, domesticated half-wit whose only escape was to leave home every night to go wagering with the few pennies I'd managed to scrape together."

"I never asked to be married to you."

"But I wanted to be married to you. I could scarcely think of anything else. And you were correct; it terrified me. It was the opposite of everything I thought I wanted for my life, and yes, I fled. I returned to London and went directly to my uncle and apologized for my ill advised behavior. Three weeks after he wrote me back into his will, he dropped dead in the middle of the House of Lords. His heart, the physician said. I've been attempting to forget you for two years, Diane."

She could feel herself breathing, but no air seemed to be reaching her lungs. Of all the things she'd expected to hear, that Oliver had liked her too much had never been one of them. His keen gaze studied her face intently, as though he was attempting to decipher what she was thinking. As she had no idea what to think, she wished him good luck with that.

"Well?" he finally prompted. "Aren't you going to hit or kick or shoot me or something?"

"You . . . you left because you were *too* fond of me?" she finally managed, her voice as unsteady as her thoughts. "And all this time I thought . . ."

"You thought what?"

She shook herself. "Oh, no. That is one conversation we are not having. Not now." Perhaps not ever.

"My dear, I deserve whatev—"

"I'd like to return to our discussion about Anthony," she interrupted. "You intend on baiting him into doing something stupid. Are you certain you can manage that?"

He was silent for a moment. "I excel at leading others astray," he finally said, though he would obviously rather be continuing that other discussion. "You know that. And never fear, we will do something dastardly to him. But if he hurts you—or attempts to hurt you, Diane—I will end him. And I won't compromise about that."

"When did you become so protective?"

He shrugged, finally loosening his grip on her fingers. "I don't know. But I assure you, I am perfectly serious."

She could see that he was. The steady gray eyes, the clenched jaw, even the way he stood between her and most of the other St. James's Park visitors. For a second she allowed herself to feel cared for and protected by a man who'd once very nearly wanted to marry her, to forget that Anthony Benchley was her problem and would be dealt with on *her* terms. Oliver had already agreed to that, so he knew the rules, but for a moment it was nice—in a warm, fluff-filled pastry sort of way—to pretend.

Then she pulled her hand free and shifted the parasol to her other shoulder. "Very gallant," she said aloud, "but unnecessary. Play your part as you agreed and I will be satisfied."

Oliver fell in beside her again. "Come to my bed tonight, and *I* will be satisfied."

"We are not negotiating something you already agreed to," Diane retorted, ignoring the thrill swirling down her spine. Whatever motivated him these days, it was still . . . pleasant to be desired.

"Then come because you choose to."

And *that* was a very tempting offer. After all, she'd made doing as she pleased something of a motto these days. He was still trouble. A great deal of trouble. But God help her, she was becoming quite fond of his sort of trouble. And knowing why he'd fled Vienna made more of a difference than she would ever have admitted to him.

His reasons didn't change the fact that he'd fled in a decidedly ungentlemanly manner, and she didn't wish to make any excuses for him over that. But she knew what he'd been like before, and she was beginning to believe that he truly had changed. For the better. "Perhaps," she said aloud. "But you are not to destroy my home if I don't appear."

With a wicked grin he took her hand again. Lifting it, he kissed her knuckles. "No promises."

Oliver wrote out three drafts of the letter he, Diane, and Miss Martine had decided would be necessary to lure Lord Cameron into their net. Finally satisfied that he'd conveyed what he needed to say in terms plain enough to be understood and subtle enough that it didn't look faux, he dusted the letter, blew it off, and folded it so he could write the address on the outside.

"Myles," he called, and his footman appeared from the direction of the front room.

"Yes, my lord?"

He slid the letter across his desk. "See that someone delivers this tonight."

The servant took the letter and headed out of the small office again. "Very good, my lord."

"And Myles, stop gawking out the front window. You'll frighten away Lady Cameron's guests."

"I've never seen so many well-dressed women in one place. It's all so . . . fluttery."

Oliver snorted, turning the page of the book he'd been attempting to read. "It reminds me of the first assembly at Almack's during the Season, except no one's wearing white."

"Might I look from behind the curtains, my lord?"

"Make certain the lamps are all out first. I don't want anyone thinking it's me spying through the window."

"Thank you, my lord."

"Yes, well, one of us might as well have some fun with chits this evening." Standing, he pulled on his dark blue coat. "I'm going out for a time. I'll see you in the morning."

Even if Diane did decide to call on him that night, it would be well after midnight. And while rumors that the two of them were lovers didn't trouble him in the least, both Appleton and Manderlin had lately been intimating that he was being pulled about by his cock. He had the strong suspicion that they were aiming a good eighteen inches or so too low, but he could do without hearing it, anyway.

With three hours to wait for an answer to his letter, he directed his driver to take him to the Society Club. Both the games and the company there bored him, and after less than an hour he moved on to White's. It wasn't much of an improvement. Forty minutes earlier than he'd intended he found himself at Boodle's. By then he had to admit that it wasn't the clubs. He was the problem, restless and uncomfortable in his own skin and scarcely able to contemplate anything other than returning to The Tantalus Club.

It wasn't even that the games were better there, though they were. Hell, he'd barely played for more than a quid in a fortnight. No, the games weren't the lure of The Tantalus Club. Not for him. Of course, a good portion of the club's members had joined because of the chits running the games and carrying the drinks and serving the meals. For him it was one chit—or rather, one challenging, sophisticated lady—who kept him returning, who made him want to be there every night even when he had obligations elsewhere, and even when men weren't invited.

Whatever the devil had happened to him, she'd done it. And not by waving a damning letter from someone whom, if need be, he could track down and squash like a bug. Two years ago she'd been an attractive, compelling, but very vulnerable woman. Now she was a remarkable one. And he couldn't imagine how dull and ordinary the days—and nights—would be without her. She claimed to make a point of never repeating her mistakes, but so did he. He'd let her get away once. He wouldn't do it again.

"Oliver. You're just in time to purchase me a brandy."

Stopping his stroll through Boodle's at the sound of Manderlin's voice, he returned to the small sitting room at the front of the club. "My timing is remarkable," he noted, gesturing for two snifters.

"It is," Jonathan agreed. "Though we're likely to expire before a footman actually appears. The fellow behind the bar served drinks to Shakespeare himself, and he's the youngest servant here tonight."

All of the clubs had been short-staffed this evening. Considering where those men were tonight and Oliver's own connection to The Tantalus Club, he wasn't about to complain. "I'm not in any hurry."

"Neither am I, actually." The earl drummed his fingers against the tabletop. "Are you attending Hereton's soiree tomorrow night?"

"I accepted the invitation, but I'm not entirely convinced I want to spend five hours avoiding Lydia Hereton."

"Perhaps if you'd avoided her last year she wouldn't be chasing you now."

Oliver eyed him. "As my friend you are supposed to commiserate with me—not remind me of my mistakes."

"I'd be more sympathetic if you hadn't avoided me at Tattersall's yesterday after you specifically asked me to be there."

Damnation. "I unexpectedly decided to enjoy the company of Lord Cameron."

"Unexpectedly?"

"It's a long story, and at points I don't come out looking so well." He leaned his elbow on the table. "I couldn't even look at the damned horses. Any good prospects?"

"Several. If you actually purchase a mare broken to the sidesaddle, however, you know most people will realize it's not for you."

"If I want to purchase someone a horse, I don't see why I shouldn't do so. Especially if the someone is an old friend."

"You're not the one your peers will be looking at sideways—or turning their backs on—the first time she rides it."

Anger curled through him. "Has someone cut her?"

"Not directly. She's still a novelty. But she is willingly engaged in a rather scandalous venture. And with Lady Dashton organizing her stiff-spined cronies to hold teas and parties and book clubs to compete against Tantalus ladies' nights, it's only a matter of time, anyway."

"I dare anyone to do so where I can see them."

"Well, that's the other rub, isn't it? However scandalous

her . . . hobby, everyone's intimidated by you, so she's protected in your company. At the same time, no one will invite her anywhere for fear of either you verbally goring the other guests, or being associated too closely with scandal, or Lady Dashton cutting anyone seen to be friendly with her."

"As long as they all still want to visit The Tantalus, I don't think she cares how they view her. I, however, consider anyone who attends and then speaks against her to be a hypocrite and they, he, or she should be flogged."

"And talk like that will only encourage people not to invite *you* anywhere, either."

Oliver blew out his breath. Hypothetical conversations like this one only served to make him angry at people who hadn't actually done anything to hurt her. Not yet, anyway. And if she couldn't go out to be the ambassador for The Tantalus Club, then that task fell to him. "Hence the reason I'm talking only to you about this. No one pays attention to you."

"Oh, thank you very much. Now you owe me another brandy." Manderlin waved at the ancient footman.

Swiftly Oliver checked his pocket watch and sent a glance at the front door. Five minutes, unless the recipient of his letter arrived early—which he likely would. Oliver leaned forward. "I require your assistance, Jonathan," he said in a low voice.

"I'm not killing anyone with you."

"I find it interesting that that's the first thing that sprang to your mind, but there's no murder involved. Not yet, at any rate. In a few moments I'm going to tell you to go away. I need you to look troubled and uneasy and then get up and leave."

"Leave the room, or leave the club?"

He considered that for a moment. "The room. Leaving the club might be too suspicious."

Manderlin swirled his drink. "Are you up to something evil, or something benevolent?"

Hm. At least Jonathan thought him capable of benevolence. "Something the recipient deserves, and something that will hopefully aid a very dear friend." Except that Diane wasn't only a dear friend. The dictionary simply didn't hold enough words to describe her.

"Very well. And if I may say, this dear friend of yours seems to be having an unexpected effect on you. I can't say I disapprove."

"I'm still undecided myself."

"Then why aid her?"

He didn't want to consider his answer to that question too closely at the moment. "You know my fondness for mayhem," he said instead.

"That's a damned understatement."

A figure walked into the Boodle's sitting room, fingers twitching with either nerves or anticipated wealth. Oliver lifted his brandy. "And thus the play begins," he murmured, taking a drink of the amber-colored liquid.

Manderlin followed his gaze. "Cameron again?"

"Hush."

Anthony Benchley stopped in front of the table. "I'm here, Haybury. Though this is an odd place for a meeting."

Oliver sat forward. "Manderlin, go away. I have something to discuss with Lord Cameron."

A fair imitation of uneasy disapproval on his face, Jonathan stood. "Good evening, then," he said. With a backward glance over his shoulder he headed into the gaming room.

When Cameron remained looking about suspiciously, Oliver pushed out the opposite chair with his boot. "Sit."

"I've had a day to consider our discussion, and I'm not convinced that you don't have some plan to publicly disgrace me. You clearly dislike Greaves and Larden, and everyone knows you're fond of Diane—whatever you said to me about her."

Patience, Oliver reminded himself. "I thought I might need to clarify a few things. That's why I asked you to meet me here. Sit. Please."

Still eyeing him skeptically, the earl seated himself. "I've made an appointment for tomorrow to see my solicitors. I'm doing this for the express purpose of putting forward my claim to Adam House and The Tantalus Club."

"As I mentioned before, I wouldn't advise that."

"And *I* would advise that you continue providing me with advice and insight, or not only will you not be one of my partners, but I'll see to it that you're included right alongside Diane in any criminal proceedings."

"I *am* advising you, if you'd just listen for a moment. And I'm attempting to explain a rather convoluted set of circumstances," Oliver returned. "These circumstances require both of us to keep our voices down."

A footman arrived with Manderlin's second brandy, and Oliver nudged it toward Cameron. After yesterday he would have rather thrown it, snifter and all, into the man's face, but he'd decided to follow a more subtle path. That was the route he'd agreed on with Diane, and so he would proceed—however hard he had to grit his teeth to do so.

After a moment the earl cleared his throat. "I'm listening," he murmured, taking a too-large swallow of the drink. "And you'd best be very persuasive."

"Firstly, I assume Diane truly did inherit Adam House legally. At the least she's never said otherwise."

"I am not going to sit here simply to listen to her version of events, Haybury. That's what court will be for."

"If you don't shut up and listen, you'll never make it before a judge."

Finally Cameron's belligerent expression dropped. "What? If you think to murder me, I assure you that I already spoke with the Duke of Greaves about our partnership, and about my requiring a monthly stipend in exchange for allowing Diane to continue managing The Tantalus Club. Killing me will end with you being hanged for it."

"I'm not talking about me," Oliver retorted. Thus far Cameron had been more predictable than a clock. He only hoped that would continue. "I'm attempting to explain that you have no idea how much is involved in skimming blunt from this enterprise. Adding you to the equation—well, you've given us no choice, really, but it's going to complicate things even further."

"Adding me? You're stealing from Diane already?"

"No, I'm not. We—and there are two of us currently involved, and three when we include you—have simply . . . reorganized the way the money flows through the club. To our benefit." With a grimace he leaned over the table, with Cameron matching him on the other side. "You were correct in thinking that Diane had no money when she returned to London. And that we were . . . friends in Vienna, which is why she came to me initially. But together we knew several influential people willing to use their funds to produce additional funds."

"Which influential people?"

"I can't tell you that. I can tell you that Diane and I decided the income they were offering to us for our efforts here wasn't quite adequate. So we made a few alterations, and, well, let's just say that money is no longer a problem. But then you came along and threatened to bring the entire thing to the attention of the courts, and when I couldn't dissuade you, I decided you needed to be included."

Good God. What a cartful of shit, yet from Cameron's rapt expression he was swallowing every word of it. And so if this ploy stung Oliver's pride a little, then so be it.

The prize he intended to gain at the end of this play was more than worth his current discomfort.

"Then I will be receiving three thousand pounds each month. Because otherwise—"

"To begin with, we'll hand you two thousand pounds per month," Oliver broke in. This bit had been Diane's idea, and he thought it rather brilliant. "That's equal to Diane's and my portion. In three months, if no one's become suspicious, we'll add another thousand."

Cameron frowned. "The Tantalus Club is making enough money that it can afford to lose seven thousand pounds each month?"

"Money goes in, and money goes back out. We merely hold our hands beneath the spigot. Of course it's much more complicated than that, but you have the general idea. And you must swear to be absolutely discreet about it. There are people inside the club who can't have any idea what we're doing. If they did . . . well, public embarrassment would be welcome compared to what would happen to us all." He sent a glance around the room. "Do I have your word?"

"I want to be admitted to the club and see its inner workings for myself," the earl returned. "The Diane who married my brother wouldn't have dared to do something as audacious as opening a gentlemen's club. I find it difficult to believe that she's now stealing from her investors."

The Diane her brother-in-law once knew didn't exist any longer. Her husband, debt, and abandonment—both by Frederick and by himself, Oliver reflected—had made her stronger and more determined. And completely irresistible. Nothing could be allowed to harm her again, whether she ever chose to include him again in her life, in her heart, or not.

"Very well," he said aloud. "You don't leave me much choice."

A smile touched Anthony's face before he managed to banish it again. Oliver kept his own expression neutral, though he was rather tempted to smile himself. Greed, the lure of an unworked-for pound—he saw those faces seated across the gaming table from him every time he wagered. As for him, it was the game he loved. The money was secondary.

"No, I don't suppose I do. Make me a member of The Tantalus Club."

"I can't push that point without arousing suspicions," Oliver returned, unsurprised by the demand. "I'll put you forward, but with the base membership established, the process will take a few weeks."

"I am not—"

"Until then, you may attend as my guest. But for Lucifer's sake, be discreet."

"Don't worry about that, Haybury. Just keep your promise."

Oh, he would. Just not the one he'd made to Cameron.

Chapter Nineteen

Diane paced back and forth in the front room of Oliver's apartment. Going by the strictest of definitions, she shouldn't have been there without his express permission; after all, while she owned the house, she'd forced him to take up residence there, and to pay her rent for the privilege.

But for heaven's sake, she'd put the future of The Tantalus Club in his hands. A man who'd broken her heart and whom she'd sworn she would never trust again. A man whom she'd blackmailed into assisting her in the first place. What the devil was wrong with her that she trusted him now? Because there was no denying that fact, least of all to herself. She trusted him. Worse still, she liked him. A great deal more than she cared to admit.

His front door opened, and Oliver walked into his rooms. "Hello," he said, pausing as his gaze found her.

Just his damned voice made her pulse speed. "Hello."

He turned and hung his greatcoat and hat on the hooks by the door, then faced her again. "I actually thought I would be spending the night alone."

"You will be. I'm here because I want to know what happened with Anthony." If she fell into Oliver's embrace again, she would no longer be able to convince herself that this was merely a physically satisfying business arrangement. She wasn't prepared yet to give a name to the . . . connection that was developing between them.

He moved past her to sit in one of the pair of chairs set before the fire in the hearth. "He thinks he's found the proverbial golden goose. If we play our parts, he'll be finished by the end of the fortnight."

That seemed overly optimistic, especially coming from someone as cynical as Oliver. But she wanted to believe him. After a hesitation, Diane sat in the chair opposite him. "That sounds splendid, but I'll believe it when I see it. I need him dealt with before the end of the Season; once everyone leaves London he'll have far too much time to reconsider his legal options."

"Very pragmatic of you." Oliver sat forward, reaching out his hand as if he wanted to touch her, then slowly lowered it again. "Speaking of the end of the Season," he said after a moment, "I wondered if perhaps . . . that is, I would be glad to have you stay at Haybury. It's close by London if you should need to return to see to the club—if you decide to keep it open."

"You want me to live in your home?" she asked, not quite believing what she was hearing. "With you?"

"I'm living in your home as we speak."

"In separate quarters. With thick walls in between."

"As if that's stopped me." He tilted his head at her. "Haybury is five times the size of Adam House. You may have an entire wing to yourself, if you want it."

"What are you trying to do? Purchase my presence? Impress me with your wealth? When I knew you in Vienna, you had to cheat at cards to pay your rent. I'm more worried over your character."

"*My* character? You're the chit who opened a gentlemen's club. We've both caused raised eyebrows. I'd go so far as to say we're both a little wicked." Oliver shifted. "I don't think you're worried over what people will say. And I like being close to you. I like knowing I'll see you each day. And I'm fairly certain you enjoy my company as well."

Her thoughts spun in a thousand directions. His suggestion sounded naughty and romantic, and very appealing. If she agreed to it, then they would both know that she'd forgiven him. *He* would know that he'd won her trust. Perhaps he had done so, but she simply wasn't certain she was ready to announce that to him. Or that she was prepared to completely let go of the tangled knot of anger and determination that had kept her going for two years.

"What do you say to that?" he prompted.

Diane stood, moving closer to the fireplace so she could stare down into the flames. She did like Oliver, very much. If she didn't, she wouldn't have been there, and she wouldn't have been contemplating what she very much wanted to tell him. If she didn't say anything, though, the two of them would be stuck precisely where they were. And in her heart, she knew she wanted either more of him or none of him at all.

"When I was a young girl," she began, hearing him rise and move up behind her, "I thought that being promised to someone was terribly romantic. Even on my wedding day I was so excited I could barely contain myself."

"How well did you know Frederick before you married him?"

"Barely at all. I thought he was shy and sensitive, and even knowing the Benchleys didn't have a great deal of money, I was certain I was embarking on a fairy tale." She took a breath. "Frederick wasn't evil. He never struck me; he never had an affair; he barely spoke a cross word until we were literally penniless. I just . . . I wasn't important to him. He wanted to be one of the suave, charming, wealthy aristocrats he saw at his clubs. He wanted to be you, I suppose."

"Diane, you don't have to—"

"Stop interrupting me. I'm nearly at my point."

"I thought you'd have one."

"Aggravating man." She mentally shook herself. "By the time Frederick sickened and died, I'd had nearly four years to consider how ridiculous I'd been. That's when I finally acknowledged what I'd slowly begun to realize: there was no such thing as love and true, deep passion. And then I met you, and I thought perhaps that stupidly naïve little girl had been correct, after all." She turned around, looking up to meet his serious gaze. "Until you left, of course."

For a long moment he simply looked into her eyes. "What can I do?" he finally murmured.

"You can't do anything." Moving around him, she headed for his front door. The very last thing she wanted to do was begin crying in front of him.

"Diane. What I did to you is the greatest regret of my life. But by God, I would have made you an awful husband back then."

One hand on the door handle, she faced him again. "I know that. And I am treading upon every instinct I possess by trusting you now." She retreated into the hallway. "I will see you tomorrow. And you will not take an axe to any part of my house tonight."

"I'll be thinking about it, though."

"Good."

When she returned to her own part of the house she intentionally removed her shoes, slipping past Jenny's door to avoid waking her. There were only so many times Diane could be reminded that she might well be making the largest mistake of her life, particularly when she'd already made far more than her share of them.

Why Oliver pulled at her soul even more strongly now, after he'd broken her heart and then returned to London to apparently take up with every woman he could manage, made no sense. Her logical mind certainly knew better than to let him close, yet her heart no longer listened.

That was the reason aside from Anthony that she needed this mess to be resolved quickly. With her club doing so well and her untouchable status well known, the logical, reasonable solution to her confusion was to distance herself from Oliver. Yes, she would still owe him money, but he didn't need to live beneath the club's roof in order for her to repay him. And the farther away he was, the less torn she would be about what she wanted and what she should never want again.

Wednesday morning meant her usual staff meeting; with Parliament in early session, Wednesday breakfast was the slowest part of the entire week for The Tantalus Club. The ladies informed her of the usual odd goings-on and reported any gentlemen who were gambling too desperately, drinking too much, or otherwise not behaving themselves.

"Emily has been entertaining a gentleman in her room," Pansy Bridger said in the middle of another of their ongoing conversations about how to deflect unwanted advances.

Diane and Jenny glanced at each other. "As long as there is no money changing hands and any gentlemen are there at the lady's request, you may all do as you will. We are not a bawdy house, but we are not a nunnery, either."

"Thank goodness for that," one of the other girls said feelingly.

"Some discretion is appreciated," Diane added, noting that not all of her staff were amused. But then as far as she knew, at least one of them *had* fled a nunnery. "And for heaven's sake, be respectful of those who may not feel the same way."

As the meeting ended, Sylvie Hartford approached. A petite blond girl who looked barely eighteen followed close behind her. "My lady," Sylvie said, "this is Mary Smythe. We met at finishing school. I told her you might have a place for her here."

With a slight frown, Diane took the roulette dealer's arm. "Sylvie, we don't actually need any—"

"Please, my lady," Sylvie whispered. "Her parents are dead, and now that she's of age her aunt turned her out. She has no experience, and no letters she can present to claim a governess position. If she can't work here, she'll end up on the street."

Diane looked over at the petite, frightened thing. Whether The Tantalus Club had begun as her bid for independence or not, it was so much more than that now. If Anthony Benchley took over the club he would have the girls . . . God knew what he'd have them doing, but they certainly wouldn't be bringing by friends in desperate need of shelter.

Whatever Oliver chose to call it in jest, fighting for the club wasn't a game. Someone needed to look after these ladies. And that someone was her. "Take her to see Emily and find her a bed. Jenny will speak with her after luncheon and we'll figure out where to put her."

Bobbing in a curtsy, Sylvie grinned. "Oh, thank you, my lady." She hurried over to whisper to her friend.

"Thank you, my lady," Mary Smythe echoed, tears running down her cheeks. "Thank you so much. You have no idea."

"Thank you for joining us," Diane said, and with a smile went to find Jenny at the other end of the room.

"I thought we weren't a charity," Genevieve muttered, her eyes dancing.

"We're a very odd kind of charity."

"An odder kind of family, I think." Jenny handed over a cup of tea. "Have you spoken with Haybury?"

"Yes. He said Anthony seems to believe our tale and they would be by sometime today."

"We should do this without the marquis. You couldn't trust him before, and neither of us trusts him now."

"I trust him in this," Diane returned, surprised that she could say the words aloud in a steady voice. "He'll see this through. And his assistance will make things much easier."

"Unless you're wrong about him."

"I'm not." If she was wrong about him, she would lose much more than The Tantalus Club.

It wasn't that unusual for Oliver to see the dawn; the quiet hours surrounding sunrise frequently made the best time to leave a woman's bedchamber or a flagging all-night card game. Much less usual were the times he simply sat and watched the night leave.

Rolling his stiff shoulders, he sat up straighter and nudged the half-empty glass of whiskey away from himself. The lamp at the corner of his desk had sputtered and gone out an hour or so previously, but he'd barely noted it.

He was supposed to be attending the House of Lords with all his fellows in two or so hours. It would be dull, almost intolerable, because he would be counting the minutes until they adjourned for the day at luncheon.

Before he'd become the Marquis of Haybury two years earlier, he'd been aware of Parliament's schedule because it dictated when soirees would be held and when husbands would be away from home. Oddly enough, once he'd inherited he'd actually enjoyed Parliament and the game of politics.

Today, however, it was at best a distraction and at worst an impediment. He needed to meet with Cameron, and he couldn't do it while the House was in session. He'd already scrawled out a note to be delivered to James Appleton's residence, asking to reschedule their luncheon for tomorrow. A second letter to one of his own solicitors followed. Cameron might be set on taking money from Diane, but every cent she'd earned and borrowed was tied into the club. If payments needed to be made, Oliver would be seeing to it. And that had nothing to do with any blackmail or loan agreement. Cameron had no right, and he needed to be stopped.

But all of it, even the business with Cameron, wasn't what occupied his thoughts. That honor went to Diane and what she'd told him last night.

Two years ago she'd been in love with him—or near enough to it that he'd been able to break her heart. He knew she'd been hurt and angry, but at the time it had been more important that he couldn't breathe, that looking at her had meant looking at a wife, children, domesticity. He'd panicked, and he'd fled.

He'd wanted a more unconventional life than that. In all his imaginings, he would never have thought that two years later he would encounter her again and that she would be even more unconventional than he was. Perhaps that was why the idea of keeping her in his life no longer terrified him, or perhaps he'd realized that no one he'd met before or since could match her—or the way he felt about her.

His footman, Myles, walked into the office, a quartet of clean glasses in his hands. When he turned toward the desk, he jumped. "Oh, I beg your pardon, my lord. Your bedchamber was unused, and I thought you'd spent the night elsewhere."

It wouldn't be the first time he'd done that. Far from it. "I'll be going out shortly. I'd appreciate a cup of tea and some eggs, if you can manage it."

"Of course, my lord." The footman set the glasses down on the liquor tray, then hurried from the room.

Taking a deep breath, Oliver rose to go and change clothes. He had time to go downstairs for breakfast, but at the moment his thoughts were still too raw and he didn't want to encounter Diane when his armor was falling apart.

"Hubert," he asked as his valet finished knotting his cravat, "do you like it here?"

"In your employment, my lord? You're a generous master and rarely yell. Of course I like my employment."

"Thank you, but I actually meant living here. At Adam House. There are a great many chits."

"Yes, there are, my lord. It's certainly unusual, but also quite . . . nice, actually. Myles and I share a room, I'm welcomed in the kitchen and the common room, and several of the ladies, well, they're quite friendly."

Oh, good God. "That's good to know."

"If I may be so bold, my lord, do you like it here?"

"Yes. I think I do."

Two minutes after he took his seat in the House of Lords, he spotted Lord Cameron arriving, and then Oliver spent the next five hours running through his mind the various ways someone like him could possibly prove himself to someone like Diane. He alternated that with berating himself for acting like a henpecked husband around her.

"I forgot to ask," Manderlin muttered from beside him. "Am I still uneasy in your company?"

"Why should we alter things now?"

"Very funny. What the devil are you playing at with Cameron?"

"It's complicated. I wouldn't make friends with him if I were you, however."

"I wouldn't anyway. The man puts me in mind of a leech, waiting about in the mud to attach himself to someone and bleed them dry."

Oliver knew there was a reason he considered Jonathan a friend. He grinned. "You may be more astute than I give you credit for. Suffice it to say that Cameron is after something that doesn't belong to him and I mean to prevent him from succeeding."

"The Tantalus Club, I presume?" Manderlin glanced in the earl's direction. "Just keep in mind that he's been known to travel in lofty company."

"I'm not concerned about Greaves or Larden."

"I hope you remember who *your* friends are. Let me know if you need my assistance for anything other than looking frightened."

"I'll keep that in mind. And thank you."

The moment the session adjourned, Cameron appeared beside him. "I've been thinking," the earl said chummily. "Whatever your scheme is, I want proof that you aren't overstating things simply to put me off. I want my first two thousand pounds today."

"Today? That's—"

"I have to insist. See to it, Haybury, or I'll be contacting my solicitors."

If Cameron had been a fish, he would already be choking on the worm and hook. "Very well. Care to accompany me to The Tantalus for luncheon? I'll arrange it while I'm there."

"Excellent."

Inside the crowded Demeter Room, Sophia White showed them directly to one of the tables reserved for the club's founding members. As he took his seat, Cameron looked more puffed up than a peacock. For the moment, Oliver took that as a good sign; if the earl had any inkling of what lay in store for him, he wouldn't have been nearly as pleased with himself—or anyone else.

A few minutes after they ordered their luncheon, Diane strolled into the room. Oliver pretended to be occupied with taking a drink of Madeira, but in reality all of his attention was on her. The tilt of her head as she greeted other club members, her smile as one of her chits approached to tell her something. Desire stirred through him, hot and heady. He would be allowed to get that close to her again, because he couldn't imagine not doing so.

Finally she appeared to notice them and strolled over. "Lord Haybury, Anthony," she said.

"Don't frown at me, Diane," Cameron returned, "simply because I've deciphered your little game."

"Yes, Lord Haybury told me that he decided to include you. Don't expect me to like your being here, however."

"Like me or not. I don't give a damn. Today I want two thousand pounds. In cash. I have several debts to pay."

Diane glanced at Oliver. "Surely Haybury told you the process is more complicated than simply handing over a purse."

"I did tell him, but he's very insistent."

The French twist walked by, sending Oliver an unfriendly glance as she crossed the room. "Diane, I need to speak with you when you're finished here," she said.

"Of course, Genevieve." Diane blew out her breath. "I can get you one thousand pounds today," she continued in a low voice, facing Cameron once more.

"No. Two thousand."

Oliver leaned toward her. "The next . . . You'll be short for a few days, but I certainly don't want any solicitors hanging about, for all our sakes."

"Oh, very well. Wait here."

"The next what?" Cameron queried, pouncing as soon as Diane left.

"I don't know what you're talking about."

"Come now, Haybury. This is the first day of our partnership. It's certainly not the time to begin keeping secrets."

It *did* seem like a very good time to punch Cameron in the jaw. Oliver closed his eyes for a heartbeat. This was for Diane. There was no other reason he would tolerate having such a self-concerned leech in his presence. "The funds from the . . . investors arrive at irregular intervals. It's been over a fortnight, so the next allotment should be here soon."

"Then it'll be time for you to give me another two thousand pounds."

"Not immediately. This requires some subtlety, you know, unless you'd care to end up at Newgate with us."

The color left Cameron's cheeks, and for a moment Oliver thought he'd pushed too hard. Vague worries were one thing; threat of prison was another. He motioned at one of the chits for a bottle of wine.

"It's a fair trade, don't you think?" he went on. "A bit of subtlety in exchange for two thousand quid a month?"

The earl poured himself a full glass of wine. After he'd finished off half of it, his color began to return. "If I'm risking prison, I want more reward."

"I told you, if no one notices anything odd, by the end of the year you'll be up to three thousand a month. After that, who knows?"

"It all sounds delightful, but I haven't seen a penny yet."

At that very opportune moment Diane walked back into the room, a book in her hands. "Here you are, Anthony," she said, handing over the tome. "*Robinson Crusoe.*

You said it was Frederick's favorite, and I wanted you to have it."

"I don't want—"

"Open it," Oliver murmured.

"Oh. Oh. Well done, then." He opened the cover, and his eyes actually widened before he slammed it closed again. "What do we do now?"

"We enjoy our luncheon, and then we part company for a few days."

"No. I want to be seen wagering here. And I want everyone to see that I'm welcome at The Tantalus Club."

Oliver sent a look at Diane, who lifted an eyebrow at him. "Diane," he said, "I'd like to sponsor Lord Cameron for membership. Until that decision is made, he'll be my guest here."

"Very well. But you must follow the rules, Anthony."

"Yes, I know, I know. Subtlety. I am the soul of subtlety and discretion, I assure you."

After quite possibly the longest luncheon of his life, Oliver walked Cameron outside, lent the earl his carriage for the ride home, and sent the villain on his way. For God's sake, he'd played all-night games of whist that had left him less exhausted.

"Oliver, please meet me in my office," Diane said from the crowded foyer, then retreated into the club's depths again.

The half-dozen men crossing through sent him swift glances full of everything from knowing cynicism to outright amusement. She'd made it clear early on that she wanted the world to think they might be lovers, but the fact that she was still willing to be seen that way left him oddly hopeful. Unless it was only that she wanted to be seen snapping her fingers and having him jump.

She sat behind her desk, making entries in a ledger as he entered the room. "You summoned me?" he said, dropping into the chair opposite her before she could tell him to remain in the doorway or some such thing.

"You can't keep paying him like that," she said, closing the book and leaning both elbows on it. "Aside from the fact that I dislike the idea of giving Anthony any money at all, two thousand pounds is a fortune."

"He's already asking for the next two thousand. But as I told you, I can afford it. A gift to you."

"It's one thing to . . . convince you to lend me funds when I know I'll be repaying them. Which I am, I hope you've noticed."

"I have noticed. And you're doing so more quickly than necessary." And almost as if she was anxious to be finished with him. "After the Season, you may need additional cash. You shouldn't—"

"Don't tell me what to do."

"Are we back to that again?" he asked, torn between amusement and frustration.

Diane grimaced. "No. It's just that I feel I'll owe you. And if I'm not to repay you for the money you're giving Anthony, I'll owe you . . . me."

"If only it were that simple to win you," he commented under his breath.

"Beg pardon?"

This was a conversation he should not be having with her. Not until he'd deciphered the odd tightness he felt in his chest when he recalled their conversation of last night. Yet there he was, jaw flapping.

"I will admit that since our last conversation I have become aware that there is a certain common villainy both in what I did to you and in what Cameron is currently attempting. Perh—"

"Do tell," she interrupted, folding her fingers together and resting her chin on them. "Care to elaborate?"

"No, damn it all." He scowled at her.

Emerald eyes gazed back at him steadily. "I want to trust you, you know."

Oliver stood. "Then do so."

"I've had two years to consider all the reasons why I shouldn't. And then there is you, who apparently didn't have a single thought about me until two months ago."

Oh, that was bloody well enough of that. Stalking around the desk, he grabbed her by the front of her black gown and pulled her to her feet. Then he lowered his mouth over hers. "I thought about you every day," he said roughly, lifting her in his arms and setting her down on her desk. "Every damned day."

The scent of her, the taste of her, aroused him more than any other woman he could ever conjure. And while she might not be able to admit that she needed his help, from the way her fingers tangled into his hair, holding him close against her, she at least wanted him.

Oliver shoved her skirt up, bunching it around her waist. Then he unfastened his trousers, pushed them down to his thighs, and drew her forward onto his cock. Diane moaned as he entered her, her ankles locking behind his hips. He pumped into her hard and fast, listening to her moaning breaths.

If only they could solve all their arguments this way. Though if she would allow him into her heart as readily as she did her body, perhaps they could. He kissed her again, hot and openmouthed. Her body began to tense around his, and he sped his pace. He wanted them to come at the same time, to share that moment. And he wanted her to remember how well they fit together—physically at least.

With a breathless moan she shattered, and he met her in that white-hot haze of pleasure. Panting, he rested his head against her shoulder while she did the same with him. Perfection. He wanted to give it another word, as well, but he couldn't. Not yet. Not until he'd earned it from her.

"I'm giving him the money," he said, not moving, not wanting her to leave his embrace. "And we're getting rid of him."

"Very well," she returned, a sigh in her voice.

"I'm not going to be so easy to do away with." Slowly he kissed her neck, ran his mouth along her throat, felt her pulse shiver beneath his lips. "I give you my solemn word, Diane: I am not going to run this time."

Chapter Twenty

I am not going to run this time. He hadn't apologized directly, but he had acknowledged that he'd done something that needed to be corrected. And he seemed intent on doing precisely that.

The next evening Diane stood in the doorway of the Ariadne Room to watch her former brother-in-law play faro. He didn't seem to have much more skill at it than his late brother. Quite possibly the only thing that had held Anthony back from complete ruin was the fact that until now he hadn't had any discretionary funds to spend.

"How much has he lost so far?"

The low drawl behind her sent pleased shivers down her spine. Sternly she ignored them. After all, Oliver could claim that he wasn't running, but he hadn't asked her if she even wanted him about or not. Of course at the moment that answer would have been a very strong "yes"—all the more reason to wait until everything was finished and she'd regained her senses.

"From what I can tell," she said quietly, "he's down approximately eighteen hundred pounds."

"That's why I had Manderlin sit at his table; Jonathan's

a fair player, so Cameron won't think the club's somehow cheating him or the table."

"How do you know he'll keep losing?"

"I've seen him play. He doesn't have the gift for it." Oliver's hand brushed against her skirt.

"The gift to be able to wager without losing everything in one's possession?" she asked, fighting the urge to lean back against him.

"The gift to know when to stop playing."

"My lady."

Startled, she turned to see Juliet approaching in her crisp black and yellow livery. Whatever had caused the lady butler to leave her post at the busiest part of the evening couldn't be anything good. "What is it, Juliet?"

"Lady Dashton is outside. She and her friends have signs, and they're chastising anyone who enters the club."

" 'Chastising'?" Oliver repeated, putting an exaggerated hand to his throat. "Good heavens."

"You may not care for Lady Dashton's opinion, but there are those here who do." Diane strode through the club, Oliver and Juliet at her heels. She'd known she would have to deal with Lady Dashton and her Ladies of Moderation, but the timing certainly couldn't have been any worse.

"Might I suggest that a stampeding herd of horses would disperse the crowd?"

Diane stifled a grin. "I'll keep that in mind. But you stay back, Oliver. If there is anyone the Ladies of Moderation could possibly dislike more than me, it's you."

Jenny was already waiting in the foyer. "Several gentlemen have stopped on the drive and then realized they have business elsewhere," she reported. She turned her gaze back to Oliver. "You should not go out there."

"So I've been told." He inclined his head. "I think I'll go see how my good friend Lord Cameron is faring. I'll give you a word of advice you likely don't need: do not make them your enemies, Diane, or they'll never let you or your club be."

She lifted an eyebrow. No, she didn't need that advice, but at least it was good advice. "Don't let Anthony out of here with any blunt, or he won't need us."

Oliver flashed her a grin. "Point taken. Good luck." He slipped back into the depths of the club.

"Arrogant man," Jenny muttered.

"At least he's attempting to be helpful," Diane noted, favoring Lord William Jensen with a smile as he entered the foyer, frowning. "My lord."

"That devil of a woman threw an egg at me," he grumbled.

"I'll see to it, my lord."

"Make certain you do."

Well, that was rude. And he'd just moved a step toward being uninvited from the club. Something else for her to see to later. "Jenny, can you join the crowd of ladies discreetly?"

"*Mais oui*. Give me one minute." Genevieve headed toward the servants' entrance at the side of the house.

"If I may ask," Juliet said, "what are you going to do?"

"Use them to help the club."

Diane finished counting down the minute, gave Jenny a few extra seconds, then pulled open the front door and stepped outside.

Two dozen ladies marched back and forth across the foot of her drive. Several of them held lettered wooden boards over their heads. In the scant lamplight reading them was no easy feat, but she managed to make them out. Her favorite was the one that read: "A bawdy house by any other name is still a bawdy house," followed by "A woman's place is in her own home." Either they didn't realize or they didn't care that this *was* her home. And it was home to all her girls as well. Her new, very unusual family.

"Lady Dashton," she called.

The viscountess, leading the chant of "Shame, shame, shame" directed at the passing coaches, turned to look at her. "Lady Cameron," she said in a carrying voice. "I'm surprised you have the courage to show your face."

"It seems we have a disagreement," Diane returned easily, continuing her approach.

"Of course we do. You invite our husbands into this place, take their money, and tempt them with women."

The small crowd jeered.

"Well, I could tell you that we take very little of their money compared to what they lose to each other, or I could say that none of them are allowed to touch my employees— but clearly you don't wish to listen to that. So instead I have a proposition for you."

"You couldn't possibly say anything that I care to hear."

"On Sunday afternoons once a month, I shall open The Tantalus Club to you. Any money made during that time will go to the charity of your choice. Or you may use the premises to hold luncheons or other charity events on that day. Unless you're only paying lip service here and you don't actually wish to accomplish anything useful."

"How dare you?"

"I shelter a number of well-bred, well-educated young ladies who by chance had less fortunate lives than you and I. That is how I dare."

"So you claim. I have my doubts."

Diane closed the distance between her and the viscountess and lowered her voice. "I wouldn't turn away a chance to do good works, my lady. Particularly when the alternative is standing about in the dark doing nothing but shouting at people and accomplishing nothing." She glanced up at the sky. "And with rain on the way."

"Our protests wouldn't end tonight."

"And if you succeeded, then The Tantalus Club would close and all these gentlemen would simply go elsewhere to lose their money and be tempted by every pretty girl they come across. And you wouldn't have a monthly charity event to host."

"You think to bribe me, then?"

Diane inclined her head. "I think to allow me to continue with my club and keep my employees protected, and to do that I am willing to give over my club and part of my earnings to the causes of your choice. That isn't bribery; it's compromise for our mutual benefit."

Lady Dashton looked at her for a long moment. "I think you will see to it that I will look very poorly if I refuse this compromise."

"If you wish to continue this disagreement, you will find me a formidable opponent," Diane said carefully. And one who literally couldn't afford to retreat.

"And they say only men are qualified to negotiate treaties and govern countries," the viscountess commented, brief humor touching her expression.

"Who says that? Men, I would imagine."

"Very true. I would only agree to this . . . compromise in exchange for ten hours on the first Sunday of each month."

"Six hours. My ladies deserve the evening to themselves."

The viscountess blew out a breath. "I won't meet with you here to discuss it."

"Perhaps we could have luncheon at the Preston Bakery on Friday."

"Very well."

Diane stuck out her hand. Oliver wasn't the only one who'd learned how to decipher people. She'd made an overture to which Lady Dashton had just agreed. If the viscountess refused to shake hands, she would look petty. And that wouldn't sit at all well with her.

A moment later Lady Dashton's gloved fingers loosely gripped hers, then lowered again. "I have to speak to my group," the viscountess said.

"Of course. I shall see you on Friday."

After some muttering and chattering the Ladies of Moderation began to disperse, and Diane turned and went back inside The Tantalus Club. A few minutes later Jenny met her at one side of the Demeter Room. "Well done," she said with an uncharacteristic smile. "They had no idea which way to turn. Refusing to fund a charity? Oh, they could never."

"And hopefully, now that they'll be patronizing the club, they'll stop protesting our existence. We may even see their husbands now."

One challenge met, but none of her maneuvering would matter if they couldn't drive Anthony Benchley away from the club. Because Oliver was correct; neither of them had a spotless reputation, and Anthony was a blood relation to the former owner of Adam House. Even if Frederick *had* legitimately signed over the property, she might not have been able to keep it. If her fraud was discovered, she'd be fortunate if she didn't end up transported.

She gazed across the full dining room, darker men's jackets interspersed here and there with lighter-colored silks and muslins. A woman could take weeks and weeks to plan a single soiree at her home; at The Tantalus Club, she held a soiree every night.

For the better part of two years she'd planned, and there it was. The clamor of mostly male conversation, undercut by the clink and clatter of plates and utensils. With the club going so smoothly and some of the other girls learning how to manage things, she didn't need to be in attendance every evening, but she enjoyed being there. She liked being reminded that she'd accomplished what she'd intended. And deep down, she liked knowing that wagering was finally earning her money. Not only her, but all the ladies in her employ also.

Through the door on the far side of the dining room came the other thing she was enjoying much more than she planned. Oliver caught sight of her, smiled, and began making his way through the crowd of tables. He was the one part of the equation that she couldn't control, and while initially that had annoyed her mightily, now she found it oddly exhilarating.

"Langtree told me how you dealt with Lady Dashton," he said, taking Diane's hand and lifting it to kiss her knuckles. "You are brilliant, you know."

"It seemed a bit more practical than having her trampled by horses."

"And whatever money you lose to the charity, you'll likely more than recoup by admitting the stiff chits' husbands." His grin deepened. "Of course you realized that, though."

"I did." Belatedly she withdrew her hand from his. It wasn't that she worried what the other gentlemen would think. It was more that the contact felt too comfortable. She liked touching him, liked when he touched her, and he was far too distracting. "How is Anthony?"

"He left the faro table, and is now attempting roulette. At this rate he'll have spent the two thousand pounds within the hour." Reaching out again, he straightened her sleeve. "The trick will be to get him to spend more than that."

A shudder ran through her. She'd done her best to ensure that no man lost more money than he could afford, but some of them seemed terribly determined to be ruined. Considering that Anthony first was unmarried, with no wife to drag down with him, and second was attempting to steal her club from her, she felt less sympathy for him than she might have otherwise. But she still didn't like it.

"How much money are you going to pay out to him before we close the trap?" she asked, nodding as Jenny joined them.

"I presume he'll ask for another two thousand tomorrow, if not tonight. Once he's spent most of that, we'll have him."

"Then let's get on with it."

"Well, it would proceed more quickly if I played directly against him, but that would also make him suspicious. So at the moment we'll have to rely on his own lack of skill and judgment. It will take more time, but he won't be able to say we drove him to it."

"Are you going to offer him credit?" Jenny asked.

"The club's limit is two hundred pounds," Diane returned. "I don't want him thinking he can go beyond that and simply keep running up his debt."

"If he doesn't feel that touch of panic that he's lost more than he can repay, he won't follow the path we want," Oliver agreed.

Diane took a breath. "Shall we go have a public argument then, Jenny?" she asked.

Genevieve glanced at Oliver. "*Oui*. I believe I have a topic in mind."

The topic didn't matter, but if he was what Jenny wanted to discuss, Diane could hardly avoid it. Leaving her position at the back of the room, she slowly made her way through the club's members toward the Ariadne Room. While she didn't relish chatting with Anthony, it was important that he realize his activities were not going unnoticed.

Yes, it was all very elaborate, and yes, there were simpler, more brutal ways to be rid of her former brother-in-law. But her keen sense of irony preferred that he meet his demise through the perils of wagering. Frederick had never learned his lesson, not even at the end. Perhaps Anthony would do so while he still had a chance to alter the way he lived his life. If he didn't, well, at least she would have given him the opportunity to do so.

Anthony had small stacks of money on several different numbers and both colors of the roulette table, a sure sign that he had no idea where the best odds lay. She stifled a sigh as she stopped beside him. "How is your evening?" she asked.

"Bloody wretched," he snapped, cursing as the ball stopped on a number he hadn't chosen. "You need to make certain my luck runs more favorably."

Diane frowned. "That is entirely up to you and to luck," she returned. "All my tables are honest. I wouldn't be in business if it were otherwise—or if anyone thought otherwise."

"This isn't good enough, then."

And there it was. "I beg your pardon?" she whispered. "I am not going to fund your wagering. I paid you what you asked. I can't do any more than that."

"I believe you can. I've lost nearly two thousand quid in one night. Multiply that by what, two hundred other men here this evening? You can damned well afford to give me another two thousand pounds. And I want it."

"Not everyone loses, and not everyone loses to the bank. The greatest amount of money simply changes hands."

"That is not my problem. And *your* problem is whether you're willing to risk this establishment."

"Fine. But I can't give you two thousand pounds every day. That's absurd. People would notice."

"Which people?"

Diane put a hand to her throat. "I can't tell you that. And keep your voice down. Come by for breakfast tomorrow and I'll get you what I can."

"Diane."

Jumping, she turned around to see Jenny approaching.

"Don't mention any of this," Diane hissed at Anthony, then went to see her friend. "Ready?"

"Has he asked for more money?"

"I'm to give it to him at breakfast."

"Then let's discuss that man, shall we?"

"This is only supposed to *appear* to be an argument. I don't want to actually fight."

"Neither do I. I only want to know why you're trusting him now."

Diane frowned, making a helpless gesture with her hands. "He had a very good idea, you have to admit."

"That only means he's an expert at being devious. I don't trust him."

"I may not trust him with my heart, Jenny, but he's proved himself several times over in the past weeks. Do a pointing thing."

Jenny jabbed a finger at her. "I feel like a complete idiot. Do you love him?"

That stopped her for a moment. To hear it said so directly . . . "I find him extremely aggravating."

"That's not an answer. Shake your head."

Diane shook her head. "It's not an answer I can give you, regardless."

Scowling, Genevieve gazed at her. "He's very quick-witted. I'll grant him that. But you need to figure out what it is you want of him. Aside from his money."

"He offered to put me up in my own wing at Haybury Park after the Season."

"What? What did you tell him?"

"I told him that I didn't want to be that near him." She took a breath. "Because I *do* want to be that near him. It's very complicated."

"Not as much as you think." Giving a hostile wave of her hands, Jenny took a step closer. "Decide who you're punishing, and why."

"I thought you hated him."

"I hate him because you hate him. We are friends, yes?"

Just barely, Diane kept from smiling. "Good friends."

"*Bon*. Lord Cameron has been watching, so be afraid of me now, and I'll see you upstairs for tea later."

"Thank you, Jenny." Grimacing, Diane backed away, then turned toward the roulette table just in time to see Anthony swiftly look away. "Will you excuse me, Anthony? That French b—" She stopped herself, swallowing. "I need to see to my books."

"You will give me what I want in the morning, yes?"

"I will try."

"No. You will do so."

"Anthony, I told you that this is very complicated. I need to be careful."

"Do what you need to. I'm not a part of your scheme. But I want my two thousand pounds, or you'll be meeting with my solicitors by the afternoon."

"No!" She put a hand over her mouth as if to stifle her protest. "No solicitors," she said much more quietly. "Very well. I'll manage it."

"Good."

Once Diane left the club for the privacy of the Adam House sitting room, she allowed herself to grin. Tomorrow was going to be quite fun.

A knock sounded at the half-open door. "You could be on the stage," Oliver's low voice came. "Magnificent."

She sat in the chair beside the table lamp. Very likely she should be asking how he managed to get past Langtree, but he'd made it into her home so many times now that questioning his methods hardly seemed worth the effort. "I'm to give him the money during breakfast."

Dropping into the chair by the fire, Oliver stretched out his legs and crossed his ankles. "What were you and Miss Martine pretending to argue about?"

"None of your business."

"Ah. Me, then. Not so pretend, was it?"

He looked magnificent taking his ease before the fire, relaxed and still alert, a lion waiting for its prey to move into reach. "What am I going to do with you?" she murmured, half-smiling.

"What do you want to do with me?"

"I'm divided fairly evenly between wanting to kiss you and wanting to strangle you," she returned.

"I consider that an improvement." Oliver kept his gaze on her. In the dim firelight that reached her from halfway across the room, her black hair looked almost bronze, her skin warm and enticing. "I want you."

"And I want to know what you'll do when you've tired of having only one woman. Or when you decide that you like me more than you're comfortable admitting."

He was already well past that point. "I told you that I'm not running."

"You're assuming that I want you to stay."

"I believe according to our agreement you have two years each to repay my loans to you." Something abruptly occurred to him, and he frowned. "That's why you're making additional payments, isn't it? To be rid of me."

"I didn't expect the club to be going so well already. You were to be a shield and a lure. You've succeeded at the first part, and you're no longer necessary for the second."

"Necessary," he repeated. "That's an interesting word."

"Is it?" she returned coolly. "How so?"

She wasn't going to give him an inch of space to maneuver. But if she meant to justify having him about because he was "necessary" to the club, then once they disposed of Lord Cameron he would likely be asked to move away. Then he would only see her when he visited the club and only until the end of the Season. Haybury Park had been his property for only two years, and he couldn't spend the autumn and winter in London just because he was mooning over some chit who didn't want him.

Uneasiness ran through him. It went against every part of his being to leave himself exposed, but he'd begun to realize that until he could make things right with her they would never be able to move forward. And he wanted to move forward. With her.

Slowly he stood and went over to where she sat. "I said we would talk after we were finished with Cameron," he said, sinking down onto his haunches directly in front of her, "but I'm finding that your jibes about ridding yourself of me are beginning to draw blood."

"You aggravate me. I haven't made a secret of that."

"Yes, I know, but I'd hoped you were jesting about your relentless dislike. Perhaps you were, and perhaps you're serious, but I'm not willing to sit and watch another chance pass me by."

She shifted, her gaze narrowing. "Oliver, I'm tired. I don't—"

Diane started to stand, but he put his hands on her thighs and kept her where she was. Wanting to touch her, Oliver curled his fingers into the black material of her skirt.

"I am sorry," he said, trying to keep his voice low and measured. "You were looking for hope, and I was looking for a bit of fun, and when I realized I'd began to care for you far more than I was willing to acknowledge, I ran. Like a scalded dog, I believe you said. I apologize. It's not nearly enough to say the words, or to confess that leaving you in Vienna stands as the greatest regret of my life, but there you have it."

For a moment she sat silently. Then she leaned forward over his hands and slapped him. Hard.

"Your greatest regret?" she repeated, shoving him onto his backside. "That's ridiculous!"

Throwing herself forward, she landed on him, punching

at his face and chest. Oliver tried to hold her away from him but couldn't shield himself completely from the blows without hurting her. "Diane!"

"For two years I thought you left because I was some weak, weeping chit, so helpless I could barely stand myself."

"You were not helpless. You've never been helpless." He grunted, wincing as her knee dug into his groin. "You were lost and angry, but by God, you were never weak. And that part of you I could see, that was the part that drew me to you. And frightened the devil out of me. The part that told me I'd met my match."

"If you regretted leaving so very much, did it never occur to you to, oh, return to Vienna? You knew I was penniless, but once you inherited your fortune you didn't consider sending me ten pounds? I suppose you regret that, too. Regret does me no good, you stupid man."

"When I saw you again here," he retorted, attempting to ignore her very apt barbs, "I knew. That strong, defiant spark in you was so . . . You were on fire. So yes, I regret my stupidity, but I'm . . . proud that you did all this yourself. You don't owe anyone anything."

"Ha. Certainly not you."

"No, you don't. I don't want to tell you what to do, order you about, make you stop what you're doing. I only want to be a part of it. I . . . I love you, Diane. I always have."

"You broke my heart!" she yelled, slapping at him again.

"I know. And I'm sorry. I'm so sorry I hurt you. I was only thinking of myself. I thought you would forget about me. My not being able to forget you—that was my own trouble to bear. Or so I thought."

Abruptly she collapsed against his chest, her breath hard and broken against his neck. Cautiously he released his grip on her wrists, and she curled her hands into his jacket.

"Are you crying?" he whispered, ready to begin defending himself again.

"No!" she said, her voice muffled and damp against him.

Slowly he put his arms around her, holding her close against him. "We are two bullheaded, wicked people who have lived very unconventional lives," he murmured into her hair. "Personally I think we belong together."

"You're a very aggravating man," she whispered.

"Yes, my love. I know." He blew out his breath. "I'm going to ask you a question. I don't want you to answer it until we're finished with Cameron and until you don't have to worry about losing the club. And after I ask this question I'm going to take you into your bedchamber, where I will be a perfect gentleman and stay with you until you fall asleep."

"What question?" she demanded, her face still buried against him.

"Diane Benchley, will you marry me?"

Chapter Twenty-one

D iane opened one bleary eye. "Shh. I'm asleep," she muttered, and closed her eye again.

"My lady, please. You said I should wake you at seven o'clock," Mary whispered, shaking Diane's shoulder again.

"Why are you whispering?" she whispered back at the maid, forcing both eyes open this time.

"Because of him, my lady." The maid pointed behind Diane at the opposite side of the bed.

Diane turned her head, abruptly remembering why her eyes felt so dry and crusty. She'd been crying. Close enough to touch, eyes shuttered beneath long lashes and a day's growth of beard stubbling the lower half of his face, lay Oliver Warren. The man who'd last night said he loved her. Who'd proposed to her.

She sat up, rubbing at her face. Beneath the blankets she still wore her shift, and while Oliver had shed his boots, jacket, and waistcoat, he was nowhere near naked, either. He'd said he would be a gentleman, and he'd behaved as one.

"Thank you, Mary. Fetch us some tea, will you? And if Lord Cameron should appear downstairs, please let me know immediately."

"I'll see to it at once, my lady." The maid hurried from the room and closed the door softly behind her.

"Is she gone?" Oliver muttered, otherwise unmoving.

"Yes."

Gray eyes opened, meeting hers. "Good. I was worried she would try to smother me with a pillow if I moved."

"Mm-hm." Diane had the oddest desire to simply sit there and gaze at him, so instead she slipped from under the covers and pulled on the dressing robe draped across the foot of the bed. "Do you think we'll be able to coax Anthony into wagering his next two thousand pounds this morning?"

"All business, eh? Very well." Oliver sat up, stretching. "I suggested to several friends that they might wish to gamble after breakfast this morning, so he won't be alone in the gaming rooms."

"It might work. I just don't want him to be overly suspicious."

Oliver stood up in his bare feet and walked around to her side of the bed. "If he balks I'll turn him away until tonight. Or conceivably he could lose the blunt at any other club in London. I just prefer to see him do it here."

They'd planned this as best they could, but she hated that so much had to be left to chance. To hope—for their good fortune, and for Anthony's ill fortune. "What if he wins today?"

"Then I imagine some street thugs will attempt to rob him on his way home."

She squinted one eye. "You know street thugs?"

He grinned. "You'd be surprised."

"Not as much as you might think."

Whatever he'd said about not wishing an answer to his question until they'd dealt with Anthony, the words still seemed to hang in the air between them. Not heavy or dark but soft and pleasant, like lace curtains or laughter. It terrified and enticed her all at the same time.

Oliver brushed a finger along her cheek. "Penny for your thoughts."

"I'm worried about Anthony's new friends," she improvised. "Larden may not return, but the Duke of Greaves seems to be nearly everyone's welcome guest."

"If he appears, I'll deal with him."

"I doubt a brawl would aid our plan."

Oliver put a hand to his chest. "Please. A brawl? Me? I have a great many cards in my deck, my dear."

"I don't doubt that."

Mary knocked and came back into the room, her arms filled with a tea tray. "Lord Cameron hasn't yet arrived, my lady," she said, sending glances in Oliver's direction as she set the tray on the dressing table. "Shall I stay and help you dress?"

"Give me fifteen minutes, Mary."

The maid curtsied. "Very good, my lady."

Once she left, Oliver poured two cups of tea. "Fifteen minutes is hardly enough time for anything worth doing," he commented, indicating the sugar and lifting an eyebrow.

"One, if you please. No cream."

He handed her the cup of tea, then leaned back against the dressing table to sip at his own. "You know," he said conversationally, gazing at her over the rim of his cup, "with most people I can tell what they're thinking, or even what they're about to say. With you, most of the time I haven't a clue. It's fascinating. You're fascinating."

"Yes, well, stop looking at me like I'm some insect you're about to stick with a pin."

"It's not a pin I want to stick you with, my dear." He glanced at the clock squatting on her deep mantel. "I should go make myself handsome," he said. "I think I'll breakfast here at the club. How close do you want me sitting to Cameron's table?"

"Nowhere near. But be ready to leave for the gaming rooms when he does."

He set aside his tea, then swept a deep, elegant bow. "He won't harm you; I won't allow it." Before she could reply to that, Oliver stepped up and softly kissed her.

She took a breath as he stepped away. "Don't distract m—"

"No, that won't do," he interrupted.

Sliding one arm around her shoulders and the other across her hip, he dipped her. To keep from falling, Diane flung her arms around his neck. Bending his head, he covered her mouth with his in a deep, hot kiss that left her breathless.

"Much better." With a last, swift kiss he set her back on her feet, strode over to collect his jacket, waistcoat, and boots, and left the room.

For a long moment she looked at the closed door. "Impossible man," she muttered, shaking her head and pushing away the urge to smile. That would have to wait until she knew her Tantalus Club was safe. Only then would she worry about her heart.

Mary was just putting the last pins in Diane's hair when Sarah, one of the footwomen, knocked at her bedchamber door. "My lady, Lord Cameron is here. Camille has seated him."

"Thank you, Sarah. I'll be down in a moment. Please inform Lord Haybury that Lord Cameron is here."

"Lord Haybury is already in the Aphrodite Room, my lady. I believe he's dining with Lord Manderlin and Mr. Appleton."

He'd said he'd asked friends to come by and add to the morning gaming crowd. Oliver had been keeping his word with alarming regularity lately. In fact, since she'd blackmailed him into assisting her. And while he was very vocal with his opinions, he'd never attempted to force her into anything. Of course she would have shot him if he had, but he'd certainly been less an unwilling slave or even a dictator, and more a . . . a partner.

Her legs wobbled, and she took a hurried seat at the dressing table.

"My lady, are you well?" Mary asked, her voice concerned.

No. "Yes, I just need a moment. That will be all, Mary."

Looking distressed, Mary left the bedchamber and closed the door behind her. Diane scarcely noticed; all her thoughts centered around the realization she'd just made. A partner. Him. Oliver Warren.

Was that what she wanted? She'd acquired an unexpected family in the young ladies who flocked to The Tantalus Club as a last chance for a semirespectable life. All of this had been *her* plan, her hard work, her responsibility, and her failure if she couldn't manage everything. After Frederick had died, she'd sworn that she would never rely on anyone else for anything. She hadn't counted on people beginning to rely on her.

She lowered her face into her hands. It was too much to consider. For heaven's sake, she'd approached Oliver for help because she reckoned he owed her, she could control him, and she would certainly know better than to ever trust him again. What she'd never considered was that he would be trustworthy, that he would be a better man than the one she'd known before.

Diane straightened and took a deep breath. *Later.* The number of things she would have to decipher later was certainly stacking up, but so be it. First she needed to save The Tantalus Club—with help that, two months ago, she never would have expected.

The book in which she chose to secret Anthony's payment was Dante's *Inferno,* though she was certain he would never understand the threat or irony of it. She did, however. And Oliver certainly would.

Shaking thoughts of the Marquis of Haybury out of her mind yet again, she went downstairs to the club and entered the Aphrodite Room. Oliver had outdone himself; the room was twice as busy as it generally was on a Thursday morning. Apparently every titled member had stopped by for breakfast on his way to Parliament.

Anthony sat alone, his expression that of a cat who'd found a bowl of cream as he looked about the breakfast room. He clearly already considered this his own private bank and believed the more money coming in, the more would go out to him. She hoped he enjoyed the feeling; it wouldn't last much longer.

"Good morning, Diane," he said, not bothering to stand as he gestured for her to sit down opposite him.

"I hope you enjoy the book, Anthony," she said, handing it over to him. "This one will have to last you for a month."

"Yes, we'll see about that." He opened the book to the title page, saw the money, and with a smile closed it again. "Is the club always so busy in the morning?"

"A great many members enjoy breakfast and then an hour or so of cards before they leave for the House of Lords," she replied, stopping herself from glancing in Oliver's direction.

"An excellent idea."

"Anthony, you need—"

"Do not tell me what I *need* to do, Diane," he snapped, then smiled once more. "Frederick had no idea, did he? If he'd allowed you freer rein, he could have been living on Park Lane. It's a damned shame I can't marry you. I'd certainly allow you to continue managing The Tantalus Club."

"Yes, a damned shame," she echoed, clenching her jaw.

Oliver watched the exchange from across the room. As before, every time Cameron gave his smirking smile, he had to clench his fist against his thigh to keep from stalking over and punching the man unconscious.

"How much blunt do you want him to lose?" James Appleton asked in a low voice, following Oliver's gaze.

"Two thousand pounds."

"This morning? That's a bit ambitious."

"It'd be easier if he played whist or something where the other players could take his money," Manderlin put in. "Losing to the club takes longer."

Considering that it was his money to begin with, Oliver actually preferred that Cameron lose to the club, but Manderlin made a good point. "See what you can do to influence him, but for Lucifer's sake, don't make him suspicious."

"You're going to a great deal of trouble to help a chit," Manderlin said in a low voice.

"*My* chit," Oliver corrected.

Appleton blinked. "Beg pardon?"

"You heard me."

His friends glanced at each other. "Very well, then. We'll do our damnedest. You . . ." Jonathan trailed off as his gaze lifted. "Bloody hell."

Oliver didn't turn to look. "It's Greaves, isn't it?"

"Yes. That damned fool Trainor has brought him again. How did you know?"

"Because today will likely be the most difficult day of my life. I imagine the ghost of Uncle Phillip will appear next."

James and Jonathan undoubtedly thought the difficulty of the day was Lord Cameron. That greedy toad scarcely concerned Oliver at all, however. Today the earl would cease bothering Diane, one way or another. No, the trouble ahead was Diane herself. She was proud and stubborn, and terrified of being dependent on anyone. Of needing anyone. And he had no idea how to convince her that he would never, ever let her down again.

"He's walking this way," Appleton muttered from behind a forkful of ham.

And he'd promised to be subtle, damn it all. Oliver rolled his shoulders, ready for whatever his former friend might attempt. To his surprise, though, Greaves continued past him without pausing. At the same moment a folded note drifted down to the table beside him.

Oliver swept it into his lap with his napkin and looked down as he opened it. *The library. Now. G,* he read to himself.

"What is it?" Manderlin whispered.

"An invitation to trouble," Oliver returned, and pushed away from the table. "I'll be back in a moment. Keep your eyes on Cameron."

"Oliver, y—"

"Please."

Taking a deep breath, Manderlin nodded. "Don't get caught, whatever you're up to."

Unable to resist a swift glance in Diane's direction, Oliver made his way to the Athena Room, nearly deserted at this hour. Greaves stood by a window, his gaze out over the garden. "Your Grace," Oliver said, unable to keep his jaw from clenching.

"I had a thought," Greaves commented, unmoving.

"Just the one?"

"When I heard Cameron grumbling about how his former sister-in-law had stolen his property and his intention to reclaim it, I could not have cared less. Until I learned of your rumored involvement with Lady Cameron, of course. Then it all became a bit more interesting."

"Perhaps I should mention that if you do anything to harm Diane or this club, I will murder you," Oliver said evenly. "Even if I hang for the deed."

"That's very dramatic of you. I remember you being more understated and cynical."

"That was before I realized I had something to lose. Why are you here this morning?"

"Because last night Cameron lost more money than I was aware that he had and this morning he seemed very confident that he would have more. He's blackmailing your chit, isn't he?" Finally Greaves turned to face him.

"That's it," Oliver said, balling his fist. "You're going through the window."

"Wait." The duke took a half step back. "I'll be more direct. I'm not going to interfere with whatever it is you're planning on doing to that fool."

Well, that was unexpected. Oliver stopped his approach. "This is the last time I'm asking: why are you here?"

"Because while I don't believe in apologies, I *do* enjoy handing someone a well-deserved comeuppance. Cameron's a snake, worse even than his brother, and I never liked Frederick, either."

"Ah. So you're offering your services if I should be attempting to roust Lord Cameron, then? Interesting how often you seem to betray the trust of people who call you friend."

"I only befriended him because . . ." The duke took a breath. "Perhaps I feel that I do owe you something. Trust me or not; I don't give a damn. But I thought I might do a bit of wagering here this morning. How much do you need him to lose?"

There was absolutely no way that Greaves could know

precisely what Oliver and Diane were planning, but if he knew about the money going to Cameron it was entirely possible that he'd deciphered at least part of the plan. Oliver could deny it all, of course, but that would likely only gain him more trouble. "Somewhere in the area of two thousand quid," he said shortly.

"Good to know."

"This doesn't make us even, and it doesn't make us friends," Oliver retorted. "And if you cross me today, I'll—"

"Yes, I know. You'll murder me."

As they left the library, Cameron was on his way to the Persephone Room, Oliver's friends on the earl's heels. While the snake wandered about the room looking for the best game, Oliver and his two companions sat at a table to play vingt-et-un. It wasn't his favorite, but playing well did require a modicum of skill. And he wouldn't be directly challenging Cameron, since the wagering passed between a player and the bank. Now he had to hope that the earl would be interested in attempting to show him up by playing at the same table.

Ten minutes after play began, Cameron settled at the roulette table. Oliver cursed under his breath. Most of his fellows would only be here for an hour at most, and he doubted even Cameron could play roulette deeply enough to lose two thousand quid in an hour.

The Duke of Greaves appeared and threw his arm across Cameron's shoulders. *Damnation.* Oliver stilled. Whatever they'd discussed, at best the duke wouldn't set himself directly against Oliver and Diana, but he had ceased expecting the best of any circumstance. If Greaves misbehaved, it would mean a fight. Anything to keep Cameron and his allies separated.

Somewhat to Oliver's surprise, the duke looked over at him, then guided Cameron toward the table where he sat with his companions. "You have room for two more, I assume?" Greaves drawled, taking the chair farthest from Oliver.

"The more, the merrier," Appleton commented, and cleared his throat.

Oliver nodded at Mary Stanford, one of four Marys employed by the club, and the day's vingt-et-un dealer. She dealt out five cards facedown, then turned up the one in front of her, a seven. The second pass delivered her a four, while Oliver had an ace and a three. He made his wager and asked for another card, most of his attention on Cameron.

The earl was wagering conservatively, and Oliver stifled a frown. The entire plot would only succeed if Cameron lost everything in his pockets. By the time of the third round, Oliver had won thirty pounds, while Diane's former brother-in-law had lost only nineteen. *Damnation.*

"Good God, Cameron," the Duke of Greaves said with a chuckle, "you wager like an old woman. Show some spleen, why don't you?" As he finished speaking, he placed a two-hundred-quid wager on his cards.

As Cameron looked down at his cards again, Greaves's gaze met Oliver's, and the duke gave a slight nod. *Hm.* Whatever it meant, Oliver intended to take advantage of it. He chuckled. "Well said, Greaves. Thirty damned quid isn't worth my time." With that, he matched the duke's wager on his own cards.

Appleton and Manderlin followed suit, all of them chuckling as if they were playing some amusing prank. With a scowl, Cameron matched the wager—and promptly lost, as did everyone but Appleton.

Thirty minutes later, with Greaves goading the earl whenever Cameron looked ready to balk, Oliver finally let himself relax a fraction. He glanced toward the doorway to see Diane gazing at him, and surreptitiously he waggled his fingers. She vanished.

A moment later she reappeared, striding directly up to Lord Cameron. "Anthony, I need a word with you."

"Not now. I'm occupied."

"No, Anthony. Now," she repeated, twisting her hands together. "And you as well, Haybury."

"Damnation," Oliver cursed, and, gathering up his winnings, he nodded at the other players and stood. "Shall we, Cameron?"

The earl nodded and left the table, but grabbed Oliver's arm as they followed Diane toward her office. "I'm down nearly seventeen hundred quid," Anthony whispered. "I need more money."

Oliver shrugged him off. "You've gone through nearly four thousand pounds in less than three days? Good God, man."

"What do you need more blunt for?" Cameron continued, scowling. "You're wealthier than King Midas. I should have your share. This place belonged to my family, after all."

"I am not—"

"Hush," Diane hissed, closing the door with the three of them inside her office. "She was looking at the ledgers this morning," she continued in a low voice, her gaze on Oliver. "I think she's suspicious."

And his lady was a consummate actress. "We've been very careful," he returned. "There's nothing for her to see."

"There certainly is, if she figures out where to look."

"What the devil are you two talking about?" Cameron asked. "And I've lost the blunt you gave me. I need more."

"Losing four thousand pounds is not like losing a horseshoe," Diane retorted. "I can't simply replace it."

"I don't think you understand," the earl said in a low voice. "I want more money. If you want to keep your club, you'd best get it for me."

She shot a glance at Oliver again. "Perhaps we should tell him," she muttered.

"Absolutely not. I am not risking getting my neck stretched because your idiot former in-law has a hole in his pocket."

"Tell me what?"

Diane took a deep breath. "The club's investors," she said slowly, backing toward the windowsill. "The ones from whom we've been . . . pilfering a little money."

"What about them? They're your friends; it's certainly not my problem."

"That's the thing," Diane continued. "They aren't my— our—friends."

"Then whose friends are they? And why are they financing your gentlemen's club?" Cameron asked dubiously.

"I told you, it's very complicated. And until she stops hunting about for discrepancies, I can't give you any more money. Not even The Tantalus Club is worth my life."

"Your life?" he repeated. "You're exaggerating. Do you think I don't know you're simply trying to escape our bargain? How stupid do you think I am?"

They were about to find out. Oliver cleared his throat. "She has to realize that we expect something for our troubles," he offered.

"I've taken out four thousand pounds in three days, Haybury. Not even *I* consider that to be reasonable."

"Who the devil is this 'she' you keep referring to? You're not frightening me, if that's your g—"

The door from the morning room slammed open. Genevieve Martine, her blond hair pulled back as severely as ever, gazed at the three of them. "I knew it," she said in a thicker French accent than Oliver had ever heard her use before.

"Who the devil are you supposed to be?" Cameron demanded. "I've seen you about. You're Diane's companion."

"I can explain, Genevieve," Diane said, backing away until she came up against the wall.

"You can explain theft? I very much doubt that, mademoiselle. And you—I knew you couldn't be trusted." She jabbed a finger at Oliver.

"Listen," the earl put in, the confusion plain on his face. "Whatever farce you think you're playing at, I am not—"

"Shut up, you. We have planned this for three years. And you three are not going to ruin it for us—for him—because of your greed." She slammed her fist down on the desktop. "We put the money into this club, and the money that comes out is ours. You will repay what you've taken."

Cameron crossed his arms over his chest. "I'm not doing anything."

"He doesn't have the money, Genevieve. I gave him four thousand pounds, to keep him from going to court to get The Tantalus Club."

Miss Martine whipped around to face Cameron once more. "You will not bring this club to the attention of any authorities. Is that clear?"

"I hardly think you're in a position to stop me."

Diane swallowed audibly. "Perhaps we should explain the situation to him, Genevieve. For all our sakes. Once he realizes what could happen, I'm certain he'll be more understanding."

Slowly Miss Martine faced the earl again. "Very well. One time, I will explain. If you say anything—*anything*—about this, I will know it came from you, and I will have you killed."

" 'Killed'? What is—"

"Lady Cameron lost everything when her husband died," Genevieve said in her newly found heavy accent. "We knew she had some knowledge of wagering and clubs, and we needed a way to raise money without garnering suspicion from the English. So we put the money into the club, and she holds the money the club earns for us, to be used at the right moment. To return the emperor to power."

For a moment Oliver thought the chit might be overplaying her hand, but Cameron blanched. "The emperor? You can't mean . . . Bonaparte?"

"Mon oncle, Napoléon. Oui."

"This . . . Your *uncle*? You can't do this! Someone must be told."

"You've taken four thousand pounds from The Tantalus Club, monsieur. If you speak a word of this to the authorities, I will make certain the world knows that you were a part of this. You will hang for treason."

"I . . ." Anthony Benchley sat down heavily on a chair, his face white. "Good God."

"He truly didn't know, Genevieve," Diane offered. "He only thought he was taking advantage of a widow. I know that wouldn't matter to the government, but surely you don't need to kill anyone because of that."

"I don't know why not. Three years, Diane. And you and Haybury and this . . . imbecile think you can upset our plans?"

"I didn't know. Diane is telling you the truth."

Miss Martine glared at Cameron. "You will go away," she stated flatly. "I do not want the attention your death would bring to this establishment. And know that I am not the only one in London involved in freeing my uncle. And some are more lethal than I am. One word, *one word,* Lord Cameron, about Bonaparte or The Tantalus Club or our arrangement here, and you will never be seen again."

"Yes, yes. Very well."

"And when you leave, you will tell our guard at the door that you will not return. If she sees you again, she will put a knife into your heart."

"Oh, God. The chit in trousers?"

"Oui." She snapped her head around to glare at Diane. "And you will pay back every penny you gave him. You do not get to escape this so easily." She pinned her gaze on Oliver. "Nor do you. You wanted wealth, and now you will work for it."

Oliver lowered his head. "You can't blame a fellow for wanting some compensation for his hard work," he muttered.

"Yes, I can." Genevieve looked again at Lord Cameron. "I told you to go. Now."

Stumbling to his feet, the earl backed up for the hallway door. "Thank you, my lady. I . . . You won't hear from me again. I swear it. This is none of my affair. I had no idea."

"Shut up and leave."

"Yes, my lady." He slipped through the door and slammed it closed again.

In the ensuing silence, Oliver looked from one chit to the other. "Bonaparte's niece?" he finally said.

Diane shrugged. "He does have seven siblings. It seemed reasonable."

"Do you think he believed it?" the French twist asked, her accent back to its usual mix of European languages.

"We'll know in a moment. I asked Juliet to stand at the front door this morning. She's to inform me if anything unusual occurs." A slight smile tugged at Diane's mouth.

The sight mesmerized Oliver. *She* mesmerized him. "Diane, y—"

"What was Greaves doing?" she interrupted.

"Helping Cameron lose a great deal of money, actually," he returned. "And before you ask, I have no idea why. He realized we had something planned. I suppose the idea of beating a toad like Cameron might have amused him." Whether it truly was about making amends Oliver wasn't willing to admit. Not without more proof than simply the shared bloodying of a snake.

"Even so, I think I may have to consider his membership request."

"If you must. I'll abstain from voting."

A knock sounded at the door. "My lady? It's Juliet."

"And here we go. Come in, Juliet."

The butleress entered the room. "My lady, you said you wanted to be notified of anything . . . odd. Lord Cameron just ran past me, saying that he was terribly sorry and he would never return. I assume this is what you were talking about."

"Yes, it is. Thank you very much, Juliet."

With a nod Langtree exited again. Finally Oliver let out the breath he'd been holding. "Congratulations, Diane. The Tantalus Club remains in your hands."

She nodded, turning to gaze out the window. "Jenny, would you give us a moment?"

"Mais oui." Sending him an unreadable glance, the French twist left the room through the door through which she'd emerged.

"Do you think she's still listening?" Oliver asked after a moment.

"I wouldn't be surprised. She remembers what a sad wreck I was two years ago. It worries her."

Uneasiness ran through him as well. Had he treated Diane too poorly to ever be forgiven? He couldn't think of anything more he could do to prove himself to her. If what he'd done wasn't enough . . . He didn't even want to consider it. He would have to become some recluse, living at Haybury and never leaving, because seeing her again and knowing he could never have her would be too much to bear.

Slowly Diane faced him again. "Do you have anything to say?"

"What do you want me to say? I asked you a question last night. I'll ask you again, if you wish. I'll apologize again, if you wish. I'll tell you again that I love you, because I do. The answers are all up to you."

For a long, quiet moment she gazed at him. "Oliver, I d—"

"I will remind you," he interrupted, his heart tearing loose in his chest and beating into his throat, "that we do work quite well together."

"Y—"

"And that if you're worried about your property going to me, I'll happily sign anything you wish to make certain this house and this club remain in your hands."

"Oli—"

"You said you'd stopped believing in such a thing as love and passion until you met me. What I didn't say was that you made me believe in them, too. I thought love was a farce until you proved me wrong." If he kept talking, then at least she couldn't say no. She couldn't tell him he'd been a mistake, and one that she truly meant never to repeat. "You don't need to repay the loan. It's yours. I can help you fund whatever you want for The Tanta—"

She strode forward and put a hand over his mouth. "Do be quiet," she said. "I believe it's my turn to talk."

He still couldn't read her expression, but he nodded. This was the moment when he paid for all his past misdeeds. He needed to face it, even if it meant he wouldn't have the chance to be happy. Not like he'd been over the past two months. Not like he'd been when he'd seen her again.

Her fingers across his lips shook a little. "Two years ago, you shattered me," she whispered. "You broke my heart into a thousand pieces, just when I'd realized I had a heart that could break."

Oh, God. "Diane, I—"

"Hush."

He subsided again, trying not to shake.

"In the past two months you've annoyed me, aggravated me, challenged me, argued with me . . . and you put my heart back together again. I tried to tell myself that I had what I wanted, I had my independence, and that I didn't need anything else."

Slowly she lowered her hand, twining her fingers into his lapel. He scarcely dared to breathe. At the moment it sounded promising, but he'd ceased attempting to anticipate what she might be thinking.

"These girls need me, and I . . . I like looking after them. They'll never have to be alone and lost like I was. And I've discovered that I like sharing things with you. I like chatting with you; I like sharing my life with you. I don't want someone to tell me what to do, or what not to do. I am willing, however, to take on a partner. An equal."

"May I speak now?"

"Yes."

Oliver cleared his throat. "Does this mean you'll marry me?" he murmured. "Or is this a professional partnership? Because I won't take one without the other. Those are my conditions."

"Are they now?" she asked softly. "You don't mind helping me manage a gentlemen's club, but you won't do it unless I agree to marry you?"

"Yes. That's it exactly."

Her lovely emerald eyes filled with unshed tears. Silently Diane nodded. "Very well, then."

Thank God. "I would prefer that you say it."

She drew a soft breath and, lifting on her toes, touched her lips to his. "Aggravating man. Yes, Oliver, I will marry you."

He slid his arms around her, pulling her close against him. The club, the money—he didn't care about any of that. All he wanted was this strong, fierce woman in his arms to care for him as he cared for her. "I love you," he whispered, closing his mouth over hers again.

"I love you, Oliver," she whispered back, smiling against his mouth. "I've only ever loved you."

Oliver chuckled. "This is going to be a very scandalous life, you know."

"I can't wait."

"Neither can I."

Read on for an excerpt from Suzanne Enoch's next book

Taming an
Impossible Rogue

Coming soon from St. Martin's Paperbacks

Camille lifted her left hand straight into the air, fingers spread. All the ladies knew the signal, though she, unfortunately, had used it more than any of the others. Even in the less-crowded, less-inebriated mornings at the club. The perils of a publicly ruined reputation, she supposed. Thankfully, while Lady Haybury might have preferred to have only female employees, it hadn't taken much to convince her that a handful of very large former boxers might be helpful to have about.

However, as she faced the ogre again, a fist and a nicely jacketed arm crossed directly in front of her—and connected with Farness's chin. The round fellow fell to the blue-carpeted floor on his arse.

"When I was last in London," a low, cultured drawl came from beside her, "men did not insult women in such a manner. I can only assume, then, that either you were mistaken, or you're not a man."

Camille sidestepped as the tall, dark-haired man attached to the fist bent down to haul Farness to his feet.

"Which is it, then?" he murmured. "Were you mistaken, or are you simply not a man?"

The ogre raised shaking fingers to touch his cut lip. "Good God. You're Blackwood. Bloody damned Blackwood."

"I'm aware of that. Answer my question."

"Mistaken," Farness rasped. "I was mistaken."

"Then I suggest you apologize," Blackwood pursued, in the same tone he might ask for an additional card while playing *vingt-et-un*.

Farness looked over at her. "I apologize."

"For?" her supposed rescuer prompted.

"For . . . for insulting you, my lady."

"Well done." With a light but unmistakably serious shove, he deposited Farness into the grip of Mr. Jacobs. "Shall I leave as well?" he asked, looking over at her for the first time.

Light brown eyes, one of them circled by a faint, fading bruise, gazed levelly at her. Stifling the abrupt impulse to straighten her hair, she shook her head. "As long as there's no more punching, I can't fault you for defending my honor—unnecessary though it was."

A slow smile touched his mouth. "Thank you. And I've never found defending a lady's honor to be a frivolity."

Just as she realized that she seemed to be staring at the man, the circle around them stirred and parted. Diane, Lady Haybury, emerged into the small clearing. "I will not have fisticuffs in my club," she said, ignoring Mr. Farness being led away and instead focusing her attention on the punching man. "Whose guest are you, sir?"

"Mine."

The Duke of Greaves moved into the circle, his expression as cool as if he were discussing the weather. "Lady Haybury, Keating Blackwood. Keating, the proprietor of this establishment, Lady Haybury."

Oh, dear. Camille resisted the urge to back away. She'd only wished to stop a man from pinching her hindquarters.

Involving Diane and dukes and disrupting the running of the club . . . Perhaps she should have simply accepted the pinch for what it was; after all, of all the ladies employed by the club, her fall from grace was by far the most public. With some of the things said to her back—and even to her face— whenever she ventured out of doors, at the least she should have expected such discourtesy from time to time within her sanctuary's walls.

Diane glanced in her direction. "Is any further action warranted, Camille?"

She shook her head. "I believe there's been enough fuss, my lady." More than enough.

Diane nodded, returning her attention to the rather tall Keating Blackwood. "If His Grace is willing to vouch for you, Mr. Blackwood, then I will allow you to remain. Your motives in this instance seem gentlemanly enough. Have a good day, sir."

Keating Blackwood inclined his head. "Thank you, my lady."

Feeling in need of a strong glass of spirits, Camille excused herself and returned to her station close to the front door of the dining room. Wasn't she supposed to have become accustomed to such assaults by now? To being ridiculed and abused because she'd done what she still considered to be the most sensible thing she'd ever managed in her life? For the most part, the Tantalus Club had been her safe haven for the past year.

As Camille looked up again, faint uneasiness touched her. Keating Blackwood, his gaze on her face, approached her podium without even making a show of being interested in some possible thing or person in her vicinity. "Thank you again," she said as he stopped before her, hoping to forestall his asking for a kiss or something as a reward of his so-called heroics. "How are you finding your breakfast?"

"Exceptional," he replied, leaning an elbow on the lectern the hostesses had taken to using to keep their table charts and lists of names and menus and the preferences of individual gentlemen safe. "You're Lady Camille Pryce."

Hiding her flinch, Camille shuffled through her papers. "That's hardly a secret. Now, is there something you need? A bottle of wine, perhaps? We have a fine bur—"

"I'm Keating Blackwood."

"So I heard." She looked at him for a moment, catching the expectant look on his lean face. "You have a black eye."

"Nearly gone, now." He brushed a negligent finger against his left cheek. "You don't know who I am."

"You're Keating Blackwood. My memory extends past one minute, I assure you."

A quick smile curved his mouth. It was a very attractive mouth, she noted peripherally. But it wasn't the first attractive mouth to decide that as a fallen woman she must be in need of a lover or a benefactor, or worse, that she made a habit of engaging in self-destructive behavior.

"Stephen Pollard is my cousin."

The ground beneath Camille's feet seemed to turn to pudding because she swayed alarmingly. Gripping the podium hard, she forced a breath through her lungs. "I—"

"I'm only telling you so that you aren't taken by surprise later," he continued. "I'm making an attempt at honesty."

Camille swallowed the lump of coal in her throat. "I . . . appreciate your candor," she ventured, using every bit of her self-control to keep from backing away.

That faint smile touched his mouth again. "My cousin is a stiff-backed buffoon, my lady. That said, I don't believe he's ever been the sort to pluck the wings off flies or . . . hurt anyone intentionally. This makes me curious. Did he harm you? Is that why you didn't wish to marry him?"

The question took her completely by surprise.

"If you aren't going to answer the question, I wish you'd say so," Blackwood prompted. "I have a fine plate of ham and cheeses and an annoyed duke waiting at the table for me."

"Then you should return to them." She picked up her seating chart and went to greet the next arrival.

"Do you ever go walking?" Blackwood's voice came from directly behind her.

Oh, dear, now he was trailing her about the room. "No."

"You should. At what time do you finish your hostess duties?"

"I—at—I don't believe that's any of your concern, Mr. Blackwood. Now please cease accosting me, or I shall be forced to have you removed."

"I mean you no harm, my lady," he returned in a low voice. "I've been away from London for six years, and you've made me curious. Few people stand against Fenton. I'd merely like to know your reasons."

Her parents hadn't even asked her that question. Camille took a stiff breath. "I will be free after one o'clock," she said in a rush, before she could change her mind. "But I don't leave the club's premises. You may find me in the rose garden."

He sketched a shallow bow. "I shall do so."

She pretended to return her attention to the club's late-arriving breakfast guests, and after a moment, the warmth shielding her back was gone. Of all the things she'd expected, it hadn't been the cousin of the man she'd jilted a year earlier appearing and being nice to her. And she'd never expected anyone to ask what Lord Fenton might have done to cause her to flee rather than to question why she'd lost *her* senses. Because she hadn't lost them. Not then, and not now.

Camille gave a tight smile in response to some lordling's greeting. Yes, she was quite aware that she'd ruined her life. What no one else—men, in particular—seemed to realize was that she had no intention of making things any worse. Ever.